Praise for *The Objects of Her Affection*

"Sonya Cobb combines the rarified atmosphere of museum scholarship, illegal art trafficking, and the sticky desperation of young motherhood to craft a superbly written thriller. Sophie Porter, the novel's fierce, flawed heroine, leads readers on a heady downhill race through the world of white-collar crime, where her high-risk gambles to secure the objects of her affection might mean losing them all."

—*Karen Engelmann, author of* The Stockholm Octavo

"A tautly plotted and elegantly written debut about the shame of secrets and the power of home. I held my breath with every twist and turn—and marveled over each effortlessly beautiful sentence."

—*Kelly Simmons, author of* Standing Still *and* The Bird House

"Sonya Cobb's *The Objects of Her Affection* is a smart, entertaining book that had me pinned to my chair until the end. An insightful and moving new voice."

—*DeLauné Michel, author of* The Safety of Secrets

THE OBJECTS OF HER AFFECTION

THE
OBJECTS
OF HER
AFFECTION

A NOVEL

SONYA COBB

Sourcebooks and the colophon are registered trademarks of Sourcebooks, Inc.

Published by Sourcebooks Landmark, an imprint of Sourcebooks, Inc.
P.O. Box 4410, Naperville, Illinois 60567-4410
(630) 961-3900
Fax: (630) 961-2168
www.sourcebooks.com

Library of Congress Cataloging-in-Publication data is on file with the publisher.

Printed and bound in the United States of America.
VP 10 9 8 7 6 5 4 3 2 1

For my grandparents, Jo and Ed, and their Ono Island dreams.

Prologue

Hastings-on-Hudson, NY
May 28, 1936

Frederick Howard
Library
Pennsylvania Museum of Art
4231 Avenue of the Republic
Philadelphia, Pennsylvania

Freddie,

I'd first like to convey my heartiest congratulations, not only for landing your marvelous job in these desperate times, but for keeping it! I could not be more pleased that it affords me the opportunity to correspond with you after all these years.

I apologize for the crate; I know it's absurdly large. Your great aunt Hester, who, you probably know, died in April of encephalitis, specified in her will that all of her silver should go to a museum. She did not specify which museum, nor did she mention why she considered her family less deserving than some arbitrarily selected institution, but perhaps that is a question best left unanswered. As the executrix of her estate it is my duty to execute and not to exhume.

I wish I could tell you more about this charmingly eclectic collection, but Hester was not what I would call a meticulous archivist. I believe she acquired some of these pieces during her travels in Europe, where her passion for collecting decorative arts was surpassed only by her zeal for collecting decorative companions. The silver-framed mirror, if you must know, was a gift from that German duke whose family was so inconvenienced by Hester's existence. I'm frankly surprised Daddy let her hold on to a souvenir from such an embarrassing episode. Memories fade; silver hangs around and tarnishes.

If you still have any curators on the payroll, they must be horribly overworked, so I implore you not to waste their time with our family knickknacks. Sell them, put them on a shelf, leave them in the crate; I place the decision in your very capable hands.

Thank you, dear Freddie, for your help as we scatter Hester's remains. I wish I could say you inherited more than this task, but alas, Hester died as she lived: with tightly clenched fists and a swollen head.

With best wishes for your continued success, I remain, as ever, your affectionate

Martha

New York Central Railroad
Bill of Lading

RECEIVED

at <u>New Rochelle, NY</u> *From* <u>John Lucas & Co.</u> March 2, *1936*

Destination: <u>Philadelphia: Pennsylvania Museum of Art</u>

State of: <u>Pennsylvania</u>

Quantity	Description of articles
2	candelabras
2	saltcellars
3	trays
2	coffeepots
1	inkstand
23	souvenir spoons
4	champagne buckets
1	silver-framed mirror

This is to certify that the above articles are properly described by name and are packed and marked and are in proper condition for transportation, according to the regulations prescribed by the Interstate Commerce Commission.

<u>John Lucas & Co.</u> _____*Shippers.*

Per <u>PLT</u> _____

One

L ike most Philadelphians, Sophie had always bought her produce at Superfresh, or, if she found herself on the other end of town, the ACME. It had never occurred to her to drive to an actual farm and pick it herself. But now she had children, and apparently, produce picking was an indispensable part of any happy childhood—like trick-or-treating or hunting for Easter eggs. You went peach picking in August, pumpkin picking in October. You introduced your children to the concept of agriculture, and took hundreds of pictures for the grandparents; or in the absence of grandparents, for the other moms in Music for Me class.

Now it was strawberry season, and the moms were all taking their kids to Shadyside Orchards, just outside the city, among the rippling, subdivided hills of Chester County. "It sounds nice," Sophie said to Brian. "A day on the farm—it's the sort of thing we're supposed to do. As parents." But Brian had been skeptical, pointing out that if this was really what all the moms and kids of Philadelphia were doing, they could hardly expect a quiet day immersed in the hush of nature.

"More like the crush of Sesame Place," he'd predicted. But

when he'd seen Sophie's face, carefully arranged into a combination of disappointment and dogged hope, he'd relented, as usual, even though it meant missing his Saturday ride. But Sophie had figured that out, too. The farm was only two miles from the cycling team's training route. If he timed it right, he could pick some strawberries with her and the kids, then jump on his bike and catch up with his team for the second half of the ride.

Brian had a lot of opportunities to say "I told you so" that morning—starting in Shadyside's vast, SUV-choked parking lot, where they were greeted not by a flock of ducks or even a stray barn cat, but by a sluggishly waving giant strawberry and a man with a walkie-talkie. He could have said it as they joined the crowd pushing their way to the ticket booth through a forest of loudspeakers. And he probably came close to saying it when he bought full-price tickets for themselves and for Lucy, age two and a half, and Elliot, a mere seven months. But he didn't.

As they followed the signs to the wagon-boarding zone, Sophie consoled herself that Lucy was still too young to form permanent memories; she wouldn't necessarily grow up thinking farms were the folksy cousins of amusement parks. There would be plenty of other farms to visit…plenty of time to get it right. She looped her arm around Brian's, grateful for his stoic good humor, hoping he wouldn't take off before they got the call from Steve, their real estate agent.

She was pretty sure Steve was going to say their offer on 2224 Hickory had been refused, and she didn't feel like absorbing this depressing news alone. She knew Brian would be relieved—delighted, even—to hear they weren't going to empty their savings into a 150-year-old fixer-upper. But at least he could still be counted on to provide the silent, consoling hug she was desperately going to need.

On the wagon, the strawberry pickers sat on scratchy hay

bales, facing each other like subway passengers. Unlike people on the subway, however, they all looked directly into each other's faces, excited about the adventure, impatient to start moving, making little jokes about traffic jams. A grandmother sitting on the opposite side of the wagon looked at Lucy and then up at Sophie.

"She looks just like you!" she said.

"Thanks!" said Sophie, as she always did, even though she knew it wasn't really the right answer. "I know" sounded unfriendly; "Really?" sounded disingenuous. She figured it must be true, because she'd heard it countless times since Lucy's birth three years ago. Nevertheless she often found herself looking into Lucy's wide-set brown eyes and thinking, "Is that me?" She also wondered when Lucy would first ask herself, with amazement and possibly a stab of horror, "Am I turning into her?"

The tractor started with a jerk; everyone swayed and grabbed on to each other, laughing. They pulled out behind another wagonload of people and staggered up the rutted road toward the strawberry field. "Faster!" cried Lucy, kicking her legs against the hay bale. Sophie looked down the row to where Brian was sitting, Elliot strapped to his front like an underdeveloped Siamese twin. Elliot was all baby fat and Brian was taut with lean muscle, but their heads were perfectly matched, with hair like the grain of a pine floorboard and a look of impassive forbearance in their pale eyes. Brian caught Sophie's gaze, raised his eyebrows in mock glee. She smirked in answer, then turned to watch the slow approach of the strawberry field.

In the distance she could see a row of houses on a low rise just beyond the edge of the farm. They were large and identical, with layers of peaked roofs arrayed over a jumble of mismatched windows, the largest of which was two stories high and arched at the top. The houses huddled above the field as if whispering to each other about its quaintly inefficient use of space. Just that morning, on the drive from Philadelphia, Brian had said he'd like to widen their search to include some of the suburbs close to the city. "Not like this, of course, but maybe one of the older towns. We could get a lot more space in Mt. Airy or Germantown. And a backyard." Sophie hadn't responded to this. As far as she was concerned, the Philadelphia Zoo was their backyard. And the Azalea Garden, where Elliot could practice crawling through the thick, cropped grass. And the Horticulture Center, with its delicately landscaped Japanese Tea House, where they would exchange their shoes for white slippers and clap their hands to attract the koi, who would lumber up to the side of the pond looking for treats. A backyard sounded, to Sophie, like an excuse to stay home.

The wagon stopped; a step stool was proffered; the pickers climbed down and accepted empty pint baskets from the sun-burned teenager just starting his summer job. The strawberry plants grew in long, bushy lines, with hay scattered on the ground between the rows. On the other side of the dirt road, at the bottom of a slope, ranks of young spruce and pine trees waited for December, when crowds of jolly executioners would come for them, wielding their red-handled saws.

Lucy broke away from Sophie and hurtled into the field, plunging her hands into one of the plants. She pulled out a large red fruit and looked up at her mother for permission.

"Go crazy," Sophie said, and the look of ecstasy on Lucy's face as she bit into the berry more than repaid the drive, the loudspeakers, the overcrowded wagon. Brian unstrapped Elliot and set him on the ground, where he began picking up hand-fuls of straw and moving them toward his mouth. Brian pried the hay out of Elliot's clenched fists and tried directing him toward a fruit-heavy bush, but Elliot was transfixed by the loose yellow stuff, so lightweight and abundant, so easily scooped and crushed in his hands. "You might as well just let him taste it," Sophie said, knowing that the easiest way to keep Elliot from doing something was to let him come up with the idea himself. But Brian made a face and picked Elliot up, batting his hands away from his mouth and making him drop the hay. Elliot's arms shuddered and his face reddened as he gathered himself for an explosion of cries. Sophie dropped her strawberry basket next to Lucy and reached for Elliot.

"I've got this," said Brian.

"It's okay." Sophie took Elliot and bounced him in her arms, cooing in his ear, searching for the rhythm and tone that would calm his fury. Brian looked at his watch again. Standing there among the strawberry plants in his red-and-black cycling spandex, he looked like a futuristic scarecrow. Sophie felt a twinge of regret for having swooped in so quickly. She'd done it that morning, too—snatching a diaper out of his hand because he was taking too long with it. She knew it was a bad habit; it wasn't fair to Brian. On the other hand she did wonder, sometimes, if he was exaggerating his clumsiness just a bit, offering himself up for the swoop-in.

"You've got great weather for your ride," she said now, feeling around for a thread to draw them back together. She genuinely wanted Brian to enjoy his afternoon away; he was here, after all, even though the farm visit was her fantasy, not his. But that was Brian—letting her get the pale yellow upholstery she loved even though they had two kids in diapers; letting her get the eight-foot-tall Christmas tree even though their apartment ceilings were only seven feet high. He was too good to her; she knew that. He wanted nothing but her happiness, and she kept trying, in spite of her mistakes, to provide it.

"I'll be home in time to make dinner," Brian said. He pulled a strawberry from a bush, wiping it on his jersey and holding it up to her lips. "Grilled shrimp rémoulade?" Sophie bit slowly into the berry's red flesh; Brian ate the other half with a suggestive eyebrow raise. She laughed gratefully. Dinnertime was the moment she looked forward to every single day, Brian stirring at the stove, Sophie keeping him company, Elliot in the Pack 'n' Play, a bottle of wine on the counter. She couldn't cook—she hated the messy panic of it all—so in the kitchen Brian was fully in charge. Without Sophie swooping in, he was free to create elaborate meals so full of depth and complexity, they were like a window into his soul—or maybe, Sophie liked to think, his feelings for his wife.

"Why do you think Steve isn't calling?" she asked, wanting Brian to share the savory mixture of hope and dread she'd been nursing all morning.

"I don't know. The twenty-four hours are just about up. He'll have to call one way or the other."

Sophie tried to detect a hint of anxiety in his voice, but was unrewarded, as usual. "Should we call him? I think we should call him."

"He must not have anything to say, or we would've heard from him."

"Maybe we should've come in a little higher," Sophie said. "What if there's another offer?"

"I don't even think we can afford what we did offer," Brian said, adjusting his bike shorts. "With the renovations—it's serious money. It's crazy."

"I can make it work. I'm not worried. I've already got two jobs lined up for this summer." Sophie set Elliot down between two strawberry plants, then stepped into the next row to check on Lucy, who was pushing strawberries into her mouth as fast as she could pick them. Red juice stained her shirt, her chin, her teeth; even her hair looked sticky. "Lucy, we're supposed to take some of these home, you know. Here, start putting them in this basket. I don't think you should eat that many. How many have you had?"

Lucy held up both hands. "Lots?"

Sophie helped her fill the basket, teasing the ripe berries away from the greenish-white ones that dangled from flimsy stems like bowed heads. The sun was hot on her neck, but it was still early enough in the season for the heat to be dry and welcome.

Her mind turned back to the house, as it had for the last few days, trying to reassemble the rooms within the three stacked stories of brick, patching together her memories of the fireplace mantels, the high ceilings, the heavy, ornately faceted doors. It was a sharp architectural retort to the apartments and rental houses she'd grown up in, with their hollow-core doors and drop ceilings, the acrylic bathtubs that flexed and thumped when you stepped into them. This was a house made to last; a place to stay put.

As she toured it in her mind, she peeled away flocked wallpaper and shag carpet to reveal plaster walls and wood floors. She flaked paint off of chestnut, porcelain, and iron. She hung a fanciful light fixture in Lucy's bedroom, and installed shelves for Elliot's bins of toys. She renovated her childhood and offered it, freshly painted and outlined in crisp white trim, to her children.

"Here, Soph." Brian handed her the baby carrier. "I'm going to catch that wagon back so I can change shoes and all. Call me when you hear from Steve, all right?" He reached around and patted the phone-shaped lump in the pocket on the back of his jersey. Sophie nodded, spreading the fingers of one hand across her belly. Seeing this, Brian stepped forward and pulled her into a hug. "It's going to be fine." His smile hovered between apology and reassurance as he stroked his thumb across her cheekbone. "Try to have fun. Call me if you need me to come back, okay? I'll come right away."

"No worries!" Sophie rubbed his shoulder briskly. "Have a great ride. I'll let you know what Steve says." She waved to him as he rode off in the wagon, wishing, too late, that she'd boarded it with him, realizing now how crucial he was to her enjoyment of the outing. Without him there, the whole thing seemed silly. Lucy loved eating the strawberries, of course, but she could do that at home, and Elliot didn't care if he was on a farm or in the playground around the corner from their house.

She pulled out her phone, checked for missed calls, then slid it back into the diaper bag. Elliot had crawled into another row and was headed toward the Christmas trees. Sophie scooped her arm between his legs and set him down facing the other direction; he continued crawling without missing a beat. She followed him in circles around Lucy, redirecting him when necessary, until she began to feel her breasts becoming uncomfortably full—which probably meant Elliot was becoming uncomfortably empty. She lifted him up and fed his thighs through the leg holes of the baby carrier, clipping it shut against her now-aching chest. "Come on, Lucy," she said, crouching to pick up the few strawberries that had made it into the basket. "We're getting the next wagon." Lucy nodded, suddenly sapped of energy. Her expression had turned inward, as if she were monitoring some kind of development in her mood. "You okay?" Sophie asked. Lucy nodded again.

Back at the farm market, Sophie found a small fenced playground with two empty benches in the shade of some oak trees. A sign was nailed to an honor box at the entrance: "Playground admission $5." Sophie snorted and shoved a five-dollar bill through the slot. She would call Steve while Elliot ate.

Lucy ambled indifferently toward the jungle gym, while

Sophie untangled herself from the baby carrier, her blouse, and her nursing bra. Elliot huffed and grunted; he was shuddering with hunger. As he started to nurse, she pulled her phone out of the bag and checked it for missed calls. Nothing.

A shriek came from the direction of the jungle gym. "Mommy!"

"What is it?" called Sophie, squinting at Lucy, who was standing next to the glaring metal slide, arms straight out, legs wide apart, her body stiff. "Come over here. What's wrong?"

But Lucy was crying, and it wasn't tired crying or plaintive crying or nobody-loves-me crying. It was gasping sobs, raw and edged with fear. Sophie threw the phone back in her bag, pulled Elliot off her breast, and lurched toward Lucy. The smell told her everything before she got close enough to see what was dripping from Lucy's shorts. Lucy, champion potty trainer, enthusiastic consumer of toilet paper, avid proponent of toilet seat covers and antibiotic gel, was frozen in horror, tears streaming down her face, her juice-stained mouth turned down and quivering.

"It's okay, honey," Sophie said, trying to button her blouse with one hand. "Don't worry. You just ate a few too many strawberries. Let's go to the bathroom and clean you up." Elliot began to snuffle desperately at Sophie's neck. When she lifted him into the baby carrier, his confusion coalesced into outrage; his screams drowned out the sobs of his sister. Sophie stabbed uselessly at his mouth with a pacifier, then gave up and hoisted the diaper bag over her shoulder, pulling Lucy toward the bathrooms.

The women's room was at the back of the market, requiring a slow walk down long aisles of pickled rhubarb and apple butter, Elliot wailing, Lucy bent stiffly at the waist and whimpering. Sophie was half expecting to find an honor box nailed to the restroom door, but this part of the experience, at least, was free.

Sophie led Lucy into the handicapped stall, feeling, for the first time in her life, legitimately guilt-free about this incursion, and used the handrail to lower herself slowly into a squat, knees cracking. It would have been silly to bring a stroller on a tractor ride, but she really could have used a place to store her son. She gingerly removed Lucy's soiled underpants and socks, then lifted her onto the toilet seat, holding her as far from Elliot's hands and feet as possible, her back twanging with pain. "Hold on to that rail."

"I don't want to touch anything!" screamed Lucy, digging her fingernails into Sophie's arms. Lucy's scream startled Elliot, whose sobs shattered into shrill, breathless shrieks. Then, from the depths of the diaper bag, mingling with the children's cries, came a more reasonable and musical sound: Sophie's phone.

Sophie pried Lucy's fingers open and planted them firmly on the safety bars. She reached into the diaper bag for one of the plastic grocery bags folded up inside the central pocket and dropped Lucy's shorts and underwear into it. She knotted the bag shut and wrapped it in two more grocery bags, which she shoved into the diaper bag. This did nothing to dispel the swampy stench that filled the stall; nor did it muffle the trill of the phone. She pulled out a packet of wet wipes and used them to swab Lucy's legs as well as she could while Lucy balanced on the toilet seat. "You done?" she asked Lucy, who shook her head miserably. Sophie stood and awkwardly leaned over to kiss Lucy's forehead, then left the stall to toss the wipes in the trash and wash her hands.

After a few more tries she persuaded Elliot to accept the pacifier, which transformed his shrieks into furious grunts and sucking noises. Sophie checked on Lucy one more time, then dug out her phone and flipped it open. Steve. Of course. She dialed in to voice mail.

"Sophie, hey, sorry this is so last-minute, we were having fax machine problems. Anyway, good news, they have counterof-fered, and I think it's reasonable. Call me back ASAP."

Sophie felt herself levitate, momentarily, above the echoing bathroom stall, then become heavy again with the realization that the counteroffer would, by definition, be way over their budget. "Ready to get up?" she asked Lucy. Lucy shook her head, so Sophie leaned against the wall and called Steve back.

"I think it's fair," he said. "For the neighborhood, the size, it's a good price." Sophie could hear the optimism in his voice, and she allowed herself to be lifted back up by it, away from the stink and ache, into a pearly cloud of excitement far above the creeping suburbs of Chester County. The number wasn't bad… the number was just a number, really. Bland, silent, you could invite it into your life without too much disruption. You could learn to live with it, move some things around, make space. "You should look into one of those new low down payment loan products I told you about," Steve said. "My mortgage guy can work wonders. Call Brian, then get back to me."

But Lucy was inching her way off the toilet seat, so Sophie stood her up and finished wiping her legs. She had a pair of clean underwear in the diaper bag, but no shorts, so she had to persuade Lucy that her T-shirt, thankfully on the large side, was long enough to pass as a dress. Lucy seemed too drained to pro-test, and even consented to put on her sneakers without socks. On the way out of the market, Sophie bought her a bottle of Gatorade, which cheered Lucy enormously because it was blue and it wore a garish, neon-scrawled label.

Sophie led Lucy back to the playground. "I just need a chance to finish feeding Elliot," she said. "Then we can all go home and take a long nap." She held the gate open for two boys with buzz cuts and sleeveless camouflage shirts. They barreled past her and began chasing each other in circles around the jungle gym while their mother pulled five dollars out of her wallet with exaggerated slowness and stuffed it in the honor box, making brazen eye contact with Sophie.

"I paid before," said Sophie, but this sounded feeble, and the woman pulled back one side of her mouth and hooded her eyes. "Oh, whatever," Sophie muttered, hurrying to the only bench that was still in the shade. She situated Elliot on her breast and called Brian, but the call went right to voice mail. She tried again; same thing. One of the boys came to stand in front of her and watch her breast-feed. His mother stalked over, slapping her platform flip-flops on the dusty ground, and grabbed him by the arm.

"Don't look at that," she said, turning him toward the jungle gym and hitting him on the rear.

Sophie tried Brian again but it was useless; he'd ridden out of range. Anyway, she knew how the conversation would go. He'd want to walk away. But Brian had not seen the same house she'd seen. He'd seen water damage, knob-and-tube wiring, an oil-gulping furnace. Sophie, on the other hand, had seen an address for their future. She'd walked through dozens of other houses in the past months, but this one had set something vibrating in her, some long-forgotten string that was now playing its note in her head day and night.

She switched Elliot, now in a limp daze, to her other breast. Her mind seesawed between excitement and preemptive guilt, feeling the thing she wanted so badly just within reach, knowing she should sit back and wait just a little bit longer. With time and persistence, she knew she could win Brian over. She just needed to find the words to explain why, exactly, this house was so necessary. Why she believed it could protect her from the lonesomeness of her childhood. Why she felt it could anchor her to the earth in a way that would ease that whirling, plastic-bag-in-the-wind feeling she'd had all her life. She needed him to know that buying this house was her way of giving Lucy and Elliot the childhood she'd missed; that the house might even serve as tangible proof that she was doing this thing right—this maddening, baffling, improvisational performance called parenting. She needed to make him understand that some day she wanted to look upon her grown children with pleasure and satisfaction, maybe even pride, instead of the sort of acidic regret that would force her to turn away from them forever. And that this house—with its honest proportions and solid bones—had somehow become home to this motley collection of yearnings.

Eventually she'd figure out how to explain it all in a way that actually made sense. And Brian, she knew, would get that soft look, and he would say yes, if it will make you happy, yes, of course, yes.

It seemed a little ridiculous to delay things, just so he could cautiously sidle up to a decision she'd already made.

A decision made in the wrong way, perhaps, but for the right reasons. She only wanted what was best for her family.

Sophie opened the phone, her blood buzzing with a cocktail of adrenaline and oxytocin. With a rubbery pop, as if crushing a tiny bubble, her thumb pressed the green button. Steve answered on the first ring.

Two

The sun was already sizzling like a snare drum as Sophie climbed the seventy-two stone steps to the museum, her back to the wide swath of Parkway that led to downtown Philadelphia. In front of her, butterscotch columns stretched into the hard blue sky, supporting a huge triangular pediment on which verdigris griffins perched like overgrown pigeons. Groups of campers in matching T-shirts scattered across the wide-open plaza, their shouts echoing off the museum wings.

Inside the east entrance Sophie gave the security guard her name, and he called Brian's office to announce her arrival. She waited at the base of the Great Stair, looking up toward the entrance to the European Decorative Arts galleries. A group of chattering children galloped down the wide steps, carrying folded stools under their arms. Behind them, negotiating the stairs more deliberately, came Marjorie, a volunteer who worked in Brian's department. Sophie watched her slow descent, smiling encouragingly.

"You're early," Marjorie said when she reached the bottom. Her straight gray hair was cropped into a boxy bob, her acrylic cardigan squared off at her hips, and her flat-front skirt fell straight to her knees. Even her wide, sturdy loafers were composed of right angles. "Brian's still in his committee meeting."

"Oh, I'm sorry," Sophie said as they started up the stairs. "I could have waited for him. I just wanted to go over some insurance stuff. Did he tell you about the house?"

Marjorie nodded but didn't answer, either because she was winded or because she was just being Marjorie. She paused at the top of the stairs, patted her chest, and briefly closed her eyes, then escorted Sophie through the galleries and into the warren of offices and workrooms hidden behind a set of locked steel doors. To Sophie, it was a journey that felt like wandering behind the set of an elaborate opera production. Up front it was all soaring, gilded spaces and artful lighting, whereas behind the scenery, among the pulleys and catwalks, it felt cramped and dank under dingy fluorescent lights.

Turning the corner into Brian's low-ceilinged hallway, Sophie almost crashed into a line of bulky carts parked along one wall. Roughly constructed of wood, they were mottled with dents and scrapes that suggested many run-ins with heavy doors and filing cabinets. Their upper and lower trays were lined with grimy gray carpet, and within the trays lay a tarnished jumble of inkstands, spoons, snuffboxes, and saltcellars—a collection of elegant silver that, to Sophie, looked dismayed by its ignominious surroundings.

"What's all this?" she asked Marjorie, who stopped, looked at the carts, then looked at Sophie as if trying to decide whether Sophie was actually asking her what silver was. "I mean, why's it all out in the hall?"

"They're emptying this storage room," Marjorie said, indicating a room opposite Brian's door. "Turning it into an office."

"That'll be nice, to have more space." Sophie peered through the door, which she'd never seen open before. Two women wearing thin purple gloves stood among rows of tall steel shelves. One of them was turning a coffeepot over in her hands while the other sorted through a stack of Rolodex-sized cards. "Who gets the office?"

"Someone other than me," said Marjorie, unlocking Brian's door. "You can wait in here. I have to get back to Ted's files."

Brian's office was a long, narrow room lined with book-shelves on one side and a large metal cabinet on the other. The department's copier occupied the wall to the right of the door, and to the left, Brian's tuxedo, draped in dry-cleaner plastic, hung from the top of a framed poster. Sophie cleared a pile of books off of a chair next to Brian's desk and sat down. She squared the stack of insurance quotes on her lap, know-ing Brian probably wouldn't have time to go over them with her. But the agent's office was just down the hill from the museum, and anyway, she'd always enjoyed dropping in on Brian during the day. Here, among the dusty typewriters and exhibition catalogs, surrounded by scholars and conservators and old Philadelphia money, Brian was always at his best: happy, absorbed, as close to giddy as his reserved personality would allow. Also, he was less likely to be made irritable by house-related conversations.

"Hey there." Brian rushed into the room balancing a laptop on a pile of file folders and bent to kiss her on the forehead. "My committee gave me the green light on that vase."

"The..."

"The Milan vase. The majolica. Now I just need to raise the funds. The auction's coming up quick." He surveyed the hill of papers and books under which, somewhere, his desk lurked.

"Oh right," Sophie said. "Congratulations." She was sure Brian had told her about the vase, had detailed its condition and provenance, had probably even shown her pictures at some point. He was like a cat, bringing her dead mouse after dead mouse, seeking her approval in the best way he knew how. To her the mice all looked the same, but this didn't diminish the pleasure she took in seeing him so proud and excited. "I knew they would love it."

Brian sat down, putting his laptop on the floor next to his chair. "Where are the kids?"

"With the sitter. I had a meeting with the insurance guy. I thought you might want to look at the options." She began paging through the stack of papers, trying to explain structure limits and deductibles in a way that was helpful but not condescending, ushering Brian as gently as possible toward her already-made decision. At first he seemed interested, but whenever his email pinged he leaned over the side of the chair to look at his screen, and when the phone rang he snatched it up with a semiapologetic eye roll.

"It's not a good time, is it," Sophie said after he'd taken two more calls.

Brian wiped a hand down his face. "I didn't realize all this would be happening today. Do you—I mean, do you feel like you have a handle on all that?"

"On the insurance?"

"Because I really don't mind if you just take care of it. I mean, if you don't mind."

Sophie slid the papers back into their folder. It had always been her nature to manage their finances, and it had always been Brian's nature to let her. But in matters related to the house—a house that meant everything to Sophie, and nothing but headaches to Brian—he was sinking to new depths of passivity. "All right," she said, helping him to shore up a sliding pile of CDs. "I'll figure it out."

"Thanks, Soph. I promise I'll have more time for this stuff after the auction." He reached out and tucked a strand of her hair behind her ear. "I've been waiting such a long time for this."

"I know." She knew. Most people had a hard time understanding Brian's relationship to his job—the way his work was woven into his very being; the way his life could never be compartmentalized into "work" and "home," or "job" and "life." The objects, the chase, the careful detective work, and the diligent pursuit of donors to pay for each acquisition—it was an obsession, if not a full-blown addiction. Just the other day Sophie's friend Carly had asked if she ever felt jealous or resentful of Brian's job, but in fact the opposite was true. She loved Brian for it. It might have been different if he'd been obsessed with pork futures or golf balls. But Brian's work made her proud. He knew more about art history and cultural expression and stylistic movements than she could ever fathom, and she found this deeply attractive.

Sophie kissed Brian, then left his office to find Marjorie. Along the way to Ted's office she found herself drawn to the object carts lined up against the wall. Brian often talked about the vast quantities of artwork in museum storage: unwanted gifts left in people's wills; objects rotated out of the galleries to make space; entire collections bought and stored, just so one good piece could go on display. He'd also told her that his department could barely keep track of the good stuff, much less the rest of it, with their antiquated system of yellowed object cards and a computer database too slow and clunky to be of any use. Sophie picked up a tall silver candlestick, marveling at its weight. An embarrassment of riches.

"Excuse me?" One of the purple-gloved women had emerged from the storage room and was frowning at Sophie. Sophie flushed and returned the candlestick to the cart. "Are you with someone?" the woman asked.

"Brian Porter," Sophie said. "I was just—sorry. I like silver. I mean, not *this* silver, of course. Although, this silver is very nice, I just mean—" She shook her head. "I'm leaving now." She turned and hurried down the hall to find Marjorie, careful not to bump into anything on her way.

Three

Twenty-two twenty-four Hickory was a brick row house on a hill, in a neighborhood that climbed slowly away from downtown: just far enough to allow young families to afford three or four bedrooms and a tiny patio, just close enough to smell the breath of the city. Ginkgo trees lined both sides of the street, alternating with lampposts neatly papered with sidewalk sale announcements ("baby clothes, toys, jogging strollers"). The pavement swirled with pink and purple sidewalk chalk. In window boxes, the houses held out prim bouquets of pansies, sweet potato vines, and the season's first begonias and geraniums.

Brian walked over from the museum on his lunch break to meet Sophie, Steve, and Gary, the diminutive inspector from ProValue, in front of the house. Sophie watched her husband recall the dented aluminum awning, the crumbling brick, the squeaky, paint-scabbed storm door. He hadn't been to the house since their first visit with Steve; she'd already been back three times.

"Look at the ginkgo," she said, taking his arm. The tree stretched tall and svelte, its branches starting at second-story height. Delicately splayed leaves hung thick along the length of each swooning branch and waved slowly in the slight breeze, like a thousand green fans.

"It's probably going to drop those foul-smelling berries all over our sidewalk," Brian said, looking up.

"That's a male ginkgo," said Gary from inside his ProValue cap. "No fruit." Sophie gazed into the tree's spreading height, pondering the idea of a male tree. Gary tucked his aluminum-clad clipboard under his arm and motioned for Steve to precede him up the steps and through the protesting door.

Inside, a thin shaft of light penetrated the heavy front drapes, illuminating a dense haze of dust floating among the doily-draped furniture. The brown flocked wallpaper, dark red wall-to-wall carpet, and acoustical tile drop ceiling stank of cigarettes and cats. Over the yellowed marble mantel, Jesus stared down at them through drops of blood.

"Well," said Steve, stepping carefully over a dark stain in the carpet, "it really is a great space. You don't usually get a living room this large in Philadelphia. And a formal dining room!"

Sophie tapped one of the walls, listening to the hollow crunch of paint and wallpaper ready to be picked and peeled away. She lifted a corner of carpet and brushed away some crumbs of foam padding; underneath, she found a yellow newspaper with strange writing. Russian? Ukrainian? She lifted the dusty paper away.

"Nice," Gary said, his flashlight illuminating the gray floor-boards. "Quarter-sawn oak. That grain'll come up beautifully when you sand."

"Or we could recarpet," offered Brian. "Until we can afford, you know, to refinish."

"Quarter-sawn oak?" Sophie squeezed Brian's upper arm. "I don't even know what that is, but I don't think you can cover it up."

She pulled him into the dining room, which was crowded with heavy furniture and cabbage rose wallpaper. "Thanksgiving," she said, holding out her arms.

"We don't have a table," Brian said.

"We'll get one. Do you remember the kitchen?" She led him through a pair of swinging doors. Greasy brown cabinets lined one salmon-colored wall; the other sides of the square room were furnished with a jumble of tables and open shelves. "Not too much cabinetry to pull out. It's a blank slate. Think of the counter space." Sophie peered through the yellow glass of the back door. "We could put a double door back here, to the patio, and eat outside in the summer."

"Mmm."

"Okay, maybe it's a little hot right now. But in the spring." She continued staring at the yellow-tinted yard.

"Do you really think they can just open up a supporting wall like that—"

"Let's look upstairs." She turned away from Brian and headed back toward the front of the house. She climbed the carpeted stairs, running her fingers along the carved balusters made vague by layers of paint. She could picture Lucy and Elliot peering through them, spying on a grown-up party below.

The front bedroom had two large windows; Sophie pushed the water-stained curtains aside and looked into the branches of the gently swaying ginkgo. "This will be Lucy's room," she said. And it would be Lucy's in every sense, she thought, without someone else's thumbtack holes in the walls, someone else's stickers on the light-switch plate. The room would change over the years, growing up along with its inhabitant, but it would never be packed up and left behind.

Brian had stopped just inside the door and was prodding a makeshift closet built with wood paneling, which bowed inward when he pressed on it. "See how easy that would be to tear out?" said Sophie. "We could do it ourselves. We'll use wardrobes, the way they do in Europe." She crossed into the adjoining bedroom. "This is Elliot's room, I think. It's smaller, but not by too much. Crib. Changing table. Nursing chair."

"Water damage." Brian poked at a bulge in the plaster. Paint was flaking off the wall in potato-chip-sized curls. Sophie pulled him to the window, which looked over a concrete patch piled with rusted trash cans.

"Look out there. The kids could have a sandbox," she said. "A few potted plants? A grill? Think about it."

And he seemed to be, until he tilted his head back and she realized he wasn't looking out the window, but at it. He plucked a shard of paint from the frame and sniffed it tentatively.

"Just *try*, okay? Put that down. Can you try to see this the way I'm seeing it?" Sophie pressed her hand over her belly, fingers splayed. "I know I shouldn't have done this without you. I should have waited." She took a deep breath. "I just wish you could see all the potential I see here." She stared into his face, smooth and pale, his brow tranquil, his eyes barely able to summon the energy required to be an actual color. The sole hint of feeling, perceptible only to Sophie (and perhaps, if she had been alive to see it, his mother), was a slight stiffening of his nostrils.

"It's not too late," she said, more gently now. "We can still walk away. I can go downstairs right now and tell Steve. All we'd lose is the deposit." She felt a tiny flicker of nervousness, but she knew that the combined weight of the house, the paperwork, the insurance, the inspector, the real estate agents, the grateful sellers, and her own excitement would require too much energy for Brian to dislodge on his own.

He looked down and toed a hole in the carpet. "It scares me." He looked at her. "Financially. I can't help but think we're being a little reckless with this. I want you to be happy, you know I do. But this scares me."

"Okay." Sophie waited a beat. "Okay. Do you want me to—"

"I'm not sure what to do."

"Okay. We can call it off." She stared at him; he didn't flinch. "Just know that I believe in this, Brian. I believe I can get enough work, I can make enough, I can get a good payment plan. Steve said he knows a guy—he said we qualify, no problem. We're good to go."

"Really."

"Really. Brian, this house, I wish I could explain it to you. It's just meant to be ours. I feel like it wants us as much as we want it. And living here…it will make me so happy. Everything will work out. I'll make sure it does."

Brian leaned his head back and stared at the ceiling for a moment. "Show me where your office will be."

She held out her arm. "Right this way." It was a relief to settle into their familiar dance step—Sophie deciding, Brian acquiescing. Perhaps the dance mostly worked to her advantage, but she knew they both heard the music. She led him down the hall to the large rear bedroom. Two cobwebbed windows faced west; one, broken, faced south. A trio of fat flies loitered in the center of the hot room. "I figure an L-shaped workstation over here, with all my monitors on it, and maybe a mini station in that corner." She paused, mentally organizing her bookshelves. In their apartment, her workspace was a sticky corner of the kitchen table, with a few laptops balanced on chairs. Here, in a room like this, she knew—she was *sure*—work would be efficient. Professional. Abundant. "See?" she said, seeing the backup arrays, the CPUs, the neat stacks of project briefs. She'd never had a real home office before. The thought filled her with eagerness to reclaim her career—to push it to new heights, to pursue new satisfactions. She looked over at Brian, who was examining a brown stain on the ceiling. She knew he was thinking like a curator, cataloging condition problems and losses. It was, after all, his job to look to the past, to understand what something once had been, to lament what it had become. But when it came to real life outside the museum, this struck Sophie as a waste of time. It was more realistic—more inspiring—to look forward, to the attractively hazy possibility of what could be.

⚜

"Don't leave me," Sophie whispered as Brian draped his jacket over his arm. She was lying on her side within a complicated arrangement of pillows, Elliot propped against her breast.

"Sorry," Brian said, leaning over to kiss her on the forehead. His tie brushed Elliot's cheek, but Elliot kept his eyes closed, comfortably suspended between sleep and milk. "Milan awaits."

"To hell with Milan. I want to stay in bed."

"I know. But just wait till you see this vase in person…"

"I don't need to. I know it's spectacular. Go. You'll be amazing."

"Thanks," Brian whispered. "Do you need anything? Want me to put out Lucy's cereal?"

"You're sweet. We're fine. I hope you get your vase."

"I hope you get your mortgage. Sorry I couldn't be there."

Sophie closed her eyes. Steve had set up the meeting with his buddy Ron at AmeriLoan a week ago, and now Brian couldn't come. One of his committee members had come through with purchase funds at the last possible minute, and now he had to spend his morning on the phone, waiting to bid on the majolica vase that would fill an "egregious gap" in the museum's collection.

Sophie propped herself on one elbow and carefully eased herself over Elliot's body to the other side, rearranging pillows and lifting his head to her other breast. She should probably reschedule the AmeriLoan meeting. Brian had urged her not to, but now she wondered if she was just reinforcing his financial helplessness—his inability to remember passwords, his refusal to figure out online banking. She also suspected that he was further distancing himself from the matter of the house. Which was fine; the truth was that Sophie didn't want him anywhere near their finances, with his shoe box filing system, his dresser drawer full of receipts and crumpled paycheck stubs. It was probably safer to just add the mortgage to her neatly arranged bin of responsibilities, and let Brian focus on what he did best: curating ceramics.

Sophie lowered Elliot into his crib, then shuffled into Lucy's room to usher her through her morning routine. She was actually looking forward to the meeting at AmeriLoan. The sitter was coming in an hour, which would give her some time to shower and dress. Maybe she'd even blow-dry her hair for a change. Then, after the meeting, there was always the possibility of lunch. Out. Alone.

But nine o'clock came, and the sitter, a Penn sophomore on summer vacation, did not. Sophie tried to rouse her by phone, by text. She left a voice mail, trying to walk the line between stern employer and sympathetic friend, but just ended up sounding frantic. Finally she had to make a choice: take the kids to her meeting, or cancel the meeting and take them to the playground.

"Put on your shoes," she told Lucy. "We're going to buy a house."

The meeting went as poorly as possible by parenting standards, and surprisingly well by any other measure. Elliot was awake and angry the whole time, refusing the car seat, straining against the baby carrier, consenting only to be bounced, at a precise angle and rhythm, in Sophie's arms while she paced in front of Ron's desk. Meanwhile, Lucy cheerfully raised and lowered the venetian blinds in the front window while singing a tuneless, syncopated dirge.

"The bottom line," explained Sophie, raising her voice over the slapping of the blinds, "is that we need our savings for the renovations, so we can't do much of a down payment. But I'm worried about going too high on our monthly payments, because my work is kind of unpredictable."

Ron paged through the paperwork she'd brought, jiggling the oversized watch that slipped around his wrist. "You freelance, am I right?"

"Yes. If you look at my returns from before 2003, you'll see how well I was doing before kids. I plan to get back to that level…soon. Once I have a real office to work in. Lucy, put that back on the shelf."

"Okay, no problem. Any chance Brian's getting a raise sometime soon?"

"Oh, God, I doubt it. Museums these days…"

"Gotcha. Well, hey, that's okay." Sophie felt absurdly grateful to Ron for his unflappable cheeriness, despite the chaos unfolding in front of his desk.

"I can see you've got some years in your field, that's awesome. Technology is where it's at, right?"

"Lucy! Can you stop with the blinds? Please?"

"Tell you what. I've got an interesting new product here that seems perfect for you guys. Well, not totally new. It's been around since the eighties, but folks like you didn't always have access to it. It's called an option ARM." Ron leaned back and gently patted the crest of his gelled hair.

"Option arm?"

"Go as low as you want on the down payment—one percent? Two percent? Up to you. Then every month, you decide what to pay. There's a minimum payment, of course, or you can choose the whole interest-only payment, or the full PITI."

Sophie switched Elliot to her other arm, provoking a fresh wail. She resumed bouncing. "Okay…"

"For a freelancer like you? Perfect. Gives you a chance to get back on your feet after—well! Obviously, you're on your feet quite a bit."

"Yes, I am."

"But you catch my drift. Anyway. Here's just a back-of-the-envelope look at your minimum monthly payment, if you put one percent down, no points." He pushed his legal pad across the desk and showed her a number.

"Really?"

"Great, right? These rates are insane right now…it's such a great time to buy."

Sophie extracted a lock of her hair from Elliot's sweaty grasp. "I didn't know, I mean, the calculator we used online made it sound like this house would be more of a stretch. Especially with the renovations…"

Ron shook his head. "Those calculators don't have all the angles. They can't…massage. That's what I do. I'm a massager. Whaddaya call it—a massoose. I'm a massoose."

"Wow. Okay, well, let me show this to Brian and we'll—"

Ron grimaced. "This rate won't be around for long. If I were you, I'd get the application in now. Just submit it, then talk to your hubby. At least that way we lock in the rate. You change your mind, fine. We'll work it out."

"I'm not committing to anything?"

"Nah, you're good. Just get these papers in, and when you're approved you can pull the trigger."

Elliot arched backward in Sophie's arms, and almost succeeded in getting himself dropped. "Okay, okay," Sophie gasped, her lower back a tangle of pain. "You're the expert."

"Trust me. You'll be happy you locked this in."

And afterward, as she sat at Johnny Rockets, Lucy coloring her menu and Elliot finally dozing in the car seat beside her, Sophie realized that she was, as a matter of fact, happy. All around her the great apparatus was in motion; gears were turning smoothly, slick with silicone and ball bearings. The mechanism was fantastically complicated but breathtakingly silent, gently conveying an entire generation to new heights of prosperity and comfort. And now here was a trio of mini cheeseburgers being delivered on a red tray, no pickles for Lucy, fries, a smiley face painted in ketchup on a paper plate. As they bit into the pillowy buns, the jukebox started playing "Last Dance," and suddenly the waitstaff dropped everything to shimmy and lip-synch along with Donna Summer's soaring voice. Twirling, grinning, dapper in bow ties and soda jerk hats, the waitresses and busboys looked as buoyant as root beer floats. It was early; Sophie, Lucy, and Elliot were the only ones in the restaurant. It was a show just for them, and Lucy clapped along and laughed: delighted, appreciative, but not the least bit surprised.

Brian pointed out, quite rightly, that they could probably hire two guys to pull up the carpet for less money than they were paying the babysitter. But Sophie wanted to be the first one to tear into the wrapping and finally see what the house was made of. She didn't mention that she was also planning to take a crack at the drop ceiling, and maybe the wallpaper, if they had time.

It was hot, filthy work. They started in the master bedroom, on the third floor, where the summer heat pooled under the roof. They tore the carpet away from its tacks with a shuddering jerk, releasing plumes of dust into the air, then sliced it into manageable pieces with utility knives and heaved the rolls into the rented Dumpster out front, along with the padding and Ukrainian newspapers. "I feel like we're waxing the house's legs," Sophie said as they caught their breath, surveying the smooth, grayish floor in Lucy's room.

"If the house were a one-hundred-and-fifty-year-old woman," said Brian. He pulled his dust mask down around his neck.

"Just wait until it's sanded and varnished. It'll come back to life." Sophie picked up a crowbar and began prying the toothy nail strips from the perimeter of the floor, energized by thoughts of darkly gleaming planks. She wondered if she could do the refinishing herself—she loved the idea of smoothing polyurethane into the wood like a salve, slowly coaxing supple beauty out of the grain. She thought about the floors of her childhood—thin, buckled carpet, reeking of mildew and cigarette ash. In the St. Louis apartment, when she was twelve, she'd ripped out the bedroom carpet herself, but underneath there was nothing more substantial than a plywood subfloor, which she'd painted black. The landlord, Mr. Crowley, didn't return their deposit.

Creepy Crowley. She remembered how he used to let himself into the apartment when she was there alone, pretending he had to fix a leak or check the thermostat. He'd stand in her bedroom doorway, jiggling the keys in his pocket and sucking on his teeth while she played Atari. She always ignored him; after a while he would leave. Eventually she discovered that if she sneaked into the apartment through the bathroom window and didn't turn on any lights, he wouldn't come.

Sophie struggled to pry up a stubborn nail strip, working the crowbar around its edges. She had almost no memory of her parents in that apartment. Randall must have worked at an office in St. Louis. And Maeve, of course, rarely made it home in time for dinner. She was like Brian—oblivious to the passage of time while she worked, lost in her world of wing flaps and wind tunnels. Sophie remembered eating peanut butter sandwiches in the fading gray light that slouched through the kitchen's louvered window, never knowing exactly when to expect her parents. Normally she would have turned on the radio for company, but she didn't want to risk attracting Mr. Crowley. She wasn't sure if she'd felt, then, the sense of unfairness that now dogged her—that she'd wasted so many afternoons dreading the sight of Crowley's yellowed, short-sleeved shirt in her doorway, unable to articulate the menace it contained, but feeling it nonetheless. She'd mentioned it once to Maeve, but when Maeve asked if Crowley had ever said or done anything, Sophie had to say no, and that was the end of it.

She gathered a pile of nail strips and maneuvered them into a trash bag, trying not to tear the plastic. Then she stood staring at the floor, lost in thought. "What's going on in there?" asked Brian, gently lifting her dust mask over her head like a bridal veil.

Sophie laced her hands across her stomach. "Just thinking about my parents. Wondering what they'd think of this place. But I guess it wasn't really their thing, renovating." Randall had always picked their apartments sight unseen, from the newspaper, based on some algorithm of price per square foot and distance from Maeve's lab. It was the most efficient approach, Sophie knew—the quickest way to get them settled into whatever new place required Maeve's services. Maximize lift, reduce drag. Maeve designed wings for commercial aircraft, and

Randall freelanced, writing about consumer electronics. Sophie just followed in their slipstream.

"It's going to be beautiful," Brian said. "I'm sure they would've been proud." He brought her a cold bottle of water from the cooler, then went to the corner deli to buy sandwiches. They ate on the front stoop, butcher paper spread on their knees, and Brian filled Sophie's silence with stories about the museum. He'd bought the Milan vase, but his boss, Ted, had gone by himself to give the news to the director, and Brian was sure Ted had taken credit for the whole thing. Also, the clean out of the storage room had stalled.

"Conservation started getting everything ready to move to off-site storage, but they started having trouble matching the pieces with their object cards. So they need Michael to go through everything and figure out the cards, but of course Michael just left on his sabbatical." Brian gave a little laugh and shook his head.

"So they'll just have to wait."

"Yeah. Except nobody told the art handlers, who kept coming every day and loading the stuff onto object carts. I didn't say anything 'cause it's all silver and crystal—not my domain. But stuff shouldn't be sitting around in limbo like that. Michael's going to have a conniption when he gets back."

Sophie had heard the stories about Michael's fits of rage, usually provoked by mislabeled objects or misinformed art handlers. Ted, who was supposedly Michael's boss, was known to take sick days during Michael's more prolonged rampages. But Brian refused to be intimidated by his colleague, knowing that the majority of Michael's fury was born of impotence. He'd never come close to actually getting anyone fired.

"Where are they putting all the carts in the meantime?"

"They crammed them into our offices because they have to

be locked up at night, and they don't all fit in the storage room. Don't be surprised if you hear I've been found dead under a pile of candelabras."

"So what's going to happen to it all?"

"I'm sure it's going to stay that way until Michael gets back. Conservation's washed their hands of it, and anyway, they're working twenty-four seven on the Dalí show now. Lord knows I don't have time to deal with it."

This was classic Brian: placidly observing the chaos around him, unmoved by any urge to intervene. It wasn't coldness, necessarily, or even arrogance. It was simply an ability to remain engrossed in his own work, letting others wring their hands over everything else.

This suited Sophie's temperament perfectly, of course—but she worried that over time their tendencies were becoming more exaggerated, her yin swelling along with his yang. She'd seen this in older couples, like Brian's parents. His mother had always been talkative, his father reticent. But in their later years her chattiness metastasized into a nonstop monologue, while Brian's father lapsed into complete silence.

That was the risk, she supposed, in marrying the person who let you be your fullest self. No other man had been completely comfortable with Sophie's insistence on picking up the check and carrying her own groceries, or her habit of disappearing on long road trips without telling anyone where she was going. With Brian she was free to continue living as an unfettered twelve-year-old with a ten-speed, no curfew, no dinner cooling on the kitchen counter, no one calling the hospitals when she didn't make it home before dark. Even on their honeymoon in France, she'd spent the first day and a half teaching herself to drive stick because she refused to let Brian be the sole driver of the rental car. "I need to know I can get away," she'd joked, and he'd laughed, and let her drive the whole time, translating signs for her, reading maps, pointing out Gothic architecture. It was almost impossible to get the cranky Peugeot into reverse, but eventually she succeeded. "*Now* you can get away," Brian had said with a slow smile as she backed out of the parking lot of the Château de Sully-sur-Loire. She'd always assumed it was his way of holding on to her, this insistence on letting go.

And then her babies were born and pulled everything inside out. Instead of needing to know she could get away, Sophie needed very badly to know that she wouldn't. But that's what the house was for, wasn't it? Putting down roots. Making promises she had no choice but to keep.

She folded her butcher paper into a square and smoothed it flat. Their babysitting hours were slipping away, and her breasts were beginning to ache, but they sat a little longer, shoulder to shoulder, knee to knee. They watched the mailman shove piles of catalogs into slapping mail slots, and listened to the idling thrum of delivery trucks on the avenue. They waved to the old woman across the street who kept stealing peeks from behind a lace curtain. It was a rare moment unhooked from nap schedules and tantrum management; it could almost, Sophie reflected, be a moment lifted from their life before children. But this time she felt the weight of appreciation, and the creeping prickle of guilt.

"Back to work," she said, putting her hand on Brian's shoulder and heaving herself to her feet.

The block was lined with jack-o'-lanterns by the time Sophie and Brian finally brought the kids to see the house for the first time. It felt strange, after months of stepping over chunks of plaster and rusty nails, to carry their children across the threshold and set them down on the gleaming wood floor. Sunlight poured through the freshly cleaned front windows, illuminating the butter-yellow walls that were were, for a splendid moment, free of crayon marks, handprints, and fire-truck-shaped dents. The trim, stripped to its youthful profile and painted white, outlined each feature like glossy meringue icing, and the chestnut banister stretched upward through the house like a strand of pulled caramel. Elliot pointed at the living room's new pendant lights, hooting appreciatively. Meanwhile, Lucy marched straight to the locked door of the powder room. "We don't go in there, honey," Sophie said. "It's not finished yet." They didn't have enough money to renovate the small bathroom, and the floor was in danger of collapsing, so for now it was off-limits.

They took the children to the second floor to see their bedrooms. Lucy stood uncertainly in the middle of her pale blue room, gazing up at the windows filled with sunny yellow leaves. She peeked into the shallow closet where people had once hung their clothes on hooks, and where, Sophie imagined, Lucy would someday hide her diary, or a Judy Blume book, or worse. Lucy looked up at her mother with a worried expression, and finally asked, hesitantly, if she was going to sleep on the floor. Sophie laughed and picked her up, carrying her around the room and helping her imagine her new big-girl bed against this wall, a wardrobe over here, a table and chair in this corner, some shelves. Later, posters and headphones and a mirror. Slumber parties and heartbreak, rock anthems and rage. A place where Lucy could be alone but not lonely. A place where, Sophie half hoped, a mother might be occasionally resented, but never longed for.

Elliot's room was smaller, and Sophie worried that this inequity would somehow become nourishment for a lifetime of low expectations. But Brian had assured her that Elliot would never suffer from his sister's grasping need for rank and privilege. As an only child Sophie generally deferred to Brian on sibling issues, but she also wondered anxiously if it was already too late, and that Elliot's noncompetitiveness was due to a nascent understanding that he just couldn't win.

Up another flight of stairs, under the roof, Sophie and Brian's room had a view of the northern sky through the upper branches of the ginkgo tree. Sophie had chosen a soft taupe for the walls, a color that seemed compatible with deep, uninterrupted sleep. She knew it would be months—possibly years—before that dream would be realized. But this tranquil aerie felt full of promise.

Sophie took charge of the move, marshalling tape, Sharpies, and the best kind of cardboard boxes—double walled; taped or stapled but never glued. The sound of packing tape being pulled, shrieking, from the dispenser was as familiar as her children's voices. It brought back memories of another set of boxes, labels written, crossed out, written again. A set that had followed her from Seattle to Saint Louis, from Chicago to Bethesda, then to Los Angeles and, briefly, Montreal.

Sophie and Brian moved quickly—racing between the apartment and house in a borrowed truck while a babysitter watched the kids—and unpacked slowly, at night, after the kids were in bed. This was Sophie's favorite part: finding a satisfying spot for every lamp and picture frame, filling the living room's built-in bookshelves, nudging furniture this way and that, arranging, organizing, claiming every corner and cabinet. She sank fully into the house's embrace, the way she had once melted into Brian, back when they were young and well rested. At night she dreamed that the house was alive, its furnace whooshing blood through its veins, radiators sighing and moaning, the smooth plaster walls warming to her touch.

She knew it was crazy to be in love with a house, but that was exactly how it felt—the dazed disbelief slowly blossoming into cautious joy. The obsessive circling of the mind back to the object of its fascination, again and again, accompanied by a private, shuddering jolt of adrenaline. How could she explain it? It was exactly how she'd felt when she and Brian had first started dating seriously, when she finally let herself stay the night, when she finally shed her casual, playing-the-field bravado and submitted to another person's caring attentions in a way that felt simultaneously alien and normal. Brian was her first; she'd never even known what it meant—"falling in love"—until she found herself plummeting into that vacuum of utter vulnerability. And then, before long, the falling had turned into floating, and over the years it had eased into a gentle sway, holding her like a hammock, exactly the way she liked to be held, yielding yet secure, not too tight, not too loose.

So here she was again, letting herself fall in love—that strange, plunging feeling—only this time it was with a house, and it wasn't scary, because while people could abandon or hurt her, a house, she was pretty sure, could not.

Four

2006

Wherever there were children, there were Music for Me franchises, so naturally there was one right around the corner from the new house. Sophie took the kids to Music for Me twice a week—an experience that, on the spectrum of parental obligations, fell somewhere between the three a.m. feeding and the episiotomy. The parents (mostly mothers, with one or two bearded stay-at-home dads thrown into the mix) would sit in a circle on the floor, singing songs, clapping hands, and shaking maracas with strenuous glee while the babies dozed and the toddlers wandered off to investigate the room's light switches and door hinges. The teacher, a deeply dimpled young woman in a bright yellow vest with a ponytail on the very top of her head, sang everything. "Registration is now open for the next session," she would croon. "We take MasterCard and Visa, fa la la." Sophie couldn't look at her while she was doing this; it was too embarrassing.

Sophie spent the majority of the classes in a state of acute discomfort, counting the minutes until the ordeal would end. But Lucy seemed to like it, and sometimes Elliot waved his fists in a way that looked vaguely rhythmic, so Sophie continued taking them, knowing how important music was to their developing brains, and wishing someone had done the same for her so that she wouldn't have so much trouble hitting the notes in "Good Morning, Farmer George."

It also turned out to be a good way to meet other parents in the neighborhood. She met Amy there, and her melancholy daughter, Mathilda, who would follow Lucy around with a look of wonderment on her face. Amy was a social worker embroiled in local politics, and her husband, Keith, was an architect who dressed the part, from his old-school Pumas to his black-framed, ostentatiously nerdy glasses. They invited Sophie and Brian to dinners with other families in the neighborhood, and introduced them to a new way of socializing: the noisy playdate with cocktails, plain pasta at the kids' table, braised lamb shanks for the adults, gossip continually interrupted by shrieks, demands, and tantrums. Eventually somebody would put on a DVD in the playroom, and the kids would get quiet while the adults, moving on to dessert wine, got louder.

Brian was the star of these dinners, with his tales of auctions and collectors, of treasures found in attics and fakes found in museums. Their new friends pressed him for details about the millionaires on his committee, basking in the borrowed glow of the cable magnate, the football team owner's wife, the newspaper scion. Sophie appreciated those stories as social capital, but she knew they had nothing to do with Brian's actual work—what pulled him to his office early each morning, what made him forget to eat lunch or return Sophie's calls. It was the objects: the glaze, luster, relief, and reserve…it was the masterful brushstrokes consigned to brittle time capsules, which managed, through some miracle, to stay intact through wars and fires and ocean crossings. Brian was helplessly, embarrassingly in love with ceramics. He didn't bring that up at parties.

People didn't understand Sophie's work, mistaking her for a web designer and running out of questions once she explained that she worked strictly on the back end. She didn't mind; she had no interest in talking about her job outside her circle of colleagues. There was too much explaining, too much baffled admiration. Brian's job was firmly rooted in the material world, but her work had no shadow, no heft, and she found she could make a conversation evaporate with the mere mention of ASP.NET data binding or dynamic validation controls.

Besides, thinking about her work had begun to produce small twists of anxiety in her stomach. Things were not picking up the way they were supposed to. Sophie had long learned not to try to see around corners; the trick to the freelance life was to accept the inscrutability of the future and wait patiently for the job that would, inevitably, come along. But she'd only had a few small jobs since the summer, and it was becoming increasingly clear that during her brief maternity leave, most of her clients had managed to forget about her.

So while Lucy was in preschool and Elliot napped, Sophie filled her time reading web dev blogs and emailing friends in the business. She called her old clients, letting them know she had "bandwidth," even though she knew somehow that this would make things worse. Clients wanted the busy freelancers, the ones who took too long to call them back, the ones who negotiated with aloofness. She'd been one of the busy ones, before having children, and had seen how busyness always spiraled into hecticness. Now she saw that it worked the other way as well. Slowness spiraled into nothingness. It was hard not to feel like the lonely girl on the edge of the dance floor; she knew she shouldn't take it personally. It was just a matter of learning the latest software, getting to know the new project managers, letting her old friends know she was working again. It would happen eventually.

In the meantime, thanks to all the renovations and their attendant surprises (bad wiring, corroded plumbing), she'd had to perform some financial sleight of hand to get through the month: shifting balls in and out of cups. Send a payment to the plumber, put the cable bill on a credit card, make the minimum mortgage payment, write the babysitter a bad check for now, make up for it with cash the next week. She didn't say anything to Brian, not wanting to worry him; she knew it was a temporary situation. She also wanted to avoid giving him the opportunity to complain about the house.

To make things worse, Elliot had begun climbing out of his crib and scaling the changing table, bookshelves, and dresser, requiring Sophie to come downstairs several times a night to put him back to bed—silently, with no eye contact or cuddling, as directed by the child-rearing experts. As if cuddling were actually a temptation, after being yanked awake at the hard-won, blissful moment sleep arrived. Exhaustion and anxiety sharpened the edges of Sophie's mind, the way it had in the first sour-milk-scented weeks of her children's lives. She felt like she'd been scrubbed all over with steel wool. Lights were too bright, voices were too loud, the clutter of toys and shoes all over the house was a personal affront. Details slipped out of her mental grasp, and making any sort of decision, whether she was choosing pizza toppings or health insurance, left her quivering with confusion. Her voice took on a sharp edge that made the children wary. Brian kept his distance.

One airless June night, after several rounds of returning Elliot to his crib, Sophie retreated to her office to wait for his next foray. She turned on her desk lamp, and a moth fluttered into the room; they still hadn't ordered screens for the third floor windows. She picked up a stack of envelopes and started sorting them into piles: bills…credit card statements…

credit card offers worth considering...refinance offers... junk mail....

She came to an envelope that read: "An important message about your mortgage." Again? How many times could one mortgage change hands? She neatly sliced the top edge with her letter opener and scanned the dense type: "...to inform you... adjustable rate mortgage...London Interbank Offering Rate plus margin..." She shook her head. At the bottom, a box that said "Your new minimum payment, as of August 1, 2006" was set apart from the rest of the text. Was this some kind of offer? If so, it was laughable. The new payment was double what she was currently paying.

She set it aside, not sure what pile to put it in, and turned to the credit card statements. Scanning the charges, she was amazed by how many times she bought diapers at the corner market, where they were twice as expensive as anywhere else. She needed to get a membership at one of those bulk stores.

She returned the statements to their pile and picked the mortgage letter back up. It didn't look like an offer. She tried to decipher the words. It was definitely from her mortgage company, MortgageOne, and it was specific to her loan: there was her account number. She found the words "your new interest rate" buried in the final paragraph. She couldn't remember exactly what the original rate had been, something with two or three digits after the decimal point, but she was sure it was much lower than this one.

All right, so their interest rate had gone up. It seemed crazy that it had happened so fast; hadn't Ron told her it was good for a few years? Or was that something else? She fanned herself with the envelope, blinking away her exhaustion. It was so hard to remember what had happened in that cubelike, acoustic-tiled room so long ago. She recalled bouncing Elliot in her arms until her shoulders ached, but that was about it.

She squared the edges of the piles of envelopes, arranging them in a symmetrical pattern on her desk. Clearly, she couldn't make the new payment. It was absurdly high—and with virtually no warning! But wasn't there always room for negotiation? She'd been scrupulous about making payments on time, which should count for something. She pulled a colorful envelope out of the recycling bin: "REFINANCE TODAY!" Of course—that's what you do. She vaguely remembered hearing Ron tell her this. She looked at her watch. Five fifteen. She could call him in four hours.

⁂

"Well, hey, Sophie! Of course I remember you. How are those kids?" Ron's voice had the same cheesy-but-reassuringly-bouncy quality Sophie remembered. She explained the letter, the new payment.

"Yep," he said. "Well, as you probably remember, we went for the one-year ARM, 'cause you were looking for a lower payment at the time, while you got your business going again. And I got you that awesome promotional rate at the time…I do remember that."

"Okay, but this is ridiculous. We can't pay this. We need to refinance."

"I hear ya. I hear ya. You did an option ARM, right?"

"Yes."

"Have you been paying the whole enchilada every month?"

"Well, the minimum. It's all I can do right now. I haven't missed any."

"You did some work on the house, right? Any new bathrooms? Add any square footage? Deck?"

"We did a lot. Took care of the lead paint, fixed some walls, did the roof. Finished the floors. Electrical stuff."

"'Kay. 'Kay. Tell you what. Why don't you call the lender, explain your situation, see if you can put your heads together and craft some kind of solution."

"Craft—but can't you help us refinance?"

Ron coughed. "That's not gonna be an option for you. Look, I don't have access to your account, but it sounds like you've been tacking interest onto your balance this whole time. Your home's worth less than a year ago, your balance is higher; you're in, you know, you're in a tough spot. It sounds to me like you might be underwater."

"What?!" Sophie cried, her sluggish thoughts flailing. "Our house is not worth less. We put every penny of our savings into it; we did the electrical, the pipes. You should see the floors! You haven't seen it, Ron. You don't have any idea!" Her throat tightened, and tears moved into position.

"Hey—I'm just sayin'," Ron protested. "The market's tanking. I'm sure you've done amazing work... Just call your loan servicer. I'm only the broker. I want to help you, but I can't. 'Kay?"

"Okay." She tipped her head back and looked at the ceiling, noticing a threadlike crack in the plaster.

"It'll work out. Call your lender, all right?"

"All right. Thanks."

She was always doing that—thanking people who didn't deserve her gratitude. It was a dumb habit. Tears rolled down her cheeks.

That night she lay awake for hours, turning the situation over in her bruised mind. She was an idiot, agreeing to those terms. She'd barely skimmed the application before signing it. And this, after promising Brian she could take care of things! Why didn't she ever learn? She shouldn't be left to handle important matters on her own.

And the house. The house was supposed to take care of

her family, and she had promised to do the same in return. Could it really be taken away from them? The very idea seemed ridiculous. It was a problem of math, a matter of shifting balls in and out of cups a little faster. She'd call the mortgage company tomorrow. There was time. A good two months before the loan reset.

Elliot's wake-up call came blaring through the baby monitor at five forty-five. Sophie lay in bed waiting for Brian to make the first move, but he stayed asleep, or pretended to, snoring lightly.

The object carts were no longer in the hallway when Sophie visited Brian this time. Instead, half of them had been crowded into Brian's office, where Sophie had to scoot sideways, holding her messenger bag high, to get to the chair beside his desk. "Sorry," Brian said, moving a pile of reference books to the floor so she could sit down. "I've left the art handlers a million voice mails about this, but apparently nobody's home."

Sophie looked at the mess surrounding her and wondered what kind of help she was expecting to find here. She felt her resolve slipping, but tightened her grip. The conversation she was here to have—about the bills, the mortgage, the shell game—this was what married people did. They shared their troubles, confessed their mistakes, accepted help when it was offered. This was normal. Nothing to be afraid of. And she knew exactly how Brian would respond—with restraint. He wouldn't yell, he wouldn't blame. He'd just sigh and press his lips together, repressing his "I told you so." And in a way, this is what she was dreading most: his tranquillity, his bottom-less well of tenderness. He would try to make her feel better, telling her it was an honest mistake, promising they'd work it out together. He was always nicest to her when she deserved it the least.

Gathering her courage, Sophie turned to face him squarely. But Brian was uncharacteristically animated, swiveling in his chair and drumming his fingers in a way that looked almost gleeful. "What's going on?" she asked.

"I think I just figured out there's a piece of Saint-Porchaire on the loose."

"A piece of what?"

"French ceramics from the fifteen hundreds. Really ornate." He played his chair arms like bongos. "There's probably only about eighty of them in the world, a few of them in museums. We don't have any. Yet."

"Is there one coming up at auction?"

Brian gave her a faint one-sided smile that, for him, represented unbridled joy. "I think it might still be in private hands." He launched into the story: how he'd dug up the records of an 1893 estate sale in France, which showed the purchase of a small collection of Saint-Porchaire by the Philadelphia shipping magnate Paul Wilder. How he'd traced three of the pieces—a cup, saltcellar, and candlestick—to Wilder's son, who had eventually bequeathed them to the Metropolitan Museum of Art. How he'd figured out that there had been two candlesticks in the original sale—not one, as everyone had always assumed.

"So one of them broke when Wilder shipped them home," Sophie said, knowing that if this were true, Brian would be acting a good deal less jolly.

"That's the thing. He didn't ship it. I found the insurance records." Brian drummed his armrests a little faster. "I figured maybe he kept it in his Paris apartment, so I wrote to his granddaughter, Eleanor. She lived there for years and eventually sold the place, along with all the art he'd been hoarding there." He snatched a piece of stationery from a pile on his desk and held it up. "I just heard back from her."

"And?"

"She says the candlestick wasn't in the apartment."

"So...it broke before she was born."

"Maybe. But it's the way she wrote it." He scanned the letter. "'The candlestick was never displayed in the apartment, and the family is not aware of its whereabouts.' That's basically all she says about it. It's not the world's friendliest letter."

"But she's acknowledging that there was one."

"Right? That's how it sounds to me. It also sounds kind of like, 'Mind your own business.'"

"Which you have no intention of doing."

Brian gave a happy little shrug. Sophie had noticed that it was the pursuit of objects that excited him even more than the acquisition. Was this a man thing?

"Well!" she said, trying to sound encouraging. From her vantage point at home, amid the crumpled laundry and spilled Cheerios and nonringing phone, it was easy to cultivate shameful pockets of jealousy. But now, seeing Brian in his element, practically trembling with excitement, a bit of hair taking its leave from the carefully gelled ranks, she chided herself for being so selfish. Brian had worked hard for his success. He deserved it. If she worked a little harder, she could surely expect, some day, to enjoy the same level of contentment.

Brian took a deep breath through his nose. "So what's up, anyway?"

"Oh, just, some issues with—um, some mortgage papers that came in the mail." Sophie wound the strap of her bag around her hand.

"I hope this isn't going to involve math." He slid Eleanor's letter back into its envelope and started rummaging through a pile of folders.

"No, well, sort of. It's just that we got this thing called an option ARM—"

"What's that?"

"Well, you have the option of paying just the minimum payment, or the whole interest payment, depending on how things are going, and to be honest—"

Marjorie appeared in the doorway. "Excuse me." Brian swiveled to look at her. "Brian, maintenance needs to move a case, and there aren't any art handlers..."

"I scheduled them two weeks ago." He held out his hands; Marjorie just stood there. He let his hands fall to his lap. "Jesus. Sophie, I'm just going to run to the gallery for a minute; it shouldn't take long. I want to hear the rest of this; can you hang out?"

"All right," she said brightly, letting the strap unwind from her hand. It left welts in the fleshy part next to her thumb.

After Brian hurried out she set her bag on the floor and moved into his chair, surveying his desk. She could never understand how he managed to get anything done amid such chaos. Books and CDs were layered into the slippery strata of papers and file folders. One pile was anchored with a large tape measure, another with a dirty coffee mug. The sight irritated her. She started straightening one of the stacks, putting books and CDs into separate piles. Behind a drift of manila envelopes, she found a picture frame lying on its back. It held a photograph of Lucy holding Elliot in her arms, her face lit up by a combination of sisterly pride and the camera's flash. Elliot was looking up at her with wonderment, his lips parted, eyes wide. The picture had been taken during his chubby phase, when his skin had seemed to rise and puff like bread dough around his joints and under his chin. Sophie couldn't believe how much he had lengthened and thinned out since then. They were turning into real people before her eyes: Lucy, with her strong opinions and keen ear, had already discovered the pleasure of making people laugh—a benign addiction that would probably be with her the rest of her life. Elliot was fearless and determined, yet mild-mannered. He'd always seemed to take after Brian, but now Sophie wondered if there was a little bit of Maeve in there too. She cleared a space and stood the photograph back up.

The kids were growing up; even Brian was maturing, coming into his own. Sophie realized that she was the only one who was stuck, who hadn't grown into her new life, hadn't learned how to handle things properly, like an adult. She could almost hear Maeve's exasperated voice: "You're more responsible than this. What were you thinking?"

She felt the fog of exhaustion rolling over her once again, threatening to condense into tears. She turned away from the confusion of Brian's desk and picked up a mirror that was sitting on one of the rolling carts. She wiped away a smudge of mascara. She stared at her red eyes, which were sunk in deep shadows. She could not remember how it felt not to be tired.

The mirror was heavy in her hand. The oval glass was set in a rectangular metal frame whose raised decorations were bluish-black with age. She ran her finger over the chubby putti flanking the glass; four women dressed in flowing garments sat in the corners of the frame. She wiped her dusty finger on her jeans, a little guiltily. She knew she wasn't supposed to touch anything without gloves on. Still, she didn't put the mirror down. She was drawn to the frame's endlessly retreating detail, the mysterious array of globes and cubes and strange devices that danced around the figures in an almost random arrangement that, when she stretched out her arm, coalesced into soothing symmetry.

Her fingers tingled. She let the mirror rest in her lap. Brian wasn't coming back; it was a mistake to try to talk to him at the museum, anyway. He was too absorbed in his work, too busy with important matters. Besides, Sophie was filled with new determination to fix things and move forward—to do what Maeve had always exhorted her to do: grow up! She needed to find her own purpose in life, rather than waiting around for others to take care of her and give her life meaning. She decided to ask Marjorie to escort her out.

She put the mirror back on the cart, but it wouldn't lie flat between the wide, spreading foot of a candelabra on one side and a bulbous coffeepot on the other. Several dozen souvenir spoons cluttered the bottom of the tray. Had the mirror been propped on something? She leaned it against an inkstand, but it tipped sideways toward the edge of the cart. She shifted the candelabra to one side, lining it up with a pair of saltcellars, then tried to move the coffeepot the other way. Its handle hooked a bronze figure of a milkmaid, making it teeter, but Sophie caught it before it fell. There were too many pieces on this cart. She tucked the saltcellars into one corner, shoved some spoons aside, and slid the candelabra further to the left. The mirror still wouldn't lie flat. She felt despair begin to tread heavily on her brittle nerves. The mirror was heavy; it was about the size of a sheet of printer paper. She turned it one way, then another, but it was impossible to find a place for it among the neglected disorder of the cart.

She picked up the coffeepot, feeling her face flush; what if someone walked in and saw her juggling the objects like this? She remembered the look on the face of the art handler in the hallway, when she'd caught Sophie holding that silver candle-stick. That was embarrassing enough; now, here she was with a mirror in one ungloved hand and a coffeepot in the other. Out in the hallway, she heard Brian giving Marjorie instructions; it sounded like they were headed toward his office. Sophie tried, once again, to fit the coffeepot and the mirror together on the cart, but nothing was working. She felt a sudden flash of anger, as sharp and unexpected as a leg cramp in the middle of the night. Why did *she* always have to be the responsible one? What if she didn't *feel like* being the grown-up all the time? And why the *fuck* wouldn't this mirror fit into the goddamned cart?

Brian and Marjorie were just outside the door. Swiftly, Sophie set the coffeepot on the cart. Then she put the mirror in the only place she could think of…a place where it fit quite neatly, where it wouldn't be jostled or forgotten: the inner pocket of her bag, right between Elliot's diapers.

Five

L ucy had decided to drop out of preschool. She had loved the first few months, which were filled with the excitement of new toys, the box of dress-up clothes, and the child-size sink where she was allowed to serve herself water. Now, having reached the advanced age of three and a half, she could not face another early-morning stroll through Center City, had no interest in another round of "The Wheels on the Bus," and was bored to tears by her cubby, which was decorated with her name, a yellow heart, and a hook where she had once proudly hung up her coat all by herself.

Now she was like a cat being taken for a walk on a leash, flattened on the ground, hissing. When Sophie tried to put shoes on her feet, she balled them into fists. She ate her breakfast in tiny bites, chewing in slow motion. When it was time to walk out the door, she would become engrossed in highly urgent tasks, such as reuniting every single Magic Marker lid with every single long-dried-out Magic Marker. Any attempt to interrupt this project would cause her to fling the markers across the room, throw herself to the ground, and pound the floor.

The morning after Sophie's visit to the museum, Lucy put on an elaborate performance as The Child Who Is Too Gravely Ill to Attend School. Her stomach hurt, her throat burned, she couldn't hear, her nose was running, she felt like throwing up, she had cavities. She began to hack like an old woman with emphysema.

"Let me see your throat," Sophie said. Lucy opened her mouth as wide as it would go, and Sophie peered solemnly inside, wondering why three-year-olds never had morning breath.

"All right. Let me feel your forehead." Lucy watched her mother carefully as she gauged her temperature. "Let's have a look in your ears now."

"Am I sick, Mommy?" she asked softly.

"I'm still checking." Sophie held a tissue to her nose. "Blow." Lucy blew as hard as she could. Nothing came out.

"I'm going to feel your tummy now." She pressed lightly on her stomach. "Okay…"

"Maybe I should take some of the grape medicine," Lucy suggested.

Sophie sat back. "In your condition," she said, "medicine will only make things worse."

"My kudishan?"

"It looks like antipreschoolitis. It's very important to dress warmly, and eat a good breakfast."

For the rest of the morning she played along with Lucy's delusions of illness, murmuring sympathetically and giving her warm milk. Once Lucy had cheerfully finished her cereal and Brian was dressed and waiting by the front door, Sophie took Lucy in her arms, felt her forehead again, and looked in her ears and her throat.

"I've never seen anything like it."

"What, Mommy?"

"You're cured! It's a miracle."

She quickly transferred Lucy into Brian's arms, along with her lunch box, then opened the door and waved good-bye.

Lucy's eyes were narrowed, but by the time she stiffened her legs and gathered breath for a scream, the front door had swung shut with a thud.

Once Elliot was dressed and installed on the living room floor with a pile of Tupperware, Sophie sat on the couch and reached into her bag for her laptop. As she pulled it out, the front of the bag slumped against her hand, heavy with the contents of its inner pocket. She pulled her hand back and pressed it against her belly, becoming still. She sat like that for a few moments, huddled inside her secret, insulated from everything around her, including Elliot, who was absorbed in his own private world of plastic towers.

She remembered now how she had told Brian she was late for a conference call, then asked Marjorie to escort her out of the offices. After emerging on the second floor balcony, she'd hurried past the monumental baroque tapestries lining the walls and quickly descended the wide, dizzying staircase in the center of the Great Hall. Striding toward the entrance, her mind already flying through the heavy doors, past the columns and down the steps, her breath snapped back into her throat at the sight of two figures silhouetted against the glass. A museum guard in ill-fitting blue polyester, his rear resting on a tall stool, was craning his neck over a dark shape, which was held out by a woman in a short dress and flat shoes. The shape, Sophie saw as she drew closer, was a purse. The woman was holding it open for the guard. He was peering inside.

Sophie had not slowed, had not hesitated; she'd merely jerked her eyes away and continued on her trajectory, giving the door a businesslike shove and trotting down the steps like someone in a great hurry to do important things.

Now, moving much less deliberately, she pulled the mirror out of her bag and laid it flat on the palm of one hand. The glass was almost absurdly small in proportion to the wide frame, which was edged in black wood. A bit of silver filigree protruded from the top edge, with a ring for hanging the mirror on a nail. She admired the casually lifelike poses of the women seated in each corner, the graceful arrangement of their muscled arms and legs, the draping of their robes. A welter of finely drawn detail—from oddly mechanical-looking scrolls to a staccato line of beads and notches forming a delicately textured border—constrained the design in a formal, balanced composition. Sophie couldn't believe the amount of effort that had gone into such a mundane object. So much labor for a simple mirror frame—those were the days!

Which days, exactly, she couldn't really say. It was pretty old—she could see that in the tarnish of the silver and the mottled look of the glass. But she had no way of knowing if it was late Renaissance or late Reagan administration. If she had to guess, she would've said it was a twentieth-century repro-duction of something from an earlier, grander time.

She shook her head, trying to clear her thoughts. What did it matter how old it was? It wasn't supposed to be here, lying on her now-sweaty hand. It was supposed to be in a museum, on a storage cart, being readied for its journey to a faraway warehouse.

Of course she would take it back. It was just a harmless prank. She was like that guy in the news who had decided to test airport security by planting a gun in the airplane bathroom. She'd just sneak the mirror back into Brian's office, and if she got caught she'd explain that she was making a point about careless storage practices.

Which would get Brian fired. It would probably be better to say it had been a mistake. She thought it was her mirror. Or, she had dumped out her bag and accidentally gathered up the mirror with the rest of her things.

She lay her head back on the couch. Lying to a three-year-old was one thing; it would be far too embarrassing to tell one of these fantastical stories to Brian's boss. She took the mirror into the kitchen and wrapped it in several plastic grocery bags. She slipped it into the back of a cupboard, between some cookie sheets that nobody was likely to use for another decade or so. She needed time to think.

The babysitter wouldn't be coming for another hour, so she strapped Elliot into the stroller and went for a walk around the neighborhood, ambling pensively through allées of ginkgos and decorative pears waving their freshly unfurled leaves. She needed to think things through logically. Working backward from her desired outcome, she should be able to find a stream of clear, rational steps that would solve her problem with elegance and efficiency.

Option A: Return to the scene of the crime and hope that Brian would leave her alone in his office. She could try to go when he wasn't at work, but she would still need an escort to get to his office—and anyone who did that would be unlikely to leave her there by herself. Even assuming they did, what if the cart was gone? She couldn't just stash the mirror in the midst of Brian's mess—that would get him in as much trouble as stealing it.

Option B: Confess to Brian, and let him return the mirror.

Option C: Throw the mirror away, bury it in the backyard, toss it into the Schuylkill River. It sounded like no one would miss it. Some old lady had probably bequeathed her silver to the museum, and some overworked curator had just stuck it all in a storage closet until he had time to assign accession numbers and object cards. If the mirror was worth anything, someone would have taken better care of it.

Her mind followed each scheme to the end of its path,

analyzing its logic and contemplating alternate sequencing. It was a process that, in her work, usually delivered her to a point of gratifying clarity. But this time she found herself getting more and more lost in forks, loops, and branches, unable to manage dynamic interactions, fogged in by confusion. She turned onto the avenue for the second time, nodded a greeting—again—to the grocer pushing his broom. Elliot squirmed in his seat; she looked at her watch. It was time to go back.

The red jersey dress, Sophie decided, was too unforgiving. At least the black one was covered in sequins, which served to create some visual confusion around the more plush areas of her waist. She wasn't sure if sequins were appropriate for the museum party they were going to—she would probably be the youngest person there, and definitely the sparkliest. But she didn't have a lot of other options. She tugged on her "foundation garment." Constructed of thick, industrial-strength elastic, the beige underthing flattened her belly into a smooth, taut drum. The waistband, which actually stopped just below her bra, was a wide strip of rubber that gripped her skin and left a red welt. The leg bands were made the same way, preventing the underwear from creeping northward. Wearing it made her feel like a tightly swaddled baby.

During the four years that she spent either pregnant or breast-feeding, Sophie's body had expanded, contracted, bulged, and cracked more often than a Philadelphia sidewalk. Both babies were large; Elliot had caused her old stretch marks to splinter into new ones—purple zebra stripes that later faded and sank, creating silvery crevices across her belly. During both pregnancies her breasts had ballooned, swollen and tender; upon weaning they collapsed, exhausted, onto her rib cage.

She'd lost all of her pregnancy weight while breast-feeding Lucy, but gained it back the minute she got pregnant with Elliot—a huge baby who'd sprawled all over her lower abdomen and seemed, toward the end, as uncomfortable with the arrangement as she was. After he was born she wore her smaller maternity clothes for a few weeks, but then, as he nursed more and more voraciously, her body had melted away like a stick of butter in the microwave.

Now that Elliot was weaned she was going back to her old weight, but her body was like a borrowed dress that had been returned all stretched out and wrinkled. She lifted her soft, empty breasts into a push-up bra, then pulled on the black dress and stepped into some strappy heels. She eyed herself in the mirror—from the side, from behind. Despite the undergarment's best efforts, her belly still swayed forward, an echo of her pregnant self. She sucked it in, mashing it with her hands. The elastic made her stomach feel oddly anaesthetized.

She rummaged among her purses and pulled out a black leather bag that was too large and casual for her dress. She frowned at herself in the mirror one more time, then headed downstairs.

"You can call me any time tonight," she said to the babysitter, who was feeding the kids their dinner. "We're right around the corner, so…" She went into the kitchen and rummaged through a cabinet, blurting instructions over her shoulder.

"Keep Elliot's monitor on after you put him to bed—he might decide to climb out. And be sure you dry Lucy's face really well. She's getting chapped."

She kissed the children's heads and placed conciliatory cookies on their plates. "Mommy, don't go. Why don't you stay?" whined Lucy. Sophie blew her one more kiss, ignored the question, and pushed through the front door into the humid night air.

Brian was waiting outside the museum's west entrance, scanning the crowd of valets and patrons milling outside. Sophie felt a nervous flutter as she approached, in the moments before he caught sight of her. When he did, his body became still and his eyebrows lifted. She felt blood gather in the tips of her ears.

"Wow," he said, lacing his fingers with hers. "You're beautiful." Sophie searched his face for hints of flattery, but she didn't need to: Brian was the most resolutely sincere person she'd ever known. She ran her fingers along the lapel of his tuxedo jacket, feeling the cautious gratitude that comes with too much luck. Brian turned and led her inside, gallantly preceding her through the heavy revolving door. As they crossed the polished stone floor Sophie walked on her toes, not trusting her wine-stem heels.

"Help me keep an eye out for Howard from Prints and Drawings," Brian said. "He promised to introduce me to this woman Mrs. Weber—she was best friends with Fifi Belmont, Wilder's other granddaughter."

"Wilder's the guy—"

"Who had the Saint-Porchaire candlestick. I'm hoping I can get Mrs. Weber to tell me some stories about the family, maybe introduce me to some of Wilder's descendants. I realize how far-fetched it all is, but I have to try." Sophie marveled at the way Brian's work filled every moment of his life, every crevice of his mind. He never stopped thinking about it. She remembered feeling that way, just out of college, when she'd been obsessed with the three-dimensional galaxies of hypertext; and later, when writing code began turning into something of an art form. But then, when she started freelancing, the work had gradually become less about exploration and creativity, and more about paying the bills. She wondered when, if ever, she might rediscover the joy in it.

They emerged into the soaring central hall, which echoed with laughter and jazz. Redwood-size columns rose to the roof and dwarfed the partygoers below; a trumpet solo bounced brassily against the stone. At the top of the grand staircase a towering statue of Diana alighted, weightlessly balanced on the toes of one long foot, her strong fist punching her bow forward, the other hand a knot of knuckles pulling the string taut. She was lightness and strength and beauty and danger, the museum's guardian huntress overseeing every opening and cocktail party.

Sophie and Brian wove through the gathering crowd toward the bar, where they met Brian's boss, Ted. Tall and thin, with long ears and sagging eyes, Ted had worked at the museum for decades, and, it seemed, would be there forever, pacing its corridors long after taking his last shaky breath. Now he was thrusting glasses of wine into Brian's and Sophie's hands, his eyes darting over their heads and into the crowd.

"Mr. Burnett is here," he said, using his head to point. "I really think you should say a word to him tonight. Plant the seeds for the Lyon auction."

"Got it," said Brian. "What about you—can I get you a drink?"

Ted shook his head vigorously, making his jowls tremble. "Oh dear no. Thanks. I saw Mrs. Paul scurrying around here somewhere. You should thank her for approving the Milan purchase. She needs to hear from the whole department—make her feel really special." Then, giving Brian a pat on the shoulder, he prowled into the crowd, sniffing out money and egos with his long, nervous nose.

"Why does he need to come to every single one of these things?" Brian muttered into his wineglass.

"Sorry," Sophie said. She knew how much Brian despised the predatory chitchat that was required of him at these parties: the tissue-thin flattery and weightless smiles, all designed to flush large checks out of jeweled clutches. He was terrible at it, or so he thought, which actually made him good at it. Museum patrons—particularly the women—were disarmed by his scholarly reserve, his devotion to the objects, his blithe, detached air in the presence of elephantine wealth.

"Let's dance a little before you go to work," Sophie said, setting her empty wineglass on a passing tray. She pulled Brian onto the dance floor, where they leaned into each other and shifted vaguely from foot to foot. When did formal dancing dissolve into this strange shuffle, Sophie wondered, admiring one septuagenarian couple that seemed to be executing actual dance steps. She rested her cheek against Brian's shoulder, feeling his voice vibrate inside his chest.

He was asking her about work, whether she was doing anything interesting. "Nothing," she said, "as interesting as this." She smiled up at him, and he brought his lips to hers, and as they kissed she was flooded, simultaneously, with the warmth of desire and the chill of dread. She closed her eyes, trying, like Elliot, to become invisible by making the rest of the world disappear. When she opened them she saw the glinting tip of Diana's arrow just over Brian's shoulder, and then, just off the dance floor, Howard, from Prints and Drawings, trying to get Brian's attention.

"There's Howard," she said, pulling away.

"Aha," Brian said. "Sorry. I won't be long."

Sipping her second glass of wine, Sophie watched her husband work. Howard had led him over to a small, plump woman in a brown dress that was embellished with black and white feathers. Her tiny mouth was painted bright red. Sophie assumed this was the woman connected to Paul Wilder; what she didn't understand was how this elderly person, who had once been friends with someone related to the guy who'd bought some candlesticks, was supposed to help Brian track down a missing Renaissance masterpiece. But to Brian no lead was ever too faint, no alley too blind, and it was often sheer persistence, more than depth of knowledge, that gave him an advantage over his less resolute colleagues.

Howard had taken his leave of them, and was chatting with a tall couple in their forties. The woman wore a simple black sheath, and the man had on a tuxedo with no tie. Their haircuts were straightforward, their faces bland, jewelry minimal, yet they shone with wealth. Sophie tried to figure out where, exactly, the sheen came from. Howard, perfectly presentable in his traditional tuxedo, didn't have it. His colleague Nancy, who had appeared at his side, didn't have it either. Sophie decided it was the graceful drape of the tall woman's dress, and its perfect length (just to the top of her shoe's delicate ankle strap), despite her considerable height. Nancy's dress, also black, pulled a little across the shoulders. But was that really it? Or was it the tall couple's bearing—watchful but relaxed. The air of creatures who knew they were surrounded by hunters, but who could, when necessary, leap swiftly into a waiting car and be whisked away to their leafy refuge on the Main Line.

This was a timeworn style of affluence, all flamboyance rubbed smooth over the course of generations. Others wore their wealth differently. Sophie's friend Carly, for example, carried handbags the size of laundry baskets, and left life-changing tips for waiters she found cute. But Carly's parents got rich in the eighties. She grew up watching them rake possessions into glittery piles, then engage in prolonged battles over the size, location, and maintenance of those piles after their divorce. Sophie figured this explained the handbags: Carly had been taught to keep her belongings close at hand. Her acquisitiveness was nervous and insulating, and Sophie didn't envy it. "But the life of these Main Line heirs, who had been born into comfort and composure—that was something she could get used to."

"Sharp as a tack," Brian said in Sophie's ear. "She said she can tell me lots of stories about the Wilder family."

"Mrs. Weber? Does she know anything about the candlestick?"

"She doesn't remember seeing it, but said there are plenty of people who could've ended up with it. I'm taking her to lunch next week to get more details."

Sophie took his arm and they circled the Great Hall. She was on her third glass of wine, and was starting to feel the way she imagined Elliot felt most of the time: jolly, unsteady on her feet, full of bad ideas. She leaned against Brian and whispered in his ear, "Phone call." Brian's mouth opened in surprise, then he looked around and pulled her behind a column.

They'd come up with the code word years ago, early in their relationship, when Brian was an assistant in the department and Sophie was working at an advertising agency on Broad Street, back when the idea of going somewhere to answer a phone call had not yet become ridiculous. It was a time of endless parties— gallery openings, agency happy hours, karaoke night with the art handlers. Sophie would be leaned up against the bar with a beer in her hand, listening to some kid designer going on about the typography in *Ray Gun*, when Brian would come up and murmur "phone call" in her ear. Then he'd saunter off down a dark hallway, where she'd meet him for some moments of frantic, rugged kissing. Over time the phrase became shorthand, depending on tone of voice, for "you look amazing," "I love you," or just, "let's go home."

Neither one of them had said it in a while. These days kissing felt strange; almost embarrassing. This was a man who had seen her with vomit in her hair, who came to bed every night with socks on. Their intimacy during the last few years had been of the most ruthless kind; kissing required them to reintroduce the membrane of romance, like putting on gloves and a hat.

Pushing her against the column, Brian slipped his hand under Sophie's hair, sliding it along the back of her neck almost furtively, the way it would sneak under a skirt or a blouse. His stubble gently scratched the skin around her lips. Sophie's nerve endings felt overwhelmed, every cell awakening at the same time. She squirmed against Brian's hands, the electric discomfort driving her to seek more pressure, more muscle, more skin. "Let's go to your office."

Brian stepped back a moment, searching her face, then took her hand and led her around the corner. He knew as well as she did that it was important to move quickly, before the fragile moment slipped through their fingers and flitted off into the night. They hurried down a hallway and into a freight elevator.

"I'm glad I didn't turn in my keys," he said as they passed through the elevator doors to his department. An exit sign barely illuminated the narrow hallway.

"Ted's not coming up here, is he?" she whispered.

"I guess you never know. Kind of adds to the thrill, right?" Brian unlocked his office door and ushered her in, his hand warm against her shoulder blades. She felt her way through the darkness to his desk, veering slightly to the right in the hopes of colliding with an object cart.

Brian turned her around and pushed her up against the desk, his hands already full of bra padding. He kissed her hesitantly, then insistently, his hands tugging at the bottom of her dress.

"What the…" He rubbed the sheet of elastic that encased her belly. "Where does this thing end?"

She squirmed away. "I'm sorry. Jesus."

"Is it Kevlar?" He laughed, pushing her dress up further. "Let me see."

"Yeah. Bulletproof underwear. Get off me."

"Come on…" he said, grabbing her around the waist. "I love this. I love coming up here with you. It's like before. Only less…accessible." He snapped the elastic around her thigh.

Sophie rested her forehead on his shoulder, and gathered her courage. "Brian, could you…do you mind going in the hall for a minute? I don't want you to…you know…see."

"See? I can't see a thing. C'mon. Let me help."

"I'm embarrassed," she hissed. "Just—"

"Really?" He stepped back. "All right, I'm sorry. Tell me when you're ready."

When she was alone, Sophie grabbed her purse and pulled out the bundle that was stuffed inside. The grocery bags rustled as she shakily unwrapped the mirror. She felt for the cart among the shadows around his desk, but her hands met only air. It didn't make any sense; Brian's office was never this empty. She couldn't even find a pile of books to set the mirror on.

Out in the hallway, fluorescent lights fluttered on. "Brian!" she hissed. "No lights!"

"Oh, hey, Ted!" she heard Brian say with a little laugh. "Mrs. Paul." Sophie crammed the mirror back into her purse, holding it against herself to muffle the sound of the bags.

"There you are," said Ted. "I was going to give Mrs. Paul a copy of your article in the *British Art Journal*."

"Oh! All right," said Brian. "I was just showing off my clean office to Sophie. It only happens once a year, so…" Brian's hand snaked through his office door and flicked on the light. Sophie backed against his desk, blinking, her purse behind her back. The door pushed open and Ted and Mrs. Paul peered in, Mrs. Paul's blond coif forming a golden halo around her tight, acid-peeled face.

Sophie gave them a little wave.

"Aha," said Ted, his mouth slack.

"Well!" said Mrs. Paul. "You have been hard at work, haven't you." Her eyes were wide, but her eyebrows didn't move. "I think I'd rather look at the article in your office, Ted, if you don't mind."

They left. Brian bowed his head, shaking it back and forth. Was he laughing? She couldn't tell. "Oh, Sophie." He wasn't laughing.

"What?" she said, casually slinging her purse over her shoulder, checking to see if it was closed. "Nobody caught—" And of course it was only then that she looked down and realized that her dress was still pushed up around her waist, giving the world an unimpeded view of her elastic-encased bottom half.

Six

MortgageOne, it turned out, was not their lender; it was their "loan servicer." It took Sophie three phone conversations with uniformly uninspired MortgageOne representatives to figure out that her loan actually belonged to Dayton Loan Services, a company with no web presence, but whose number she managed to find by calling, on a hunch, directory service in Dayton, Ohio.

"Sorry," said the affable young man at DLS, who sounded like he was operating out of his dorm room. "Your loan is with…" He tapped some keys, then tapped some more. "New Century Mortgage."

New Century Mortgage played an endless recording about high call volume, encouraging callers to try again another time. Sophie did this daily until, exactly a week after her first attempt, a real person actually picked up the phone. "I'd be happy to help you," said the representative, with a veneer of professionalism that was a relief to Sophie's ear. "What's your account number?"

Sophie read out the number, slowly, and the representative read it back.

"Hmmm," she said. "Normally our account numbers have three more digits. Let's try your address, phone number, and social."

Before long, Sophie had given the representative so much information about herself, the woman could have assumed her identity, moved into her house, and started raising her children. Still, she couldn't find any record of Sophie's mortgage.

"Why don't you call your loan servicer," she suggested.

"That's where I started. They sent me to DLS, who sent me to you. I have no idea how this works, but clearly my check is going somewhere—right?"

"Of course. If I were you, I'd write a letter to your servicer. Start putting everything in writing. You might get further that way. Good luck!"

"Okay, thanks," Sophie said, wondering what she was thanking her for. She felt dwarfed by this vast web of mortgage lenders, servicers, and brokers. These people were tied to her by the most gossamer of connections: a telephone call to anonymous banks of customer service representatives. They knew that if they could get her off the phone, she'd call back later and get someone else. Never mind that the shadows around her eyes were beginning to resemble bruises. Never mind that every hard-earned hour of sleep was interrupted by nightmares of homelessness. Never mind that she was a good person who had simply made a mistake and was now trying, as hard as she knew how, to unmake it.

Carly wanted to walk the bike path because it made her feel like she was exercising, so Sophie strapped the kids into the double stroller and went to meet her behind the museum. The sun glowered through the sycamores that lined Kelly Drive, and joggers heaved themselves through the humid air. She could see Carly coming around the bend, striding through the bobbing crowds like a limousine with tinted windows: aware that she was drawing stares, returning none of them.

"Glad to see the SUV is holding up," Carly said, dropping her water bottle into the stroller's cup holder. She always had to mention the stroller. It had been her shower gift, presented to Sophie along with every possible accessory: cup holder, rain cover, the detachable "foot muffs" that zipped onto the seats and covered the kids' legs in cold weather. It was the kind of shower gift that took up too much space in someone's living room, making all the other gifts look small.

"It's great." Sophie stretched upward into a mist of YSL Paris and espresso and kissed Carly's cheek. "You look amazing, as usual."

"How's life? How's the house?"

Sophie leaned on the stroller to get it going, trying to keep as far to the right as possible so she wouldn't take out any Rollerbladers. "The house is fantastic," she said, ignoring the first question. "It feels really good, being anchored—you know? It's what I've always wanted for our kids."

"Do they appreciate it?"

"In their way, I guess. It's their normal. The other day Lucy drew a picture of her home. And instead of the usual, you know, pointy roof, chimney, she drew a tall skinny rectangle with a flat roof and six windows."

"How very Philadelphia."

"I know. I was so happy—it's part of her iconography. Right along with her stick family." She patted her belly. "I aspire to be more like my stick self." She tried for a lighthearted chuckle, but it came out sounding forced. The mortgage situation kept leaking into her thoughts, darkening her mood. How long before they would have to move out, and Lucy would have to learn to draw a new kind of house?

"How's work?" Sophie asked quickly.

"Oh, you know." Carly began doing stretches, folding one long arm at a time behind her head and pressing down on her elbow, looking like the world's most elegant broken umbrella. "I'm doing a gig at Hexagram, which is fine, except they keep throwing last-minute revisions at me and expecting me to turn them around overnight. I've basically been living at the agency." Unhampered by mortgage payments or cable bills, Carly didn't have to work; she chose to. She loved code and information architecture and, Sophie was pretty sure, being surrounded by men. Carly was also engaged in an ongoing battle against boredom—a symptom, probably, of being single, childless, and financially comfortable. But Sophie supposed boredom was as legitimate a problem as any other, and she had to admire Carly for putting up a good fight. Carly could be vain and self-involved, but she was firmly in charge of her life, and Sophie had never, in their ten years of friendship, seen her mope or complain or indulge in the luxury of aimlessness.

"What're you working on?" Carly asked.

"I'm kind of between things right now. Waiting to hear back on a couple of bids."

"You're not working on that huge Vidontrin project at Pixelhaus? I thought they were using everyone in the city." Carly uncapped her water bottle and drank deeply.

"That's not really my kind of job. Too many layers, too much busywork."

Carly had a face like a crossbow: long, slender nose leading to wide, languidly curving lips. She shot Sophie a sharp look. "Really."

Sophie shrugged. "Really. Dating anyone new?"

"No. What're you bidding on? Anything juicy?"

Sophie shoved the stroller's sunshade down over the kids' heads. "Nothing special."

"Why don't I call my friend at Whirlygig, in New York. I just turned him down for a job. He's probably still looking for someone."

"New York? No way."

"He said off-site was okay."

"Thanks, Carly, but I've got everything under control. Really."

Carly rolled her eyes. "Give me a break. Just let me help you out for a change, all right? You look terrible. Have you slept at all in the past year?"

"Thanks. No, I haven't."

"Okay then. I'm calling Whirlygig. I'll have Dan get in touch with you." She tweezed a blob of mascara from an eyelash. "How's Brian?"

"You know. Job-obsessed. He's on the trail of some mysterious ceramic candlestick that went missing in France. I think he's nuts, but he's convinced it's sitting in someone's attic waiting to be discovered." Sophie was relieved to be off the subject of her foundering freelance career, but realized she didn't particularly feel like talking about the museum, either.

Just then she noticed a man jogging toward them, looking straight at her. Her brain spun the wheel of social contexts, ticking through possible connections: Museum guy? Client? Ex-boyfriend?

"Keith!" she exclaimed as he pulled up in front of them, hands on his hips, panting. "I didn't recognize you without your glasses."

He grinned. "They fog up when I run. Hey, little guy." He wiggled his fingers at Elliot. "Hi, Lucy." His chest heaved under a sweaty T-shirt, which clung to his decidedly unnerdy pecs.

"Carly, this is Keith. He feeds us. Keith, Carly."

"Hey," he said, with a little wave. "I'm sweaty, sorry."

"That is not a problem," Carly said to his chest. She slowly angled her head to one side, then straightened it, found Keith's eyes, and unleashed a wide smile.

"Keith is married to Amy," said Sophie.

"Do I know Amy?"

"She's our new friend. Married. To Keith."

"Mmm." Carly was still smiling.

"So we'll see you Saturday?" Keith said to Sophie.

"Yep. Six o'clock."

"What can we bring?"

"Wine, I guess? Italian? Brian's making pork ragu."

"'Kay. See you then. Nice meeting you, Carly."

"My pleasure. Keith."

Sophie and Carly walked on.

"So—" Carly began.

"No."

"What?"

"Just, no. I'm not telling you where he lives, where he works, or what his last name is."

"What? You're acting like…like…"

"They're our new friends. If I decide I hate Amy's guts, fine. I'll give you his number. But she's a social worker."

"Excuse me? He was wearing Lacoste."

"Architect," muttered Sophie.

"Ooooooh—"

"NO."

Lucy twisted around in her stroller to see who was being bad, and Elliot waved his arms, crowing his new favorite word: "NONONONO!"

Dan wanted Sophie to come to Whirlygig on one of the days she didn't have a sitter, so she asked Brian if he could take the day off.

"I guess so," he said. "I'm kind of supposed to be keeping an eye on Marjorie and the storage situation, but one day won't hurt." They were lying on the couch, heads at opposite ends, legs intertwined, watching *Antiques Roadshow.*

"You're sure you don't mind? I can try to reschedule."

"It's fine."

"I owe you one." She slipped a hand into the cuff of his jeans, running it up his knifelike shinbone. Brian shifted his legs over and motioned for her to come to his end of the couch. She nestled against his shoulder, and as he stroked her hair she felt her tension sluice away.

"Does it sound like a good project?" he asked.

"I think so. I trust Carly's judgment—about work, anyway."

"Good. You seem a little…stressed. I was wondering if your clients were making you crazy, or what."

"I can't say I have any clients making me crazy right now," she said truthfully. "I'm just crabby from not sleeping. I'll be fine once Elliot goes back to sleeping through the night. Anyway, how was your lunch with Mrs. Weber? Did she tell you anything about the candlestick?"

"She just wanted to talk about her engravings. I don't think she really got that I'm a ceramics guy."

"Sorry."

"It's okay. She did mention one thing." On the television, a plump woman in a turtleneck was showing her cross-stitched sampler to a dealer. "Apparently Wilder didn't just go to France to shop for art. She said it was an open secret that he had a girlfriend over there."

"Aha."

"Yeah. Who knows where that'll lead…"

The woman on TV looked stricken. An animated treasure chest rolled across the bottom of the screen, trailing the words "Early American Sampler: $10,000–$15,000."

"Jesus," Brian breathed. Sophie blinked at the screen.

"It's amazing what people have hidden away," she murmured, her face warm. She twisted around to face Brian, her heart beating fast, seeking reassurance in the firm pressure of his chest against her chest, his hips against her hips. "Phone call?" she said softly. Brian reached around her shoulder, flicked off the TV, and let the remote fall to the floor.

Sophie felt lighter than air as she pushed through the heavy, brass-fitted doors of Thirtieth Street Station and hurried past the food stalls and newsstands that were already thronged with wingtip- and slingback-clad commuters. In the vast, marble-lined central hall, the clacking information board flipped its letters and numbers, stubbornly refusing to join the twenty-first century, while quaintly outfitted redcaps pushed carts of luggage and tipped their hats at ladies. At least they'd finally installed automated ticket kiosks, Sophie observed. She was less heartened to find that ticket prices had almost doubled since her last trip to New York. She'd just have to expense it when the job was over.

Once settled into the luxurious embrace of her seat on the Metroliner, Sophie pulled a warm paper bag out of her briefcase, holding it on her lap for a moment. There was a toasted sesame bagel inside, which she was going to be able to eat at her leisure without anyone's chubby hands trying to tear it from her mouth. After that she could daydream, look out the window, close her eyes for a nap. She could visit the restroom and relax in its solitude, without a small person crowded against her knees, staring at her.

In the seat facing her, a woman in lavender houndstooth was maneuvering thick stacks of paper in and out of her rolling briefcase, periodically writing notes in a leather folio. Her companion, a man in his late twenties with shaggy hair and an ill-fitting suit, idly paged through a copy of *People* while holding a one-sided conversation.

"Could you believe that con call yesterday.

"I thought Jenkins was going to have a stroke.

"Those rookies in DC have screwed things up royally."

Flip, flip.

"I hope they bring in lunch today.

"I like that place they order from…Donagans?

"The roast beef is off the hook."

Sophie was impressed by the degree to which the woman was ignoring him, and by the man's compulsion to keep talking anyway. Why didn't he just shut up? Couldn't he see how busy she was, doing the work he was probably supposed to be helping her with? At one point the woman looked up and met Sophie's eye; Sophie gave her a little smirk, and a raised eyebrow; a sisterly moment of shared contempt. Then she turned to the window.

When she looked back, the woman was packing up her belongings. She gathered her trench coat and folio into her arms, pulled out the briefcase's handle with a snap, and moved to another seat. Strangely, her companion stayed where he was. Even more strangely, he continued to talk.

"…heartburn sometimes…probably the horseradish.

"Whaddareya gonna do.

"Dude. I know.

"Yep. Yep. Okay. Later."

Bluetooth. Sophie finally spotted the earpiece; it was an accessory she didn't see much at playdates and Music for Me. She pulled out her bagel and started to eat, her pleasure now tinged with the discomfiting sense that the professional world was leaving her behind.

When the train finally heaved to a stop in the tunnel under Penn Station, the car's collective stored energy exploded into a bustle of bag retrieval, tray table stowage, and tie straightening. Passengers crowded into the aisle, poised to sprint off the train, up the stairs, and into the mad rush of Manhattan. Sophie felt her pulse quickening to the pace. Here, hours and minutes were shot at you out of a gun. There were no aimless mornings or endless afternoons, no strolls to nowhere, no Tupperware housing developments being built up and torn down. There was work to be done.

She'd timed her trip perfectly; she walked into the Whirlygig offices at eleven on the dot. There was some confusion when she told the receptionist she was there for the briefing with Dan. Calls were made; coffee was offered. The girl promised Sophie someone would be right out. For the next hour and fifteen minutes, however, nobody came. Sophie stared at the lobby TV, which was showing a special about the Iraqi insurgency, and tried to hang on to her buoyant mood. A caterer brought in lunch for a meeting in the glass-walled conference room just off the lobby; Sophie's stomach growled.

Finally, she was greeted by a thick-necked man in his twenties wearing a khaki jacket and a chunky class ring. "I'm Craig," he said, half to his BlackBerry and half to Sophie. "Come on back." He led her to a windowless, cubelike conference room that was too small for its six Aeron chairs. "Sorry about the confusion," he said. "Dan just moved to a different team, and he didn't tell us you were coming in. I think he was going to use you on the Intactin project?"

"He didn't actually say... Um, I was referred by Carly Gregorio? Does that help?"

Craig shrugged. "I guess. I think she worked on Intactin before. Well, let's see whatcha got."

Sophie wasn't sure what he meant at first, but after an embarrassing pause she realized that her briefing had just turned into an interview. She pulled out her laptop and started it up. While she was waiting for it to boot, she rummaged in her bag. No résumés, of course. She found a slightly creased business card and slid it across the table to Craig.

"Philadelphia?" he said. "Wow. I guess you'll be working off-site."

"Dan said it wouldn't be a problem."

"Huh."

"Anyway, here are a few things I've done recently. Here's a Flash intro I did last year... It just takes a moment to load."

"Did you develop the rest of the site as well?"

"Not really—they kind of brought me in at the end for the animation."

"Can we see something a little more robust? We're looking for dynamic content, mobile development, SEO..." He leaned back and smoothed his tie over his belly.

"Well, I don't consider myself an SEO expert... I've usually worked with partners on that."

"Fair enough."

"Here's an e-commerce site I did with a 360 product viewer."

"Have you done any custom CRM platforms?"

"Well, let me see..." Sophie moused through the files on her laptop, opening windows and closing them. Craig looked down at his BlackBerry.

"Here's a site for a packaging company. I built them a back-end data management tool, for storing client files."

"'Kay. Any CMS? I assume you're up on all the new platforms out there." His thick thumbs danced across his tiny keypad.

Sophie snapped her laptop shut. "You know, I didn't actually bring all my files with me. I didn't realize—"

"Can't you just show me your live stuff?"

"If you tell me exactly what you're looking for, I'll be able to pull together the right examples and talk about how they apply. I just didn't know that's what we were doing today. Dan didn't say anything about—"

Craig sighed elaborately and put his BlackBerry on the table. "Dan left his shit in a mess. I'm sorry he didn't tell you the deal. Can you just email me some links? We need CRM, CMS, and SEO would be a major bonus. Oh, and we'll need a mobile version of everything, of course, so I'll need some small-screen samples."

"Well, of *course*—"

"Awesome. Hey—thanks for coming in. Sorry about the wait."

"Oh, no problem. I'm sorry. Thank *you*."

⊱✦⊰

Sophie stood out on the sidewalk, trying to get her bearings in the humid, noisy air. She squinted up and down the avenue; was she facing north or south? She wandered for a bit, her slow pace clearly annoying the people who were actually trying to get somewhere. For the first time that day she felt like an impostor. All around her, people were rushing toward real responsibilities, whereas she was merely playing at it, in her outdated shoes and too-small skirt. She walked into a deli and, feeling overwhelmed by the vast menu hanging over the counter, ordered the first thing she saw.

As she chewed a dry turkey wrap (when was it decided that

sandwiches would be better rolled up in something with the texture of a commercial paper towel?), she tried jotting down old websites she could send Craig to show how "robust" her portfolio was. Her best work was from before Lucy's birth, and she knew none of it would interest him. She doodled on her napkin, leaning her cheek on her fist, despair bearing down fast through a fog of dumb disbelief. Nothing was working, and she was trying, goddamn it, she was trying as hard as she knew how. Her mortgage payment was going to reset in fifteen days, and while she might be able to pull together enough to pay the first one, there was no way she could do it a second time, and a third, and a fourth. At least then her mortgage company might come out of hiding, she thought ruefully. But by that time it would be too late to undo the damage.

They were underwater, Ron had said, and that's exactly how it felt. She recalled the feeling, when she was a child, of being tumbled by a wave at the beach: the roiling, watery confusion of not being able to get her legs under her, not knowing which way was up; the roar in her ears, the scrape of salt inside of her nose and down the back of her throat. She was going to lose her house, one way or another. The smart way would be sell it now, get out quick. The painful way would be to have it pried out of her grasp by a series of threatening letters and legal notices, and eventually, she supposed, the sheriff. For a moment her mind lingered on the scene: their belongings piled high on the sidewalk under the ginkgo tree, the kids weeping, her neighbors standing around shaking their heads, feigning concern but secretly relishing the spectacle.

She needed a walk. She left the deli and headed south, toward the less-hectic blocks of Murray Hill. She strolled slowly down Second Avenue, through a dull blur of drugstores and dry cleaners, sweating into her silk blouse. Something about the city's midsummer smells—exhaust, urine, impatience—brought back memories of her first visit to New York, when she was ten years old. Randall had brought her on one of his trips to visit his editor and go to a trade show. Maeve must have been out of town, and somehow it was decided that leaving Sophie alone at home for three days, while completely acceptable to her parents, might be frowned upon by the neighbors.

So Sophie was left, instead, in a New York City hotel room, along with ten dollars and a subway map. Randall suggested a few places she could visit while he was in his meetings: the Met, the Empire State Building, Bloomingdales. Sophie got lost on her first day, ending up in the Bermuda Triangle of Times Square, and had to take a cab back to the hotel. After that she'd stayed inside, watching TV and feeling the excitement of the trip drain away. She'd been looking forward to spending time with her father, thrilled to accompany him on one of the many trips that normally took him away from her. But she was embarrassed to tell him about her reluctance to leave the hotel room, so at the end of each day she didn't have much to offer in terms of conversation. Randall would take her to a bar down the street, where she drank soda while he explained the vagaries of the consumer electronics industry. Then they'd get broad slices of pizza draped over flimsy paper plates and eat them, folded in half, on the way back to their room, where Sophie would fall asleep in the flickering light of the evening news. How she hated that hotel room, with its musty smell, textured wallpaper, and thick windows that wouldn't open. It was a feeling that stayed with her for the rest of her life: a deep dislike for hotels and their halfhearted attempts at hominess, as if a cheap floral bedspread and bolted-down brass lamp could supply what a traveler was missing.

All of New York, in fact, had seemed stingy and unsatisfying on that visit, especially compared with Seattle, where she was free to ride her bike for miles, having memorized the orderly lay of the suburban land. She had her favorite hangouts there: the cat-draped bookstore, the coffee-scented diner, the mall. She'd figured out which parking lots harbored the kinds of aimless, cigarette-puffing kids who would eagerly home in on a small girl on a ten-speed. She also knew which underpasses to avoid.

On subsequent visits to New York, though, she'd developed a grudging respect for the city's hard edges, the anonymous remove of the high-rise apartment buildings, the brittle slap of fast-moving feet. There was a lonesome toughness about New York that felt very familiar to her.

Crossing Fifty-Sixth Street, Sophie was about to turn onto one of the tree-lined blocks to the east, when she stopped in front of a low shoe box of a building: the Manhattan Art & Antiques Center. The large plate glass windows were stacked high with armoires, marble busts, and regency chandeliers. Through the double doors she could see richly carpeted corridors lined with individual shops; a group of Japanese tourists mingled in the lobby, dwarfed by a pair of grandfather clocks.

Sophie pushed through the doors into the hushed coolness. The Japanese murmured quietly; the clocks ticked; Sophie's heels sank into the carpet. The low ceilings and recessed lights provided a humble backdrop for the piles of jade carvings, Russian icons, eighteenth-century paintings, and heavily gilded furnishings behind the floor-to-ceiling storefront windows. She wandered the halls, taking in the plunder of centuries, grateful for a retreat from the bland midtown heat. She climbed a wide, curving staircase to a second floor of galleries, which were smaller and more specialized: antique books, estate jewelry, coins. At the end of one corridor she paused in front of a cluttered shop whose door was propped open. A sign in the window read "McGeorge & Fils, Antique Silver."

Sophie peered inside, her eyes struggling to take in the scintillating jumble. Mirror-lined mahogany-and-glass cases shone with candlesticks, coffee sets, and elaborately decorated urns. Antique occasional tables, their inlaid wood surfaces polished to a high gloss, held large silver candelabras and coveys of life-size partridges and quail. Mirrored trays displayed mother-of-pearl-handled butter knives, tortoiseshell combs, and silver-and-ivory napkin rings. The air clanged with reflected light.

Toward the back of the shop she spotted a slender man seated at a delicate wooden secretary, his forearms resting on the desk, the tips of his fingers pressed together. His reddish hair, brushed back from his forehead, came to his shoulders, framing a boyish alabaster face. He was the most beautiful thing in the shop, Sophie thought. She gave him a quick, embarrassed smile, then turned to head back down the corridor. She had no business walking into any of these places.

"Oh, come on!" came the man's voice, exasperated and British. "Don't go!"

Sophie turned back; the man was hurrying toward her. "You don't have to buy anything. But dear God, you're the first friendly face I've seen in a week. Come on, then."

Sophie stepped into the shop, holding her laptop bag close against her hip so as not to bang any of the spindly tables.

"D'you like silver?" the man asked. "Need a wedding gift? I've got all kinds of stuff. If I don't have it, I can get it." He had a quick, worried smile, and his pale cheeks were spattered with freckles.

"Just window-shopping today," said Sophie.

"You know, in France they call it 'window licking,'" he said. "Normally things sound better in French, but not really in that case, eh?" He cracked his knuckles: first the left hand, then the right.

Sophie smiled, allowing herself to be entertained. She'd met plenty of these dealers, whenever Brian dragged her to the Antiques Show at the Armory, or to museum parties. They were usually stiff, defensive, humorless; worn down by years of catering to wealthy clients who treated them like shopkeepers. She liked this one, though.

"What d'you think of this?" he asked, holding up a large drinking horn whose tip was capped with a long, curling tail of silver, and whose midsection was held aloft by a pair of silver chicken feet. Sophie laughed.

"That's...wacky."

"Vikings. Everyone thinks they had no sense of humor." He set it down. "So what brings you here?" He gestured toward the laptop bag. "Sneak out of the office, did you?"

"I came up from Philadelphia for a meeting."

His eyebrows popped upward. "I've got a few clients in Philadelphia. Great town. Good museum. Reeeeally good. Not a bad restaurant scene either, eh? Buddakan, Le Bec-Fin. What d'you do there?"

"I'm a web developer."

"Computer stuff? Don't know much about that, myself. You like it?"

"Mmm." Sophie pointed to a two-handled tray that was rimmed with an elaborate border of grapevines, leaves, insects, and snails. "So how much is something like this?"

"You like that?"

"It's incredible," she said truthfully.

"You've got expensive taste. This here is an exceptional English Sterling silver tray with a cast border, and here—" He picked it up and showed her a tiny mark on the back.

"You've got the maker's mark, that's Vander." He set it down. "Nineteen grand."

"Wow."

"Yeah, but look." He crossed the store to another table, where he picked up a round, footed tray. "This one's nice; you've got some beautiful vines, trees, also English, also marked. Nine hundred." He held it out to her. "Have a look."

Sophie held the tray, feeling its cool heft, turning it over to see the mark.

"We're running a special for web developers from Philly. Fifteen percent off."

"What makes this one so much cheaper than the other one?" she asked, running her finger over the border.

"Well, to put it bluntly, that other one's a masterpiece. Really unusual to see all those little figures, so finely detailed and naturalistic, with piercework, chasing…and of course, it's a big name. This one's a bit thick, really; everything's very heavy, rounded, stylized." He turned the tray over and pointed to one of the feet. "You've got a repair here; it's been welded back on. And the whole thing's been polished half to death." He leaned in and spoke from one side of his mouth. "I don't really like this one, to be honest. You could do better."

Sophie laughed, and handed it back. "Not much of a salesman, are you?"

He sighed and pressed his index finger into his palm. "Terrible."

"Well, I can't afford anything in here anyway," she said, taking one of his cards from a dainty holder on the secretary.

"That's all right," he said. "You can come browsing any time. My name's Harry, by the way." He held out his hand.

"Sophie."

"Sophie. Sophia. Wisdom! I like it. I'll see you soon, then?"

"Maybe."

On the train home, Sophie tried to dodge thoughts of Craig and his fat thumbs, dwelling instead on the glimmering, finely wrought world she'd discovered inside Harry's shop. But her anxieties about work, money, and the mortgage kept intruding on her reverie. She leaned her head back and closed her eyes, trying to breathe deeply.

In the far reaches of her mind, there was an idea signaling her through the fog. She tried to ignore it, but there was a swift current pushing her toward the beam, which swelled and receded in the darkness like something breathing. It was an illusion, she told herself; the idea was foolish, dangerous. But it was also mesmerizing, and the more she stared at it, the brighter the world around her seemed to become. She studied the idea for a while, passing the time behind her closed eyes while the real world rushed by outside the window.

When she got home Sophie found Brian sitting at the table with the two kids, who seemed to have just finished dipping their faces in bowls of yogurt.

"Mommy, we're having yogurt for dinner!" announced Lucy, waving her yogurty spoon in the air, sprinkling her hair with white specks.

"Yaaaah!" agreed Elliot, imitating his sister's spoon-waving technique.

"What's for dessert?" Sophie asked, kicking off her shoes. "Ice cream?"

"You and I are having beef burgundy," Brian said.

"Did you go to Music for Me?"

"God no. I'd rather gouge my eyes out."

"But Brian—"

"Mommy, Daddy let me watch TV this afternoon, and I wanted to watch the *Supreme Dream Girls*," Lucy said. "He said no, but then I threw a fit and he said okay. I like Daring Darla the best." She scraped some yogurt off her nose with her spoon.

"Brian, I thought we decided the *Supreme Dream Girls* were too S-L-U-T-T-Y."

"I had to write some emails, and she was being a P-A-I-N I-N T-H-E B-U-T-T."

"Yeah, well, T-O-U-G-H S-H-I-T."

"Stop spelling! Stop spelling!" Lucy cried.

"Look," Brian said. "I did what I had to do. She wouldn't take a nap."

"She didn't sleep? Oh my God."

"Everyone's fine," Brian said.

"We're great!" Lucy said.

Sophie sighed and sank into a chair at the table, reaching for the yogurt container and a spoon. "I can't believe you let her watch TV instead of napping. Brian, seriously."

"How'd the briefing go?"

"Fine," she said, hating the way Brian always managed to slip out from under her aggressions, smoothly avoiding a fight when a fight was exactly what she needed. This was how her life had begun to feel recently—reaching out for something solid, something that would make her feel alive, but grabbing air. "It went great."

She paused, revisiting her daydream on the train. "I need to go back up there in a few days to work out my estimate," she said, slowly scraping out the last of the yogurt with her spoon.

"Is it a big job?"

"I hope so. It might turn out to be small, though. I'll find out for sure when I go back."

Seven

The next train ride to New York felt less triumphant. At the station Sophie had bought some magazines, anticipating the pleasures of solitude when she was once again seated on the train, but she found herself unable to focus on them. She stared out the window of the slow-moving, midmorning Clocker, watching the weedy remains of Philadelphia's industrial past roll by: crumbling brick factory buildings, rusted trestles, ravines filled with strollers, shopping carts, and the occasional tent. She felt guilty about the unreimbursable train ticket and the extra hours of babysitting, and of course Brian—she didn't even want to think about Brian.

Draped over the guilt like a scratchy wool blanket, though, was anxiety: What if the mirror turned out to be worthless? What if Harry laughed her out of his shop? What if he knew exactly what the mirror was, and where it came from? She leaned her head back against her seat and closed her eyes. She needed to stay focused on the facts: The mirror was good enough to be in a museum, even if it wasn't good enough to be on display. There was no possible way for Harry to know where it came from. So far, no one had noticed it was missing. The sooner she got it out of her house, the better.

The Art and Antique Center provided a chilly refuge from

the fug of sewer smells, exhaust, and hot dog steam that had trailed her across Midtown. Once inside, Sophie hurried upstairs and stopped outside the window of McGeorge & Fils. Unlike the other day, the door was closed. Through the window she could see Harry talking with an elegantly dressed couple in their sixties. Gone was Harry's expansive air; today he appeared soberly thoughtful, nodding and narrowing his eyes as he listened to his clients. Sophie turned away, wondering what to do. She couldn't change her mind now; she'd come all this way. Nor could she intrude on this intimate, burnished scene of gravitas and wealth. She glanced back through the window, and this time Harry caught her eye. He acknowledged her with the faintest lift of his chin. In an agony of indecision, Sophie stepped back, turned to flee, then circled around and yanked open the door.

"...the valuations are absurd, you know; I don't know who they think they're fooling." The older man spoke with the low, plummy intonations of East Coast wealth: not quite British, but just around the linguistic corner.

"Quite right," murmured Harry.

"But you've got to deal with them. Lord knows we can't go to Christie's at this point."

"Oh, no, no."

Sophie picked up a creamer from a tea set, and turned it over. The hinged lid flopped open unexpectedly; she jumped and abruptly righted it with a loud clang. She returned it delicately to its tray.

"Well, old man, I'll let you get back to work."

"Thank you *so* much for stopping by," said Harry, shaking his hand. "Madame. Always lovely to see you both. Give my love to Sarah."

"Of course, of course."

Sophie was unnerved by the way Harry was acting. She realized she'd been looking forward to his charming banter. She didn't get a lot of charm in her life these days, much less banter. But this version of Harry was as stiff as a British upper lip.

Having escorted the couple out, Harry appeared at her elbow.

"Wankers."

"Excuse me?"

"Bloody wankers!" he said, gesturing toward the door with his head. "Horribly stuck-up. Painfully boring. God! Kill me now."

Sophie laughed. "Isn't that your core customer?"

"Of course, you're right." He sighed heavily. "But they never buy anything, that lot. They just come in to air their grievances about Sotheby's and tell me how much they miss my dad."

"Was this your father's shop?"

"It was, yeah. I am *le fils*. Dad's been gone a year now."

"I'm sorry."

"Horrible man. Used to throw saltcellars at my head."

"Oh."

"Anyway. You're not here to buy anything, are you? Let's go to lunch! I fancy a martini."

He took her to a mahogany-paneled tavern on Fifty-Eighth Street. It was the middle of the day, but inside it was dark, with tiny lamps puddling warm light on the walnut tables. They sat in a booth in the back and ordered truffled cheese fries, duck sliders, and Bombay martinis. Harry spent most of the meal telling long, rambling stories about his disastrous upbringing, his brother's defection to Australia, and his lover Jeffrey's penchant for bad electronica.

"You know—vvvpp vvvpp vvvpp vvvpp. He buys it in the subway. God-awful stuff. Thank you." Two more martinis had appeared.

"This is terrible!" Sophie exclaimed. "I've got to relieve the babysitter. I can't go back like this."

"Sure you can! Parenting's much easier when you're drunk. Just ask my mother."

"Stop it."

"It's true!" Harry slurped his drink. "I don't know how she would've survived motherhood without being thoroughly embalmed. Don't look so shocked. I take it your parents are perfect?"

"No, they weren't."

"Past tense?"

Sophie ate an olive, chewing slowly. "My father died in a plane crash when I was eighteen, and after that my mother kind of went missing."

Harry cracked his knuckles under the table. "Sorry. How awful. I didn't mean to—"

"No, it's fine, I mean…" She shouldn't have been so specific.

"So you've got kids?" Harry asked brightly. "What're their names?"

"Lucy and Elliot. One's three, one's a year and a half."

"Pictures?"

"But of course." Sophie pulled some photos out of her wallet.

"He's cute. And she certainly looks like she can take care of herself."

"What do you mean by that?" Sophie asked, a little too sharply.

"Nothing, really. Just that she looks bright. Self-sufficient. Like her mum."

"Oh, well. I'm not so great at taking care of myself, to tell you the truth." She took a steely sip. "I should get back."

"What. You had a meeting today, right? Tell the nanny it went long."

"Actually, no. No meeting. I came to see you."

"*Moi?* So you *did* want to buy something. Second thoughts about that Vander tray?"

"God, no."

"Didn't think so."

"I wanted to show you something, actually." She pulled the wad of grocery bags out of her purse. The martinis were making this easier than expected. "Maybe you can tell me what it is. I picked it up at a sidewalk sale for next to nothing."

"I see. And you're hoping it'll put your kids through college, that it?"

"Actually, there's this island I've got my eye on."

"Right! Education's overrated. OK, let's have a look." Harry peeled the bags away and put the mirror on the table in front of him. He pulled a pair of glasses from his shirt pocket and put them on. "Oh, all right."

"What?"

Harry picked up the mirror, held it close to his face, turned it over, angled it to catch the light. "That's a nice little piece."

"I thought so."

Harry stopped turning the mirror and gave her a sharp look over the top of his glasses. "Yeah? What d'you know about it? Any idea whose it was?"

Sophie gathered the grocery bags and balled them up in her hands. "I know enough," she said finally. "What I want to know is, what do *you* know about it?"

Harry blew out a puff of air, his bottom lip protruding. "Well...I haven't seen many things like it. I'd need to do a bit of research, maybe show it around..."

"No, that's all right. I just thought you might be able to tell me something, but if you can't..."

"Well, here's what I can tell you." Harry set the mirror on the table and drummed his fingers lightly on either side of it.

"It's a nice antique. Good condition. It's got a mark, which I don't recognize right off the bat. With a little gentle cleaning it'd make a nice wedding gift, a nice decorative accent, you know. I have clients who like this sort of thing."

Sophie crossed her arms.

"If I had to offer you something right here," he continued, "without further research, but seeing what a beautiful piece it is—and it really is very, very nice—I'd say I could do, oh, how about a thousand. And by the way, my father is now doing pirouettes in his grave."

Sophie sat unmoving, staring at Harry, making stacks in her mind: things she knew, things he knew, things she knew he didn't know. Among them, the fact that she'd heard detailed accounts of exactly this sort of negotiation with exactly this sort of dealer. Also: his upper lip was glazed with sweat. "You know, I think maybe I'll just hang on to it." Sophie reached for the mirror.

Harry threw himself against the back of the booth, raised his hands in the air. "What can I do, without any research? At the very least I need to look up the mark. Can I snap a photo, get back to you later?"

"No! No photos. I think, actually, that's all right," she said, bundling the mirror back in the plastic bags. "I'm not really interested in selling. Thanks for looking at it." She tipped the last drops of gin into her mouth.

Harry took off his glasses and looked at Sophie for a minute, tapping them against his top lip.

"Right. Perhaps I came in a little low."

"A *little*! I realize you barely know me, but please don't take me for an idiot."

"Look, let's pop around to the shop, talk some real numbers. I'll write you a check and you can be on your way."

He was trying to get her onto his territory, and Sophie was content to let him think this would work. Ultimately, though, she knew she held the greatest advantage, which was ambivalence. The longer she engaged in this unseemly negotiation, the more uncomfortable she was with the entire idea. If Harry wasn't going to make it worth her while, she would just have to dispose of the mirror some other way.

"Fine," she said, folding her napkin into a perfect square and centering her martini glass on top of it. "Let's see what you can do."

The cash was a problem. She'd told Harry she couldn't take a check ("for tax reasons"), so he'd paid her out of an old-fashioned-looking safe in the back of his office. The money didn't take up that much space—the stack fit neatly into one of the smaller Adobe software packages on her office shelf. The problem was the denomination. Sophie and Brian were not hundred-dollar-bill kinds of people; she usually kept her wallet stocked with twenties from the cash machine. Brian, in turn, used her wallet as his personal ATM, since he could never remember to get his own cash. She knew he would find it odd to come across wads of hundreds in her purse.

She tried to remember to take a couple of the bills with her every time she went to the grocery store, but while she was getting good at remembering to bring her reusable cloth bags, she almost always forgot the hundreds. So she would end up putting the groceries on her credit card, whose balance, since the beginning of summer, had been growing at a steady pace.

She considered getting some money orders at the post office and using them to pay her bills, but she didn't like the paper trail this would generate. Finally she took the hundreds to the bank and had them changed to twenties. She tried to act casual, passing the bundle through the window as if she did this every day, but she was painfully aware of the cameras staring at her and the people in line shifting their feet while the teller counted and recounted the hundreds, then counted and recounted the twenties. As each twenty was peeled off the pile, Sophie felt the charges stacking up against her. One count of art theft. One count of selling stolen property across state lines. One count of husband endangerment. One count of dishonesty. One count of trusting someone she barely knew. One count of being the world's most irresponsible mother.

Sophie rushed home with her envelopes full of cash and hid them inside her software packages. There was enough in the bank to make the new mortgage payment and pay a few bills; the rest of their expenses would have to be paid out of this stash. By the time it was gone, she reasoned, work would pick up again. It would have to.

Of course, it was summer—a time when everything, including website development, tended to slow down. So instead of writing code, Sophie spent her days taking Lucy and Elliot to the public pool, five blocks up. This meant smearing them with thick white sunscreen from head to toe: a greasy, squirmy process that seemed to take hours, their small bodies covered in surprisingly vast quantities of skin. Then she would stroll them up the pulsating sidewalk, trying to stay in the quickly narrowing strip of shade on the east side of the street. It wasn't a steep hill, but it was a hill, and after about ten minutes there would be a drop of sweat clinging to the end of her nose, and she would feel that at any moment the double stroller was going to roll backward and crush her into the concrete like a wad of gum.

The pool was a rectangular hole punched in a field of

concrete, heartlessly devoid of shade, chairs, or grass. By ten o'clock, though, it was already boiling over with neighborhood kids. After spreading out towels, stowing clothes and shoes, and touching up sunscreen, Sophie would stake out a corner in the shallow end and hold on to Elliot's slippery body while Lucy splashed and played nearby. Still breathless from her exertion, still sweating, Sophie longed to melt into the blue water, pushing off against the wall and shooting across the pool, her body nothing but a shadow, bursting out at the other end, grateful, at last, for a gasp of air and sunshine. But she could not take her eyes off the children for an instant, could not move beyond arm's reach. Everyone knew what happened when you did that.

An hour and a half later she would reverse the process: peeling off the wet swim diaper, pulling on sun-baked clothes, letting herself be yanked down the hill by the stroller, the shade scrubbed away from the glaring sidewalk, the kids irritable, emptied out of anticipation. Every time they did this, Sophie wondered if there was any net benefit of going to the pool at all.

Personally, she would have been happy to spend the rest of the summer at home, in the rattling cool of the air conditioner, finishing up some home improvement projects. She'd found a collection of porcelain keyhole covers, and she needed to screw them on to all the doors. She also wanted to strip the paint off the decorative heating vents, and add some bronze sash pulls to the window frames. But the kids never left her alone long enough to accomplish anything. After about twenty minutes they would tire of their toys and markers, and focus their full attention on the only other living, breathing, and thus potentially interesting presence in the house. They wanted her to read to them. They wanted her to play with them. They begged her to become a queen, a horse, a puppeteer. She would oblige them for a little while, forcing herself to be fun when she didn't feel fun, finally decreeing that they were now going to play "sick mommy," a game in which she lay on the couch in a dead faint while Lucy ministered to her and Elliot draped himself over her hot torso, occasionally touching her lips with utmost care and whispering, "Shhh, sick."

At least when they were going places the kids would occasionally turn their gaze away from her and out into the world. And so she would take them on long walks through the city, the huge, rubbery stroller like an extra appendage she had grown used to hauling around. It wouldn't fit through most café doors, and couldn't squeeze between clothing racks in any store, so she kept moving: past the neoclassical porticos of Spruce Street, under Delancey's decorative pears, through the sprinkler-soaked lawns of Washington Square. Sometimes she would announce a destination, just to give the day a sense of purpose. They would walk to the Falls Bridge, collecting sticks and leaves along the way, then throw them into the water and watch them float away. Or they would walk to the Italian Market, where they would buy a pint of strawberries to eat in the grass at the Palumbo ball field. Every day it became harder for Sophie to summon enthusiasm for these outings, and when Lucy would ask, at breakfast, "What are we going to do today?" Sophie would say, "I don't know, what do you want to do?" and Lucy would shrug and return to her cereal, comfortable in the knowledge that something would eventually be decided by some adult.

Sophie tried to engineer a social life for her children, inviting other kids to the house for playdates. She herself hadn't had many friends growing up; she realized, now, that her nonchalant independence had probably made her unapproachable. And of course, whenever she discovered like-minded kids her age and started to experience the thrill of budding friendship, her mother would get that moody look, and Sophie knew it would soon be time to haul the cardboard boxes back out of the basement.

Of course, Lucy and Elliot were too young to make real friends; they played alongside the other kids, not with them. But Sophie liked to imagine some of them walking to school with Elliot in a few years, or taking Lucy to a dance. She imagined Lucy saying of her husband, "We've been friends since we were four." Sophie's oldest friend was Carly, and they'd barely known each other ten years. Her kids, she decided, would form lifetime friendships, starting now. She and Brian would become close with the parents; they would take group vacations, have the kids over for sleepovers, weave their lives together in a way that seemed to belong to a previous, less transient era.

Of course, these friendships would have to wait until Brian stopped traveling so much. First there was an auction in London, then a collector to visit in Italy. He went to the National Library of France, then spent a week in Connecticut, looking for clues among the Wilder family correspondence, which was being maintained by one of the magnate's descendants. Brian felt guilty about the travel; he apologized constantly, and always came home burdened with silk scarves, fancy chocolates, and oversized stuffed animals. "It's okay," Sophie reassured him again and again, wincing at the price tags he always forgot to cut off. "We're fine."

But when he wasn't around, the days lost their shape completely—afternoons melting into evenings, evenings evaporating into night. Sophie allowed herself certain indulgences to make up for her loneliness. She ate dinner with the kids—fish sticks, mac and cheese, chicken nuggets—and put them to bed half an hour earlier than usual. She poured herself extra helpings of wine, let the dishes pile up, watched bad TV late into the night. She stopped shaving her legs.

She also found herself thinking more and more about her trip to New York: the cold, biting martinis; Harry's redheaded charm; the oily twirl of the dial on his safe. These thoughts had a tinge of pornography to them…a complicated mixture of shame and excitement, disgust and desire. They were only thoughts, she reassured herself, as she turned to them again and again. Thoughts never hurt anyone.

Her listlessness was compounded by lingering anxieties about the mortgage. The irony did not escape her: in her eagerness to create a stable home, she'd created a mess that could end with her family being thrown out into the street. She'd managed to make the last two mortgage payments, but there were no freelance jobs in sight. Her phone calls and letters to the mortgage servicers continued to go unanswered. And the latest electric bill, thanks to the air-conditioning units, was an assault on reason.

She went online and found a list of local firms on the American Association of Advertising Agencies website. She'd worked with most of the big ones in the past, but she was amazed to find hundreds of tiny shops she'd never heard of, scattered throughout office parks in suburbs she'd never visited: Malvern, Exton, Conshohocken. She went to all of their websites, narrowed down which ones were doing digital marketing (or claimed to be), and sent messages to whatever email addresses she could find—in the best cases, a director of web development; in the worst cases, she just sent it to "info@QuirkyAgencyName.com."

It took several evenings to get through the list, from 11point Design to ZeroSum Marketing Solutions. She got a few polite emails in return, promising to keep her information on file. The creative director at Big Red Ball Communications called to ask if she did design work, too; she told him sure, she could do whatever he needed, but that her background was in code, not design, and she didn't really have a portfolio. He told her he'd keep her information on file.

"The problem," said Carly one day over coffee, "is that the big shops with serious web business have their own developers on staff now. And the small shops want more bang for their freelance buck, so they're looking for designer-developers who can do it all."

"Lame," said Sophie, stacking creamers into a tower for Elliot to gleefully knock down. "You can't be good at both."

Carly shrugged. "I'm doing a lot of design these days, actually. I did some as a favor for the people at Skunk Design, and then that turned into another job, and another, and now I've got a little mini portfolio. So…"

"It's hard enough trying to learn the new version of Silverlight without having to become a designer at the same time," grumbled Sophie. She tried to direct Elliot's attention to the toy basket.

"Don't knock it till you've tried it. And don't take this the wrong way, but people are more used to the idea of a girl designer than a girl developer."

"Shut up."

Carly raised her hand. "Just sayin'."

"That's the worst reason I ever heard for giving up my coding cred."

"Fine. Keep your cred. Cred won't buy diapers." She cocked her head at Elliot.

"Pfffff…" Sophie let out a long exhale. She wondered what Carly would say if she told her about the mortgage debacle. Carly probably had no idea what an adjustable rate mortgage was, having lived her whole life in houses that had been given to her as birthday presents.

"Do you really think that's why people aren't calling me? 'Cause I'm a girl?"

"Are you kidding?"

"What?"

"Sophie, please, don't be naive. Of course you're up against that."

"Well okay, being the caregiver and taking time off has hurt me. But a guy would have the same problems. It's not the fact that I'm a woman; it's the logistics of parenthood. The logistics suck."

"I'm not talking about that. I'm talking about the tech world. The geek club. No girls allowed. Hello?"

"I don't know...maybe."

Carly rolled her eyes and went to the counter for more coffee. Sophie sank back into the couch. Carly was probably right. Sophie had never been bothered by the testosterone-rich atmosphere of her field. Even in college, while her dormmates were starting a campus charter of NOW, and women's studies was the hot new major, Sophie had cheerfully ensconced herself in the computer lab with her fellow geeks, where reproductive rights and equal pay were the furthest things from her mind. Naturally, she enjoyed some benefits of being one of the only female computer science majors: she became the exclusive focus of her classmates' romantic attentions, which she enjoyed on some level, but consistently rebuffed. She preferred liberal arts men.

It only occurred to her now, her forehead thumping against something that was beginning to look like a glass ceiling, that her mother had utterly failed to prepare her for the possibility that some women got a raw deal in the working world. This was probably because Maeve had always flown above the glass ceiling. Once she'd made a name for herself with the Boeing 747SP's single-slotted flaps, she'd had her pick of dream projects: the DC-10 Super 60, the Lockheed L-1011 TriStar. Nobody seemed to care that she was a woman; they just wanted a piece of her aerodynamic artistry.

Maximize lift, reduce drag: it was an approach Maeve applied as diligently to motherhood as she did to her career. Sophie went into day care when she was six weeks old, and as soon as she could reach the kitchen counter she was expected to pull her weight at home: washing dishes, mowing grass, answering the door when the guys from the electric company came.

Carly's loud, ringing laugh exploded on the other side of the café. Sophie turned to see her friend resting an elbow on a high two topper, languidly stirring her latte while directing the full force of her tall blond charm at a man seated on a stool. Sophie didn't need to see his glasses to know it was Keith. "Shit," she muttered, waving frantically at Carly, who ignored her. She slumped back into the couch. She knew what she was up against. Introducing Carly to married men was like planting a bomb with a three-to-six-month timer.

Eventually Carly came sashaying back to her seat. "Sorry," she said. "I got to chatting…"

"I hope there was no exchange of information."

"What? We were talking about running. I think I'm going to start. I need to get in shape."

"Please. If you lose any more weight you'll evaporate."

"There are cardiovascular benefits. It'll be good for my heart." Carly busied herself with sugars and creamers.

"Carly, I am telling you, I will not be able to stay friends with you if you have an affair with Keith."

"What. I'm not having an affair. It's innocent flirtation. Anyway, how long have you known him and his wife? Are they like your best friends now?"

"No, that's exactly the point. I want to be friends with them.

Their daughter is the same age as Lucy, they live in the neigh-borhood, they know everyone."

"Well, I don't see what I have to do with any of that."

"Just—don't."

"Okay! Okay! Calm down."

Sophie narrowed her eyes at Carly, who looked more annoyed than she really had a right to be, considering the damage her previous romantic collisions had caused. Carly needed to work on her heart, all right, but taking up running was the wrong way to go about it.

Eight

One oppressively humid morning in late August, Sophie dropped Lucy off for a playdate with Mathilda, then strolled Elliot to the Azalea Garden behind the museum. She spread a small blanket under a magnolia tree and emptied Elliot's travel bag of toys onto the blanket. Elliot ignored the jumble of brightly colored plastic and headed straight into a nearby flower bed, trampling hostas and coral bells and digging his fingers into the mulch. Sophie picked him up and redirected him toward the grassy lawn, but this became a funny game, Elliot running shrieking back into the flower bed and Sophie pulling him back out, her stern "no" an occasion for more delighted laughter. It irked her more than it probably should, to be laughed at when she was trying to be serious. But where was there to go, after delivering her meanest face and deepest growl? Was a smack on the rear the next logical step in the arms race?

Sophie left Elliot in the flower bed and began gathering all of his toys in the travel bag. Then, without a glance backward, she walked out into the middle of the grass and began tossing toys to and fro. The cheerfully smiling fire truck landed with a clatter; the Duplo blocks sailed through the air like candy from a parade float; stacking rings whizzed like Frisbees. From the flower bed, an enraged howl; she didn't even have time to turn around before the bag had been snatched from her grasp, and Elliot began staggering across the lawn to retrieve his toys: it was like an Easter egg hunt, only angrier. Sophie retreated to the shade and sat on the blanket, feeling partly triumphant and partly guilty. Maybe it was wrong to exploit her son's controlling, tidy nature. But he shouldn't have laughed at her.

Elliot finally sat down in the grass, absorbed in arranging the stacking rings in the proper order, and Sophie lay back, propped on her elbows. Small spots of sun pricked the dense mat of waxy leaves overhead; long knobby branches, mottled with lichen, created a low canopy. It was a good climbing tree. As a child, Sophie would not have hesitated to clamber into its branches, searching for a comfortable joint where she could lean back, legs dangling, and gaze into the high-ceilinged rooms of her shady mansion. So much of childhood, she realized, was spent imagining or assembling shelter: the blanket-draped chairs in the living room; the cardboard box castle; the large, hollowed-out boxwood in the backyard in Bethesda. Even Lucy had created a nest in her bedroom closet, piled deep with blankets and stocked with dolls and markers and a lovingly curated collection of business reply cards.

An airplane crawled across the shimmering sky and disappeared into the branches, drawing her thoughts to Randall. She'd never even had a chance to see his personal effects. She'd always wondered what they'd recovered. His Casio watch? His wedding ring? Whatever was left of him, it had disappeared along with Maeve after the funeral. There had been a few sporadic postcards for a while; Maeve was "taking time off," living with friends in the Southwest, experimenting with alternative lifestyles, whatever that meant. Sophie assumed Maeve was running from her guilt, which was ridiculous. Her father's plane was a 747, but not the variant her mother had helped design. Just an evolution of it.

She glanced back at Elliot. He was walking with an all-too-familiar hitch in his step. "Come here, babe," she called, spreading the changing pad out on the blanket. Elliot toddled over, and she realized his face was bright red from the heat. She gave him a sippy cup of water to suck on while she changed his diaper; he drained it within seconds.

"Let's go visit Daddy," Sophie said. "It'll be nice and cool in his office, and we can get some more water."

Marjorie greeted them at the museum's handicap-accessible entrance, where Sophie pushed the stroller up a ramp into the bracing air-conditioning. All of the curators were in a meeting with the director. "They should be out soon," Marjorie said, leading Sophie to the elevator. When they got upstairs, Sophie set Elliot on the floor, swung her diaper bag over her shoulder, and collapsed the stroller. Propping it against a wall, she led Elliot down the hall to the watercooler, where she refilled his sippy cup. Four object carts lined the hallway on the other side of the cooler; Elliot reached toward a shiny crystal chalice, but Marjorie grabbed his hand. "No touching, please!" She shook her head, sighed, and pulled a pile of small cards from her jacket pocket.

"What have they got you doing now?" Sophie asked, nodding toward the cards.

"I'm trying to match each piece to its object card so we can put it into off-site storage," Marjorie answered. "Then I have to submit paperwork for it all, so they can keep track of what's been moved. These are all good to go." She indicated the cart nearest the cooler, which held a footed crystal bowl, some silver pieces, and a carved wooden clock. Each object had a small yellowed card propped against it. Marjorie walked further down the hall, pointing to three more carts. "Halfway there. No cards to be found. Haven't even started." She turned back to Sophie. "It's a mess."

"Why is it so hard to match the cards?"

"Well, let's see. The object number is worn off half of them, and some were tagged, and the tags have fallen off. And then these—" She held up the stack in her hand. "Mystery cards! Look—this one says 'silver spoon.' There's no photo, and we have a hundred silver spoons." She pulled a stack of cards from her other pocket. "These are things I just can't find. Yet. I'm sure they're in there somewhere, but I'm only one person." She smoothed her already smooth bob.

Sophie widened her eyes. "Is anything missing?"

"Oh, I doubt that. Of course it's possible—in this state of disorganization, yes, I suppose some things could wander off. But nobody really has access back here. To be honest, I think most people have forgotten this storage room even exists. It's quite unusual to have storage near the offices. Quite unusual, and definitely not a good idea, if you ask me, which nobody has."

"And why do they have you doing this?" Sophie asked. "I mean…volunteers don't usually do this stuff, do they?" Elliot tugged on her shorts, and she picked him up. He handed her his sippy cup and laid his head on her shoulder.

"Oh, I'm qualified," Marjorie huffed. "I worked at the Atwater Kent for fifteen years, in the registrar's office. Brian never told you?"

"I didn't know that."

"Well, I did. But you're right, Brian and Michael were supposed to be doing all this. But it wasn't getting done, and I started to get concerned. You know. Objects all over people's offices. Michael gone. You never know what could happen."

"True."

Marjorie shook her head. "It's impossible to get it all done in my ten hours a week, but somebody has to try. Anyway, I'm going to take these down to Art Handling to be packed up.

Brian should be here soon." Marjorie maneuvered the finished cart down the hall and into the freight elevator at the other end, leaving Sophie and Elliot alone among the treasures.

Sophie picked up one of the object cards on the half-finished cart. The brittle yellow paper had been typed on with an old typewriter; all the capital letters floated slightly above the rest of the text.

```
31-145-1
Dutch
18th Century
METAL
Brass and Copper
SMOKERS' EQUIPMENT
TOBACCO BOX
SOURCE: Dr. Robert H. Landon
Collection
SIZE: L. 0.165m W. 0.05m.
DESCRIPTION: Ornamented with
inscriptions and figures. Copper body.
```

In one corner, a fuzzy black-and-white photograph showed the box, which appeared as little more than a dull oblong shadow. Sophie didn't envy Marjorie's job, considering the scant information on each card. Shifting Elliot to her other arm, she picked up the small box and turned it over. The number 31-145-1 was painted in faint red numbers. She returned it carefully to the cart.

Elliot was going limp and heavy in her arms. "You sleepy, babe?" she murmured. She carried him into Ted's office, where a small love seat sat under the department's only window. She laid him down, then rummaged in her diaper bag for the blanket.

She wrinkled her nose, remembering that she still hadn't thrown out Elliot's dirty diaper, which was loosely wrapped in a plastic grocery bag. She pulled out the blanket and draped it over Elliot, then headed toward the restroom to throw away the diaper. As she passed the carts in the hallway, her eye browsed the objects. On the second cart, among some candlesticks and platters, she noticed a small, flat silver box with no object card. She picked it up; the cool touch of metal reminded her of Harry's shop, and the taste of gin. She turned it over. The size of a deck of cards, the box was ornately decorated on both sides; the metal was coppery-black with tarnish. There was no place that a number could be painted, and there was no tag dangling from it. Sophie popped it open, and widened her eyes: the smooth interior surface, broken only by two small stamped marks, gleamed with the unmistakable warmth of gold.

She snapped the box shut and cradled it in her hand. It was so small, and so lost among the jumble of unwanted objects. She felt a wave of tenderness… In a strange way, she felt almost protective of the little thing.

She considered the diaper in her other hand, then hurried back into Ted's office.

Sophie spread the changing mat on the floor beside Elliot, pulled the diaper out of its plastic bag, and peeled back the Velcro strips that were holding it closed. She exhaled through her nose; Elliot's older, solid-food-based poops were a lot less endearing than the tiny newborn squirts that had smelled like baking bread. Sophie positioned the silver box above the brown smear, then thought better of it, and wrapped the box tightly in the plastic bag. Then she pressed the small package into the poop, and with practiced neatness, rolled the diaper back up and fastened it into a tight bundle with the Velcro strips. She folded up the changing pad and dropped it with the diaper into her bag.

"Pyoo," she heard behind her.

"Sorry! Sorry," she said, standing up with the diaper bag. Ted stood in the doorway, fanning his nose. "I should have changed his diaper in Brian's office. I had no idea it was such a bomb. We just stopped in to get some water and say hello."

Brian appeared behind Ted. "I thought that was our stroller," he said. "What are you doing in here?"

Sophie indicated the love seat. "He passed out, so I thought I'd put him down while you were in your meeting. It's so hot outside. We can get going now."

"That's all right, that's all right," said Ted, sitting down at his desk. "Leave him be. I'm just going to catch up on some memos."

"You're sure?" She picked up the diaper bag. "I'll get out of your way." She followed Brian into his office and, once he'd sat down at his desk, nudged herself into his lap. He wrapped an arm around her waist and scrolled through emails with his other hand.

"Where's Lucy?" he asked.

"Keith and Amy's. Playdate."

"Marjorie let you in?"

"Yeah. Elliot was dying of heatstroke out there."

"Why don't you take him to the pool?"

"Mmm. Good idea."

Brian stopped scrolling. "Look at that. Madame Viellefond wrote me back." He stared at the screen for a moment, his fingers lightly tapping the top of the mouse. Sophie tried to remember who Madame Viellefond was. She knew that Brian had found a stack of postcards among Wilder's personal papers that were signed by someone named Sandrine. From the way the postcards were written, Brian assumed Sandrine was Wilder's not-so-secret French lover.

"Is she the woman you found in Collonges-la-Rouge? Sandrine's relative?"

"Her great granddaughter."

"What does she say?"

"She knows about Wilder."

"You mean—his affair with Sandrine?"

"Yes. She says Mr. Wilder was a benefactor of the family. He made sure her great-grandmother was very comfortable."

"Must be nice."

"And he gave her many gifts."

Sophie raised her eyebrows. "Impressive. I can't believe how far you've come based on a hunch and a couple of postcards."

Brian kissed her shoulder. "I know. It's exciting."

"Something tells me you're going back to France."

"Yeeeeeah. Just for a few days. Is that okay?"

"I'm kind of busy, you know, with the Intactin job."

"I know, I'm so sorry. You know I wouldn't ask if it weren't important…"

Of course it was important. Even Sophie wanted to know what Sandrine's great-granddaughter had to say about Wilder and the missing Saint-Porchaire. But the prospect of spending another week alone with the kids filled her with dread. Her only consolation was the small, tightly wrapped secret tucked into her bag. Maybe it could cast a little light on those dull, aimless days.

"All right," she said. "But tomorrow I have to go up to New York. For a meeting. So…"

"Can you get a sitter for the afternoon?"

"Yeah, but you need to get home by five thirty in case I get held up. Deal?"

"Deal. Thanks, Soph."

Extracting the silver box from its hiding place, it occurred to Sophie that the task probably should have filled her with some amount of revulsion. But once she'd plucked it from the plastic bag and thrown the diaper away, the bad smell quickly dissipated and she became absorbed in the box's beauty, which was even more lovely now that it was freed from the confusion and fluorescent lighting of the museum hallway. Sophie pulled off her rubber gloves and turned the slim box over in her hand, admiring the intricate relief work. Bell-shaped flowers climbed along the edges, framed by orderly patterns of stylized vines and leaves. In the center, under a beribboned canopy, a man and woman danced with joined hands, their figures enlivened with billowing hair, lace, skirts, a feathered cap. At their feet, a pair of putti played a tune: one on trumpet, one clapping a tambourine.

On the other side of the box, a woman wearing some sort of elaborate headdress stood lightly poised on one foot, framed by swags of ribbon and flanked by a pair of sphinxes with long, snakelike necks. The scene was odd, mysterious, but pleasingly symmetrical.

Sophie called the number on Harry's business card.

"Darling! Thank God you called!" His tone was so affectionate, so intimate, Sophie felt a pleasant rush of warmth. "You're my favorite person right now. My absolute favorite, and I didn't even have your phone number."

Sophie laughed. "Well, here I am!"

"Here you are! You must come immediately so I can give you champagne and...and massage your feet. Whatever you want. I am your humble servant."

"You sold it."

"God, yes. My client was over the moon. Absolutely over the moon. Please come soon, love. Can I buy you dinner?"

"It's going to have to be lunch. Tomorrow."

"I'll take you somewhere posh. All right?"

"Perfect."

❧

Harry took her to a sleek vault of frosted glass and stainless steel, where they sat at the foot of a tower of wine bottles that glowed with eerie blue light. "I feel like I'm on a spaceship," muttered Sophie after the six-foot-tall hostess had led them to their glossy white table.

"We've been abducted by aliens," Harry said. "They're going to probe our wallets."

"Ha-ha."

"Champagne?" Harry waggled his eyebrows at her.

"You're really out to spoil me, aren't you."

"Who else is going to do it?"

"You have no idea. I have many lovers."

"Really?"

"No."

"Well, you should. I can arrange one if you like. What's your type? Tall and dark? Short and sweaty?" Harry leaned toward the waiter without breaking eye contact with Sophie. "Taittinger Brut, please."

"That's sweet of you, but I'm happily married."

"Right. Mr. Sophie. And what is it that he does?"

"Brian…is…in import-export." Sophie studied her menu. "Everyone's eating cheeks these days, aren't they? Veal cheeks. Fish cheeks."

"I'm more of an ass cheeks man, myself."

"Harry! I'm going to send you to the naughty spot."

"No need. My life is one big naughty spot. So what does Brian import and export?"

"Mmm…decorative items. The skate sounds good. But does it have cheeks."

"From China? India? That sort of thing?"

"Not really." Sophie snapped the menu shut. "So why are you spoiling me like this? You barely know me. The last time I had a meal this expensive was at my wedding."

"I just happened to do really well with that little mirror of yours, and I wanted to thank you."

"I take it you did your research."

"Mmm. You could've done a little better for yourself if you'd've let me do a proper appraisal. The whole thing was a bit seat-of-the-pants."

"I'm new at this myself, Harry, but I'm pretty sure you're not supposed to feel guilty about making a huge profit off someone."

"Quite right. Quite right. I've got a big mouth. Don't know if you've noticed. Anyway, I like you."

"I don't know why."

"Well, you've got excellent taste in objects of virtu. And you're interesting. I don't really know what it is yet, but there's something intriguing about you."

Sophie fussed with her napkin, caught off balance.

"Plus, I deal with such assholes all day long," Harry continued. "I mean, real assholes. And you know, I only moved here a year ago, when I took over from my dad. I haven't got any friends." He made a sad-puppy face.

"Well I don't know why, if this is how you treat them," said Sophie, raising her champagne flute. "Cheers."

She was actually glad to hear that Harry had made out well with the mirror. The quantity of cash he'd given her was enough of a hassle; a greater amount, all at once, would have created logistical problems. And now the mirror was gone, continuing on the journey of its now-troubled provenance, having passed through Sophie as if she were a ghost. Part of her was curious where it had ended up, and part of her wanted to forget she had ever seen it.

At the end of the meal, Sophie sat back and savored her wine—something dark and pleasantly earthy, several years her senior, unlike anything she'd ever drunk in her life—while Harry provided a steady stream of commentary on the restaurant's clientele, his own clientele, and Sophie's hair, which he had decided needed highlights. "Nothing stripy," he said. "Just some glints, a little dimension. Know what I mean?"

"I have something else for you, Harry," she said, putting her glass down.

"What's that?"

"Another piece."

"Aha. You've…been to another sidewalk sale?"

"Same sidewalk sale." She pulled the box out of her purse and laid it on the table in front of Harry.

"Lots of old money in Philadelphia, I hear," said Harry, cracking his knuckles. "That's a pretty little snuffbox, in'it?" He opened it, squinted at the marks, closed it, turned it over in his hands. "French rococo. I'm thinking early seventeen hundreds. Not sure what that mark is—maybe Guynot? Anyway…" He rubbed his lips.

"Do you like it?"

"Well, sure, I mean…" He laughed. "You kind of knocked my socks off with that mirror. This is a little…"

"Small?"

"Late. D'you have anything else? Perhaps a bit older?"

"What? No!"

"All right, all right. It's just, my client—the one I sold your mirror to? He's rather fixated on the Renaissance." Harry turned the box this way and that. "This is a nice piece, though. It's very pretty, finely worked, classic rococo. People do love snuffboxes, God knows why." Harry popped his knuckles. "Tell you what. I could probably sell this for five grand. Why don't we split it? Twenty-five hundred?"

It was Sophie's turn to make the sad-puppy face.

"Oh, come on, love! If it was anyone else I'd offer them two hundred. But I'm investing in our…" He waved his hand around. "Relationship."

"I don't know. I was hoping it was worth more." It was easy enough to research snuffboxes on the Internet. What did he take her for?

Harry took off his glasses. "Why'd you think that?"

"Well, to begin with, it's gold inside."

"Good lord, so are most of my teeth. That doesn't make them masterpieces. Seriously, though, what's all this about? Are you sure you don't have anything else up your sleeve?"

Sophie shifted in her seat. "Did you want dessert? Because I'm seriously considering it."

"You are the queen of the redirect, aren't you."

"It's a parenting thing."

"All right, well, I'll give you three grand for this, in the hopes that you will continue to grace me with your presence, and whatever else you might decide to bring me."

"Four."

"Brute! Just tell me—is there more?"

Sophie stared at him for a moment. "That depends on you."

Harry drained his wine. "All right, fine. But remember. Renaissance."

"Noted."

The midafternoon Metroliner wasn't crowded, so Sophie was able to raise the armrest, take off her shoes, and curl up with her feet in the next seat. She gazed out the window as the train crossed the Hackensack River, wondering at the stretches of grassy marshland all around, with narrow two-lane roads seeming to float on the greenish water. It was unaccountably wild here, right at the feet of Manhattan, the sandy landscape delicately crisscrossed with power lines and abandoned train tracks, but no buildings, and few cars: only a lonesome pickup truck parked, strangely, on a narrow spit of land that stretched into the water. Here and there, birds dotted the grasses; an egret, a puff of downy white speared on spindly legs, stood in the shallows. Sophie felt a rush of delight. Right here, bubbling up through the tangle of highways and runways and train tracks fighting their way toward Manhattan, nature was asserting itself, against every odd.

A violent jolt concussed the window, and she jerked her head back. Another train passed with a roar, inches from her face, rushing toward the city. In a moment it was gone, leaving a vacuum of sound behind. Outside, the landscape had changed back to office parks, parking lots, and warehouses with tractor trailers nosed up to them like baby pigs at their mother's belly.

Sophie stretched out her legs and savored her drowsy good mood. She was looking forward to seeing the kids. For once, she missed the warm weight of Elliot's body in her arms, and Lucy's chattering voice. Separation, she realized, was crucial to the mother-child bond. If she spent too much time with them she developed a crackling force field around herself, resisting their intrusions. But now, after a day of luxury, gloss, drinks, charm, she was ready to sink back into the marshmallowy world of motherhood.

At home she found Brian grilling shrimp and corn while the

kids drew on the patio with sidewalk chalk. Sophie hugged him, resting her cheek against his chest; she loved feeling the warmth of his skin through a crisp cotton shirt. He smelled of sweat and smoke, with a faintly lingering whiff of aftershave. "Thank you for coming home early," she said into his chest.

She pulled away and bent to pinch some wilted blooms from the geraniums growing in pots along their fence. Up above, two squirrels chattered and tumbled through the branches of the neighbor's sycamore tree. It was rare to have such a pleasant, shady outdoor space in the city; Sophie had grown to love it as much as any of the rooms inside the house.

"I was happy to get away from Marjorie this afternoon," Brian said. "She's so grumpy these days, always going on about how much better things are at the Atwater Kent. Today I thought about calling them and asking them to take her back."

Sophie laughed, and Brian raised his eyebrows at her.

"Red wine? Must've been a fun meeting."

Sophie ran her tongue over her teeth. "We had a working lunch."

"Nice! Sounds like they're treating you right. As they should."

"I guess." She felt her good mood begin drifting away, joining the dirty smoke from the grill as it wafted into the sky.

"So they were okay with your estimate."

"Yes. It's all fine."

"Good money?"

"It's fine, the money's fine. You sure have a lot of questions."

"Just making conversation."

"Your corn's going to burn."

While Brian addressed the corn, Sophie knelt and kissed the kids. Lucy's breath smelled sweet and crackery. "Did you give them Goldfish?"

"They were hungry."

"Well, they're not anymore, are they?" She brushed orange dust from Elliot's cheeks and stood up. "Now they won't eat dinner."

"Sorry."

"You know how that works, right? Food goes in their stomach, they feel satisfied, then you put more food in front of them and they turn up their noses. Parenting 101." She wasn't sure why she'd decided to go for the extra thrust. She was just getting impatient with Brian's seeming lack of curiosity…his willingness to believe that she'd had a few glasses of red wine with a client. Why didn't he press for details? Didn't he want to know what she was really doing?

"Sorry…sorry," he said lightly. "Always screwing up the parenting, I know. Do you want something to drink? There's a bottle of Muscadet in the fridge."

"Quit trying to distract me! I'm not a two-year-old."

Brian turned back to the grill, saying nothing.

"Do you know how much sodium is in those crackers?" she cried.

Brian began snatching the corn from the grill and plopping it onto a platter with the shrimp. A piece of shrimp fell to the ground. Brian bent, picked it up, and, with a furious convulsion of his arm, threw it in the direction of the street. The shrimp sailed through the alley, over the wrought iron gate, and landed on the hood of a Subaru Outback parked out front.

That, Sophie thought, is more like it.

Nine

Barnes and Noble story hour was like a gift from the gods. It was air-conditioned. It was free. The kids loved it. And most important, it was every Thursday morning, at the same time as Music for Me. Sophie had decided to replace a portion of the kids' musical education with some literary enrichment, making them more well-rounded people, and reducing her Music for Me attendance to just one hour per week.

It was a Thursday morning in late August. Sophie deposited the kids on the story rug, then sat nearby to leaf through a pile of home renovation magazines. The magazines were one of Sophie's guilty pleasures: she could spend hours gazing at beautifully lit photographs of Victorian kitchens, Asian bathrooms, and cavernous whitewashed lofts. Staring at those spreads, her mind detached itself from the real world, and she would float from fantasy to fantasy: here's what it would be like to live in the woods of Washington state. Here's a life sheathed in glass and corrugated steel. This is how it would feel to live in a two-hundred-fifty-year-old farmhouse outfitted with restaurant-grade appliances.

She stared wistfully at a stunning Brooklyn bathroom. Someone had converted an antique walnut dresser into a sink, topping it with marble and setting the copper faucet into the barnwood-paneled wall above. They'd found the industrial light fixture in a factory; the crackled, cream-colored tile had been painstakingly excavated from a Parisian bistro. An elaborately compartmented pharmacy cabinet held towels and apothecary jars behind wavy glass doors with porcelain knobs. It was the kind of bathroom that cost a fortune, but looked like it hadn't been touched since the turn of the century. It was, she realized, exactly what they needed on the first floor, in the closed-off powder room.

She quickly flipped to another page. Obviously, the bathroom would have to wait until her business picked up again. For now she was saving every penny for the mortgage payment. Each time she wrote that check, it felt like she was placing her claim on one more brick, one more floorboard, slowly easing her house out of the bank's grasp. With a few more payments, she was sure she would start to feel more anchored, more certain of her new life's validity. That was worth every penny she'd "earned." Anything beyond paying the mortgage wasn't worth the danger.

She picked up another magazine. Maybe danger wasn't quite the right word. The stuff was sitting there for the taking—unwanted, uncared for. The museum's few cameras were reserved for the real treasures, the Duchamps and the Warhols. The rest of the place, as Brian had complained many times, was enclosed in a perimeter of trust and hope. Trust that no one would doubt the museum's security practices; hope that the guards were alert and motivated. Trust that visiting scholars and family members were museum allies; hope that the curators were actually taking care. Sophie had penetrated the perimeter, but so far, no one had gotten hurt. In fact, no one had even noticed.

Sophie let the magazine drop into her lap. Across the store she noticed a familiar head bent over a table of poetry books.

Sophie rose to say hello to Carly, but sank back into her chair when she saw who was standing on the other side of the table, his black-framed glasses aimed at a slim chapbook, his gaze intently focused on Carly. Sophie quickly raised her magazine in front of her face and peeked over the top. Carly rounded the table to look at the book in Keith's hand, standing too close, her interest in the book about as scant as her tank top. She brushed the side of her breast against Keith's arm. Keith flushed, and leaned in to say something in Carly's ear. These two people, Sophie realized with a jolt of horror, had been naked together very recently—probably in Carly's nearby condo, and probably, judging from the sheen on Carly's unmade-up face, within the last hour. And now here they were, putting on this disgusting display—over poetry, of all things! During story hour! Sophie gathered her magazines and crept over the story rug, keeping her burning face turned away.

Afterward, shoving the stroller up the hill toward her neighborhood, Sophie counted the ways that she hated Carly. There was the blond hair, of course, and the height: tall enough to command attention, not so tall that she intimidated men. There was that damned belly, untroubled by pregnancy, unaffected by her diet of rotisserie chicken and Manhattans. That belly was a miracle of nature, and Sophie had always studied it with fascination: How did it disappear when she sat down? How could it possibly contain any organs? Wasn't the human intestine over twenty feet long?

Normally Sophie could grant a friend her beauty, could even enjoy it. But what she really couldn't stand was the thuglike way Carly threw her good looks around, taking out everyone in her path. And she didn't have to. She didn't need to pluck the low-hanging fruit of aging, anxious married men. She could do so much better, and she was too stupid to see it.

As a colleague, of course, Carly had always been unfailingly generous, even deferential to Sophie's years of experience. But now her career was in full bloom while Sophie's died on the vine, and it was getting more embarrassing every day to even talk about it. Again, Sophie would not begrudge a friend her success, but in this case it was almost impossible to tolerate, since Carly had never worked a day in her life out of necessity. Carly had never struggled to come up with the mortgage payment on her three-bedroom condo, had never had to choose between a gym membership and a cable subscription. She supposedly only worked because she loved computers and information architecture—something that had immediately endeared her to Sophie when they first met, ten years ago. Now Sophie found it irritating, and dubious. Wasn't it just a party trick—the cashmere-clad blond who would swoop into the bull pen and dazzle everyone with her JavaScript and MySQL skills? And now she was dipping into design—as if she needed the extra work. What she really needed, Sophie realized, was more approval and admiration. It was pathetic.

And now this. Sophie had made herself perfectly clear: Keith and Amy were not to be messed with. They represented her fragile new life; she had just been granted entrance to their world. Plus she genuinely liked Amy, with her hilarious stories of Philadelphia politics, and her kindhearted charm. There had been talk of an early September weekend at the beach together. Now Sophie was saddled with this terrible knowledge, their friendship barely begun.

Sophie pulled out her phone and considered calling Brian. He would be sympathetic, but did she want him to be burdened as well? What if he became too uncomfortable to socialize with Keith and Amy? Or worse—what if he decided it was his duty to say something?

She scrolled through her contacts and came to Harry's name. He'd keyed his number into her phone at their last lunch date, urging her to call any time. And of course, he was the perfect one to call. He didn't know any of the parties involved, he would probably have a lot to say about Carly and her money, and he might even manage to cheer Sophie up.

At the first "Sophie, darling!" she felt her mood improve. She sat on a bench at the playground and told Harry the whole saga, and he pressed her for details at every turn, like a medical student doing a thorough workup. She told him about the time Carly had freelanced at the agency where Sophie was working, and had an affair with Sophie's boss, only to dump him once the devastation to his marriage was complete. Her boss couldn't stand having Sophie around as a reminder of the whole episode, so he concocted a reason to move her onto another team, where she didn't get along with the designers. She ended up quitting a few months later.

Then, when Sophie was pregnant with Lucy, and Brian had to spend three weeks in Italy, Carly had accompanied her to her obstetrician appointment. It was while Carly was holding her hand, and Dr. Hanson was feeling her cervix, that some current had passed through Sophie's body and connected her doctor and her friend. Before the day was over, Carly and Dr. Hanson had made cramped but passionate love in the backseat of his Lexus. The whole thing made Sophie so uncomfortable she was forced to change obstetricians in her eighth month of pregnancy, requiring revisions to her birth plan and causing undue anxiety during a time that was supposed to be spent lovingly folding onesies. She was still angry at Carly for that one.

And now Keith: dinner party host, husband of her new friend, and a clearly stated member of Sophie's "off-limits" list.

"Well, you've got no choice," Harry decreed. "Break up with her!"

"Really?"

"God, yes. I mean, number one, she's a bitch. They all are, these entitled rich girls—especially the good-looking ones. Number two, she's out to get you. This is the third time she's done it, right?"

"Well, this is the first time I specifically told her to back off."

"Yeah, but it's no coincidence she keeps going after men connected to you. Has she ever had a go at your husband?"

"God, no. I mean, I don't think so…" Sophie's stomach clenched; she'd never even considered the possibility. Brian loved her too much to cheat on her. Didn't he? And anyway, when would he find the time?

"Well, look, naturally it's up to you what to do," Harry continued. "But what are you getting from the friendship at this point?"

"I talk to her about work. She helps me get jobs."

"And how's that working out?"

"Right."

"Anyway, you can talk to me about work. I'm extremely knowledgeable about computers."

"Really."

"I have a Mac. And you may not know this, but Mac is short for Macintosh, which is a type of apple. And Apple is a computer company. They make Macs."

"You do know your stuff, Harry."

"Just let me know if you have any questions."

Breaking up with a friend was easy—there was no need for finality, no announcement, no drama. Just a cooling off, a pulling away. Harry was right, she realized now. Carly's romantic exploits always had a tendency to sideswipe Sophie's life, leaving dents. Who needed a friend like that? Why hadn't she done this sooner?

The breakup also represented one more snapped fiber between Sophie and her career, which, she had to admit, felt all right—it was even a relief. Without Carly she wouldn't constantly be reminded of the world that was no longer available to her, and she wouldn't be set up for any more embarrassing interviews for jobs she had no chance of getting.

Sophie leaned her head against the back of her reading chair, absently stroking Elliot's hair as he dozed in her lap. She watched the afternoon sun walk across the dark wood floor of her office. She was becoming familiar with the light's routine in the house from day to day, season to season. The way it sneaked in sideways through the southern windows in the morning, then banged hotly on the dining room windows at noon. The way it draped itself among the branches of the gingko in early evening, the sky going soft and purple above the roofs of the houses across the street.

She needed to go back to the museum. It should be soon, before all the objects made it down to Art Handling. She also needed time alone in the department, so she could select carefully. She wanted to please Harry.

Gently easing Elliot from her lap, she got up and rummaged through the papers on Brian's side of their desk, making a pile of all the heavy, expensively printed envelopes she could find. Brian constantly received invitations to museum parties, but he seldom opened them since, for him, the dinners and receptions represented an extended workday—and it was the kind of work he despised.

Many of the invitations had expired, but there was an

upcoming banquet in one of the Medieval galleries that sounded interesting. Guests would eat in the museum's cloister, whose marble archways and Romanesque fountain had been brought from France and reconstructed in a room just off the tapestry balcony. There would be medieval music and a performance by a tenor from the Philadelphia Opera. It was black tie.

Otherwise, there was the One Big Family Party: an annual event for museum members and their children. They had gone to it a year ago, and regretted it. Elliot was too small and squirmy, and Lucy had been unnerved by the throngs of older kids jostling her at the craft stations. They'd quickly made a paper shield in the Arms and Armor gallery, gulped down some cupcakes, and fled at the crest of a double tantrum.

"Why, exactly, do you want to go to this?" Brian asked that night, when she showed him the invitation.

"The kids are older now. I think Lucy would really like it. She's very into arts and crafts right now. And the theme is China!" She didn't mention the other reason: that she was counting on the party's chaos to provide certain opportunities and distractions.

"Don't you remember how packed it was? You can't even use the stroller. They'd have to walk."

"Elliot's great at keeping up these days. And I really think he'd love the music. And look—Chinese acrobats!"

"You're crazy."

"Please, Brian? It would make me happy."

Brian sighed. "'It would make me happy' is becoming your version of batting your eyelashes."

Sophie smiled and slid the invitation back into its envelope. "We'll meet you there at five thirty."

The evening of the party, Sophie felt energized but calm. Over the past two weeks, her anticipation of the event had provided a welcome distraction from her financial anxieties. She'd toyed with different plans in her head, idly playing out scenarios, enjoying the way her heart flared in her chest every time she imagined herself alone in the darkened offices. The whole fantasy was made more alluring by the knowledge that she could skip the whole thing and just enjoy the party with her family; she didn't actually have to go through with anything.

When she got to the museum, Sophie pushed the double stroller up the ramp at the handicap-accessible entrance, where Brian was already waiting. "Why'd you bring this?" he asked, as he helped Sophie untether the kids.

"I couldn't make them walk all the way here," she said. "They'd be dead on arrival."

With Elliot in one arm, Brian maneuvered the stroller toward the others already parked along the hallway.

"Wait, no," Sophie said.

"What?"

"Do you know how much this thing cost? I'm not leaving it here."

"Where do you want to put it?"

"Your office?"

"Really?" Brian paused, then handed Elliot to Sophie. "Okay, you take the kids upstairs. I'll take the stroller, and then I'll find you."

"I can take it," she offered.

"Then we'd all have to go. Ted's still up there."

"Oh. Okay. Well, let me fold it up so it's easier to get through doors." Sophie collapsed the stroller with a swift click of the release lever and jerk of the handle, and Brian wheeled it away through the crowd.

Sophie led the kids up to the Great Stair Hall, which was vibrating with the clamor of children and the twang of Chinese music. Elliot fastened himself to Sophie's leg and Lucy looked around anxiously, fingers in her mouth. The stairs had been turned into stadium seating for the acrobatic performance, which was taking place in front of the main entrance. Along the sides of the hall, craft stations were choked with children busy scribbling, cutting, and pasting. The food tables were upstairs on the balcony, but Sophie couldn't imagine navigating the crowded, dizzying staircase with her two nervous bundles. "Let's sit down," she finally suggested, finding a spot near the bottom of the stair. "We'll wait for Daddy here."

When Brian returned from his office and joined them on the steps, Elliot scrambled into his lap. The acrobats were like brightly colored rubber bands being shot across the room, piling on top of each other in endless combinations, stepping on each others' knees, shoulders, and heads and smiling broadly the whole time. Elliot bounced appreciatively, and Lucy pointed at one of the spangled girl acrobats and cried, "That's me! I'm her!"

After the performance they climbed the stairs to the mezzanine, where they sat around a small table with a red tablecloth and ate egg rolls and lo mein. Lucy wielded her chopsticks like knitting needles, carefully lifting noodles to her mouth one at a time. Brian fed Elliot by lowering the wiggling strands into his grasping mouth like a mother bird. Sophie watched them with her chin in her hand. "If we ever went to China, we'd starve to death."

Brian snorted and put the rest of the noodles in front of Elliot so he could eat them with his hands. At the table next to theirs, a redheaded girl about Lucy's age was objecting strenuously to the noodles her mother had placed in front of her. She pushed them away and her mother, smiling and cajoling in a low voice, pushed them back. "Uh oh," said Sophie under her breath as the mother pushed the noodles toward the girl one too many times. The girl grabbed the plate and Frisbeed it in the direction of one of the Baroque Rubens tapestries hanging on the wall. A sleepy-looking guard, who happened to be standing to the left of the tapestry at the entrance to the Medieval galleries, casually reached out one long arm and caught the plate, a fraction of a second before East met West with a greasy splat.

Brian and Sophie quickly averted their eyes from the horrified mother and bent over their plates. Brian choked on his egg roll, his eyes clenched shut against a wellspring of laughter, and the sight of his reddening face made Sophie convulse with silent mirth.

"What's so funny?" demanded Lucy in a loud voice.

"Nothing!" Sophie hissed. "We're just happy you're eating your noodles." And then they were off again, helplessly passing the disease of inappropriate laughter back and forth, no longer sure what they were even laughing about. Finally they shuddered to a stop, and Sophie collapsed against her chair feeling warm and almost postcoital.

"Let's go make some stuff," she said. "Lucy, do you want to make some stuff?"

"Make stuff NOWWWWWWW!" sang Lucy operatically.

They found their way to the Asian Art galleries, where Lucy barged through the crowd to the paper lantern–making table. Sophie and Brian followed, but before they could join her Elliot slipped away and ran in the other direction. "Stay with Lucy," Sophie called to Brian. She followed Elliot, who barely slowed as he ran through the dark and looming Chinese temple, past rooms of furniture and vases and a wheeled dog cage, and finally into the Japanese period room. She let him stay a few steps ahead of her, enjoying his moment of discovery as he crossed the threshold and came to a halt, disoriented. They had emerged from the shadowy galleries into a sunny garden whose stone paths were lined with leafy bamboo. The paths framed a ceremonial teahouse and Buddhist temple: two rustic buildings of cypress, pine, and plaster. The teahouse formed an L around a simple dirt courtyard, while the temple was surrounded by a bed of wood mulch; above its simple square frame, a tiled roof swooped into a cloudless blue sky. Elliot ran delightedly along the paths, seemingly untroubled by the surreal scene. Sophie wondered if he understood instinctively that it was not daytime, and they were not outside; or if he thought he had indeed exited the building into the sunshine, and simply accepted the strangeness of the situation the way he embraced strangeness every day of his life.

"Stay on the path, Elliot," she called, as she studied one of the labels on the wall. The building in front of her was named the "Temple of the Attainment of Happiness." Through its square doorway she could see a large, lacquered Buddha, resplendent with gold leaf and draped in an elaborately carved robe, sitting serenely atop a garlanded base. Arrayed around him was a collection of smaller sculptures and brass devotional objects. The Buddha had definitely mastered attainment, Sophie decided, but was he happy? Perched there in his little house, among his shiny knickknacks, he actually looked kind of lonely.

Elliot crashed into her leg, breathless from his romp through the galleries. He raised his hands in the air and Sophie lifted him onto her hip. "Let's go find Daddy," she said, and Elliot squirmed in excitement.

"Daddy! Daddy! Daddy!"

She exited the gallery and almost bumped into Marjorie,

who was walking with a tall woman in a seersucker pant-suit. "Marjorie!"

"Hello." Marjorie was holding a cardboard box filled with construction paper and Magic Markers; she raised a knee to support the box for a moment. "Sophie, this is my friend Helen. She volunteers at the Met—in the registrar."

Sophie shifted Elliot to her other side so she could offer her hand. Helen's grip was surprisingly strong.

"Sophie's married to Brian Porter, our ceramics curator. He's quite the rising star, even if he's not the world's most organized person."

"I've heard of him," Helen said in a deep voice.

"Helen was just telling me how different things are at the Met," Marjorie said. "It sounds like another world."

"New York is where the big money lives." Sophie smiled. "And the big budgets."

"Mmm," said Marjorie. "Sophie is a stay-at-home mom," she said to Helen, nodding at Elliot.

Sophie was almost too surprised by this to respond. "Actually, I—"

"Good for you," intoned Helen.

"I *work*," Sophie said.

"Of course you do," Marjorie said. "The most important work isn't always paid, right, Helen?" They smirked knowingly at each other. "I've got to put this box down," Marjorie said. "I'll see you later, Sophie."

"I write code," Sophie said to their retreating backs. But they didn't hear.

Sophie put Elliot down and led him back into the shadowy galleries. She knew Brian never talked about her work, but couldn't he at least let people know she *did* work? Was that so hard? And Marjorie—pretending to put Sophie on some kind of homemaker pedestal while reserving her true admiration for Brian; it was disgusting. Sophie had talents; Marjorie had no idea what kind of talents she had. No idea!

She finally found Brian at a scroll-making station downstairs, where he was helping Lucy practice calligraphy with a long-bristled brush. Lucy was seated on his lap, and he was murmuring into her ear as she carefully daubed black ink onto a piece of rice paper. Something he said made Lucy laugh, and she twisted around to squeeze his nose. Brian feigned outrage, which made her laugh even more. A smudge of glitter sparkled on his cheek.

"Having fun?" asked Sophie, trying to sound brighter than she felt.

"Show Mommy what we made!" demanded Lucy, and Brian held up a painted lantern encrusted with glitter and plastic jewels. "The jewels aren't real, but they are very beautiful anyway," Lucy explained. "Daddy said he would talk to them about getting real jewels next time."

"Now we're writing Chinese poetry," Brian said. "Well, Lucy is. I don't know Chinese."

"I do!" said Lucy.

Elliot leaned out of Sophie's arms, reaching for Brian. Brian moved Lucy onto the bench beside him and took Elliot into his lap. "He looks tired," he said.

"Yeah, I think he's ready," Sophie said. She thought a moment. "Why don't I go get the stroller."

"I need to get it."

"You're having a good time. Hang out with them a little longer."

"Yeah, but you know you're not supposed—"

"Daddy, you make one," Lucy said. "I'll teach you. Here's your brush."

Sophie nudged him. "Come on. Look how good they're being. Enjoy this."

Brian kissed Elliot on the head and reached into his pocket. "Do not tell anyone," he said, handing Sophie his keys. "I could get fired."

Upstairs, the offices were dark and hushed. Sophie squinted down the hallway, which was dimly lit by two faintly buzzing exit signs. The carts were no longer lined up next to the water cooler. She found the door to the storage room and jangled through Brian's keys, trying each one in the lock with shaking fingers, until finally the knob turned and she pushed through the heavy door. As it swung shut behind her, she turned on the lights and surveyed the scene. Six or seven carts were jumbled in the front of the room, blocking access to the storage shelves, half of which were empty, save for a coffee cup stained with a dark pink lipstick mark. The rest of the shelves were still dense with objects. Sophie knew she had to move fast, or Brian would come looking for her, or worse, Marjorie would come back upstairs. She also wanted to get to the shelves beyond the carts, where she would find the pieces that were still untouched and unexamined—the ones least likely to be missed.

Sophie tried to squeeze between the carts, but they were jammed into the tight space, and no matter how tall and thin she tried to make herself, her thighs stubbornly refused to get through. As she jostled the carts, something fell over with a clang. She backed up, heaved the door open, and pulled one of the carts into the hallway while holding the door with her foot. The cart was heavy and hard to steer, and as she wrestled with it, a ewer tipped over the edge; she reached out and caught it before it hit the floor. She parked the cart next to the doorway, then paused for a second to listen. Silence.

Back in the storage room she pushed through the remaining carts and hurried down the narrow alley between two of the tall steel shelving units. Objects offered themselves up on every side: vases and urns, crosses and clocks, bowls and boxes, chalices and goblets. She paused in front of a huge footed silver monstrosity, an assemblage of lacy bowls held aloft by curling vines, the whole thing dripping with tiny bells and flowery garlands. Too big.

On the shelf below, a silver and glass decanter caught her eye, but the scrolls and flowers decorating its base seemed too fat and clumsy. Next to it sat a squat, plain tankard with little embellishment aside from an etched coat of arms on the front; Harry would probably find it "unassuming." And anyway, wasn't she supposed to be looking for something from the Renaissance? Realizing she should have done some basic research before coming, she thought back to her art history elective. Leonardo da Vinci…humanism…the Sistine Chapel…statues of gorgeous naked men. That class had ruined her grade point average, she remembered now. She should have studied harder.

She moved down the shelf, angling her neck to get a view of the pieces pushed back in the shadows. Minutes were passing like slippery fish through her fingers. She reached for a strange, lumpy shape hidden behind a set of tumblers. Pulling it out, she saw that it had four legs, and a head that was lowered submissively, with long ears and a low-slung tail. It was an Irish setter, complete with a coppery coat of tarnish. Its fur rippled over its muscled flanks, and its legs were feathered with short, curled tufts. About a foot long, it felt heavy and solid in her hand. It reminded Sophie of her neighbor's Irish setter, Jeremy, when they'd lived in California. He'd always greeted Sophie by standing on his hind legs and putting his front paws on her shoulders. This one was more guarded, though, with a hint of wildness in its wary eyes and half-crouching stance. It looked like a biter.

Gripping the dog around its middle, Sophie pushed through the carts and pulled open the door. She tried bringing the cart from the hallway through the door with one hand, but it was too heavy. She set the dog on the hallway floor against the wall, and yanked the cart into the storage room, the door shutting behind her. She did her best to reproduce the original logjam of carts, jostling them back and forth with much rattling and clanking. Finally she turned and reached for the doorknob, then stopped, blood flooding her head, her heart straining as if it had been grabbed and squeezed hard.

The faint click of the department's steel door latch, barely audible from the end of the hall, was followed by a languid squeal of hinges and a decisive thunk. Sophie's finger flew to the light switch and turned it off; she winced at the click. She waited in the darkness, her head buzzing, her arms feeling strangely disconnected from her body as they hovered at her sides. A sharp metallic taste flooded her mouth. She heard the muffled rattle of keys going into a pocket; the mutter of a walkie-talkie; the quick tap of doorknobs encountering locked latches. Sophie carefully backed away from the light switch, past the doorknob to the hinges. She imagined the dog crouched just outside the door, its head low, eyes on the intruder. She hoped its dull brown body was melting into the shadows. She hoped…

The doorknob turned and the door pushed open slightly; she swiveled her shoulder an inch to the right to avoid touching it, biting back her breath. The walkie-talkie clicked and whispered while its owner paused in the darkness. A hand pushed the door open wider, a foot braced it, another hand flicked on the light.

A rustle of jacket sleeve as fingers dialed down the walkie-talkie. Silence. Then a single, disapproving click of the tongue, and a brusque sweep over the light switch. The door slammed shut. A key turned in the lock.

Sophie didn't move until she heard the stutter of the freight elevator door and the hum and whine of cable. She waited another moment to be sure, then flipped the dead bolt and escaped. She picked up the dog, unlocked Brian's office door, and found the stroller leaning against his desk, still folded. She pushed the release lever with her thumb and gave the handle a shake, popping the stroller open. Reaching into the basket, she located a zipped compartment under the seats and pulled out one of the foot muffs that were folded inside. Sophie stuffed the dog into the quilted sack, then rolled it up and shoved it back into its pocket. She zipped the compartment shut, pushed the release lever again and collapsed the stroller, trapping the dog deep inside.

She rolled the folded stroller into the hallway and locked Brian's door. Inhaling deeply through her nose, she savored the adrenaline that was charging through her veins. Ahead of her, the exit sign was rimmed with an exquisite halo of light. The rubbery stroller handle felt plush; the large wheels cushiony. Through the darkness, Sophie was aware of every angle formed where walls met ceiling, where doorjambs met lintels; she was dazzled by the pattern of planes running headlong toward the end of the hallway; she imagined the wall disappearing, and the planes continuing into space, converging in a point that moved infinitely onward.

Downstairs she found Brian sitting on the stairs, cradling Elliot in his arms while Lucy skipped up and down the steps. Sophie apologized, explaining that she had run into a client who had gone on and on about a new project. They left through the west entrance, Elliot asleep on Brian's shoulder, Lucy holding Sophie's hand as Sophie wheeled the folded stroller through the crowd to the guard station. The guard fist-bumped Brian, gave Sophie's diaper bag a quick glance, and wiggled his fingers at Lucy.

On the walk home, Sophie linked her arm through Brian's and relished the first touch of autumn coolness in the air. She admired the pink and green neon sign in front of Nero's Pizza; why hadn't she noticed it before? It was an old one, full of retro charm. She chattered happily about the evening: Lucy's lantern! Elliot's romp through the Asian galleries! Could you believe the turnout? And the acrobats—so beautiful, so daring!

Ten

In November the ginkgo tree went off like a firecracker, its leaves turning bright yellow, filling the second and third floor front bedrooms with their noisy glow. At the end of their run they fell, practically all at once, like a shower of sparks all over the cars and the sidewalk and the worn marble stoops.

Lucy was four now, and went to preschool every day. Sophie put Elliot, now two, into day care on Monday and Wednesday mornings. Those two mornings were more luxurious, more restorative and liberating, than she imagined any tropical vacation could be. With no one else in the house she was free to wander its rooms at her leisure; free to eat a snack at any moment without explanation; free to sort through the kids' toys and throw out the rocks, sticks, and headless dolls. She finally installed the porcelain keyhole covers, and touched up the paint where the stroller had marred the vestibule wall. She sat in her reading chair and browsed through shelter magazines, dreaming of marble counters and built-in bookshelves.

They continued to see Keith and Amy. Sophie scrutinized them for signs of marital distress, but couldn't pick up on anything. One night at their house, Keith had made everyone drinks and left a kitchen cabinet open, and Amy, who had been leaning down to talk to Mathilda, straightened up fast and banged her head on the corner of the cabinet door. She cried out and bent double, clutching her head and groaning while Mathilda laughed. Keith swiftly filled a small bag with ice and guided Amy to a chair, rubbing her back while she rocked in pain. Sophie imagined that if Amy had been harboring any hidden anger toward Keith it would have burst out at that moment, in the form of a sharp remark about the open cabinet door, or at the very least, by brushing his hand away. But Amy accepted his tender ministrations, and after icing her head for a while she came to the table and made a joke about needing a hard hat.

During her time at home Sophie tried to contemplate her career, but found it difficult to focus. She did miss her work, but was filled with resentment toward her field: she had dedicated so much of herself to it, for so many years, and the minute she slowed down it had sped off without her. She knew she could catch up, with hard work and one or two successful projects, but for now she preferred to sulk.

She also resented that when Brian asked her about work she was forced to be evasive and dishonest. If her field were not so impatient, so sexist, she wouldn't be in this position. "How is that New York project going?" he would ask. And she would answer that it was the perfect client, they were totally understanding of her schedule, and they were keeping her busy with a steady stream of revisions and additions. "That's fantastic," he would say, genuinely pleased and probably grateful that she hadn't gone into a lengthy explanation of the project's back-end dynamics.

Brian may have been a detective at work—searching for clues and following leads—but at home he seemed blithely content to accept whatever Sophie told him. He failed to notice that she never got client phone calls, never had to work at night or on the weekends. Nor did he notice that even though their bank balance kept dipping close to zero, they always had enough for groceries, and that there were always twenties in Sophie's wallet when he needed them. Brian was happily absorbed in his own career, whose skyward trajectory seemed limitless. His journal article had been well received; the Milan vase got a small mention in the *Times*; he'd secured a place for the museum in the will of an elderly collector of majolica.

Above all, Brian was caught up in his quest for the missing Saint-Porchaire candlestick. He'd come back from his visit to Madame Viellefond practically trembling with excitement: apparently Wilder's lover, Sandrine, had passed down several works of art to her family. Madame Viellefond showed him a small Dutch painting that he felt certain was important, although he wasn't planning to put the Paintings curator on its trail just yet. Sophie knew he was waiting until he'd finished his own plunder of the family treasures; no need to send them scurrying to the appraisers just yet. Madame Viellefond had given him a list of Sandrine's progeny and he'd written to them all, presumably asking, in the most casual way possible when writing letters in French, whether any of them had seen a fancy candlestick lying around.

Sophie, too, was spending a lot of time thinking about museum-quality antiques. Harry had not been thrilled by the Irish setter. "Nineteenth century?" had been his exasperated response. He'd paid her reluctantly, grumbling that he'd never be able to sell it, but Sophie didn't really care. Her real payment was the small thrill that trembled in her throat every time she imagined the rest of the objects waiting in the storage room, or recalled those silent, terrifying moments in the dark. She could still taste the strange, exciting rush of fear that felt like the mirror image of desire.

During their usual gin-soaked lunch at the tavern, Harry had an idea. "Let's pop over to the Met," he said. "I'll take you around, show you the good stuff. Yeah?"

"I don't know, Harry, I need to relieve the sitter."

"Just give me an hour. I want to show you some of my favorite things, give you a little brushup on sixteenth century versus, say, nineteenth. So the next time you see something at a sidewalk sale, or your grandmother's china cabinet or whatever, you'll know what you're looking at." Harry laced his fingers together and turned his hands inside out, cracking all ten knuckles.

Sophie stared at him for a moment, turning things over in her mind. "All right," she said slowly. "To the Met."

Once they were inside the museum, it became clear that Harry was well acquainted with the labyrinthine floor plan. He led her quickly through the throngs of people crowding the Great Hall and into the moody, churchlike Medieval galleries, eventually emerging into a tapestry-lined gallery of Renaissance art. "Augsburg and Nuremberg," he said briskly, pulling her toward some display cases filled with gleaming objects made of gold, silver, glass, and shell. "All of this was made for the courts of Northern Europe; the German silversmiths were like the Lagerfelds and Louboutins of their time." He showed her a drinking vessel in the shape of a stag; a tankard swirling with vines and flowers and topped with a naked putto; a footed cup engraved with pastoral scenes. He drew her eye to the imaginative wit of the decoration, and the natural attitudes of the miniature creatures that sprouted from handles and lids. He pointed out the feats of perspective in the tiny, intricate scenes, and explained repoussé, damascening, fire gilding. For a brief time Harry slipped from behind his droll facade, and surprised Sophie with a level of earnestness she hadn't thought him capable of.

"You should be a docent!" she teased him.

"Maybe I will someday. As penance for my sins." He drew her into an English period room lined with dark oak paneling, and pointed out a pair of silver ginger jars in a small case. "See those?" he said. "Seventeenth century, English, cast and chased." He cracked the knuckle of his forefinger. "Just gorgeous." He turned to the label. "They belong to someone I know."

"One of your wanker clients?" Sophie asked. The label read, "Anonymous Loan."

"One of my dad's clients. Someone with great taste, but terrible manners." Harry shook his head.

"Why did he loan these out?"

"With something like this, impeccable provenance, bought at auction for a ridiculous sum, the insurance is ruinous," Harry said. "But if you loan it to a museum, they pick up the insurance. Of course, some people also do it for the bragging rights, but my man's a bit more discreet than that. He keeps his best stuff hidden away where no one will ever see it."

"Who is he?"

"Also, these are English. Normally he's got more continental taste. But I think he couldn't resist the workmanship on these."

"Is he French?"

"You know what we should look at?" Harry brightened. "Storage!"

"How—"

"Follow me." Harry strode through several small galleries, then led her to a glass elevator that deposited them on a mezzanine in the American wing. "Visible storage!" he announced grandly, as he swept through a pair of doors. "This is just the American stuff—some of it, anyway. You've never been in here?"

"Never," Sophie breathed, her eyes struggling to take in the sight. As far as she could see, acres of simple glass cases were filled with shelf after shelf of tightly packed objects, furniture, and paintings. Along one aisle, Tiffany glass was stacked on stepped shelves like crayons in a box. Down another aisle, ranks of grandfather clocks stood as humorless as palace guards. Paintings were hung in jumbled rows, ornate gilded frames butting up against bare canvas. In another case, empty frames gaped strangely, displaying the utilitarian lattice on which they were hung.

"Museums are like icebergs," Harry said, standing in front of a floor-to-ceiling pile of chairs. "You only see the top five or ten percent. But some museums are starting to show the work in storage like this—no labels, no precious arrangement. Look over here." He led her around a corner to a row of cases thickly stocked with hundreds of silver tumblers, creamers, chafing dishes, and flatware. Arranged by type—dozens of identical coffeepots followed by dozens of identical saltcellars—the effect was of an assembly line, or a shelf at Target.

Sophie walked slowly down the aisle, struck by the depreciation of the objects once they were placed in this dizzying, hall-of-mirrors display of accumulation. What could be more anonymous than fifty monogrammed tumblers? Did anyone care where these endless tallies of spoons came from; whose mouths had they been inside?

"It all becomes sort of meaningless, doesn't it?" she said. "When you see it like this."

Harry shrugged. "If you collect pie servers, it's nirvana. You can see every kind of American pie server ever made. But yeah— for the average person, it all sort of bleeds together, doesn't it?"

"Mmm." For a moment Sophie had a strange, floating feeling, as if the floor had dropped away, and everything—the silver, the glass, the paintings, herself and Harry—had become mere molecules bobbing about in an invisible and immeasurable puff of air.

❧

Sophie became aware of someone looking at her from across the café. She was sitting on a flabby, coffee-stained sofa, waiting for her new friend, a real estate agent named Janice she'd met at a dinner party. But now she found herself locking eyes with Carly, who gave her a small smile and a half wave. Sophie frowned into her mug. She didn't want her pleasant afternoon interrupted by some kind of confrontation. But now Carly was standing in front of her, and after an awkward moment, she helped herself to the spot Sophie had been saving for Janice.

"Hey," said Carly. "What's going on?"

"Nothing."

"No, really—what is going on?"

Sophie had once enjoyed Carly's bold, entitled directness. Now she found it obnoxious. "What do you mean?"

"I mean, why the cold shoulder?"

"You know why."

"What did you hear? Or see?"

"What do you think?"

Carly pushed air through her nose in exasperation. "If you're talking about me and Keith, it's long over. Things got weird really fast…"

"Things got weird the minute you decided to ignore my wishes." Sophie instantly regretted the phrase "my wishes."

"Look, I'm sorry about that. But it wasn't about you."

Sophie looked into Carly's face for the first time, surprised by the anger she found there.

"It had nothing to do with you," Carly continued. "It was between two consenting adults."

"I don't think Amy and I were consenting."

"Why do you keep trying to insert yourself into this situation? You're not Keith's wife."

"But I asked you not to! I was clear! I didn't want you fucking with our friends!"

"And what about me? Aren't I your friend? What if this was something I needed?"

Sophie let out a short, hard laugh. "You don't need that. You don't need anything. You have everything already. You took someone's husband, just for kicks, and that's wrong."

"Excuse me? How do I have everything?" Carly crossed her arms and leaned her head to one side, apparently expecting an answer.

"You're kidding me."

"No, really. How can you, with your husband and your children—these people who *belong* to you, who are *part of* you—tell me I have everything."

"That's not—you have everything else. Oh, please, don't pretend to be jealous of me."

Carly narrowed her eyes.

"Anyway," Sophie continued, flustered, "that's beside the point. You took Amy's husband."

"Come off it. It's just sex, for Christ's sake, and I didn't 'take' anyone's husband. She still has her husband. Nobody got hurt."

"I did."

Carly grimaced in confusion. "How?"

"You basically made it clear you don't give a shit about my feelings."

Carly rested her forehead on her fingertips, eyes skyward. "Sorry."

Sophie said nothing.

"Anyway," Carly continued, more softly, "we all have stuff to resolve."

"What's this 'we' business?"

Carly snorted.

"No, really. What?" Sophie's breath shrank in her chest. Heat gathered in her head.

Carly straightened. "Nobody's perfect, all right? I've got issues, you've got issues…"

"Excuse me? What *issues* do I have?"

"I don't know, let's start with control freak?" Carly pressed her lips together and let her words settle for a moment. "You want to control everyone around you, you want to control me, you want to control yourself—*especially* yourself. I mean, my God. You've got everything locked up behind this big, black iron fence, and you won't let anyone in. Just, you know, as an example."

Things were sizzling, now, in Sophie's ears. How dare she? "How dare you?"

"What?"

"You think you know anything about what I have quote-unquote locked up? What's with this psychoanalysis bullshit? You're the one we're talking about. You're the one with an addiction to stealing people's husbands." She must have been getting loud. People were turning their heads and laughing nervously. "Because no one ever gets hurt. Because it's a *victimless crime.*" Sophie drew out the phrase, furiously finger-quoting. "Such bullshit. There are victims all around you."

"Sorry I'm late!" Janice had breezed in, oblivious to the room's crushing barometric pressure. "My buyers wanted to see the place a third time. I told them I'm going to have to start charging them rent."

Sophie laughed loudly. "Hey, Janice. No problem. This is Carly. She was just on her way out." She landed hard on the last word.

Carly stood and silently walked back to her table. Janice raised her eyebrows, but Sophie just shook her head and patted the couch beside her. "How are you? How's Tim?"

From the corner of her eye, she saw Carly gather her coat and bag and walk out the door, leaving behind an uneaten bagel.

A few days later, much to her surprise, Sophie received a letter from MortgageOne. The unsigned, fuzzily photocopied note invited her to apply for a loan modification; application forms could be downloaded from the MortgageOne website. Sophie searched the site, but there were no loan modification forms to be found. Once again, she called the 800-number and spoke with a woman who took such long pauses during their conversation, Sophie wondered if she were conducting simultaneous conversations with other customers on other lines.

"You'll need to get those forms…

"…from the bank that owns your loan."

"I don't know who that is," Sophie said. "I wrote you a letter to find out, and you sent back a letter telling me to get the forms from your website. And there aren't any forms on your website."

"We're the loan servicer…

"We need authorization from the investor…

"…to modify your loan."

"Fine. Tell me who that is."

Long pause.

"Dayton Loan Services."

"No! Listen! They sold my loan to New Century Mortgage, and New Century Mortgage, as I have mentioned many, many times, can't find any record of it. They sent me back to you." The phone felt hot in her hand. "But hey—since my mortgage has been lost, why don't I just stop paying? Nobody would notice, right? How would you even know?"

Long pause.

"Hello?"

"Nonpayment of your loan will result in foreclosure."

"Then tell me what to do."

"Why don't I send you…

"… the loan modification forms…

"…in the mail."

"Thirty seconds ago you were saying that wasn't possible."

"Would you like the forms?"

"Hey, you know, I'm going to go with 'yes.' Is that the right answer? Because I don't even know anymore. But sure. Knock yourself out."

What the hell? Wasn't property ownership supposed to be the most reliable way to anchor a life? You entered a three-decade-long relationship with a bank, you sent them a check every month, you filled your shelves with photo albums. Nobody had ever mentioned this tangled world of brokers, servicers, and investors, or the emperor's-new-clothes nature of a loan. Why *didn't* she just stop sending checks? It certainly seemed as though her name and address had long ceased to exist in their files. But the representative's robotic voice echoed in her head: "Nonpayment of your loan will result in foreclosure."

Sophie let herself take a quick peek inside the locked room where that word lived, where her darkest fears made their plans. She slammed the door quickly, but the chill lingered. There was enough in the bank to make ends meet for a few more months, but their day-care and preschool costs had gone up, and Sophie could see the graph in her head: savings trending downward, expenses trending upward, neither showing any sign of stopping.

Eleven

Brian liked his sandwiches the way they were made in France: a split baguette with butter, a few tissue-thin slices of ham, and those tiny pickles whose price, Sophie had noticed, was in inverse proportion to their size. Sophie packed two of these sandwiches into a mini cooler with two bottles of Perrier and a bag of sweet-potato chips. She walked to the museum and called him from outside. The museum was closed to visitors on Mondays, so there were no guards on duty, and the entrances were locked.

When Brian poked his head out of the door, Sophie held up the cooler with a smile. "I made food!" she announced. "Your favorite sandwich."

His answering smile was more of a wince. "Oh, God. You're so sweet."

"I brought one for me, too," she said, pushing past him into the museum. "Picnic in your office!"

"It's kind of a crazy day," he said as he followed her toward the elevator. "And technically we're not supposed to have food in the offices—"

Sophie waved her hand. "Please. You eat at your desk all the time."

She could tell immediately, when they got upstairs, that

something had changed in Brian's department. Instead of the usual hush, the hallway was filled with loud voices. Marjorie scurried out of the storage room without acknowledging Sophie and disappeared into Ted's office, shutting the door.

"...fucking *ridiculous*," she heard from the storage room. "It's like a fucking flea market. Get—what is *this*? I mean, are you fucking kidding me?"

"Michael's back," said Brian.

"Oh." Sophie slowed as they passed the storage room, looking in to see Michael amid the carts, his chest heaving. Ted was busily sorting through a pile of object cards, head lowered. "Hi, Michael," said Sophie with a little wave.

Michael stared at her, blinking. He was like a young incarnation of Ben Franklin, all chin and dome, with round wire-frame glasses.

"Sophie," she said. "Brian's—"

"Sophie. Hi. I just got back."

"I see that."

"Excuse my language. But as you can see, things have *fucking* fallen apart around here." Ted cringed.

"Sorry to hear that," said Sophie, hoisting the cooler up and cradling it against her belly. "Well, we'll get out of your way."

In Brian's office she ate her sandwich while Brian whispered about the maelstrom that had struck upon Michael's return. "Poor Marjorie's been taking the brunt of it. He actually accused her of stealing some things."

"*What?*"

"I know, it's ridiculous. There are so many cards without objects, and it's been that way since...I don't know. The thirties?"

Sophie chewed a bite of baguette, unable to swallow. "Poor Marjorie...that's really unfair."

"Yeah. He'll calm down eventually. Michael's just a control freak."

"Is he going to…report her?"

"I don't think so. I mean, I hope not. I don't know what he would be able to report. And then we'd all be screwed, for letting things get so bad with our inventory."

"You think you guys would get blamed?"

"Absolutely. I mean, remember those carts that were in my office? That never should've happened. I had all kinds of people in and out of here. Thank God there wasn't anything really important on them."

"Anyway, you guys wouldn't have had something important just sitting in storage, right? With no object card? Don't you keep track of the good stuff?"

Brian massaged his forehead. "We try. But with the turnover we've had, it's hard to know what's been studied and what's been just stuck on a shelf without a second thought. That's why I wanted to wait for Michael before we started shipping everything out. I wanted him to go through it all." He rubbed his eyes. "I should've put my foot down."

Sophie sipped her water. "Don't you want your sandwich?"

"I have zero appetite. Sorry. It was nice of you—I mean, it's a beautiful sandwich. My God, you practically *cooked*."

"I know!"

Ted appeared in the doorway. "Brian, do you have a moment?"

"You finish eating," Brian told her. "I'll be right back."

But instead of waiting, Sophie tossed the rest of her lunch in the trash, took the empty cooler, and let herself out through the department door. Walking past the tapestries to the Great Stair, she found the silence of the near-empty museum oppressively lonesome. She changed direction and headed toward the vast front window, which was swathed in white floor-to-ceiling curtains. She slipped behind the curtains, set the cooler on the floor, and stood admiring the view of the city skyline, which shone under the cold blue sky. Cars swirled around Eakins Oval; joggers bounced in place at stoplights; a helicopter paced the sky over the Vine Street Expressway. Sophie felt very still. She was aware that everything had changed, that she was being nudged off her track, but for the moment she had not decided what new direction she would take.

Behind her, she heard Brian's voice calling her name. Standing behind one of the fat columns flanking the window, she peeked through the curtain and saw him leaning over the balcony rail, searching the Great Hall. He hurried to the stairs and ran down them while she remained motionless behind the curtain. A few minutes later he returned, climbing the steps two at a time, and disappeared into a side gallery. She heard a door slam.

Sophie waited. Two young employees carrying file boxes emerged from another gallery and walked to the balcony elevator, then disappeared behind its tall bronze doors.

Silence.

She waited a little longer, her heart calm in her chest. In front of her an enormous gray-and-white Calder mobile spun serenely over the Great Stair Hall. A car honked outside and the helicopter sputtered in the sky, but inside there was no sign of life; all the curators, art handlers, conservators, volunteers, and assistants were hidden away in their offices behind the museum's proscenium. Sophie picked up the cooler, slipped from behind the curtain, and walked slowly toward the stairs. It was over. Michael was back; he would take care of the objects. It was time to resume her life as an unwanted freelancer, playground bench warmer, fish-stick dispenser. They would sell the house at a loss. With no down payment, they'd have to rent something. A place in the suburbs with low ceilings, louvered windows, hollow-core doors. A place that would offer no solace when Brian was out of town; a place far from their friends, far from their new life. In a place like that, she imagined, she could almost evaporate, disappear, with nothing at all to tether her to the earth.

Sophie veered away from the stairs and walked into the European Art wing. She moved slowly through a series of doorways, passing period rooms whose entrances were blocked by iron railings. Navigating this dense network of galleries had always felt frustrating to Sophie, who found it hard to remember which rooms she had visited and how to get back to where she'd started. The mix of ceramics, bronzes, furniture, chandeliers, and paintings was overwhelming if she tried to cover too much ground at once, and the many styles of period rooms, from a gilded Parisian salon to a wood-paneled English lodge, left her disoriented. This time, however, she was grateful for the wing's many twists and turns: a person could disappear forever in here. There were no guards or cameras to find her.

She quickened her step, scanning the objects sitting on mantels, consoles, and side tables: they looked back at her silently, almost indulgently. She turned off into a series of smaller galleries, peeking into a mirrored French drawing room, then the sitting room of an English country manor. She took note of an ornate mantel clock, some rough pewter tableware, an endless variety of ceramics. A pair of reddish-brown vases looked like something you could get at IKEA: simple, monochromatic, completely modern. The label read "Tang Dynasty, 618–902."

In another gallery she came across a display of finely wrought silver miniatures: dozens of doll-size coffeepots, candlesticks, baskets, and chalices. If they hadn't been under Plexiglas, Sophie would have gladly swept the entire tinkling collection into her cooler.

Bent in front of the display, she became aware of a distant vibration in the air, which gradually coalesced into a sound, then a realization: footsteps. Sophie straightened and slid to the wall by the door, listening. The steps grew muffled as they passed into a further gallery; then they stopped. There was a dull metallic clank, then the footsteps reversed. Sophie moved closer to the doorway, edged her face to the jamb, and peeked out. She had a view of the next three rooms through a series of nesting doorways. A figure suddenly crossed one of the openings, startling her: it was a man in blue coveralls carrying a metal ladder.

Sophie pulled her flats off her feet and put them into her coat pockets. She quickly turned the corner and hurried through a side door, putting distance between herself and the worker, who was headed, she thought, toward the galleries along the exterior wall. She crept toward the other side of the wing, slipping a little in her tights, carefully skirting rooms with creaky parquet floors.

Suddenly, the screech of the ladder being opened tore through the silence, sounding closer than it should. Sophie ducked through a small door and found herself in a strange, claustrophobic nook. To one side of the doorway was a dark pocket of space just large enough for her to stand in, her back against the wall. The other side of the alcove opened into a small period room, the entrance blocked by a wood and Plexiglas barrier. From her hiding place Sophie could just make out the title on the room's label: "*Het Scheepje* (The Little Ship)."

Lit by a pair of tall exterior windows, soft with shadows and filled with heavy black furniture, the room seemed to come straight from a Dutch painting. A few simple metal objects had been placed on a cloth-covered table near the window, where they caught the light and gently held it. In one corner a brass birdcage hung from the heavily beamed ceiling; on the opposite wall, blue and white tiles surrounded an iron fireplace screen, flanked by stone columns supporting a carved wood mantel, on which was propped a series of blue and white plates. Between the two windows a heavy black sideboard loomed, its ebony-inlaid surface busy with carved figures. Sitting on top of the sideboard, under a massive cornice supported by elaborate pillars, gleamed a silver footed bowl.

Sophie fixed her gaze on the bowl, admiring the way its embossing caught the window light with such clarity, like a stroke of white impasto ringing through the darkness. The shallow dish perched lightly atop a fluted stem, which bulged in the middle and resolved in a gracefully spreading foot. Its delicate proportions were a welcome contrast to the dark, plodding wood, iron, and brass that filled the room.

Waiting in her dark corner, listening to the creaks and clanks of the maintenance man's work, Sophie felt herself pushing away from shore and embarking on a different sort of journey: one that was simultaneously more deliberate and less certain. Somewhere in the back of her mind something bothersome flapped in the wind, distracting her from the darkness that was luring her into its velvety depths. She turned away from it, allowing the noise to recede from her consciousness, blocking the loose canvas flap, which lashed a long tail of rope, from her mind's line of sight. She eased the cooler to the floor between her legs and pulled a pair of winter gloves from her pockets. A few rooms over, the ladder shrieked shut. Footsteps thudded quickly toward the exit.

It wasn't difficult to climb over the barrier, which was just over waist-high. Climbing back over it with the bowl in her hand was trickier but she managed, resting her torso on the wood frame and swinging her legs over, careful not to kick the label stand. The bowl almost didn't fit in the cooler, but she set it at an angle, and the cooler's pitched lid just cleared it.

She stopped right inside the wing's entrance, slipping her shoes back on and peeking out at the balcony. Her heart had finally revved up, and the strange metallic taste once again glazed her tongue. She gripped the cooler in her moist, gloved hand and willed herself to step out into the wide, exposed balcony, walking casually, swinging the cooler with the relaxed air of a wife who has just enjoyed an intimate lunch with her husband. Jauntily descending the Great Stair, she saw a figure emerge from a hallway on the first floor, headed her way. The woman looked familiar: Sophie had met her at many parties. Nancy? Ann? Their paths crossed on the bottom stair.

"Hi, Sophie!" said the woman. (Tammy—wasn't it Tammy?) "Visiting Brian?"

Sophie held up the cooler. "Yeah, I brought him some lunch."

"Lucky guy. How are the kids?"

"They're doing great. Growing like weeds. I'm actually on my way to pick them up at day care."

"Okay, well, enjoy!"

"Bye!"

Tammy seemed so nice. Why didn't they ever invite her for dinner? What was her husband's name? Bill?

Sophie hummed to herself as she jogged down another set of stairs to the employees' entrance, and pushed through the door into the cold winter sunshine.

"You can't pull that kind of stuff, Sophie," said Brian that night as he spooned pasta onto the kids' plastic plates. "You should've waited for me to come back and escort you out."

"Sorry—you just looked so preoccupied. I didn't want to bother you."

"Yeah, well, Tammy Brewer said she saw you. Made a point of coming to the offices to mention it."

"What the hell business is it of hers?"

"And no more food in the offices. Now that Michael's back, Ted's playing everything by the book. He's reasserting his authority. So…" Brian swept his hand through the air. "No more rule bending."

"Got it. Can I have some of that wine?" She was thinking about the cooler, which she had carelessly left in the middle of the basement floor, the bowl still inside. She was getting too cavalier. "What's going on with Marjorie?"

"It was pointed out to Michael that several of the so-called missing objects were actually locked in a cabinet in his office, and that he hadn't made note of it on the object cards."

"What were they doing there?"

"I don't know—overflow from the storage room, I guess? Usually we're supposed to use those cabinets for small things we're studying or writing about; it's meant to be temporary."

"So Marjorie's off the hook."

"For now. He's still pretty pissed, and storage is still a mess, but now he's spreading the blame around. Apparently I was Marjorie's direct supervisor while he was gone, and so I am being blamed for letting a volunteer touch the objects."

"Oh, please. Didn't she work for the registrar at Atwater Kent?"

"As a secretary."

"Oh."

"Anyway, Ted's determined not to let any of this get out. If our committee got wind of any of this…or the head of collections… well. But that's not going to happen. Now Ted and Michael are working their asses off to get it all sorted and out of our hands."

"And what about you?"

Brian shrugged. "It's never been my problem, I'm not about to get involved now. Silver and crystal—"

"Not my domain," Sophie finished for him. "Lucky you."

The next day she called Harry, but he'd gone to England to visit his family. "The annual pilgrimage," he explained over the phone. "Just making sure I don't get written out of the will. What's happening in Philadelphia?"

Sophie told him about her confrontation with Carly, but Harry seemed distracted and impatient. "Fuck her," was all he had to contribute. Then, "Well, do you have anything for me?"

Sophie was taken aback; this was not the Harry who was always so surprised and delighted by her offerings. She hesitated, unsure how to navigate the shift in tone.

"Hello?"

"I...might."

"Good. I'll have a look when I get back to New York."

"Okaaaaay..." For the first time in a while, Sophie felt a twinge of nervousness. This was not how things were supposed to go. She wasn't a mule. "I'll try to hang on to it for you," she said. "If I don't find someone else who's interested."

Harry snorted. "Well, well! Listen, love. Be careful. Most dealers won't be as casual about provenance as I have been."

"What's that supposed to mean?"

"I've been very generous with you, darling. You go elsewhere, you might not find people who are this...friendly. And then I'm afraid you'll be on your own."

Sophie frowned at the phone. Where was Harry going with this?

"Anyway," he continued, much more cheerily, "I'm off to dinner with this pack of miscreants that keeps insisting it's related to me. I hope your Christmas is better than mine. See you soon, love."

"See you soon. Harry."

Sophie hung up, Harry's tone clinging to her like a sticky residue. The bald greed, the thinly veiled threat—where was this coming from? He knew, yes...of course he knew there was something...not quite right about the source of the objects. So far he'd been polite enough to avoid mentioning it. But it hadn't occurred to her until now that Harry might be more aware of what she was doing than she was.

After dropping off the kids at day care the next morning, Sophie pushed the empty stroller through the gray chill of Center City, staring glumly into store windows. There was no way she could make a mortgage payment after buying gifts for the kids—remarkably expensive gifts that had been listed with great urgency by Lucy, dictating to Sophie, who then mailed the requests to the North Pole, complicit in her own undoing. Of course Santa would bring them the Playmobil palace and the Brio train set. Sophie would not, for anything in the world, miss that Christmas morning moment when the children saw their dreams come true, just like that, for the asking. Then there were the plane tickets to Cincinnati. They'd be spending the holiday with Brian's sister, Debbie, and her family; she had to buy gifts for them, too.

Sophie paused in Rittenhouse Square, as she often did on her way home, with a cup of coffee and muffin. Here in this meandering refuge from the city grid, squirrels seemed to be the only ones in a hurry. Even on a chilly day the benches were crowded with members of the slower class: retirees, students, mothers, drunks. Sophie found an empty seat on the main path and unwrapped her muffin. The argument with Carly was still bothering her. That she would even pretend to be jealous of Sophie's life was absurd; Carly had always been perfectly content with her single, childless existence. Now all of a sudden she was lonely? Wasn't that just an excuse for bad behavior?

And then deflecting the blame by bringing up Sophie's supposed issues. Okay, she wasn't blind—Sophie could see her own hypocrisy, but Carly couldn't see it, could she? It was Sophie's own fault that the argument kept coming back to poke her in the ribs, like a wayward underwire. She reminded herself that Carly's affairs were destructive—to marriages and friendships. Sophie's little habit affected no one, it was temporary, and there were good reasons for it.

A pregnant woman walked by, then another. There was probably a Lamaze class across the square. She watched the bellies pass, idly inventorying the types: high and proud, wide and spreading, pointed, lopsided. She remembered when she had first started to show, feeling like a fat peony bud, clenched tight and shiny around her secret beauty. As her belly swelled, so had her sense of importance. It was saintly work, putting a heavy child, literally, before yourself, sharing every meal, breath, and heartbeat. The world had been eager to grant her special status, quick with chairs and glasses of water. The cruel joke, of course, was that the heroic work actually came later, when the hormonal buzz had faded and her belly had crumpled, when she was heaving the double stroller around—then where were the chairs and glasses of water? But that, she supposed, was when the rewards of motherhood became more private and hard-won. When the kids showed flashes of intelligence and good sense. When she watched her son reach out to a goat at the petting zoo, his head cocked with curiosity, his hand descending gently onto a flank, where others might grab or pull, his gesture filled with pure kindness.

Sophie smoothed out her muffin cup, folded it into quarters. Across the path a homeless woman settled onto a bench, resting a tattered duffle bag beside her. Sophie looked away, started to get up, then paused, looking back. There was something about the woman's cheekbone, jutting like a shelf beneath her dark eye. Her skin was scorched with age and weather, but Sophie could see that she had once been beautiful, her features well proportioned, her neck long. She wore a man's blazer, the sleeves rolled up, faded jeans, filthy loafers. Her feet shuffled back and forth, as if she'd forgotten to stop walking upon sitting down.

Sophie squinted, but couldn't be sure what she was seeing at this distance. She got up and inched the empty stroller toward the other bench. She was moving so slowly, it felt like a dream. Actually, maybe it was a dream. Wasn't this a recurring vision that visited her in the crazy hours of the night? She stopped in front of the woman, dread swirling into hope and then whirlpooling back into dread.

"Mommy?"

The woman turned to look up at Sophie. The far side of her face had come unmoored, the eyelid sliding downward, her cheek and mouth slack. The good side pierced her with a sharp, suspicious gaze. Sophie fumbled in her pocket, pulled out a twenty, handed it to the woman, and hurried away. It wasn't her. *It wasn't her!* Tears bloomed in her eyes, her throat swelled, and she let out a surprised sob, cupping a hand over her mouth.

She thought she had let her feelings dry up and blow away on the desert wind, but now, strangely, she found herself filled with the same fear that came over her whenever she lost sight of Lucy or Elliot, no matter how briefly, in a crowded place. Who could say Maeve wasn't on the next bench down, or on some bench in New Mexico, her entire life balled up in a greasy bag? But of course, that was crazy. Her mother was strong, fearsome, spiny as a cactus. She'd never needed anyone, never asked for help. Why was Sophie suddenly worried about her, after all these years? Why was she suddenly thinking of her as a lost child?

Twelve

After picking them up at the Cincinnati airport, Dan parked the minivan in the driveway and carried their luggage through the garage while Debbie gave them a tour of "The Stash": shelves and shelves of spaghetti sauce, pineapple juice cocktail, potato flakes, soda bottles, whitening toothpaste, high-fiber cereal, cheese spray, antimicrobial sponges, mild salsa, Italian dressing, dryer sheets, and lemon juice.

"It's like a store," breathed Lucy, running her hand across a row of Gatorade bottles.

"And I only paid one hundred and twenty-seven dollars for the whole thing," said Debbie. "Want to see where the magic happens?"

"Magic!" cried Elliot.

Debbie led them out of the garage and through the great room to her couponing office. They crowded around a table covered with newspapers, a paper cutter, several types of scissors, a computer, and a color printer. Against one wall, a bookshelf was filled with binders marked "no expire," "no limit," "BOGO," and "Moneymakers." Debbie showed them how she searched for coupons, categorized them, and compiled them in a binder for her monthly trip to the supermarket.

"You've really taken this to a new level," Sophie said.

"All thanks to you!" Debbie said, squeezing Sophie's hand. Sophie didn't really see how she could take credit for all of it, but she squeezed Debbie's hand back. Yes, she'd been the one to set up Debbie's first computer, T1 line, and email address—nine years ago, when she and Brian had come to visit the newborn twins. Sophie remembered how they'd found Debbie, formerly a high-ranking product manager at Procter and Gamble, wandering the house with unwashed hair, her nursing bra permanently unfastened, a glazed look in her eyes. Sophie had hooked up the computer and introduced her to the nascent world of mommy blogs and Listservs, but it was Debbie who discovered the existence of coupon sites. Before long she was feeding her family, plus the beneficiaries of countless soup kitchens and food drives, for pennies on the dollar, and was helping others do the same with her exhaustively researched blog "Debbie Does Discounts." All signs of depression had disappeared; on the contrary, Debbie now functioned on a higher level than most people.

Having finished the tour, their suitcases put away in the bonus room, Sophie and Brian flopped on the sectional in the great room, where Dan was flipping through sports channels. Lucy and Elliot, shy at first, had quickly discovered the pleasures of the vast carpeted space, the corpulent furniture, the large-screen TV, and the bottomless bowl of Goldfish crackers sitting on the low coffee table. They ran laps through the kitchen and great room, stopping periodically to examine the cathedral-ceiling-grazing tree ("seventy-five percent off at Costco last January") and the extravagantly wrapped gifts already heaped beneath it.

Debbie added crab dip and Pepperoni Stix to the coffee table, and brought out cold beer in frosted mugs. "I got the kind you like," she said to Brian, perching on the arm of the sectional next to him, "even though it wasn't on sale, ha-ha." She smiled broadly, shrugging her eyebrows. Like Brian, Debbie was fair, with pale blue eyes and easily burned skin. Unlike him, she splashed every emotion across her face.

"Thanks, Deb."

"So how's the famous curator? Tell me about all your adventures. I'm dying to hear."

Brian told Debbie about his latest trips to Italy and France, his publications, his search for the Saint-Porchaire. She listened with her mouth half-open, interjecting "oh!"'s and "wow!"'s and "you're amazing!"'s, periodically waving at Dan to make sure he was listening. Sophie yearned for Brian to duck Debbie's praise, murmur something modest, but he accepted her admiration as his due. Sophie figured Debbie was just traveling the orbit already scribed by their parents when they were alive, with their displays of high school cycling trophies and their bulging scrapbooks of museum newsletters and exhibition announcements. Brian was used to it.

The nine-year-old twins, Kendall and Kylynn, surprised Sophie by taking an immediate interest in the younger children, styling Lucy's hair and heaving Elliot around in their skinny arms. They even offered to change Elliot's diapers, to which Sophie had no objection, even though the twins took this job too seriously and began changing him every twenty minutes. Elliot seemed happy with the attention, and Sophie was sure Debbie would be able get her some cheap diapers.

Sophie offered to help out in the kitchen, but Debbie's meals generally involved adding a cup of water to something in a casserole dish, so she found herself spending most of her time on the sectional feeling superfluous. This actually wasn't so bad. It had been a long time since she'd watched daytime TV; she was amazed there were so many shows about women having babies. Didn't the people sitting at home—women with babies—want to watch something else? But she found that she couldn't take her eyes off the young, excited couples as they decorated the nursery and talked about names, then rushed to the hospital and eventually descended into sweaty, face-distorting agony. Like clockwork, Sophie burst into embarrassed tears every time a slimy blue infant was placed, flailing, on its exhausted mother's chest.

Dan went to his job at Ashland Chemical every day, and Debbie and Brian stayed busy showing the kids around their hometown. They took them to see the tree at Fountain Square, the Festival of Lights at the zoo, and Cincinnati's best-decorated front yards. Sophie never felt like going along; she was finding it harder and harder to look into Brian's eyes, and Debbie's gushing niceness made her uncomfortable. She retreated further into the folds of the couch, napping and channel surfing, making occasional forays into the garage for bags of chips. Despite her calorie intake she felt pleasantly hollow. Now and then she would think about her house—its cramped living room, its excess of stairs. Then she would change the channel without looking, having memorized all the buttons on the remote control.

On Christmas Eve, Debbie wanted to go to the mall to catch the last door-buster deals at Circuit City. "Come on, it'll be fun," she said to Sophie. "There's nothing like the mall on Christmas Eve! The kids can see Santa!"

"I don't know," Sophie said. "They're showing a *Baby Story* marathon."

"Mommy!" cried Elliot with a gurgling laugh. Sophie sat up and looked over the back of the couch to see him running ecstatically into Kylynn's arms.

"All right," Sophie said, peeling off the afghan that was twined around her legs. "I'll come."

The eight of them boarded the van, the stroller comfortably

stowed in the back, and the doors oozed shut with the push of a button. Christmas music played on surround sound as they pulled out of the cul-de-sac. Sophie marveled at the van's spacious, soothingly beige interior. She'd never sat in such firm-but-yielding, buttery leather seats. The armrests were generous and adjustable. Warm air flowed over her feet. Let's keep driving, she thought; let's skip the mall. Why leave this paradise and endure the indignity of walking?

Too soon, they arrived at the Tri-County Mall, which was ringed with news vans and reporters filing their Christmas Eve reports. "Is he really here?" asked Lucy as they hummed around the parking lot searching for a spot.

"Oh, he's here," said Debbie. "Getting everyone's last-minute requests before he starts flying around the world."

"Wow…" breathed Lucy, craning her neck to see out the window. "I can't believe he's *here*." Sophie allowed herself to rise out of her funk just enough to enjoy her child's happy acceptance of the impossible. Here among plastic trees and prerecorded church bells and manufactured magic, Lucy's four-year-old heart, barely the size of a clementine, was large enough to welcome it all inside.

Once inside the teeming mall, Debbie and Kylynn peeled off toward Circuit City, while Dan and Kendall took the escalator to the Sharper Image; they'd all agreed to meet for dinner at Ruby Tuesday. In their stroller Lucy and Elliot swiveled their heads in amazement, taking in the flood of shoppers' knees streaming past, the fistfuls of shopping bags, the blinking jewelry and sparkling sweaters. A fleshy old man in a Santa hat buzzed by on his mobility scooter and winked at the kids. "Santa?" inquired Elliot, twisting around to watch the man disappear into the crowd.

"No, honey," said Sophie, struggling to keep up with the

stroller, which Brian was pushing with grim determination. "Santa doesn't ride on a scooter. He's up here, I think. In Section E, by Abercrombie and Fitch."

They found the line: a long, winding queue of red-faced, overdressed babies, wailing toddlers, and blank-faced parents. At the front Sophie could just make out a hugely fat Santa sitting on a couch with a small boy seated beside him.

"Really?" said Brian, eyeing the line.

"Where's Santa?" asked Lucy, trying to unbuckle the stroller straps.

"Stay there, honey," said Sophie. "We just have to wait in line for a while. Are you sure you want to do this?"

"Of COURSE I want to do this!"

"Well," said Sophie to Brian. "When in Cincinnati, do as the Cincinnat...ianites? do."

"Cincinnatians. Do you mind if I run over to Banana Republic while you wait?"

"Go ahead. Just don't spend too much money."

Lucy pulled on Sophie's sweater. "Mommy, is he the real Santa?"

Sophie considered the many answers to this question: he's one of Santa's helpers...nobody really knows...he's whatever you want him to be...

"Of course he's the real Santa."

"Okay, good," said Lucy. "Because this is a very, very long line, and Santa is the only person I would wait in this line for." She paused. "Is Santa a person?"

"Um, he's a magical person. A person with magical powers."

"Wow."

By the time Brian got back, Sophie was only halfway to the front of the line, and the kids were beginning to fray. Every time she pulled a new toy out of the stroller basket and handed it to Elliot, he flung it to the ground. Lucy, allowed to get out of the stroller on the condition that she stay within three feet of Sophie, was flaunting her freedom in front of her brother, who desperately wanted to get up and run. She was also trying to engage the two children behind them in conversation.

"Santa is a magical person," she said to the pair of little boys. "He has magical powers."

The boys gave her a blank stare and Sophie, as usual, found herself acting as a conversational stand-in, making eye contact with the parents and chuckling, "Thank you, Lucy, that's very interesting." The mother, who seemed to be half Sophie's age, returned the chuckle halfheartedly while her husband (boyfriend?) remained absorbed in his phone. Elliot let out a bloodcurdling shriek.

"Please," Sophie pleaded with Brian, "take Elliot. He wants to get up, but I can't chase him around."

"It's almost time to meet them for dinner," said Brian, lifting Elliot from his seat.

Sophie sighed. "Lucy, honey," she said, "we might not have time to get to Santa. It's almost time for dinner."

Lucy blinked at her. "But—Santa! You *promised*!" Her bottom lip began to grow.

"I know." Sophie looked at Brian. "We did promise."

"Look," he said, trapping Elliot's kicking legs against his chest with one arm. "Why don't I run to Ruby Tuesday and tell them we're going to be late. It'll give Elliot a change of scenery."

"Okay, great," breathed Sophie. "Thank you. I love you."

Ten minutes later, when Sophie and Lucy had almost made it to the front of the line, Brian and Elliot reappeared with Debbie, Dan, and the twins in tow. "They wanted to watch," he explained.

"This is so exciting!" said Debbie, rattling her shopping bags. "You're almost there! Dan, get the camera out."

And so Elliot had a full audience when Sophie plunked him on the sofa next to Santa, with Dan and Brian pointing their cameras at him, the twins aiming their phones, Debbie waving excitedly. Elliot took one look at the large, perspiring stranger sitting beside him, slid off the couch, and ran back to the stroller, slipping his arms into the straps and trying to buckle them himself. Dan, Debbie, and the twins rocked with laughter.

"My turn!" shouted Lucy, clambering onto the couch in Elliot's place. "Santa, I want some Polly Pockets and a Playmobil palace. And a book about fairies."

"Ho ho ho," chortled the Santa mechanically, his eyes glazed with fatigue.

"That's not funny," objected Lucy. "Why are you laughing?"

"Ho ho—ah, what's your name, little girl?" He winced a little, adjusting his position on the seat, which, Sophie noticed, seemed to offer no lower back support.

"Lucy. Don't you know that?"

"Oh, right, Lucy. Now I remember."

"Did you get my letter?"

"Of course I did."

"You know where I'm staying, right?"

"Of course I do. Now what else do you want for Christmas?"

"Tell me."

"Tell you what?"

"The address. It was in my letter."

"Lucy!" said Sophie. "Leave Santa alone. Tell him what else you want."

Santa put a finger against his nose and tried his best to twinkle.

"I just want to make sure he knows where to bring my stuff." Lucy was squinting up at Santa. "Is that beard real?"

"Okay, time to give another little girl or boy a chance to talk to me," said Santa, probably sensing what was coming next. Lucy looked out at the kids waiting wearily in line, then turned back to Santa, grabbed his beard, and pulled. Sophie was chagrined to note that it wasn't even a good stage beard; it was held on by an elastic band. When Lucy let go it snapped against Santa's face.

"You little—"

"Fake! Fake Santa! Santa's fake!" bellowed Lucy as Sophie grappled with her, trying to pull her off the couch. Lucy flailed, reached out, and grabbed Santa's hat. His flowing white hair came off with it.

"Sorry, Santa, I'm so sorry," muttered Sophie as she dragged Lucy off the couch, prying Santa's hair out of her grip and trying, awkwardly, to hand it back to him. At the head of the line the two little boys, mouths slack, watched Santa replace his hair. They turned to their mother for an explanation, but she only glared at Sophie.

"He's FAKE!" Lucy screamed at the children.

"Thank you, Lucy, I think they got it," said Sophie, depositing her into the stroller. Debbie and Dan looked stricken; the twins were laughing, showing each other the video they'd just taken on their phones.

"That was *excellent*," said Kylynn.

Sophie caught Brian's eye; he couldn't have looked happier if someone had just handed him a gift-wrapped piece of Saint-Porchaire. "Truth to power," he said, patting Lucy's head. She looked up at him, her fingers in her mouth.

"He was fake," she said, and resumed sucking on her fingers. Sophie studied her for signs of emotional distress, but Lucy seemed content. Her disappointment, after the long journey to the front of the line, had apparently been quelled by the satisfaction of arriving at the truth. Sophie shook her head, amazed, as always, by her children's ability to navigate the ever-shifting landscape of true and false, yes and no, possible and impossible, here and gone. It was something to be learned from them, she decided: the ability—not to mention the willingness—to face the beardless, hairless truth, accept its implications, and move on.

She leaned on the stroller handle, pushing it forward, and they all headed downstairs for Christmas Eve dinner at Ruby Tuesday.

The day after Christmas, Sophie lay on the sectional watching the gray sky through the high, arched window that loomed over the great room. The kids were busy with their new toys, whose molded plastic packaging was scattered around the room like cast-off cicada husks. Dan and Brian were watching football while Debbie filled lawn and leaf bags with crumpled wads of wrapping paper. Sophie cradled her Christmas stocking against her belly. The floor next to her was confettied with foil wrappers of mini chocolate bars, each one neatly creased into a small, shiny square. She opened another bar and slowly chewed the waxy chocolate, molding it against the roof of her mouth. Her fingers worked the foil, lining up the edges.

The top of the window arch, she had discovered, framed a small portion of a commercial flight path. She'd spent the morning watching planes climb through the arch, trying to imagine the people inside. It really was extraordinary that hundreds of fleshy, unruly bodies could be so neatly contained in a sleek package whose red, white, and blue logo could actually be identified from a sectional in a cul-de-sac. She imagined each package scattered across the ground, torn open like a gift handed to an impatient two-year-old.

Debbie set a small wastepaper basket next to Sophie. "Can I get you anything, sweetie?" she asked.

Sophie turned her head, struggling to focus on Debbie's pale, worried face. "No, I'm perfect."

"Do you want to go for a walk?"

Sophie blinked. People walked here?

"I don't know about you," Debbie continued, "but I could use a little fresh air."

So against her better judgment, Sophie squeezed into a pair of jeans and put on her coat and set out with Debbie. The neighborhood had sidewalks, but they walked down the middle of the street, Debbie walking fast, pumping her arms, her breath coming out in little puffs. Sophie stuffed her hands in her pockets and kept up by inserting occasional jogs into her stride.

Debbie talked for a while, telling stories about the twins' school, where she volunteered three days a week. She was in charge of obtaining donated school supplies. She described how, at the beginning of the school year, they had assembled the crayons and glue and chalk into six-foot-tall tiered wedding cakes decorated with ribbons and paper flowers.

"But why?" Sophie asked, confounded.

"Why what?"

"Why cakes?"

"Why not? It was pretty—you should've seen the teachers' faces."

"Oh."

Debbie linked her arm through Sophie's. "It feels good, you know. Making people happy. Doing something good for the world. It helps."

Sophie groaned inwardly. Debbie's very personality was a cul-de-sac. How did she avoid getting fat, living on Pepperoni Stix and platitudes? Sophie found herself suddenly longing for her cracked marble stoop and crazed porcelain doorknobs, and streets that actually went somewhere.

But now, with Debbie's arm through hers, cold air slapping her cheeks, her smugness felt empty and unsatisfying. Was her life in Philadelphia really so special? The pine floors and the lead abatement and the high utility bills—weren't they just an expensive form of vanity? And her neighborhood—in truth, it was exactly like this: a numbingly predictable housing development, with its mass-produced moldings and identical marble mantels. Hers was just older and less convenient. Why was she risking everything for that?

"Did I ever tell you about the time I let thieves into my house?" Sophie asked, knowing that she hadn't.

"What? No. When?"

"When I was a kid." Sophie pulled her arm away from Debbie's on the pretext of zipping her coat up to her chin. "I was eight. We'd just moved into a new house, and we had the usual people coming in and out—the telephone company, the water company. I was always the one who let them in 'cause my parents were gone all the time."

"They left you alone when you were eight?"

Sophie's laugh came out in a white puff. "Of course. They always said I was responsible enough to be treated like an adult, which—yeah. Anyway, I was at home one afternoon when these two guys came to the door saying they were from the electric company." In jeans and T-shirts. Knowing, somehow, how stupid she was. "They said they had to do something with the meter, but they didn't want me around. Said it was dangerous. Told me to take a walk or something, so I went out back." There was a tire swing in the backyard; it always had a murky puddle of water in it. Sophie remembered pouring the water out, then sitting in the middle of the tire and using her feet to push herself around and around until the rope began to kink. Then she let go and pulled up her knees and spun crazily, hugging her cheek against the cool black rubber, struggling to keep herself from being flung backward into the air.

"After a while I started to wonder if they were ever going to come tell me they were finished, so I went to the back door and peeked in." She remembered seeing all the way to the front door, and through it to the front yard, because it was standing wide open. "They were gone. So was half our stuff."

"Oh, no!" Debbie's mittens flew to her mouth.

"Mostly my dad's stuff. All the electronics he was supposed to write about, plus his Commodore, his Selectric, everything. Most of it still in moving boxes."

"Oh, how awful."

"Yeah." Sophie felt the crush of realization and guilt now, just as heavy as it had been that day in 1978. "I felt like the world's biggest idiot."

"But you were a child!" Debbie took Sophie's arm again. "How could you be responsible for something like that?"

"I was in charge."

"You were eight!"

"Well, anyway." Sophie took a deep, bracing breath. "I couldn't handle telling my parents what I'd done. So I took a rock and broke the window in the back door, then I locked the front door, got on my bike, and went for a long ride." Whipping through the suburban streets as fast as she could, losing herself in the unfamiliar neighborhoods, daring the universe to try to scare her now. "When I got back that night, everything was cleaned up and they'd already filed a police report."

Debbie didn't seem to know what to say to this.

"You're the only person I've ever told about that."

"Well! You were awfully…resourceful. I guess you had to be."

Sophie suddenly felt embarrassed.

Debbie asked, "Have you heard from your mother lately?"

"Not in a couple of years." There had been two postcards after Randall's funeral, from New Mexico, then nothing. Sophie had tried sending letters through family friends, then through Maeve's cousins in Texas, but nobody knew where she'd gone. Sophie remembered the way Maeve had looked at the funeral, stony and tall in her tailored black pants and gray jacket. She had squeezed Sophie's hand in a way that said, "You can do this," but not in a way that said good-bye.

"I'm sorry."

"I've tried to be different," Sophie said. "From her. But you know the saying—one day you put your arm into your sleeve and your mother's hand comes out."

"Oh, I don't think that's always true," Debbie said. "You're not about to run off and disappear. You're just not like that."

Oh, but I am, Sophie thought, horrified. I'm about to pull my own kind of disappearing act: as devastating as a plane crash, as careless as running away. Her throat began to ache. "I'm trying…." She tucked her chin and mouth down inside her parka.

"What?" Debbie asked, with a nervous laugh.

Sophie breathed deeply through her nose, forcing cold air through her clenched throat. "I think I just came up with my New Year's resolution."

"Oh! What is it?"

"To grow up."

"Oh, come on. You don't need to—"

"I just mean I'm going to stop doing some stuff that was bad for me."

"Smoking?" Debbie whispered.

"Something like that."

When they got back to the house, Sophie pulled off her coat

and tried to remember where she'd left her laptop. She wanted to start redesigning her website; she also needed to send belated holiday greetings to her old clients.

Brian came into the foyer. "I have to go back."

She smiled at him. She knew he couldn't stay away from the museum this long. "Fine with me."

"Something's missing."

"I know the feeling."

"From a period room. A Dutch tazza."

Sophie stared at him.

"A footed bowl. It's silver. Michael's freaking out. He always wanted to put it in a case."

Sophie's hands crept to her stomach. "Why do you have to go back?"

"For questioning." Brian rolled his eyes. "Michael brought in the FBI, for Christ's sake."

"Oh. Wow." She'd worn gloves, right? But what about fibers from her coat…skin cells…a hair. She'd seen the TV shows. She knew what maniacs those people were.

"Hey," Brian said, reaching out to touch her face. "Don't worry. We'll all go back together. I'll change our tickets."

"Oh, good," she said, hugging herself. "I mean, I love it here. But I have so much to do back home."

Thirteen

S he made a point of getting the phone at a store in West
Philly, on Baltimore Avenue, where she didn't know a
soul. She paid cash and threw away the receipt. The store was
sandwiched between two abandoned houses, the sidewalk lit-
tered with hair extensions, a dead tree out front garlanded with
plastic bags. Sophie, now part of the neighborhood's criminal
element, stood out front trying to get the phone to work. It was
kind of pointless, really—she'd called Harry on her other phone
just after taking the bowl. It was in the phone records. Still,
she'd decided to start acting more responsibly. Or if responsibly
wasn't the right word, less recklessly.

She didn't know Harry's number, of course, because it was
programmed into the other phone. She took it out of her bag
and looked it up, clumsily dialing the number on the prepaid
phone with her left hand. A tall man in a black leather jacket
ambled by, then stopped and cocked his head at her. She turned
and hurried to her car.

"Harry McGeorge speaking."

"It's me. Sophie."

"Sophie? That's odd. It says Daneel Brown..."

"New phone. Listen. I need to talk to you. Is it a good time?" She got into her car and locked the doors.

"For you, always! What is it, Sophie? Why so out of breath?"

"Listen, Harry. There's something we haven't talked about that, ah, we need to talk about."

"Go on."

"Okay. So. The stuff I've been bringing you. You know I didn't buy it from a sidewalk sale. You know I didn't buy it...at all."

"And I know who your husband is and where he works. Yes. And now the thing I'd like to know is, why are you calling me from Daneel Brown's phone, and how much am I going to dislike the answer?"

"How long have you known?"

"Since you brought me the mirror. I like to know who I'm dealing with."

"Huh. Okay, well..." Sophie fiddled with the gearshift, absorbing this news. "Are you back?"

"I got in last night. Now are you going to tell me what's going on?"

Sophie's mind whirled, doubt and terror chasing their tails.

"It's all right, you know," Harry said softly. "We're in this together."

She took a deep breath. "Well, until now I've been taking things out of storage—things nobody cares about. It was all being moved to a warehouse somewhere, never to be seen again. So..."

"So it was a rescue mission."

"I'm not deluded, Harry. I know there was nothing right about it. I know. But it was...safe. Safer."

"Than?"

"Than what I did before Christmas. Which was to take... somethingfromthegalleries."

"Sorry? Take what?"

"I took something from the galleries. A silver bowl. Dutch. Apparently it's, I don't know, kind of important."

"Go on."

"So the museum noticed, and now the FBI's involved, and they questioned Brian yesterday and now they're going to question me." She closed her eyes and massaged her forehead.

"I see. And why do you think they want to do that?"

"Brian said they asked him who else would have had access to the galleries while the museum was closed, and he told them about me coming on a Monday. He didn't mention that I let myself out, but this woman from Asian Art saw me…"

"Hold on, back up. I'm a bit lost here."

Sophie told him about sneaking into the galleries, the cooler, Tammy Brewer, the tazza in her basement. "I've made a mess of things, haven't I? I'm so sorry, Harry. I don't want to get you in trouble." Her breath hitched in her chest. "I don't want to get in trouble, either. I'm, oh *God*, Harry, I'm freaking out."

"All right, all right. Now listen. None of this is going to touch me, so you can stop worrying about that. My ass is covered. It's yours that's hanging out in the wind at the moment, but I think we can fix that. Now, obviously they've got nothing on camera or you'd be in jail by now. And unless you fuck up the interview they won't be searching your house."

"Okay. Okay."

"But just in case, I think you need to get rid of the piece."

"Throw it away?"

"God no, please don't do that. I'll take care of it. Can you meet me this afternoon? I'll drive down. Then we can talk some more."

"Really? I…I'll have the kids."

"I'd love to meet them. Now, bring the piece with you, but for heaven's sake try to be subtle about it."

"Of course. Thank you, Harry."

❧

She met him in the parking lot of a strip mall down on Delaware Avenue, the kids strapped into the backseat. Harry got in the front seat, twisted around, and gave them a broad smile. "Hello, Lucy. Hello, Elliot. I'm Harry. Lovely to meet you."

"I like how you talk," said Lucy.

"You're too kind. I like your dress."

"What do you say?" said Sophie automatically.

"Thank you."

"Now, your mother and I are going to talk about some grown-up things, so just try to ignore us," said Harry. Lucy raised her eyebrows, and Harry looked at Sophie. "On second thought, maybe we'll just talk outside the car. That all right?"

In the cold air, Sophie reached out and touched Harry's arm. "Thank you for coming."

"Of course. Come here, you." Harry took her in his arms and Sophie sank into his warmth, burying her face in his cashmere coat. Then she willed herself to straighten and take a step back. She couldn't afford to be seen embracing a strange man in a Delaware Avenue parking lot, even if he was carrying an extremely gay looking satchel. Plus it was making her want to cry.

"Oh, darling, you'll be all right," said Harry. "You'll see. Just keep it simple, and don't volunteer anything. All right? Lie as little as possible, isn't that what they always say? They don't have anything on you, and they won't get anything unless you give it to them. You're in control. Try to remember that."

"Right."

"Now what about the other pieces—has anyone noticed those missing?"

"No—well, Brian and his colleagues think some things *could* be missing, but they're keeping quiet about that because they don't want anyone to know how messed up the storage situation is. They could get fired."

"All right, good. So let's have a look at this thing."

Sophie opened the trunk and showed Harry the cooler, which he opened. He lifted out the footed bowl, leaning awkwardly in order to keep it concealed inside the trunk.

"Well! This is more like it. It's beautiful."

"I know." Sophie frowned.

He turned it over. "It's a tazza. Definitely seventeenth century." He straightened up. "Nicely done, Sophie. I've got some cash in my car—I'd like to give you a bit of an advance. Let me just go fetch it."

"Oh, well—" Sophie backed away from the trunk. "I didn't—I mean, you don't have to do that. I just want you to make it go away."

"Sorry?"

"Just take it."

Harry cracked his knuckles inside his leather driving gloves. "What's this—scruples? Come on, be a sport. Let me give you some cash for your trouble."

"No." She wondered how much he'd been planning to give her. It didn't matter. Even if she would have to miss another mortgage payment. Even if the tickets to Cincinnati had been ridiculously expensive, and the car was coming up on its inspection.

"Hang on, hang on," Harry said. "Just let me—" He took the cooler over to his BMW and lowered it into his trunk. Sophie shut her trunk, peeked in to the back window, and waved to the kids. When she turned around, Harry thrust a manila envelope into her hands. "Take it," he said. "I'll give you the rest next time you're in New York."

Sophie wasn't wearing gloves; the envelope felt warm. She pressed it against her belly, trying to gauge the thickness of the stacks inside. Above their heads, seagulls sailed from light post to light post.

"Call me after you talk to the FBI," Harry said, giving her a kiss on the cheek. It was a soft kiss, a moment longer than a peck. "Bye, love."

"Bye." As Harry turned and walked toward his car, Sophie called to him. He swung around just in time to see the envelope arching toward him. With the grace of instinct, he reached out one elegantly gloved hand and snatched the envelope out of the air.

"You forgot that," Sophie said, and got into her car and drove away.

※

That night, Brian made a *blanquette de veau* while Sophie sat with a glass of wine and kept him company. She tried making banal conversation, but they were both too preoccupied and eventually fell into silence. Lucy sat at Sophie's feet playing with her dolls. Snow White was driving her Polly Pocket kids around in a shoe box.

"Where's the daddy?" asked Sophie.

"In Europe," said Lucy. "Working."

"Oh."

"Come on, kids, let's drive over here now. Oh, look who it is." A plastic turtle waddled over to the car. "Hello, Cindy. Hello, Janey. I'm Mr. Turtle. So lovely to meet you." Sophie's eyes widened. Mr. Turtle had a British accent. "I like your dress." Brian turned around.

"Lucy, where'd you learn that accent?" he asked. "It's great!"

"One of the dads at school is British," said Sophie.

Lucy ignored them. Mr. Turtle continued, "Now, Cindy and Janey, your mother and I are going to talk about some grown-up things, so just try to ignore us. On second thought, maybe we'll just talk outside the car. That all right?" Snow White got out of the shoe box and hugged Mr. Turtle.

"Lucy," Sophie said, "Why don't you help me set the table. Put your dolls away."

"But Mommeeeee!"

Brian absently adjusted the apron that was tied over his work clothes. He frowned and turned back to his cooking.

Sophie was folding laundry in the living room when her doorbell rang the next afternoon. She peeked out the front window and saw a man and a woman in long coats standing on the front sidewalk. She groaned inwardly. Couldn't they have called first? She was never prepared for the unannounced drop-in. There was always some kind of unseemly mess in the living room, and she was frequently braless. She scooped the stacks of bibs and socks off the couch, dumped them in the laundry basket, and opened the door, grateful to be wearing a heavy sweatshirt.

The man introduced himself as Agent Chandler, and his companion as Agent Richardson. "We're with the FBI's art crime team," he said, showing her a badge. "Do you mind if we ask you some questions?" Sophie let them in and motioned toward the couch. Agent Chandler was lanky and middle-aged, with heavy folds between his nose and mouth, and eyelids that sliced off the upper curve of his eyes, giving him a doleful look. Agent Richardson was younger, with dark eyes, thick black hair, and assertive eyebrows. She wore an acrylic pantsuit and no makeup, and she was holding a stenography notebook. Sophie saw her notice the laundry basket.

Agent Chandler explained about the missing tazza, and Sophie nodded gravely. "Brian told me about that," she said. The agent slid on a pair of reading glasses, then pulled a calendar out of his briefcase. He handed it to Sophie and asked what day she'd last been to the museum. He asked who had escorted her inside, how long she'd been in the department, what she'd done while she was there.

"Do you often bring lunch to your husband?"

"Not too often," answered Sophie. "Technically, Brian's not supposed to have food in his office."

"But this time it was okay?"

"I thought it would be okay. I didn't think the FBI would be asking me about it." She snorted, but the two agents remained expressionless. "Brian told me not to do it again."

"Tell us what happened after you had lunch."

"Brian had to go talk to his boss, so I decided to just let myself out. I could tell he was having a crazy day, so..."

"What time did you leave?"

"I have no idea. Probably around...twelve forty-five? One o'clock? I can't really remember."

"Did you go anywhere else in the museum before exiting? To the bathroom, maybe?"

Sophie shook her head, pretending to give this question serious thought. "No...I just left." She knew Tammy Brewer would say they had crossed paths around one o'clock. She also knew that, if asked, Brian's colleagues would say she left their offices around twelve thirty. But half an hour of missing time could easily be explained away by poor memory, inattention to detail, a slow watch.

Agent Richardson consulted her notes and spoke for the first time. Her voice was low and impenetrable. "Mrs. Porter, the camera at the employee entrance shows you exiting the building at one oh three p.m. Your husband tells us you left his office around twelve thirty and that he looked for you shortly after, but you were nowhere to be found. Can you explain that?" Agent Richardson, Sophie observed, had a hairline that started halfway up her forehead. Sophie had always found this to be one of the ugliest possible traits for a woman.

"Brian has no concept of time," she said. This was true. He rarely looked at his watch, and only knew it was time to leave at the end of the day when he saw his coworkers putting on their coats. "Tammy Brewer can tell you—she saw me leaving. She'll probably tell you it was one o'clock." It seemed like a good idea to appear helpful.

"We're actually interested in what happened before you crossed paths with Mrs. Brewer," Agent Chandler said conversationally. "Why don't you tell us, in more detail this time, exactly what you did after your husband left you in his office."

Sophie sat up straighter in her chair. If they wanted a story, fine, she would tell them a story. This was much simpler than the tales she concocted for the kids on a daily basis, persuading them, for example, that the car would break down if the passengers made too much noise, or that once a year a magical bunny distributed candy-filled eggs all over the world.

"All right, well, first I cleaned up what was left of our lunch. Then I exited Brian's office into the hallway."

"What did you bring the lunch in?"

"A cooler."

"Did you take it with you?"

"Yes."

"Did you see anyone in the hallway?"

"No. Everyone was in their offices." Agent Richardson was writing something in her notebook, but Sophie couldn't see what it was. "Then I went out the door at the end of the hallway—the end opposite the freight elevator. I went out the department door, walked down the steps, walked through the Tapestry balcony, then went down the big staircase."

"Did you see anyone on the balcony?"

"No. But at the bottom of the stairs I ran into Tammy Brewer, and we chatted a minute."

"Did you see Brian coming after you? Did you hear him calling?"

"No. I was probably already on my way out at that point."

"You're sure about that?"

"I'm sure I didn't see him or hear him, if that's what you're asking."

"Go on."

"After talking to Tammy, I went directly to the mail room area, I waved to the guard at the key desk, and left through the employee entrance."

Agent Chandler pulled off his reading glasses and looked at Sophie for a moment, tapping them against his upper lip. Agent Richardson glanced at him, then said, "Thank you, Mrs. Porter. We'll be in touch if we need anything else."

Agent Chandler handed her a card that read, "Agent James Chandler, Federal Bureau of Investigation, Art Crime Unit."

"Call me if you think of anything else you want to tell us," he said, just like on TV.

Sophie assured him that she would.

Fourteen

It snowed for a whole day and a whole night—big, downy flakes that accumulated in puffy mounds on every surface. Lucy and Elliot ran from window to window, laughing at the sight: a trash can wearing a tall white hat, a car with a hi-top fade. Schools were closed, but Brian pulled a pair of rain boots over his suit and hiked through the drifts to the museum.

After breakfast Sophie dug the kids' snowsuits out of the third-floor closet and arranged them by the front door along with their gloves, hats, and boots. It was important, when the time came, to get the gear on quickly; otherwise the kids would begin to heat up, which meant that while she was trying to thread each of Lucy's fingers into a glove, Elliot would be pulling off his boots, and while she was retrieving his boots, Lucy would tear off her hat, and the whole operation would quickly devolve into an exercise in sweaty frustration.

This time, though, she managed to get them into their puffy, noisy outfits without any tears—on their part or hers. She snapped a quick picture to send to Brian, then released them into the snowy hush. The trees lining the street were bent into a glittering tunnel, each bowing branch thickly painted with white crystals. The street signs, the lampposts, the porch railings—every hard edge had turned vague and innocent.

Lucy and Elliot shrieked with delight, throwing handfuls of snow into the air, their high-pitched voices sinking quickly into the cottony surroundings. Sophie showed them how to make snowballs, and soon they were all spattered with snow and breathless with laughter.

"Let's make snow angels," Sophie said, leading them into the middle of the street. The kids followed hesitantly, gazing around themselves with wonder, and she realized that even though they were within a few feet of their house, it was a place they'd never been. "No cars!" she said, throwing out her arms. "We're safe!"

She lay on her back and showed them how to scissor their arms and legs to make angels. Elliot got stuck on his back, impeded by his Michelin Man outfit, but Lucy pulled him up and helped him draw a face on his angel. Sophie stayed on the ground, staring up at the branches laced across a bright blue sky. The cold was seeping through her nylon cocoon, but it felt clean and bright instead of damp and chilly. Suddenly, a dark shape eclipsed her view of the sky; it was a face, with glasses.

"Keith!" She sat up, brushing snow out of her hair. Keith, Amy, and Mathilda had glided up on cross-country skis, their faces glowing. Sophie stood up and marveled at Mathilda's tiny skis; the kids showed off their angels; everyone exclaimed about the beautiful day. Then the little family glided off again, looking as weightless as a flock of birds. Watching them turn down Twenty-Second Street, Sophie decided, in a fit of good humor, that she would call Carly. As long as she was putting everything else right in the world.

First, though, she wanted to spend some time working on her newest project. The idea had come to her early one morning, when she was just waking up, her mind lazily rolling around in its sheets. The museum needed new database software. The system they were using wasn't designed for museums, and it was so slow none of the curators ever bothered to make the transition from object cards. Sophie knew she could easily create something better; something more organized and efficient, that would centralize all of the information for each object and, eventually, render filing cabinets and card catalogs obsolete. She had time; she could work on it pro bono. Maybe someday she'd even be able to sell the system to other museums.

She brought Lucy and Elliot back inside, stripped off their snowsuits, sat them down to lunch, and mopped up the puddles of melted snow by the front door. Once the kids were warm, fed, and snoring under their blankets, Sophie retreated to her quiet office and began sketching out the database architecture. As she brainstormed functionalities and worked through the navigation structure, she found herself losing track of time. It seemed like years since she'd been able to unhook herself from the hands of the clock. Ever since going into labor with Lucy, when she and Brian had carefully written down the amount of time between each contraction, her life had been measured in rigorous increments of minutes and hours. Time between feedings. Duration of naps. Hours of babysitting. Now, slowly, time was regaining its elasticity, and Sophie's mind was rediscovering the habits of work.

Her email chimed; there was a message from Brian. She opened it to find no words, only a photograph of a tall, fantastically decorated ceramic piece that looked more like a wedding cake than a candlestick. At its base, four lion heads surrounded a fluted urn, above which marched a succession of columns, balustrades, cherubs, garlands, plinths, shields, sphinxes, and mermaids. The entire assemblage, rendered in creamy porcelain, was crawling with arabesque patterns and flourishes in red, blue, and pale green. It appeared to be sitting on a Formica kitchen counter.

Sophie shook her head at the sight. Magnificent and absurd at the same time, the candlestick was the Renaissance equivalent of a big-budget Hollywood movie, with every possible special effect applied to a glossy surface of starlets and plot twists. Still, its shape was, as a whole, harmonious, and in a way reminded her of the intricate sculptures she'd seen in the museum's Indian Art galleries.

"Congratulations," she said when Brian picked up his phone.

"Can you believe it? Sandrine's great-grandson's ex-wife has it in her apartment in Strasbourg."

"All those college French classes finally paid off."

"Oh, man. It's too bad no one came in to work today. I can't wait to see Ted's face."

"Does she know what she has?"

"Who knows. Her email says nobody in the family ever really liked it; it spent years packed in a crate. She said she got it in the divorce because her husband took the pressure cooker." He laughed. "So no, I guess she doesn't know. Although she's probably down at the local antique shop right now, having it appraised. So, ticktock."

Sophie knew this meant that Brian would have to fly back to France, verify the authenticity, take dozens of photographs, then return to Philadelphia to convene his committee, present his case, and campaign for purchase funds. He would overnight packages to trustees at their Wyoming ranches and Palm Beach villas, fax letters to their assistants, and gently try to provoke a competition for the right to put one's name on this momentous, collection-defining purchase. She knew he wanted to act fast, before a dealer caught a whiff of something entering the market, or the Met or the Getty heard a rumor and sent their curators scurrying to Strasbourg. The big museums had purchase funds that could be used to snap something up quickly; Brian needed to raise his own money, and that took time.

"Send me a copy of your travel itinerary," she said, before hanging up and turning back to her sketches.

❧

On the day she and Carly had agreed to meet, Sophie got to the café too early and drank a double espresso, which compounded her jitters and gave her a sour stomach. She bought a bagel to try to soak up the caffeine and the acid, even though she'd sworn off carbs. She smeared it with too much cream cheese and ate it too fast, then berated herself for her lack of self control. Did women's bodies have some kind of guilt-excreting gland that was activated by the digestive system? Could someone invent a drug to turn it on *before* the food was ingested—when it would actually be useful?

When Carly walked in, twenty minutes late, Sophie saw her eyes go to her midriff, where she'd arranged her spring jacket.

"I got fat," Sophie said, looking up into Carly's blond stratosphere. Carly's tense face released a smile, and she sank down on the couch.

"You look great," she said.

"No, I don't. Thanks. Sorry."

"I'm happy to see you," Carly said shyly. "It's been weird."

"I know." Sophie took a deep breath. "I'm sorry I freaked out on you like that."

"Forget about it." Carly waved her long hand. "Water under the bridge."

Sophie waited a moment, as Carly pulled off her jacket and set her bag on the floor. She considered prompting Carly, maybe reminding her that she'd done something that hurt Sophie's feelings, but the prospect of rehashing the whole argument was exhausting. She tried to remember what, exactly, Carly had thrown in her face that long ago day. Something about control issues. Maybe she did need to loosen up; learn to accept people the way they were. Learn to enjoy the refuge of friendship, no matter how flawed.

Carly settled back into the couch and raised her eyebrows at Sophie. "So...how's work?"

Sophie wanted a cappuccino. "I think I'm going to get a cappuccino."

"Seriously," Carly said. "I know the Whirlygig thing didn't work out. Are you working on something else?"

"Not really."

"Oh."

"Yeah." Sophie drew in her breath. "If you really want to know, I haven't worked since we first moved into the house."

"*What?*"

"Everything just dried up. And after a while I kind of stopped trying." She looked down at her hands, then gave Carly a wry smile. "See? I'm sharing."

"But what are you doing for money?"

"You know. We cut back on a lot of stuff."

Carly sat back and stared at Sophie. "I had no idea."

"Yeah, well, the whole Web 2.0 thing kind of happened without me. I had poorly timed babies."

"God, why didn't you say anything?" Carly plunged into her crocodile-size crocodile purse and pulled out her BlackBerry. She thumbed the keys. "I know of at least two projects I could bring you in on. Really straightforward. One's just a refresh for a law firm, the design's already done. The other is adding e-commerce to this beverage company's corporate site. I already told them I don't have the bandwidth; they'd be so happy if I brought you in. Here; I'm emailing you the briefs."

"Oh, that's all right. You don't have to—"

"Hey!" Carly pointed a finger at her. "Let. Me. Help."

"Jesus."

"What else is going on?"

Sophie looked over the back of the couch toward the coffee counter. There was a line. "Well…"

"What."

"Uuuuuhhhh." Sophie rubbed her face with her hands. "I can't—I haven't told anybody this."

"Spit it out."

"Okay. All right. So, there's kind of a situation with our mortgage." She did her best to keep the story compact, but digressions kept springing loose: the absurd reliance on fax machines, the phone calls to nowhere, the grammatically tortured letters. Talking about it brought her frustration back to the surface, and seeing Carly's shocked face made her want to hide her head under her jacket.

"But have you hired a lawyer?" Carly asked.

"With what money?"

"I don't know. Legal Aid? You need one."

"Why? It's all my fault. I signed up for the stupid option ARM. I failed as a freelancer. A lawyer can't change all that."

"That's not how it works. A lawyer can help you fight. They can help you get the upper hand. At the very least, they can force the bank to talk to you and work things out."

Sophie fiddled with her jacket zipper. Hiring a lawyer meant talking to Brian. Talking to Brian meant admitting that she hadn't been working. Admitting she hadn't been working meant having to explain all those trips to New York. "I think I can handle it. They're supposedly sending me loan modification forms. So…"

"What if I have my friend Joshua call you. I think he does real estate. He could give you some advice."

"That's okay."

"Sophie." Carly pointed her finger again. Sophie batted it away.

"Just get me working again. That's what I really need. Work."

"Done."

"Thanks." Sophie smiled wanly. "Still jealous of me?"

"In some ways," Carly said. "I'm sorry it's so hard to believe."

"I didn't know you wanted a family."

Carly shrugged. "Obviously I don't need two point five kids to be happy. But sometimes, yeah. The condo gets a little quiet."

"You can have my kids."

"Ha." Carly picked at her sweater. "I'm sure you don't take them for granted."

"No. I mean, I don't think I do. Sometimes it's hard to see past the day-to-day. It's not all continuous delight and amazement, you know?"

"I know." Carly smiled wanly. "Nothing ever is."

She'd almost forgotten about the prepaid phone, until it started ringing from the pocket of her winter coat, which had been put away for the season. Sophie dug through the closet of parkas, scarves, and sweaters, finally pulling the phone from the woolen depths; by the time she had it in her hand it had stopped ringing. She stared at it apprehensively, wanting to talk to her friend Harry, not wanting to think about why he was calling on this small, grimy phone. Then it rang again, making her jump.

"Hello?"

"Darling! How are you?"

"Wonderful, now that I'm hearing your voice." She hurried

back downstairs to the living room, where Elliot was stacking Tupperware containers into towers and driving toy cars through the streets of the plastic city. "How about you?"

"Can't complain. No, I take that back. I can complain; I'm quite good at it, but I choose not to."

"Oh, Harry. What's wrong?"

"You know. The usual. I hate my customers and there aren't enough of them. Also, Jeffrey's been in a beastly mood ever since I quote-unquote abandoned him over the holidays. He thinks I'm having an affair, which is utter bullshit. I mean, I've barely got the energy to deal with his tantrums, why would I want to double my workload?"

"Oh, dear."

"But that's enough of me not complaining. How are you? How are those delightful children of yours?"

"Fine. We're all fine. Sorry I didn't call you after talking to the FBI...I just wanted to put the whole thing behind me."

"I was a bit worried. But I've been keeping an eye on the *Inquirer*. There's a reward, you know."

"I heard that."

"That means they haven't got any leads. Won't be long before everyone forgets all about it."

"I hope so."

"Don't worry, love, everything will be fine." His words felt like a warm bath; when was the last time anyone had told her everything would be fine? "So the interview went all right?"

"Piece of cake. There was a little bit of missing time they couldn't account for, between my leaving Brian's office and exiting the building, but they don't have anything solid. And anyway, nobody really knows when the thing disappeared. They only noticed it missing the day before Christmas."

"All right, good. So...in the meantime."

"Yes?" Sophie tried to shield the phone as Elliot knocked over his towers with a roar.

"Have you got any more goodies for Uncle Harry?"

Sophie snorted. "You sound like a pedophile."

"Sorry. You know what I mean."

"I know what you mean, and unfortunately the answer is no." She cleared her throat. "Uncle Harry."

"Taking a little time off until the dust settles?"

"Yes, well, partly. I've actually decided to stop altogether."

"Stop? But you've barely begun. We have such a perfect little setup."

"I know, I know, and it's been very rewarding, Harry. But I can't take these kinds of risks anymore. It's crazy! I have a family."

"I would think the money has been very nice for your family."

"Of course. And I appreciate everything you've done. You've been so great. I just…I just can't anymore. I'm done."

"Sophie, why don't you just let me help you. You don't have to do everything on your own. If we work as a team we can start doing things properly. Make some real money. *Then* you can quit."

"Sorry. Sorry, Harry." Elliot had climbed into her lap; she closed her eyes and rested her cheek on his warm, silky hair. "I want to keep seeing you, though. Can we still have lunch sometimes?"

"Maybe." The charm had slid off Harry's voice. "I'll call you."

Fifteen

C arly got her the two projects—at the same time—which meant Sophie soon found herself working both of her free mornings, as well as during Elliot's naps and in the evenings. It took a few days to update all her software and review the changes in browsers and JavaScript protocols, a process that reminded her of her grandfather cleaning and oiling his gun at the beginning of hunting season. She eased herself into the methodical processes of the work, readying her mind, quieting her nervous imagination.

The law firm's site was straightforward; the wireframes and design flats were already finished and approved. Still, Sophie lavished it with the kind of care and attention she normally would have reserved for a much larger, better-paying client. She optimized it for search, without even being asked, stocking the meta tags with well-researched keywords. She finessed the linking strategy, refined the secondary navigation, and added some subtle but crucial Flash effects to the menus. She tested and retested. She optimized load times. She created a user-friendly back-end tracking system.

The e-commerce work for the beverage company was a little further outside of her comfort zone, but Carly recommended some decent new shopping cart software options and helped her with Ajax. Sophie built the pages slowly, learning as she went, adding in the customer feedback mechanisms and relationship management tools that had apparently become *de rigueur*. She trolled blogs and forums, giving herself a crash course on the latest trends in order streams and registration protocols. The hours unspooled like toilet paper in the hands of a bored toddler. She had to set an alarm on her computer to remind her to stop working and go get the kids at day care.

At night, lying in bed, she brainstormed ideas for the museum database. She created sections for cataloging each object's provenance, valuation, location, and condition notes. She added a media center for tracking photography, and a cross-referenced index of donors, artists, conservators, and curators. She filled a notebook with ideas, then started a new one.

Her newly busy schedule meant skipping a few Music for Me classes, and eventually dropping out altogether. Lucy was in preschool full-time now, so the classes were only for Elliot, and it was pretty clear he was more interested in organizing the stack of lyric sheets in neat piles than singing or dancing. Once she'd made the decision not to register for the next session, Sophie felt a sense of liberation so profound, she wondered why it had taken her so long. Where had she gotten the idea that being a good mother meant sacrificing her own sanity? Why had it never occurred to her that her own happiness might be the germ from which her children's contentment might sprout?

Brian came back from France to find her more cheerful, well rested, and interested in his successes than she had been before he left. He was brimming with his news, and they stayed up late the night he came back, in spite of his jet lag, talking and making each other laugh in a way that felt freewheeling and full of hope. The Saint-Porchaire was real. Its condition was excellent. The woman in Strasbourg was ready—eager!—to sell it to the museum. Brian had asked her to name a price, and she had shyly requested ten thousand euros.

"No," said Sophie, her eyes wide.

"Yes." Brian laughed tentatively.

"But you can't do that to her."

"Why not? She thinks she's asking a lot. I'll even get her a little more. She'll be ecstatic!"

Sophie said nothing.

"What? Imagine the uproar it would create in her ex-husband's family if she got, like, a million for it. It would tear them apart."

"That's hardly your problem. And anyway, the *real* value..."

"Value," said Brian, kissing Sophie's hand, "is a slippery concept."

Sophie shook her head, letting him kiss her arm, her neck. She felt like calling the woman to say, "Show it to everyone! Start a bidding war! You have nothing to hide...everything to gain..." Maybe a million euros would create tensions in her family, but at least she wouldn't have to deal with inconvenient piles of cash. She wouldn't have to live weighed down with secrets and fear. And for a long, long time, she wouldn't have to worry about the money running out.

As for Sophie, she wasn't going to be paid for the website work for another month, so she was back to the shell game: making the minimum payment on her credit card, delaying the last payment to the oil company, paying the day care out of her thinning pile of twenties. She'd called several times to check on the status of her loan modification application, but each time she was told it was "being processed." They also asked her, every time, to fax them another copy of her settlement papers, deed, mortgage note, tax return, and utility bill. For all she knew, the documents were sitting in the tray of a fax machine in some abandoned building in a ghostly office park, where mortgage notes blew like tumbleweeds through the empty streets.

She decided to pay a visit to some of her old clients, with muffins. She remembered, from her agency days, how art directors would swarm photography reps who brought in food. If this was what it took to lure her old colleagues out of their cubicles, she was not above it.

She picked a warm Friday morning in April, when the air was thick with the buttery smell of pear blossoms, when she knew agency creatives would be in the mood to linger in the kitchen. She stopped in to three Broad Street agencies, calling her old friends from the lobby, then handing out business cards as word spread throughout the office and people flocked to the oil-stained bakery boxes. Sophie was amazed by the number of cherubic new faces: the girls carefully draped in blazers and statement jewelry, the boys assiduously unshaven. She knew they'd be cracking open beers at their desks at five o'clock, then meeting up at McGillan's or the Standard Tap...drinking pitcher after pitcher, then wobbling home, some in pairs, others alone, for a weekend of throwing Frisbees in a ball field, changing the color of their bedroom walls, shopping. Part of her ached for those youthful, meandering days, but part of her was glad to be rid of the anxiety that accompanied such a gravity-free existence.

Walking home afterward, her mind buzzed with self-congratulatory energy. Her old friends had remembered her; had asked to see pictures of her kids; had accepted her business card without hesitation. Muffins! Why hadn't she thought of it before? Next week she'd hit the agencies around Rittenhouse Square.

She walked briskly up the hill from the Parkway, twirling her key ring around one finger as she turned down Hickory, marveling at her neighbor's cherry tree, which had exploded into thick clots of pink petals almost overnight. She pushed open her front door and dropped her bag on the floor, then inhaled with a loud, sharp noise that caught up short in the back of her throat.

"Darling!" exclaimed Harry, his greeting tinged with a razor-thin glint of irony.

"Harry? How—is Brian home?"

"No, no. It's just me. Relax." He was sunk into an armchair, his legs languidly crossed. "I love your home. It's so…working-class Victorian."

"How did you get in?"

"Back alley. Kitchen window. You really should consider an alarm system." He was holding a dingy canvas bag in his lap; the head of a claw hammer protruded from the top.

"This is a safe neighborhood. At least, it was." Sophie took off her jacket and slowly hung it up. She felt a twinge of happiness, as always, at the sight of Harry's freckled face. But she couldn't understand why he had chosen to make such an unsavory entrance.

"Look, you weren't around, and I didn't want to hang about on the front stoop."

"So you broke into my house? What the hell, Harry? You shouldn't be here in the first place!"

Harry shrugged, then folded one hand in half, using the other hand to mash the fingers against his palm. He was wearing his leather driving gloves. "Have a seat, love."

Sophie felt herself flush as she perched on the edge of the sofa opposite Harry. There were toys all over the floor, a stack of unused diapers, and a half-eaten bowl of Cheerios on the coffee table. "You could've called," she said, combing her fingers through her hair.

"I didn't want to waste any time. Listen, darling, I need your help, all right?"

"What is it?"

"It's my client. The collector who's been enjoying all of your...finds." He waved his hand in the air. "He's eager to make some more acquisitions, and he's wondering what the holdup is."

"I told you, Harry. I'm not doing it anymore."

"Right." He folded his hands over the tool bag. "Let me put this another way. My client has prevailed upon me to prevail upon you to come up with some more museum-quality merchandise. *Tout de suite.*" He pronounced this through cheerfully pursed lips.

"I'm sorry—" She was still struggling to absorb the sight of Harry—who had been walled off in a more tastefully decorated room of her life—here, among the diapers and Cheerios.

"All right, let me put this *yet another* way." Harry was turning red. "Get me some more bloody stuff, and this time make sure it's fucking *good*."

Sophie blinked at him.

"I'm sorry, but you didn't seem to be listening."

"Get out of my house," Sophie said shakily. "I don't know what's going on with you, but...but you need to leave."

"You got him all worked into a lather over that Jamnitzer. That's the problem—the fucking Jamnitzer. He thinks you've got more."

"Yam? Nitzer?"

Harry sighed noisily. "Come on, love. Really? That mirror you brought me. The Jamnitzer."

Sophie shook her head.

"Famous Nuremberg goldsmith? Sixteenth century? Worked for the Habsburgs?"

"Okay…" Sophie tried to recall the contours of the mirror. She'd known it was old, of course, but sixteenth century? Habsburgs? What was it doing sitting on a cart in Brian's office? "I guess I don't understand."

"Debt," Harry said, placing the tool bag on the floor. "Sometimes it forces us to take desperate measures." He picked up one of Elliot's fire trucks. "Let's say I'm indebted to a certain collector who is starting to throw increasingly frequent tantrums. I try to distract him with a shiny new toy." Harry turned the fire truck over in his hands. "It's called a Jamnitzer. He loves it, but he wants more. I *owe* him more." He picked up a small Matchbox car. "So you bring him a French Rococo snuffbox." He hurled the car at the wall; it bounced onto the floor, leaving a small dent in the plaster. "Not good enough!"

"Hey!" cried Sophie.

"Then you bring him some more mediocre crap." Harry hurled a plastic car at the wall; its wheels broke off with a clatter. "Not good enough!" He picked up a dump truck. "Not good enough!" His voice became a childish shriek as he flung the scissoring dump truck across the room. It crashed against the marble fireplace surround, narrowly missing a floor lamp. "I want fire trucks! I want fire trucks!"

Harry smoothed back his hair and carefully set the fire truck back on the floor. "We are dealing with someone who is accustomed to getting his way."

"I thought you liked the Dutch bowl." Sophie had backed into a corner of the sofa.

"That was definitely a step in the right direction, and I applaud your good taste. Now the question is, how can we continue to make our little boy feel loved and cared for?"

"Harry, I—"

"And just so you know—his fire trucks don't have to be silver.

Just as long as they're sixteenth century. He's open-minded! A nice Dutch painting would be perfectly fine."

"It's out of the question. The mirror was a fluke—I don't know why it was there in the first place. And all the other stuff in storage is gone. They finished moving it."

"And yet you are clearly a woman of great ingenuity and resourcefulness."

"Please."

"I would even say you have a gift. It also appears you could use a little more money." He gestured toward the unrenovated powder room. "I had a peek in your loo. You realize that toilet doesn't work?"

"I don't care. I don't want your money. I've told you, I'm done. Find someone else." Sophie had never been one of those parents who laced their reprimands with a hint of uncertainty, or ended their orders with a rising question mark. One thing Lucy and Elliot had always been able to depend upon was the clarity of Sophie's intentions.

Harry, too, seemed to be getting the message. He stared at her over tented fingers, sharp creases etched between his eyebrows. Sophie suddenly felt sad, seeing the ruins of their friendship among the broken toys. Meeting Harry, she realized now, had been the best part.

"All right." He sighed, picking up the tool bag. It made a heavy clanking noise. "I'd hoped it wouldn't come to this, but…"

Sophie shrank further into the couch. "Come to what?"

"Uncomfortable measures. I mean, bloody hell! The wife of a curator!" He grimaced and shook his hand back and forth as though he'd hit it with the hammer.

"What the hell are you talking about, Harry?"

"I'm turning you in."

"Harry, stop it. What is this *act* you're putting on?"

"Seriously. I'm going to the cops. Because you stole a beautiful Dutch masterpiece and tried to pawn it off on me, an honest dealer."

"Honest dealer, my ass! We're connected, you know. There are phone records."

"Yes. You kept trying to embroil me in your dirty little scheme."

Sophie blinked at him, struggling to comprehend the strange turn things had taken. "Anyway," she said slowly, "you have no proof. And—and! May I remind you, you're the one with the bowl."

"Am I now?"

"Okay, fine, I'm sure you've given it to your collector guy by now. But they'll find him."

"Actually, darling, when I got the feeling you were having second thoughts about our arrangement, I decided to hold on to the tazza. As leverage. And now you've got it." He drew the hammer out of the bag and spun it in his hands.

"What the hell are you talking about?"

"It's tucked away. In your house. And you made the mistake of telling me where you hid it. I guess you were showing off. Thieves are *such* braggarts."

"Here. In my house."

"That's right." Harry cocked the hammer back, then tipped it forward so that it was pointing at Sophie. "Your house."

Sophie burst out laughing. "You're insane. Harry, it's me! What are you doing? Can we talk about this like normal people, please?"

Harry let the hammer fall back into his lap. His body seemed to droop. "No, we can't talk about it like normal people. It's too late. My dad—he's so pissed."

"I thought your dad was dead."

"'Take care of it already, Harry. Quit fucking around, Harry.'

The pressure—bloody hell. I have to make things right." Harry squared his shoulders. "Anyway, unless you bring me something soon, I'm going to have no choice but to call Agent Whatsit, Chandler, and tell him exactly where you've stashed that tazza." He shoved the hammer into his bag and stood up. "I'm sorry. I hope it doesn't go that way. But if it does…" He gave a half-hearted shrug. "Don't get up, love. I'll let myself out."

She started with the powder room, since Harry had mentioned going in there. During the renovation they had peeled back the moldy carpet and chipped away the linoleum underneath, only to find that the wood subfloor was rotted through. Now Sophie got on her hands and knees and probed the spongy boards, searching for evidence that one had been lifted up and replaced. But the wood was so friable, it couldn't be moved without dissolving into splintery fragments. Sophie hesitantly felt around behind the baby blue toilet, but found no hole, no box. Just powdered rust and strange bits of waxy fluff. Next she opened the boxy, vinyl-laminated vanity and felt around among the roach traps and air fresheners. She went to the basement to get a flashlight, then came back and shone it under the sink, searching for a cutout or some other sign of tampering. Finally she lifted the toilet tank lid; empty.

Standing in the small, fetid bathroom, running her dusty hands over the brittle wallpaper, Sophie silently cursed Harry. Who would ever have thought him capable of breaking into her house and threatening her like this? Sweet, excitable, boyish Harry with his relationship issues and alcoholic mother and his irresistible, hapless charm. It was ridiculous, the very thought of him climbing in her kitchen window in his Savile Row suit.

Acting like some kind of lowlife thug. And what was all this nonsense about his client? Harry had money; he should be able to pay off a debt. It didn't make any sense.

She also suspected that the whole hidden-bowl story was a bluff. But what if Agent Chandler did show up at her door one day, warrant in hand, and walked straight to its hiding place? She tried to shoo the images from her mind: Lucy and Elliot watching their mother being led away in handcuffs; Brian packing up his office under the watchful eye of a security guard; lurid headlines; embarrassed friends, years later, avoiding her at the supermarket. And the house. She'd lose the house and the house would lose her. Someone else would move in and rip out the moldings, mantels, and fixtures, replacing everything with MDF and PVC, sheetrocking over her restorations and her dreams.

Sophie washed her hands and locked the bathroom door. She would just have to search everywhere. If it was here, she would find it. No one knew this house as well as she did.

She decided to proceed methodically, starting in the basement. She searched through bins of leftover tile, paint-encrusted window hardware, forgotten stuffed animals. She waded through piles of empty cardboard boxes, feeling for telltale heft, shaking out their Styrofoam peanuts and pawing through wads of newspaper. She opened the panniers on Brian's touring bike, and pulled boxes of tools, pedals, and bike seats from the shelves of his worktable so she could feel around behind them. She shone a flashlight under the oil tank, then hauled a stepladder across the width of the basement, peeking into each bay of the ceiling, which had moldy plywood nailed across the thick, strapping joists. At the back of the house she poked her head into a dank crawl space, shining the flashlight into its cobweb-draped depths. She ran her hand along the top of an old metal cabinet that hung on the wall, steeling herself against the invisible grit and furry remains.

She found mouse droppings, old cockroach traps, several coins, and, stashed above the plywood between two joists, a bundle of fishing rods. Behind the washing machine she found one of her favorite bras, which probably wouldn't fit anymore. She found screens for the third floor windows, and a box of beautiful antique buttons. But no tazza.

The next morning she tackled the kitchen. She hauled a ladder out of the basement so she could see on top of the seventies-era cabinets, which stopped a foot short of the ceiling. She nudged the refrigerator away from the wall, rifled through the cleaning products under the sink, and scooped armloads of Tupperware out of its cabinet. She looked in the freezer. She checked the oven.

But they were all too obvious, these hiding places. Harry had tools; surely he'd stashed the bowl where no one would stumble across it. Climbing back up the ladder, Sophie tapped the drop ceiling here and there, searching for cracks or holes. It was solid. She climbed down and inspected the edges of the linoleum floor. Glued tight.

That night, lying in bed, she combed through the house in her mind, making mental notes of radiator covers to lift, loose floorboards to check. When she finally slept, well after midnight, her brain jumped and skittered, continuing the search in her dreams, going up and down the ladder, back into the crawl space, back through bathroom's sticky corners, over the cabinet tops, again into the crawl space, up the ladder again, down the ladder again.

The next day Brian came home and found Lucy and Elliot alone on the first floor playing "circus," which involved Elliot walking the tightrope, otherwise known as the back of the sofa, while Lucy cracked a pretend whip. Sophie was on the third floor rummaging through suitcases. She'd only meant to run upstairs for a minute, just to check behind some boxes of photographs on a high shelf in the closet. But catching sight of the suitcases, she'd decided to go through them quickly, so she could cross the whole closet off her list. "What are you doing?" Brian asked breathlessly as he carried Elliot up the stairs. "This guy almost took a header off the couch into the coffee table."

"Sorry! Sorry," said Sophie, shoving a garment bag back into the back of the closet. "I was...looking for something."

"What?"

Sophie pushed the closet door closed. "What what?"

"What are you looking for?"

"A pair of shoes. I haven't seen them since, um, Christmas."

"Do you want me to ask Debbie?"

"No! Don't worry about it, all right? Just, forget it."

"Okay..."

Sophie pushed past him, ducking Elliot's outstretched hands. "I've got work to do," she muttered, and went to shut herself in her office.

Their marriage, she had long ago come to realize, was like the rim of a bowl, and the two of them traveled around it, sometimes coming together, sometimes apart, always on the same plane but not always close. These days they were both preoccupied, quiet, tired. Sophie knew they would come together again eventually; she just hoped it wouldn't be at the bottom of the bowl.

When Harry called, she was ready.

"I found it," she said.

"Well, aren't you the clever one."

"You underestimated me. I am the resident champion of hide-and-seek."

"Congratulations. Where was it, if I might ask?"

"You know where it was. You might be more interested in knowing where it is."

"Don't tell me you've hidden it in my flat. This *is* fun."

"There's a little spot on the Falls Bridge where the kids love to look at the river. We always bring something to throw into the water so we can watch it sink."

"Where I come from they call that littering."

"I think it's time for us to go our separate ways, Harry."

"Not quite yet, love. You see, I am still under a great amount of pressure to come up with another decorative item."

"I'm afraid that's your problem, Harry. Just pay him already. I don't see why you need me."

"He doesn't want money, for Christ's sake. He's got plenty of that. He wants the goods. Objects. Masterpieces. Things you can't buy in a store."

"Tell him no, Harry. Use a firm voice. It gets easier with practice."

"I don't understand why you won't help me," he wheedled. "I thought we were friends. C'mon, love."

"Friends!" she exclaimed. "What about Brian? What about my family? Would a friend ask me to do this to my family? Anyway, you've got nothing on me. I'm done with this."

"Really. Then tell me where you found the tazza, and I'll be on my way."

"I'll tell the cops everything. You'll be in just as much trouble."

Harry sighed heavily. "Make this a little easier on both of us, love. Pay another visit to hubby, slip into the galleries, nick me a little painting. Something petite. Dutch, if possible. Just do it, get it over with, and then I'll come retrieve my tazza—which, I assure you, is very cleverly hidden in your home. All right? I promise. Pinky swear."

"Harry."

"Yes?"

"Fuck you."

It was a bluff. It had to be. Harry was too confident that she hadn't found it; he should have sounded more worried.

Sophie considered the veiled gaze of a suit of armor looming above her on a roped-off platform. Maybe Harry wasn't as transparent as she'd always thought. She wished she could replay their phone conversation, to search for notes of bravado, or an edge of anxiety in his voice.

The armor had apparently been made for an overweight prince; the bulging torso's delicately engraved decoration reminded her of the visit she and Harry had made to the Met together. Those were the days, she thought ruefully; when she and Harry had been on the same side; before he started playing his ridiculous game.

And who was this mysterious collector who had such a grip on him? Who could possibly have such a thirst for stolen artwork, which could never be shown off, left in a will, lent to a museum? From what she knew about collectors, only a portion of their pleasure came from the work itself. Most of them thought like decorators, imagining the long captions that would border photographs of their homes in *Elle Décor*. Others were investors, obsessed with auction results, watching values rise and fall with the avidity of hedge-fund managers. Then there were those who were simply in love with the art of collecting, determined to assemble a group of works that would become, in itself, a work of art, carefully edited to tell a cohesive story about a time, a place, a person. What all of them had in common, of course, was the desire for others to know what they had.

At this particular museum party, the collectors were an unlikely mix of NRA members and Renaissance scholars. Brian had insisted on coming to the event, which marked the opening of a show on Brunswick armors. He was looking for donors to fund the purchase of the Saint-Porchaire. It felt strange, standing there in her party dress, champagne in hand, stiff smile on her face. What she really needed to be doing was looking inside all the radiator covers, and then, maybe, in the chimneys. But she'd promised Brian she would come, and anyway, she did need to get away from the house. It was making her feel a little crazy.

The party was in a large, cathedral-like gallery whose enormous windows offered a view of the Schuylkill River as it tumbled into the city from the green depths of Fairmount Park. The room was populated by imposing figures dressed in flamboyant armor complete with rippling puffed sleeves, flared skirts, majestic capes, and decorative roping, all wrought in gilded steel. The inscrutable figures' heads were fully enveloped in metal, giving them a menacing air; yet their outfits were decorated with twining leaves, lilies, loping animals, and graceful birds. The terrifying steel and florid decoration combined to form an eloquent expression of power.

Just beyond the portly armor, Sophie could see a tall blond woman in a gray silk dress and silver fur stole. She was talking to Ted, who was nodding vigorously between slurps of champagne. "That's Maura Pfeiffer," Brian said in her ear. "She's interested in the Saint-Porchaire."

"Who is she?" asked Sophie.

"Ex-wife of some sports…person. She lives in a palace on the Main Line. Her entire first floor comes from a castle in Italy. She literally skinned the thing and put it in her house—walls, ceilings, floors. It's incredible."

Ted beckoned them over, and introductions were made. Maura greeted them with practiced warmth, then brightened when she realized who Brian was.

"Is it true?" she asked him, her eyes wide, her high forehead immobile. "You found a Saint-Porchaire? A real one?" Her voice sounded the way Sophie imagined her stole felt.

"All true. I'll be presenting the photographs at the committee meeting on Tuesday. I hope you'll be there."

"Well, of course. I wouldn't miss it. It's extraordinary. Do you know Rob Moffett has one in that monstrosity of a house?"

"I know," answered Brian with a pained smile. "He's bequeathed it to the Met."

"Bastard. He's a mean bastard, you know," she said to Sophie, nudging her with the back of her hand. "Stingy. No loyalty. Listen, Brian, I want to buy that piece for you. I've heard it's better than Rob's, and I want to show him a thing or two."

"Well!" exclaimed Ted, sloshing his champagne.

"How much does that woman want? Never mind. We'll talk about that later. Now listen. I want my name all over this. I want Rob to know exactly who got this for you. All right?"

"Of course," said Brian. "We'll do a press release, a party…"

"Good. But it's got to have my name everywhere. Prominently." She nudged Sophie again. "A girl's got to do what a girl's got to do."

Later, Ted explained that there had been some unpleasantness recently between Rob Moffett and Maura Pfeiffer, and she'd been throwing her money around in pointed ways. "But we're not here to question anyone's motives, ha-ha," he said, patting Brian's arm. "Let's just make a big deal over her on Tuesday, make a big announcement at the end of your presentation. Larry Weber will probably be fit to be tied, but too bad. I'll find something else for him to buy."

Competitive philanthropy was a sport practiced vigorously by this crowd. Looking around her, though, Sophie couldn't find anyone besides museum staff who was under the age of sixty—despite many laudable efforts to look that way. The Young Friends of the Museum were legendary for their parties, but she wondered if they'd been bred for a lifetime of collecting and giving, and flaunting, the way these last members of the old Philadelphia guard had been.

Brian had been pulled away by the director of development, so Sophie wandered into the next gallery on her own. Here, dozens of pistols and rifles were suspended between glass, creating the illusion that partygoers were walking through a cloud of floating firearms. Contemplating their ornately inlaid stocks and engraved barrels, Sophie wondered, why bother? They were instruments of death, no matter how you decorated them. She remembered the gun she'd glimpsed on Agent Chandler's hip: black, ugly, plastic. It certainly wasn't meant as decoration.

Sophie shuddered and pushed her way out of the gallery into the tapestry hall. She wandered toward the European Art wing, placing her champagne glass on the tray by the entrance. There was only one other glass on the tray.

She walked through the maze of period rooms, moving more slowly than she had on her last visit, smiling blandly at the bored-looking guards. Passing through a Parisian hotel, an English country manor, a Fifth Avenue townhouse, Sophie felt dwarfed by the soaring painted ceilings and looming chandeliers. On this visit, her gaze no longer focused on cooler-size objects, Sophie was struck by the melancholy vastness of the rooms. Each click of her heels fluttered quickly into nothingness. In these houses, she imagined, inhabitants must have floated like dust motes, passing only momentarily into existence as they bobbed through a ray of window light.

But where was the Little Ship? She suddenly longed for its close, humble warmth. In her memory it had become impossibly dark, as if lit only by one or two candles, the furniture melting into deep pools of shadow, the red curtain on the bed alcove almost imperceptible against the carved folds of the dark wood paneling. Surely it wasn't so dark in real life? She turned right, then right again. Where was it? Maybe she would find it intact, the tazza still standing proudly on the cabinet. Maybe she had imagined the whole thing.

Finally, passing through a small room of Dutch paintings, she spotted the entrance to the alcove. She walked quickly toward it, then slowed. Someone was standing inside the doorway, leaning his elbows on the Plexiglas barrier. At the sound of her footsteps, he turned.

"Come to visit the scene of the crime?" Michael said.

Sophie moved her clutch in front of her belly.

"The stolen tazza used to sit right there," Michael said, pointing toward the sideboard. "You probably don't even remember it, such a small detail."

"No," Sophie murmured. She joined Michael at the barrier, looking into the little room, which was dimly lit but not as shadow-drenched as she remembered it. Fresh details jumped out at her: a pair of gleaming brass wall sconces; a trio of ceramic canisters. Inside the birdcage hung a colorfully painted earthenware parrot perched on a ring.

"I'm mulling over our new arrangement," Michael said. "We moved a vase onto the sideboard, to fill the space, but I wonder. It's out of whack with the rest of the ceramics." He pointed toward a high shelf lined with plates, which was at the same height as the fireplace mantel, also topped with plates and vases. Together, they created a pleasing stripe of blue across the top third of the room.

"Why not one of the other metal objects?" asked Sophie, indicating the bowls and cups sitting on the table.

"Those are for everyday use. The display area on the sideboard would have been for family treasures—like the tazza."

"Oh." Sophie looked down at the room label. "So why do they call this the Little Ship, anyway?"

"The room comes from a house in the Netherlands that was built by a sea captain. He became a brewer after he retired." He sighed, taking off his flimsy glasses and polishing them on his shirt. "I had a theory about that tazza, you know."

"What's that?"

"It wasn't signed, but I was pretty sure it was by Jansz van Vianen."

Sophie frowned. It sounded like she was supposed to recognize the name.

"He was the cousin of two famous goldsmiths. He never made it big, but he was just as good. I mean, you should have seen that tazza. It was embossed with a scene of Venus and Mars hanging out with Cupid. Venus is holding a cup with the same scene on it. It was clever."

Sophie felt a warm flood of shame; she hadn't paid much attention to the decoration of the bowl, much less to the one in Venus's hand.

"I was going to publish it, but I never found the time. Nobody realized what we had. I wanted to put it in a case where you could see the metalwork up close." He exhaled sharply through his nose. "And where some asshole couldn't grab it."

"I'm sorry," said Sophie, watching the color rise in Michael's pallid cheeks.

"You know, his career was cut short."

"Who?"

"Jansz van Vianen. He inherited his father's brewery, and I guess he was expected to take it over. So he dropped silversmithing."

"To make beer? Like the sea captain?"

"Yeah!" Michael laughed bitterly. "Poor guy. He was a real artist. And only four of his pieces survive. Well—" He coughed out another laugh. "Three."

"So it's—it was—really valuable?"

"You mean, as something to be bought and sold? It would be worth more if I had published it, drawn a clear line to van Vianen. But I don't care about that." He looked around the room as if searching for something. "Every time I came here, I would look at that tazza and think about this artist, a man with an eye for beauty, with talent. No one else was doing what the van Vianens were just starting to do with gold and silver. And I imagined him fighting with his father, wanting to be as good as his cousins, and his father saying, 'My father is a brewer. Your father is a brewer. You're a brewer too, so you can just forget about making these crazy bowls of yours.'"

Sophie absorbed this quietly. Just like the last time she'd stood staring into the little Dutch room, she became aware of something loose flapping in a far corner of her mind. Something like a corner of canvas lashing the sea air, urging her to turn and look. But it was too frightening, too erratic; she knew it had the power to knock her into the surging depths below.

Michael continued. "He would have lived in a house just like this. He lived in Haarlem at exactly the same time."

"I'd better get back," Sophie said, pushing herself away from the barrier. "I'm sorry about the tazza. It's…a shame."

Michael didn't turn, didn't answer.

That night, Sophie lay in bed with a busy mind. The house was hushed; Lucy and Elliot were finally sleeping through the night.

Rather than greedily lapping up every minute of sleep she could get, however, Sophie could only fluff and refluff her pillow, growing more and more angry at herself, angry at Harry, angry at Brian sleeping tidily next to her, his breathing deep but quiet, hands resting on his chest.

Quiet, she urged her mind. Be quiet. Think about your database design. She tried to lose herself in the twists and turns of the code, breathing deeply in synch with Brian, urging her mind to let go. But there was a pounding in her ears—was it her heart? Why was it beating so loudly?

She turned onto her stomach and put her pillow over her head, but the heartbeat only resonated more loudly. She started thinking about Michael, his shiny head, his flushing cheeks, his sorrowful tale about the would-be silversmith. At least van Vianen knew what he wanted to do with his life, thought Sophie bitterly. For this, of course, he deserved his small memorial in the loving care of a museum, where his artistic ambition would be admired and studied by at least one curator—and perhaps, in time, appreciated by two or three members of the public.

And what did Sophie deserve?

Pound. Pound. Pound. For the first time, she began to feel the tazza's presence in her house. Maybe it was here, after all. It seemed to be vibrating somewhere—under the floorboards? In the chimney? Behind a stair riser? Perhaps all she needed to do was listen more carefully. Maybe, if she were quiet enough, the house would tell her its secret.

At some point, well into the morning hours, Sophie skated over a thin spot in the crust of her consciousness and, with a muffled crack, plunged into oblivion.

Sixteen

The next day Brian went back to France, to pick up his Saint-Porchaire. Sophie was aware that recently, her most tender thoughts toward her husband had only bubbled up when he was away. When he was home, her feelings resembled something more like agitated resentment. She recognized how unfair this was. Obviously it wasn't his fault that the sight of him inspired spasms of guilt. Obviously, he deserved better.

It didn't help that money was tighter than ever. She still hadn't received her final payment for one of the websites, because the client was dithering about last-minute changes. The muffin deliveries had yielded a few inquiries about her availability, but no green lights as of yet. Unopened mail had started piling up in the tray on her desk, including envelopes from MortgageOne. She had their attention now, but she felt perfectly justified in treating their correspondence with the same level of urgency they had granted hers.

With Brian gone, she was able to launch phase two of her hunt for the Dutch bowl. This was the real search, under the surface of things, inside the cavities of the house. She started with the fireplaces, three in all, which were actually just vents for the original coal heating system. The marble mantels were inset with iron grates, cast with a design of curling vines and flowers, which led to closed-up chimneys. Sophie heaved the grates out of the marble surrounds, lay on her back, and scooted her head into the openings, shining her flashlight upward into the crumbling brick tunnel, then, turning onto her belly, peering downward into the basement.

She had her head in the third fireplace when the doorbell rang. Startled, she knocked the back of her head on the chimney, causing brick dust to rain into her hair. She shoved the grate back into the opening and looked out the front window. The two FBI agents were standing on the sidewalk. The man, Agent Chandler, saw her before she had a chance to duck behind a curtain. He waved.

Sophie jumped back from the window. Had Harry called them already? Did she have to answer the door? Would they break it down? Could she get out through the back alley?

"Have a minute?" asked Agent Chandler when she peeked her head out the front door.

"I'm just, okay, a minute, sure." Sophie's tongue struggled to navigate the sandy desert of her mouth.

Inside, the agents sat down in the same spots as before, and Agent Richardson took out the same stenography notebook. She was wearing another acrylic pantsuit, but this time it was a sort of sea-foam green that accentuated the yellowish cast of her skin. Sophie noticed Agent Richardson looking at her hair; she ran a shaking hand across it, and brick dust sprinkled onto her lap. She wiped it away, but some of the grit stuck to her sweaty palm.

"We just wanted to follow up on a few of the things we talked about during our last interview," said Agent Chandler.

No search warrant? "All right."

"Agent Richardson was just going through some of her notes, and a few things weren't adding up, so we thought we'd run them by you." He smiled in a reasonable, friendly way, then nodded to Agent Richardson, who was paging through her notebook.

"During our last interview," said Agent Richardson in her low, manly voice, "you said that on the day you brought Brian lunch, you ran into Tammy Brewer on your way out of the museum."

Usually it was Agent Chandler asking the questions. Was this Bad Cop? "Yes."

"We spoke with Tammy Brewer, and she said she went straight up to Brian's office after speaking with you."

"Okay."

"But Brian said…let's see." Richardson flipped a few more pages. "He said that he came looking for you shortly after you left his office. Right?"

"I don't know. I didn't see him." Sophie became very still.

"It seems that while you and Tammy were chatting on the stairs, you should have seen Brian. But in fact, Brian told us that Tammy came to his office about twenty to thirty minutes *after* he had gone looking for you."

"Hmmm."

"So what we're wondering is, where were you between the time that Brian last saw you, and the time that you spoke with Tammy Brewer—a period of twenty to thirty minutes?"

"Look," Sophie said, holding out her gritty hands. "I don't know anything about what Tammy did, and I don't know anything about what Brian did. All I know is that I left Brian's office, chatted with Tammy on the stairs, and went on my way." She stabbed a finger in the direction of Richardson's notebook. "Like I said before, Brian has no concept of time. He never looks at his watch, he usually forgets to ·eat lunch, he is chronically late. And as for Tammy, well, maybe she ducked outside for a cigarette before going upstairs. I doubt she would mention that. She thinks nobody knows about it." She sat back in her chair and crossed her arms.

Agent Richardson flipped to another page. "You told us you brought Brian's lunch in a cooler."

"Yeah."

"May we see it?"

"The cooler?" Sophie's mouth went dry again. Fibers. Molecules. DNA. But wait—hadn't Harry taken the cooler along with the tazza? "I don't have it anymore!"

"Where is it?"

"I...we left it somewhere. After a picnic. At the Horticulture Center. I called and they said nobody turned it in. I guess someone stole it." She shrugged and pressed out a smile.

"Mrs. Porter," said Agent Chandler, moving to the edge of the sofa. "Do you mind if we take a look around your house?"

"For the cooler?"

Chandler lifted one shoulder.

"Isn't that the kind of thing you need a warrant for?"

"Are you saying no?"

She looked into his droopy eyes. They had a look of chronic disappointment that almost made her feel sorry for him. "I've already looked everywhere, but if you want to take a crack at it, hey." She felt a bubble of inappropriate laughter pressing against the back of her throat. It burst out before she could swallow it.

"What's so funny?" Chandler asked.

"Nothing," Sophie said. "I just...hope you find it."

When Agents Richardson and Chandler had left, Sophie turned her attention toward the stairs. They hadn't thought to look there; in fact, they hadn't looked any place she hadn't already inspected quite thoroughly. They'd spent a good deal of their time with their heads inside the fireplaces. She explained that she'd been looking for a mouse, and that was why there was brick dust everywhere, but they were not dissuaded.

The stairs had never been painted; when they bought the house, they had simply pulled off the shag carpet runner, then sanded and stained the wood. At the top of each riser, a strip of molding was nailed under the lip of the tread above. Some of these had worked themselves loose over the years; she easily popped the first one off with a screwdriver. A small gap at the top of the riser allowed her to slide the screwdriver into the space under the tread and gently work the plank loose from the next tread down, where it was nailed from behind. She could see it would have been easy for Harry to pry out a riser, stash the bowl inside the stair, then nail the riser back in place through the molding. Since the stairs were unpainted, there were no telltale cracks or chips.

She shone the flashlight into the hole, looking under the neighboring steps, feeling a rush of anticipation. This felt promising. The house was finally whispering to her, telling her where to look. Two steps up she repeated the process; this time, she had to tap the riser with a hammer before she was able to pry it away from the tread below. Then she worked it out of the small space and peered inside.

By the time she had finished removing every third riser from the first set of stairs, it was time to go get the kids from day care. When they returned, Lucy and Elliot walked into the living room ahead of Sophie, stopped short in front of the staircase and stared, their eyes wide.

"Holes!" said Elliot.

"Mommy, the stairs lost some teeth!" said Lucy.

"Don't touch anything," Sophie warned them, gathering up tools, stair risers, and molding strips, trying to keep them in order. "Mommy's fixing the stairs. Come sit down and have a snack." She installed the kids at the table with some orange slices, then hurried to nail the risers back in place before the kids decided to start dropping their toys into the holes. She took the first plank (or was it the last one? She'd lost track) and maneuvered it into the space below the first tread. Once it was under the tread, though, she realized she had no way to hold it in place because there was no way to nail it from behind. She couldn't access the back of the riser without removing the tread above, which was impaled by the balusters, which were embedded in the underside of the banister. It would be impossible to replace the risers without dismantling the entire system.

"Shit," Sophie muttered, sitting back on her heels. The house had played a hell of a trick on her.

She went to the basement stairs to look at the underside of the first-floor staircase, but it was entirely plastered over. She could rip out the plaster, but she had no money to pay someone to fix the mess, and besides, Brian was coming back in three days. No carpenter had ever accomplished anything in three days.

She gave the kids bowls of crackers (they'd never eat dinner now), then took a strip of molding and a riser to the basement and located an old bottle of wood glue. After gouging dried glue from the tip, she ran a bead along the top of the riser, pressed the strip of molding onto it, and set it down with a few Styrofoam peanuts arranged under the molding to hold it at the proper angle while it dried.

That night, after the kids fell asleep, she brought the riser up from the basement and, using the molding as a sort of handle, tucked it into the space behind the tread below, holding it tight against the underside of the tread above, where she tried to attach the molding with finish nails. The problem, of course, was that it was nearly impossible to hold the riser with the fingertips of one hand while holding a tiny nail in place and hammering, upside down, with the other hand. She kept dropping the nail, then the riser, cursing more and more loudly, until she finally had to put everything down and walk away for a bit. After pacing the dining room several times, stretching her arms, cracking her neck, and taking some deep breaths, she came back and tried again. This time, she managed to get the nail tapped far enough into the molding that she could let it go and focus her left hand on the job of holding the riser in place. A few more taps and the nail was finally in. The second and third nails were easier.

She sat back and admired her work. As long as she didn't touch the riser, it looked normal. The slightest nudge, however, sent it creaking inward; she knew a good kick would dislodge it completely. But that, she decided, would be easier to explain than an entire staircase full of holes.

She gathered the remaining risers and molding strips and spent the rest of the evening gluing them together. It was hard to be patient and careful when she was nearly shaking with frustration. It would take all day to nail the risers back in place, but she didn't have all day because the kids would be home. Harry would be calling soon, probably with more threats. For all she knew, he would show up at her house again. She hoped he knew the kids' day-care schedule; she couldn't afford to have Lucy doing more Harry impressions in front of Brian.

The next day she took the kids to the pool, hoping to prompt a long nap. Carly called while she was pushing the stroller up the hill.

"Congratulations to Brian!" she said.

"What do you mean?"

"The paper! Haven't you seen it?"

"I haven't read a newspaper since Lucy was born."

"There was a story in there this morning, about some fancy candlestick they just bought."

Sophie stopped and leaned on the stroller handle. The press release wasn't supposed to go out for another couple of weeks; they were waiting for the Saint-Porchaire to be cleaned and put on display. It hadn't even made it into the country yet.

"There's a quote in here from the director, thanking Maura Pfeiffer for funding the 'collection-defining purchase.'"

"Of course. Maura. What a spotlight-stealing hag."

"I don't know. There's a picture of her looking very unhaglike."

"Is there a picture of the piece?"

"No. But it says only about eighty of these things still exist, and most of them are already in museums. Wow."

"I better call Brian. Thanks, Carly."

Brian already knew about the story, and he confirmed that Maura was the source of the leak. "I just can't believe they didn't try to get in touch with me for a quote. They have my number. I mean, hello? I found the damn thing?"

"Maybe they're going to do a follow-up story after the unveiling."

"They better! It was all fluff! There were more words dedicated to Maura Pfeiffer than to the candlestick."

Sophie tried to distract him with stories about the kids, but he didn't seem to be listening. It was his big moment at the museum, and she knew he felt cheated. It should have been his picture in the paper, his words. She ached for him, feeling his hurt through the crackling overseas connection, wishing, for a change, that she could be the one to reach out and touch his cheek in just the right, consoling way.

"I know how hard you worked," she said. "I know what you did to find that candlestick, and I'm just so—so proud of you, Brian. God, that sounds like something your mother would have said. It's true, though."

There was a short silence. "Thanks," Brian said. "I actually didn't know that."

"That I'm proud of you?"

"Yeah."

"Well—" Sophie frowned at the phone. "Of *course* I'm proud of you. What do you mean?"

"I don't know. Lately you've been so…absent. Like it doesn't matter if I'm there or not."

"What?" Sophie shook her head. "How can you not know how much it matters?" Panic began creeping over the edges of her mind; sweat slid down the back of her neck. She was too tired and frazzled for this. "You're going to have to trust me," she said, a bit too abruptly. "I love you." This came out like a bark. "I love you," she tried again, more softly. "I need you here, I need help, I need to tell you things."

Silence.

"Hello?"

But the call had been dropped. She had no idea when.

⚜

While the kids napped, she managed to fasten a few more risers in place, although a couple of the nails got bent in the process and some of the planks went in at a slant, leaving long triangular gaps where they were supposed to meet the treads below. Sophie had never been particularly good at crafty projects; her hands were clumsy, her patience limited. She just had to hope that Brian wouldn't notice the change in the stairs, and that no one would ever kick the risers.

She finished the job that night while the kids were in bed, then rewarded herself with a large helping of red wine. She tried watching TV, but couldn't sit still. She had no desire to go to bed and battle insomnia. Moving through the dark house, glass in hand, she scanned each room, trying to think like Harry, although she was feeling a little fuzzy on who he really was these days. The reddish pine floorboards in her office creaked under her feet; some were as wide as the bowl, some were wider. They were held in place by handmade square nails. Sophie loved those nails. They'd found dozens of them while renovating the house; each one was different. She tried to imagine a time when something as ubiquitous as nails was made carefully, individually, by a craftsman—a nailmaker? Nailsmith?

She took another swig of wine. Those were the days, when every little detail mattered, when people really cared about what they did. Being authentic wasn't hard—it wasn't even a *thing*. You did your job and you did it well and you never questioned the work-life balance, the mommy track, the meaning of your life; you just got on with it. The house knew these things. Sophie squatted down and ran her hands over the pocked, rippled wood. "You know," she muttered.

The floor refinishers had filled the cracks between the boards, but the filler had shrunk over time; it tended to pop out in chunks when she vacuumed. She ran a finger between two of the largest, creakiest planks. Over the years, as the boards had moved apart, some of their tongues had withdrawn from their grooves. She finished her wine and headed downstairs to get a second bottle and a crowbar.

❧

Strolling the kids to day care the next morning seemed to take forever. By eight thirty it was already hot; the sun clanged about her head like a pair of cymbals. The kids were peevish, fighting with each other in their seats, but Sophie knew if she tried to intervene she would lose her composure. She pushed the sunshade down over their heads, pretending not to hear their complaints, and deposited them at the day-care door with quick, absent kisses.

Back at the house, she slowly mounted the stairs to her office and stood surveying the previous night's work. Her desk and chair were pushed against one wall; an empty wine bottle and dirty glass sat on the filing cabinet. The floor was striped with holes where she had pried up the birch beer–colored planks, and under the windows lay a messy pile of boards, many split lengthwise, some just cracked, all with antique nails hanging from their undersides like fangs.

The floorboards ran perpendicular to the beams, so each hole revealed a series of thick joists. After pulling up the first plank, Sophie had tried to shine a flashlight down the length of each bay, but the hole was too narrow; she needed to be able to lower her head down into it. She'd pulled up two more adjacent boards, which helped. Still, she couldn't see the entire bay. Moving a few feet across the room, she'd repeated the process, pulling up more boards, surprised by how easily they cracked and split, and peered into the darkness.

Now, seeing the aftermath in daylight, Sophie felt like crying. She could probably fit the broken boards back together with the help of some wood glue and more nails, but she knew the cracks would turn into splits, which would splinter and fray, and that the entire floor would have to be refilled, sanded, and polyurethaned—if it could be salvaged at all. For now, though, she had to hurry to make everything look as normal as possible before Brian got home the next day. It was going to take hours. She hadn't slept all night, and her head was pounding. She allowed herself a quick, deep sob into her hands, then swallowed her tears, vigorously rubbed her cheeks, and went downstairs to find a hammer and a box of nails.

The prepaid phone rang while she was trying to coax the last of the wood glue onto a sharp dagger of wood that had flaked off the edge of a board. Sophie groaned. "Dammit, Harry," she muttered, as she capped the glue bottle and felt for the phone on the inside of the tissue box where she'd hidden it.

"What."

"Darling! You sound terrible. Rough night?"

"What is it, Harry?"

"I've been reading the paper." He sounded proud of himself.

Sophie pressed the wood fragment too hard against the board, and it skidded out of place. Her thumb slid forward and several splinters embedded themselves in its flesh. "Ahhh," she gasped. "Shit."

"Oh, I don't know, I think it's wonderful news. Saint-Porchaires don't come along every day, you know. Not in one piece, anyway. Brian must be over the moon."

"Leave him out of this; leave the Saint-Porchaire out of this," Sophie hissed.

"But darling! This is an amazing opportunity! I've already spoken with my client, and he is quite excited. In fact, he seems to have wet his trousers. Or something of that nature. In the trouser area."

"Are you out of your mind, you fucking lunatic?"

"No, love, not at all. Think about it. Brian will probably

bring the piece to his office—it's so convenient! He'll want to show it off, impress his coworkers. Then it'll spend some time in Conservation—less convenient, but doable. Then Photography. Possibly penetrable, possibly not. I'll leave it to you. Then maybe it'll come back to Brian's office while they build a display case? What do you think?"

"I think you need to get a life, is what I think."

"Me! Oh, that's wonderful. Listen, Sophie. There's no reason Brian should be the one having all the fun. Yes, he's a good museum boy, trotting around the world nicking treasures from people who don't know what they've got—but you! You've got actual talent, and you deserve a piece of the action. Don't waste your life changing nappies. This is your chance to get out there and—what's that delightful expression?—grab life by the bollocks!"

"Harry, you sound ridiculous. You know that, don't you?" She stared at her shaking thumb.

"You're the one who's going to sound ridiculous, trying to explain why the FBI just found a stolen Renaissance tazza hidden in your house. 'Oh, how did *that* get there? Oh dear! How terribly *odd*!'"

"Guess what?" Sophie hissed. "They've already been here. They looked—*I've* looked. It's not here, you lying fuck." She squeezed the end of her thumb, and tiny drops of blood bulged out of the purplish flesh.

"They came back?" Harry sounded genuinely surprised. "They didn't look very hard, did they? Sounds like they need someone to point them in the right direction. I'm happy to do it. Why don't I give you…a week. That should give you plenty of time to do what needs to be done."

"Whatever." Sophie snapped the phone shut and threw it into a corner. She picked up the broken board and shoved it into its space in the floor without its missing shard. She hammered the nails back into the joist below, missing periodically, pounding the wood, which cracked and dented with every blow. Pound. Pound. Pound. What this room needed, she decided, was a rug.

⁂

"Daddy! Daddy!" screamed the kids when the doorbell rang.

"Daddy's plane is still in the air," Sophie said over the din. "And Daddy doesn't have to ring the doorbell."

It was the postman, with a slip she was supposed to sign, in exchange for which he handed her an envelope from MortgageOne. Inside she found a document titled "Notice of Intent to Accelerate," which read:

> If the default is not cured on or before August 21, 2007, the mortgage payments will be accelerated with the full amount remaining becoming due and payable in full, and foreclosure proceedings will be initiated at that time. As such, the failure to cure the default may result in the foreclosure and sale of your property.

Sophie laughed to herself. "Failure to cure the default?" Like an injection of antibiotics was all that was needed. And the part about the full amount becoming due—was that some kind of legal sarcasm?

She sat down on the sofa, her knees trembling as if the postman had just handed her a three-hundred-pound package. She hadn't expected it to happen so fast. She'd been planning to make up the missed payments, just as soon as the last check came from her client. Her mistake, she realized now, had been to continue paying the electric bill and the cable company.

They could threaten her and make her feel guilty, but at least they wouldn't send the sheriff to take her house away.

Hearing Brian's key in the door, Sophie shoved the letter into her back pocket. "Okay, this time it's Daddy," she said to the kids, who rushed to the front door and attached themselves to Brian's legs as soon as he entered the house.

The sight of him—uncharacteristically rumpled, shadows under his eyes, yet still so solidly, comfortingly male—made Sophie ache with longing and sorrow. She leaned over the pile of kids and suitcases to give him a kiss. He wearily handed her a gift bag from duty-free.

"Presents! Presents!" said Lucy.

"Let Daddy catch his breath," Sophie said. "He just walked in." Part of her wanted to sit him down and tell him everything, and part of her wanted to shield his eyes from the smoking ruins of their life. "How was your flight?"

"Grueling," Brian said, kneeling down to hug Lucy and Elliot. "It's so good to be home."

"Was it a cargo flight?"

"Yeah. I sat on the tarmac for three hours, and when we were all set to go, customs came on board and got in my face about the paperwork. It took another hour on the phone with the registrar to get it worked out. Anyway. Everything okay around here?"

Sophie peeked into the gift bag: French chocolates. "Everything's fine. Why don't you go upstairs and change. I'll heat up some dinner."

Brian stood and wearily lifted his suitcases, turned toward the stairs, then dropped his bags. He leaned down and ran his finger along the gap between one of the risers and the stair tread. He straightened and rubbed his eyes, looking up the staircase.

"What the f—heck—happened to our stairs?"

This, Sophie thought, was the problem with being married to a curator.

"I'll tell you about it later," she said. "Go change."

Later, after putting the kids to bed, she found Brian in the office. The cheap kilim she'd bought at IKEA was pushed back to reveal the scarred and splintered floor. Brian turned to her with a look of weary alarm.

"Sophie—"

"I know," she said. "It's horrible. I know."

"But what's been going on?"

"It's just…kind of…hard to explain."

"Did you do this?"

She nodded slowly.

"And the steps?"

She nodded again.

"But why?" His eyes, deep in their jet-lagged hollows, searched her face.

Sophie drew a long breath. "I smelled something."

"You're always smelling things. You don't usually do…this." He waved his hand over the massacred floorboards.

"It was bad, Brian. It smelled like death. You have no idea. I had to do something."

"Did you find anything?"

Sophie nodded. "A rat. A big one. All…swollen up." She pointed to a spot in the floor. "Under there."

"Oh my God," said Brian, grimacing. "That's disgusting."

"I know!"

"But—why the stairs?"

"It was hard to tell where the smell was coming from."

"I just can't believe you didn't call a carpenter. Or an exterminator."

"That would've been too expensive. I thought I could manage on my own. I…I don't know why. I mean, you know how I am. I try to handle things on my own, and then I screw it up. I'm sorry."

Brian shook his head. "I don't understand you. I'll call the carpenter tomorrow. This floor is a disaster."

"I know. I'm sorry," she whispered, her throat swelling with the urge to cry.

"Hey, come here. It's okay." Brian pulled her against himself and hugged her hard. Sophie buried her face in the hollow between his shoulder and his chest, and then, with the force of a sail tacking hard into the wind, a sob flew out of her throat, then another, until she was wailing raggedly into her husband's body, holding him tight, refusing to let him pull back and look into her face.

"Please," Brian said into her hair. "Whatever it is that's wrong, just let me take care of you. Let me help."

Sophie shook her head violently. "You can't," she sobbed.

"Why not? Can you try to drop the whole independent, one-woman-army thing for a bit? I just feel like you might be happier if you let people help you now and then." He pulled away and looked into her eyes. "I don't want you to get so miserable you take off."

"Take off? Don't be ridiculous." She gave a little laugh. "You think—?"

Brian crossed his arms and looked down. "I don't know. I never really know what's going on with you. You're a god-damn mystery, Sophie."

"But Brian…" She felt a new wave of misery roll over her. It had never occurred to her that Brian struggled to understand her, that he felt uncertain about her intentions. That was the last thing she ever wanted to inflict on someone else. "You don't have to worry. I'm not my mother, okay? I'm not going anywhere. Please, I need you to know that—*I* need to know that!" She was crying again. Brian pulled her back into his arms, and her words sank into his warmth. "Look what I've built for our family! This was all for us—so nobody would have to wonder! So nobody would have to worry!"

"This what?"

"This house!"

Brian took her by the shoulders. "Sophie, if you and I are really okay, which I really hope we are, we could be happy living in a trailer. Come on! Don't you know our kids would feel safe with you in a homeless shelter or a refugee camp or a—a—split level—because you're a good mother?"

"But that's just it. I'm the worst mother in the goddamned world."

"No, you're not. I don't know why you would say that."

"Trust me," she said, even though she knew that was the last thing he should be doing. "I am."

Seventeen

B rian scheduled the carpenter, then Sophie called and unscheduled him, saying she was too busy with a big project, and needed quiet in the house. She called the cable company to cancel their subscription, then put some of her computer equipment on eBay. She reduced their car insurance to the legal minimum and switched to a credit card with a low introductory rate. It felt like bailing out a boat with a thimble, but at least she was doing something.

Brian wanted her to come see the Saint-Porchaire. Sophie wanted to do nothing of the kind, but at the same time, she felt the need—now more than ever—to show Brian that she cared, that she was proud of him, that everything was normal. How she longed for everything to be normal! To be able to show up at her husband's office without feeling a complicated flood of emotion…to enjoy his company without debilitating attacks of guilt, resentment, and fear. She was ready to do anything to make things normal again—even if it meant things had to get worse before they got better. Even if it meant things might get worse and *never* get better. Anything was better than this.

When she arrived at the museum she found Brian's office crowded with curators who had come to get a look at the candlestick. Brian was presiding over the large crate like a proud new father; seeing Sophie hovering at the doorway, he smiled and beckoned her in. The crate sat on a table in the middle of the room; Sophie squeezed between a curator of Prints and Drawings and a curator of Textiles to peer inside. The box was lined with dense foam that had been cut to the exact shape of the candlestick; two pieces of foam had been lifted away from the top, and a thin sheet of foam swaddling had been peeled back to reveal the candlestick nestled in its cavity.

Brian was using a pen to point to the intricate patterns that decorated the surface of the piece. "These here were stamped onto the clay, then the impressions were filled with colored paste. The stamps were used over and over, so we can relate this piece to a particular group made at the same time. Then these"—he pointed to an elaborate pattern of angular woven designs encircling the base—"what we call eternal knots—were drawn on the clay first, using a template, then scored and filled."

The photograph Sophie had seen earlier had not revealed the most delicate decorations, which were so perfect they seemed machine-made. The three-dimensional ornaments which sprang from the richly patterned surface—garlands, mermaids, cherubs, and the like—were just as finely wrought. The cherubs, perched on a small ledge, casually fingered tiny painted gold necklaces; on the pale green garlands, she could see every vein of every leaf. It was outrageous showmanship and meticulous artistry all at once.

"You know, we have a leather bookbinding with almost the same exact pattern stamped on it," said the woman from Prints and Drawings. "It came from—"

"Anne de Montmorency," Brian interrupted. "I've seen it."

"We can't have it on permanent display, but maybe we can talk about a mini exhibition? Maybe throw in a piece of armor? I know Carlos has a great breastplate with this amazing damascening, all arabesque patterns. It would be so cool." She clasped her heavily ringed hands together.

Brian gave her a stiff smile. "Interesting," he said, before resuming his monologue about decorative techniques.

Sophie's mind turned to the woman in Strasbourg who was probably, at this moment, gloating over the fifteen thousand euros the museum had just paid for her ex-husband's ex-property. Brian had told Sophie the candlestick was worth well over a million dollars on the open market. She wondered how much Harry was planning to pay her for it.

Harry. He was stuck in her head like a bad jingle. She was so sick of him and his silly game with the tazza, and the way he spoke to her these days, with that snide, condescending tone. Now, standing in the presence of this monument to Renaissance wealth and spectacle, she felt a slight shift in the arrangement of the universe around her. The candlestick had power. Perhaps it could even make Harry disappear, along with her financial woes, her insomnia, and the sudden, inexplicable urge to destroy her house.

"What's Conservation planning to do with it?" she asked Brian.

"Nothing more than a careful cleaning. It's in great condition. I'm just waiting for them to get done with everything for that American Art show. I'm next on their list."

The Textiles curator snorted. "Don't hold your breath."

Sophie measured the candlestick with her eyes. The base was a wide saucer, about five inches across; the entire piece about a foot long. It looked exceedingly fragile, with so many delicate protrusions. She could imagine how easily one of them could be snapped off if the candlestick were removed from its foam cradle. Harry really was crazy.

Sophie picked up the foam pieces that were lying on the table and held them together to see the perfectly carved candlestick-shaped hole. How had they managed to create the exact shape like that? she wondered. Lasers?

One by one, the curators congratulated Brian and filed out. Brian carefully replaced the foam padding over the candlestick, closed the crate, locked it in the metal cabinet next to his desk, and dropped the keys into his top right desk drawer. Sophie almost laughed out loud. That's it? she wanted to say. That's the extent of museum security around one of the most important acquisitions in years? A work of art so valuable, it could pay off her entire house? Granted, she was the only person who knew it was in that cabinet. And she knew where the key was, too.

She gave Brian a quick kiss, said good-bye, and hurried home to call Harry.

⁂

"You're mad," was his response when she told him how much she wanted up front.

"Cash," she reminded him. "And I'll need a little time. There's a family event at the museum in two weeks; I need to go with the stroller and the diaper bag. Try to be patient."

"Sod off."

"It's gorgeous, Harry. I wish I could send you a picture of it. It's been sitting in a box for more than a century. You don't find them in that kind of condition, if you find them at all."

"May I remind you—"

"Of what? Of how scared I'm supposed to be of you and your insatiable client? Listen, Harry. I just went and saw this thing, and it occurred to me: You have to have it, and I am the only one who can get it for you. I know where it is, and I can get in there during the party. I even know where the keys are. Don't miss out because you're too tightfisted."

"What's this all about, Sophie? A week ago you wouldn't give me the time of day, and now you're going all Thomas Crown on me?"

Sophie sighed loudly. "I've been under some…financial pressure. Which just became much more intense. Okay?"

"And how do I know you're not going to lose all of your motivation after you've got the money?"

"Then feel free to point the FBI to the location of the supposed tazza in my supposed house. Anyway, I need my entire cut. I'm not going to quit halfway."

"Hmmm."

"Look, Harry." Sophie paused, collecting her thoughts. "When I was there today, seeing that amazing piece just sitting there, I don't know. I realized I've been missing that feeling I get. When I'm taking something…it's the only time I feel completely awake. I mean, I know you can't relate, but having kids, you just empty yourself out. It all goes into them. And that's beautiful, and that's how it should be, but I'm not that good of a person. Every now and then I want something that's all mine. Something that makes me feel alive. You know?"

Harry groaned. "Just…come up here tomorrow. I'll have your cash."

"I've got the kids tomorrow. You'll have to bring it to me."

The train was packed, but Sophie refused to take the large cardboard box off of the seat next to her. She leaned her head back and pretended to be asleep, her hand resting on the box. She could almost smell the annoyance of each harried traveler who paused at her row, but she didn't care. It was an amateur packing job—nothing like the museum's custom-made crate with its perfectly carved foam lining. She wasn't about to leave it to the vagaries of the overhead rack.

She struggled to keep her eyes closed and her breathing slow. When was the train going to leave? She wanted to be there, now. She'd waited long enough. Harry, too, had been far from patient during the last two weeks. In fact he'd been downright obnoxious, calling every other day, wheedling and threatening and making life unbearable. Sophie had employed the only technique she knew for appeasing a child who must wait an unspecified amount of time: distraction. She entertained him with stories about Carly and her new boyfriend, a podiatrist with a foot fetish who, thankfully, had nothing to do with Sophie. She fed him rumors and intrigue about museum trustees. She tried telling cute stories about her kids, which did not interest him, and actually put him in a bad mood, setting off another round of threats and curses.

It was exhausting, the constant tap dancing, but eventually Harry loosened up and began to enjoy their chats, just like the old days. And now that she was finally bringing him what he wanted, he'd promised to take her back to the tavern near his shop, to celebrate with martinis. She could almost taste the briny gin that would briefly numb the inside of her top lip before sliding down her throat. She wanted to be there now.

The train started, then stopped again; there were announcements about a delay. Sophie's stomach clenched. She pulled out her phone and selected the preprogrammed number. "The train's a little delayed," she said. "Wait for me. I'll come straight to the pub."

She pulled a notebook from her purse and tried to distract herself by working on her museum database. Brian had been complaining about the lack of coordination between Conservation and Art Handling; she had some ideas for a workflow that would be triggered by a cleaning schedule established for each object. She was pretty sure she could integrate the system with the museum's calendar and set it up to send reminders to the appropriate departments when a conservation project was about to be launched.

Before long the train got going, and the landscape began to flow by her window. Sophie scribbled faster, ideas flooding her brain. She was eager to start creating some wireframes and sample pages. She decided to get to work on them as soon as she got home.

Finally, the train pulled into Penn Station and disgorged its impatient cargo. New York was hot; the late August air was swollen with bad smells. Every sewer grate and subway vent was leaking hot, musty fumes, and taxi exhaust hung listlessly in the air. Sophie hit redial on her phone and said, "I'm here. I'll be at the pub in five minutes."

The restaurant, fortunately, was aggressively air-conditioned; Sophie plunged gratefully into the chill, scanning the room for Harry's red hair. She spotted him in a booth and hurried over, apologizing.

"It's fine, it's fine," he said, kissing her cheek. "I started without you. I'm sure you'll catch up, right, love?"

Sophie slid into the booth and set the box down next to her. "How've you been, Harry? It's good to see you." She wondered how many drinks he'd already had; he seemed more slumped than usual.

"Jeffrey moved out."

"Oh. I'm so sorry."

"Enh. Fuck 'im." He leaned his cheek on his hand, pushing up the skin so it bunched unattractively around his eye.

"Will this cheer you up?" Sophie asked, pointing to the box.

"Possibly. Hand it over here."

Sophie passed the box across the table, and Harry put it on the bench between himself and the wall. He peeled off the tape that was holding the box closed.

"Don't pull it out," Sophie warned.

"I'm not an idiot," he muttered, pushing aside the crumpled newspaper and Styrofoam peanuts that were packed around the candlestick. He paused while the waitress delivered Sophie's drink, then resumed foraging in the box while Sophie took her first bracing gulps.

"It's hard to see," he complained. "Did you have to use peanuts? I abhor these things." He tried shaking one off his hand; it jumped onto his suit jacket.

"Just try to be gentle," Sophie said. "You snap off one of those doodads, it's worthless."

"You think I don't know that."

"I thought you'd be in a better mood," said Sophie. "I just stole you a rare sixteenth-century candlestick worth a million dollars."

"I know, I know," he said, turning back to his drink. "I'm forgetting my manners. Thank you, Sophie, brilliant burglaress, for saving my ass."

"You're welcome. I hope this makes you happier than the snuffbox and the Irish setter."

"You can be sure of that," said Harry. "There's a bag of cash for you under the table. Promise me you'll put it to good use. Like some new clothes. That blouse you're wearing—is that actually rayon?"

"Wow. No wonder Jeffrey moved out. Why so grumpy, Harry? Does this have something to do with your mysterious client?"

"No."

"What's his deal, anyway? Why does he have such a grip on you?"

Harry ignored this. He ordered another drink and launched into a detailed account of his breakup with Jeffrey, which included not just the specific insults he and Jeffrey had lobbed at each other, but the ones he'd come up with since then, and which he had started compiling in a devastating email that he considered his personal Manhattan Project.

"I don't know," Sophie said. "Maybe you should move on. You're very dateable, you know. You'll find someone soon."

"I'm a nightmare to date. I'm very emotionally needy."

Sophie laughed, then stopped when she realized he wasn't joking.

"It's true. I'm a mess. Fucked-up childhood. My dad—God. I shouldn't say this, but he's such a—never mind."

"What?"

"Always on my back. I cannot take a piss without him telling me I'm doing it wrong. Nothing will ever be good enough for him."

Sophie frowned. "Why do you always talk about him like he's alive?"

"Sorry. I just mean, my whole life. He never let up."

"I guess some fathers don't know how else to show they care. I mean, at least he paid attention to you, right?"

"I would have preferred a little less attention."

"Well, my parents basically ignored me growing up, and my mom has blown me off for the last fifteen years. I don't know which is worse."

Harry leaned against the back of the booth, looking at her. "Did they pour silver polish over your head?"

"No."

"Did they grab your belly fat and jiggle it for your friends' amusement?"

Sophie crossed her arms in front of her stomach.

"Did they find hundreds of ways, on a daily basis, to express their grievous, excruciating disappointment in the way you turned out?"

"Okay, no."

"I have not been neglected." Harry cracked the knuckles of one hand, then the other. "Far from it."

Sophie felt the tips of her ears turn warm. Of course there were childhoods more miserable than her own. Of course her parents hadn't abused her, hadn't even hurt her, really. Harry had the decency not to say it, but the truth was, Sophie's upbringing made a pretty shabby excuse for poor behavior.

"Dammit, Harry," Sophie said.

"What."

"It's just…" Sophie looked around the restaurant. "I'm so sorry."

"Oh, it's fine." Harry waved his hand. "My dad's always had impossibly high standards. He's always wanted me to be successful, like him." He sat back in the booth and said robotically, as if reciting the Pledge of Allegiance, "He taught me everything I know, and I mustn't forget that."

"I guess." Sophie pulled an olive out of her glass, contemplated eating it, then dropped it back in. She thought about ordering another drink, then remembered she was supposed to keep her wits about her. "Well," she said heavily, "on another note, we still have a piece of unfinished business."

"What's that."

"The tazza."

Harry brightened. "Right! Did you find it?"

"It never was in my house, was it?"

"Nah. I gave it to my client. He loved it." He laughed ruefully. "Sorry, love."

"Shithead." She pulled the olive back out and ate it. "So who is he, anyway?"

"Doesn't matter."

"Come on. I'm dying to know. Who's collecting all this stuff?"

"I told you. It doesn't matter. Why would you want to know that?"

"I don't know. I'm curious. Is he a celebrity? Is that why you're so secretive about him?"

"Trying to cut me out, my dear?"

"Harry!"

"Sorry. I'm not telling you. It's for your own good, love."

Sophie saw the waitress coming toward them; two men stood up at different tables and walked in their direction.

"Harry," she said.

"Yes?"

"I'm sorry about this. But trust me—if you tell them, they'll make a deal. Okay?"

"What are you on about?"

"Just tell them who he is and they'll work something out."

The waitress had her badge out, and so did the two diners, and then Agent Chandler and Agent Richardson walked out of the kitchen.

"You bitch," Harry said, not even looking at the badges being flourished like auction paddles. He just stared at Sophie, his lower jaw clicking back and forth under his cheeks, now gone bluish-white.

Things got confusing then, the agents crowding around the booth, diners standing up to see what was going on, people saying things to Harry about being under arrest, telling him to stay calm. The damp smell of sweat tinged with adrenaline clouded the air. Harry stood up, his eyes still on Sophie, and one of the agents attached handcuffs to his right hand. Before he could snap them on to Harry's other wrist, though, Harry lunged toward the booth, reached out with his free hand, and seized the candlestick, pulling it out of the box in a rain of Styrofoam peanuts. Sophie shrank back into her side of the booth. The agents dove after Harry's left arm and wrenched it backward; then, with a smile for Sophie, Harry relaxed his hand, letting the candlestick slide from his fingers. It hit the floor with an ugly crunching sound. Agent Chandler jerked Harry's arm backward, snapped the other side of the handcuffs closed, and roughly pushed him toward another agent, who led him toward the exit. Ceramic shards cracked under their feet.

"Thank you, Sophie," said Agent Chandler, reaching out and awkwardly patting her on the shoulder. "We got most of what we need."

"I'm sorry I didn't get the collector's name."

"Oh." Chandler dismissed this with a shrug. "We've got enough to put Harry's feet to the fire. He'll talk. We can probably get his charges dropped."

"I hope so." Sophie retrieved the tote bag from under the table and handed it to Agent Richardson, then pulled the microphone and transmitter out of her blouse and laid them on the table. Her hands, she observed with strangely detached clarity, were still shaking.

Eighteen

As Sophie yanked the red plastic shopping cart from the firm embrace of the cart ahead of it, it occurred to her that shopping carts, like portion sizes, had almost doubled in size since her childhood. She had a vague memory of Randall, an average-size man, looking slightly ridiculous pushing a petite metal cart through the aisles of the grocery store. Of course, in those days no one would have taken a shopping cart in the first place if they were only running in for a bar of soap. But in a modern-day Target it was sheer hubris to try crossing the store's acreage without a cart.

Sophie needed soap because Carly's bathroom was stocked with French soaps made of olive oil, orange peel, and lavender seeds, and the smell of them tended to linger on Sophie's skin all day, making her feel like some kind of exotic Provencal muffin. She needed white soap—cheap but not too cheap, since the lowest-tier soaps were always the most aggressively scented, presumably to make the buyer feel that she was getting more than her money's worth.

Sophie knew the soap could be found just to the left of the checkout area, but she decided to take the long way around the store. She had a feeling she needed something else, but she wouldn't know it until she saw it. Besides, she had always found it soothing to push a cart slowly through the aisles of Target, ticking through the rooms of her life and contemplating possible improvements: new pens, easier-to-carry laundry hampers, a scale that could measure body fat, chocolate.

She paused in the party-supply aisle. Lucy was turning five next month. Sophie and Brian hadn't talked about it yet. In theory, Brian was in charge of these things now, but Sophie doubted he fully grasped the amount of preparation a five-year-old's birthday celebration required. Had he reserved a venue? Had Lucy started thinking about a theme? Did he know the rule that you could only bring invitations to day care if every child in the class was invited (otherwise you had to mail them)?

The only times she saw Brian were when he dropped off and picked up the kids for their visits. That's when they exchanged little packets of information about schedules, playdates, car repairs, mortgage paperwork. There wasn't enough time to think of everything. Pushing her cart into the stationery aisle, Sophie decided she should buy a notebook for keeping a list of things to remember to tell Brian. The green sippy cup goes in Lucy's lunch box, the purple one in Elliot's. Here's the website for ordering bulk diapers. Help the kids pick out things that start with a P to bring to school this week. Next week is Q.

She scanned the notebooks, wondering what was an appropriate design for transmitting five years of maternal experience. Businesslike blue? A cool Japanese floral design? Something her kids would like, with a robot or a princess on it?

The old familiar wave of sadness washed over her, threatening to pull her back into deeper currents. She fought it off, grabbed a plain black and white composition book, then pushed further into the store. Lightbulbs? Kitchen gadgets? What did she need? Carly's condo had everything she could want; much more, in fact, than she deserved. The guest bed was made up with eight-hundred-thread-count sheets and a cashmere blanket, the bathroom was stocked with Frette towels. It was disconcerting for Sophie, who, for the last five years, had bought sturdy linens and clothing in dark, stain-disguising colors, to find herself suddenly living in a satiny world of ecru, eggshell, and pearly gray. She'd offered to bring her own linens, but Carly was unfailingly generous with her space, insisting that Sophie stay for as long as she needed to, never complaining when the kids trailed cracker crumbs through her living room, always making herself scarce when Brian came over. She had not asked Sophie a single question aside from, What do you need from me, and What do you eat for breakfast?

Sophie decided to buy a waffle iron. She'd learn to make Sunday morning waffles, just like they'd always had at home. How hard could it be? She lowered a midpriced model into the cart, making a mental note to stop in the grocery section for syrup.

The toy department was next, cleverly located just across from children's shoes. Normally she avoided these aisles, but now she felt the pull of the toys' plastic promise: buy me, and inject instant happiness into the life of a child. Buy me, and I will replace your child's confusion with the simpler, less expensive confusion of noise and lights and polyester fur sewn onto a hard molded body. Buy me, and for five minutes (ten if you're lucky), your child will stop asking questions.

Sophie picked out a set of spy equipment for Lucy, and a doctor's kit for Elliot. At least these were slightly more wholesome than the loud, flashy electronic guns, cars, and life-size robotic animals that seemed to be specifically designed to broadcast, "I LOVE YOU MORE THAN YOUR OTHER PARENT." Sophie wasn't there yet. The word "divorce" had not yet been said out loud. She'd simply moved out, without being asked, leaving Brian with the number for the day care's business office so he could call and change the kids' schedule however he saw fit.

Rugs. Towels. Bathroom decor. They needed a new shower curtain for the third-floor bathroom; the current one smelled mildewy. She picked up a sunny yellow curtain that would look great with their tile. Of course, Brian had never complained about the smell. She didn't want it to look like she was expecting to come home at some point. She put the package back on the shelf. She had to let the shower curtain be Brian's problem for now.

If they decided to put the house on the market, of course, the mildew smell would be an issue. She picked the curtain back up. She'd never told Agent Chandler about the money Harry had paid her up front; as far as he knew, the tote bag confiscated at the pub was her entire cut. She'd used the up-front money to hire a lawyer recommended by Carly—a young guy named Joshua Goldmeier, who did not even raise an eyebrow when Sophie explained she'd be paying him in cash. He was trying to help them win the slow race between foreclosure and loan modification, but so far he wasn't having much more luck than Sophie had. In fact, he said it was beginning to look like the bank had lost all of her paperwork, including her mortgage note. He seemed excited to tell her this. "We're not there yet," he said, "but I don't see why we couldn't take on your loan servicer for this. Everything I uncover points to gross negligence and misconduct. This thing looks uglier every day."

Sophie put the shower curtain back on the shelf. He'd told her and Brian not to sell for now, to keep trying for the loan modification because, in reality, they could afford the house on Brian's salary if they could just negotiate more reasonable payments. "Some people are in much worse shape than you," he'd pointed out. "I'm hearing about people just walking away from their homes. It's crazy what's going on. I honestly wouldn't be surprised if we saw one or two banks collapse after a few years of this."

Brian thought Joshua Goldmeier was a litigious hysteric, but Sophie appreciated his outrage. It had never occurred to her that some of this wasn't her fault. It had also never occurred to her that she might not be the only person in the world with mortgage problems.

She pushed her cart into the next aisle, then quickly reversed course. Amy was standing there looking at toothbrush holders. As Sophie tried to maneuver her cart backward out of the aisle, Amy looked up.

"Hey, there! Sophie!"

"Oh! Hey, Amy."

"How are things going? I feel like we haven't seen you guys in ages."

"Yeah. Well. Brian and I hit a…snag." She needed to brainstorm some better euphemisms. "I've relocated to Rittenhouse Square for a little while."

Amy frowned. "You mean…what do you mean?"

"We're separated."

"Oh. My God. I'm so sorry." Amy's face contorted itself into a combination of embarrassment, surprise, and pity.

"Yeah, well."

"I mean, I can't believe it. You guys seemed so good."

"Some stuff happened." What stuff, exactly, would not become public knowledge until Harry's trial.

Amy nodded slowly, and Sophie wondered what she was imagining. She also wondered if Amy had really been oblivious to Keith's philandering. She had a new appreciation for just how much drama could be concealed within the narrow walls of a Philadelphia row house.

"I'm looking for soap," Sophie said.

Amy brightened. "It's on the other side of the store. Over by the pharmacy."

"Oh, that's right. Well, say hi to Keith for me."

"Okay. Let me know if you need anything," said Amy. "If you want to talk or whatever. Call me."

Sophie almost had to laugh as she pulled her cart away. Sweet, normal Amy. She had no idea.

Against everyone's expectations, Harry had refused to give up his client. Apparently he preferred to go to prison, stubbornly refusing even to post bail. This baffled Sophie, but mostly irritated her. Why wouldn't he play along? Agent Chandler was equally frustrated; he told Sophie Harry's client was a "big fish," and it was driving him mad that Harry wouldn't cooperate. At Chandler's request Sophie had gone to see Harry and plead with him to make a deal, but Harry wouldn't even speak to her. He'd just stared, his eyebrows tense, his neck flushed, reeking of suppressed rage.

The next time Sophie expected to see him was when she would testify at his trial, which was scheduled to happen in a few weeks. The museum, she knew, would have preferred to have more time. They wanted to get out in front of the story with an exciting event that would, in theory, distract everyone from the impending PR disaster. They'd brought in a freelance conservator to accelerate preparations for the hastily organized gala, and invitations had just been mailed. Sophie knew this because Carly, as one of the museum's bigger donors, received invitations to every party they threw. She'd left this one sitting prominently in the middle of the coffee table. *Celebrate the acquisition of a masterpiece of Faience*, it said. Inside, a professional photograph showed the Saint-Porchaire in all its regal splendor.

Of course, Brian probably wasn't invited to the party. Sophie had heard from Agent Chandler that the museum was work-ing with the FBI to conduct a full investigation of Brian and his department. Michael, Ted, and Marjorie were still allowed to come to work, but Brian had been put on administrative leave until things were cleared up. It killed her to think that he would miss his moment of glory, when the Saint-Porchaire was unveiled before the world.

The candlestick she'd taken to New York hadn't done the real one justice. A local ceramicist had made it based on photographs; Sophie had counted on the tavern's dim lighting to obscure the piece's clumsy painting and thick ornaments. The tape she'd made during her conversation with Harry was enough to get him convicted. According to Chandler, Harry could get anywhere from twenty to forty months, depending on the sentencing judge. Sophie had been surprised by the light sentence, but Chandler just shrugged and said that in a world of drugs and violence, nobody wanted art lovers taking up space in prisons. And if Harry would just give up the name of his client, he could walk away free.

Sporting goods. Automotive. Electronics. Syrup. Sophie had almost gone full circle; she finally found herself in the soap aisle. She chose her favorite brand, something basic and inoffensive. She contemplated buying more than one. How much time did one bar of soap represent? She stood staring at the package in her hand; her thoughts began to wander.

"Finding everything okay?" asked a Target team member, a young girl as bright and full of promise as her red vest and the shelves of skin-care products that gleamed under the faintly buzzing fluorescent light. Sophie frowned at her. The question didn't make any sense. This place didn't make any sense. The soap in her hand suddenly seemed like a strange artifact from another world, emptied of its meaning, as bland and worthless as a piece of driveway gravel. She threw it into her cart anyway, and headed for the register.

"No," she said over her shoulder to the girl. "I'm not finding everything okay at all."

✾

1. *Elliot will pee in the toilet, but not poop. You can let him go without a diaper during the day, but <u>keep an eye on him</u>. You can usually tell when it's about to happen by the look on his face.*
2. *Never leave the house without a change of clothes.*
3. *No peanut butter in their lunches. No peanut products. Do not even think the word "peanut" while you make their lunches, or someone in their class will end up in the hospital.*
4. *Miss Theresa (blond hair, sturdy build) is the one who will take the time to tell you if the kids did/said anything interesting during the day. Be sure to ask how Elliot's doing with the toilet training, so you can be consistent at home.*
5. *Bring home all of their artwork from school, but you should by no means try to keep all of it. Pick out the good stuff and sneak the rest into the recycling. Make sure Lucy doesn't see it sitting on the curb on trash day.*
6. *When you take them to the grocery store, Elliot can ride in the cart but Lucy is <u>not allowed</u> to stand on the end of the cart. This makes the cart tip over. Also, watch Elliot when you're in the checkout line. He will try to shoplift candy.*
7. *When you have pried the candy out of Elliot's hand and he starts to wail, try to get as many groceries as you can onto the belt before he starts attempting to climb out of the cart. Prepare for rapid escalation. Handle it however you see fit—*

apologize to those around you, pretend nothing's happening, speak to him in your Scary Voice, but above all—and this is very important—do not give that piece of candy back to him.

8. *Release him from the shopping cart at the last possible minute, after the groceries are already in the trunk and Lucy is in her car seat. If you really can't wrestle him into his car seat, it's all right to threaten to leave him in the parking lot. What's important is not to actually do it.*

9. *I've been reading "Mary Poppins" to Lucy. We're about halfway through it; she can summarize the first part for you.*

10. *Sometimes, right after their bath, when they're shivering in their pajamas, we pile into Lucy's bed together and get warm under the blankets. Sometimes we'll pretend the blanket is an igloo, and we're Eskimos trying to stay warm during a blizzard. We'll give each other Eskimo kisses and wrap ourselves in pretend seal fur, although Lucy prefers if we use pretend faux fur. Sometimes Elliot will pretend he's a penguin, which is very cute.*

11. *I realize this is all my fault, and I understand why you hate me. And I know it's a huge burden for you to be on your own with the kids now. When you said, "I don't even know who you are, and I can't let my kids be raised by a stranger," well, that makes total sense. To tell you the truth, I haven't been completely sure who I am since the kids were born. It's simultaneously the most defining and most alienating experience I've ever had.*

12. *This list was supposed to be more helpful. Sorry.*

Sophie shyly handed the notebook to Brian when he came to get the kids after their next visit. "It's just some stuff I haven't had time to explain," she said. Brian absently stuck it into his laptop bag, and she wondered if he would actually read it. But when he brought the kids by a few days later, he handed the notebook back. His handwriting—small but messy—filled the page after Sophie's list.

1. *Elliot pooped in the potty twice this week, and once in his pants.*
2. *Lucy got in trouble at day care for hitting some kid. She said he deserved it. We had a talk.*
3. *Lucy hit Elliot, right in front of me. I don't even know why. He was just sitting there. We had another talk.*
4. *Lucy hit me when I said she couldn't stay home from day care. We were late, so we couldn't have a talk, but anyway I'm not sure the talks are working.*
5. *I need to get the zoo membership card from you.*
6. *Keith called. What did you say to Amy?*
7. *Lucy wants to have a Dora-themed party at the Smith Playhouse. I called and booked it for the 27th at 2:00.*
8. *I have a two-day ride this weekend so I was wondering if you could come home and stay with the kids. If not, that's fine; I don't need to go on the ride.*
9. *The kids won't let me read "Mary Poppins" to them because they say I read it wrong.*
10. *I'm thinking about moving their bedtime up because they don't nap at day care, and they're totally exhausted by the end of the day.*
11. *It's not a burden for me to have the kids, I like spending time with them. And believe it or not, I do know what I'm doing.*

Sophie came home for the weekend so Brian could go on his ride. Entering the house as a visitor felt odd. It smelled different; not bad, necessarily, just not familiar: a combination of rubber, fabric softener, and toast. She busied herself putting away some CDs that had been left on the coffee table and putting the armchairs back at right angles with the rug.

"Look, Mommy. I can tie my shoes," Lucy said, untying them so she could demonstrate. "Watch." Her chubby fingers worked the laces slowly, struggling to keep a loop pinched between the fingers of each hand and then to tie the loops in a knot. One hand was always losing its grip on one of the loops, though, so she had to keep starting over.

"That's the hard way, honey," Sophie said, reaching for the laces. "Just make one loop, like this, then wrap the string around and push it through."

"That's not how Daddy does it."

"I know, but it's easier. Here, try it."

"No." Lucy yanked her foot away from Sophie's hands and started over with the double loops. "I can do it. Watch."

Sophie watched for a while, clenching her hands to stop herself from grabbing the laces. But every time Lucy fumbled, her fingers became more frantic, and her face turned a deeper shade of scarlet, until finally Sophie said, "Why don't I hold that loop," which caused Lucy to rip off her shoe, throw it across the room, and scream,

"NOOOOO! I can do it when Daddy's here!"

Sophie stood up and went into the kitchen, where she stood for a moment, hands flat against her belly, taking deep breaths through her nose. It has to get worse before it gets better, she reminded herself. But just how much worse could it get? She noticed that Brian had hung up an old dish towel she had long ago consigned to the rag pile. She shook her head and replaced it with a clean one, then opened the fridge. Fluorescent colors blared from the shelves. She picked up a "yogurt on the go" package and read the ingredients, then tossed it into the trash. She studied a package of lunch meat. Nitrates *and* nitrites. She threw it away, along with a bottle of juice cocktail, a jar of maraschino cherries, and an assortment of individually packaged puddings. She slammed the refrigerator door and went upstairs.

She surveyed the kids' rooms with a prick of disappointment. The house was actually neat; the kids' bedding was clean. She peeked into Elliot's dresser. His clothes were folded, but completely mixed up: socks and underwear in the same drawer as T-shirts, pants sandwiched between sweatshirts and pajamas. How could anyone find anything? She pulled out all the clothes and began sorting them properly, feeling her thoughts slow down as she worked. Some of the pants were definitely too small. She made a pile to go to Goodwill, and made a mental note to get some more next time she was at Target.

Upstairs, their own bedroom—Brian's bedroom—was also clean. The bed had been stripped; a pile of clean sheets sat folded at the foot of the mattress, polite and cruel. Sophie sat on the edge of the bed and held the square stack in her lap. The sheets smelled like chemical sunshine and baby powder. She set them aside and lay down, her cheek against the mattress, and breathed in all that she could find of Brian, and herself, and their tangled togetherness. It was ghostly but still recognizable, like an old photograph bleached by the sun. She closed her eyes and tried to remember the last time she and Brian had woken up together in this ginkgo-dappled room, the morning before she called Agent Chandler, before she made her rambling confessions and packed her bags. But those final, innocent hours were a blur. She hadn't thought to savor the last moments of being loved, to memorize their texture and shape. She ran her hands over the mattress, and then she let go, allowing all her fear and regret and embarrassment and grief to pour down the satiny mounds and puddle in the mattress's tufted depths.

After a while she got up, dried her cheeks, and opened the windows. The air was just beginning to crisp; the ginkgo leaves had taken on a faint golden cast. Sophie stood at the window for a moment, tasting the breeze, then went downstairs and pulled the discarded food out of the kitchen trash. She washed off the packages, dried them, and arranged them on the refrigerator shelves. Then she collapsed on the couch with Lucy and Elliot, who crawled into the spaces under her arms.

⁂

That night, after putting the kids to bed, Sophie poured herself a glass of wine and pulled out the composition notebook.

1. *Elliot needs bigger pants; I'll pick some up at Target.*
2. *I think the earlier bedtime is a good idea.*
3. *I tried to read "Charlotte's Web" to them tonight, but they wouldn't let me because they said you do it better.*
4. *I got a big freelance job from one of my old clients. Three months on retainer. Yay.*
5. *The house looks great. You're obviously doing fine without me.*
6. *I know my biggest mistake was not coming to you when I first realized we were in trouble. It's not that I didn't trust you. I just felt responsible, and embarrassed, and I thought I could handle everything. It has been pointed out to me that I am a control freak.*
7. *I also realize that on some level, I created the problems between us, or aggravated them, to justify what I was doing. You didn't stand a chance.*
8. *I'm sure the museum will realize you had nothing to do with any of this. They have to.*

9. *I'm just so sorry.*
10. *I miss you.*
11. *Phone call.*

Brian's response came the following Friday.

1. *Thanks for getting Elliot pants.*
2. *The museum would feel a lot better about things if they could get their stuff back.*

The trial was fast approaching, and Sophie managed her nervousness by plunging into work. A large hospital was reorganizing its website: an unruly collection of mismatched pages and microsites administered by marketing managers scattered throughout the organization's network. The agency had asked for her exclusive availability during the next three months so that she could respond to changes and join conference calls at a moment's notice. The job fit her suddenly empty schedule perfectly. Carly was working on-site at another agency, so she let Sophie use her home equipment—a setup as luxurious as anything else in the condo, with four high-res monitors, Mac and PC towers, an assortment of laptops, and an external hard drive array. In the evenings, after dinner, Carly would help her puzzle through awkward stretches of code, and the two of them would work late into the night, drinking wine and talking in the blue and green glow of the machines.

"I guess I should start looking at apartments," said Sophie late one night, saving her files and shutting down the computer.

"Did Brian say that?" Carly was sitting on the love seat in the office, a laptop on her bony knees.

"No. But he's not showing any signs of wanting to fix things. For all I know, he's planning to stay mad at me forever. You can't blame him, really."

"Well..." Carly typed a few more words, then snapped her laptop shut. "He has a lot to be mad about. But I wouldn't go signing a lease any time soon."

"I can't stay here forever."

"Just give it a little while longer."

"And do what in the meantime?"

"What you're doing. Work."

"But what about Brian? What should I do? Should I suggest couples therapy? I thought maybe I could go to a few appointments first, check it out—"

Carly threw a throw pillow at her. "Can you stop? Can you just stop and be passive for once in your damn life? Wait for him."

"But this is all my fault. I have to do something. What if I wait and wait and nothing happens?"

"Wait. For. Him."

Sophie hugged the pillow. "You're so bossy."

"I'm so right."

Carly didn't say she couldn't go see Harry. Agent Chandler cleared her for one more visit, and she went to the detention center on the pretext of making Harry talk. She didn't expect him to tell her anything, really; she just felt an intense need to see him, to make sure he was all right, to try to figure out why she still cared.

When Harry was brought into the visiting room, Sophie's stomach clenched. He'd lost weight; his skin seemed slack. She could read a full account of his ordeal in his eyes, brow, and hollow cheeks. "Harry," she pleaded. "Why are you letting this happen to you?"

But Harry wouldn't answer this, or any of her other half-hearted questions about his client, or about his mule-headed refusal to make a deal. Finally Sophie sank back in her chair and stared at the ceiling, which was veined with exposed cables and ductwork. "Did you just see me as someone you could use?" she asked finally. "Were we ever friends?"

"If we were friends, would I be here?"

Sophie snapped her head upright; it was the first time she'd heard Harry speak since he'd called her a bitch at the tavern. "You didn't really give me a choice," she said. "You were trying to force me to do something…"

"To help me. To save my ass."

"You didn't exactly come to me like a friend in need, hat in hand. You threatened me. You were so *mean* to me."

"Yeah, well, what can I say; I learned from the best."

"What's that supposed to mean?" Sophie thought for a moment. "Your father?"

Harry shrugged. There was color in his cheeks now.

"You can't use your shitty father as an excuse," Sophie said. "You're your own person."

"Like you?" Harry sneered.

It was Sophie's turn to flush. "Yes, like me! I've tried hard to be different…to do the right thing for my kids."

"Oh really." Harry was coming to life now. He sat up and leaned toward Sophie across the table. "Come on. Admit it, love. You enjoyed yourself."

"No!"

"It fills a hole, right? That feeling of power, that glorious 'fuck you' to the universe. Looking out for yourself, doing what has to be done, taking care of business. It's delicious."

"No, it's not."

"Listen, love. The sooner you admit this about yourself, the better. Then you either embrace it"—Harry gestured toward himself with a flourish—"or control it. But you'd best not ignore it."

Sophie ran her hand along the cool edge of the steel table that separated them. This was not the conversation she had come here to have. She didn't need to hear Harry's thoughts on her character; as if he were one to judge! "Look," she said. "I want you to know how sorry I am. My intention—honestly—was for you to make a deal so they could put your guy away and we could both get on with our lives. You're the one who isn't playing along. But Chandler told me the maximum sentence is forty months, so don't worry—"

"I'm not worried," Harry laughed. "I'll still have a shred of honor left when I get out. It's snitches who have trouble sleeping at night."

"That's what this is about? Honor among thieves?"

"My dad worked too hard to build this business for me to tear it down. I have to protect his name as well as my own."

"What business? How deep into this are you?"

Harry snorted. "What business. *Our* business! You—me— our arrangement. It was really starting to come together. I was finally getting to a point where I could make my dad proud. Or at least, less infuriated."

"Your dead dad."

Harry balled up his fists and dropped his voice to a whisper. "Yes."

"The one who poured silver polish on your head."

"Do me a favor and stop coming here, okay? Just stop. You've got your life back, now go live it."

A guard appeared by Harry's side; their time was up. Sophie

watched him being led away, and felt their friendship—
imagined or real—turn to mist in the stale air. Check Harry
off the list, she thought bitterly. Just one more person
who wouldn't care if she disappeared from the face of the
earth. Harry was behind bars, and for whatever reason, he
seemed determined to stay there. But Sophie was entirely,
terrifyingly free.

As a cooperating witness, Sophie wasn't allowed to attend
Harry's trial, so on the day she was summoned to testify she felt
like someone intruding on a sensitive conversation. Fifteen or
twenty people sitting in the gallery paused and shifted on their
benches to watch as she entered behind the bailiff. On the left
side of the courtroom the jurors, who had the soft, sunken look
of people who have spent a long time in their chairs, regarded
her with dull expressions. She took her place in the front of the
room, facing Harry. He wouldn't look at her, and for this she
was grateful.

She'd never liked speaking in front of groups; the judge, a
drily authoritative woman whose black hair was pulled tight
with a bow clip, ordered her many times to repeat her answers
more clearly into the microphone. Sophie spoke haltingly, her
mind slow to find the right words. It had probably been a mistake
to come without an ally; the gallery seemed to radiate hostility.
She imagined that one of the men sitting in the front row, arms
crossed, must be Jeffrey. She also recognized Hilda Ross, the
museum's head of collections, and behind her, Marjorie.

As Sophie's story emerged, painstakingly plucked out of her
with the tweezers of jurisprudence, she enjoyed no confessional
release, no soothing balm of truth. Instead, she felt herself being

slowly transformed from cooperating witness into defendant. She joined Harry in his small, stuffy cell, walled in by the gray cement of people's revulsion, incredulity, and scorn. As she recalled each object—the little snuffbox, the wavy-haired dog, the proud tazza—she was struck, simultaneously, by the smallness of her crime and the enormity of her transgression. She had stolen from an institution whose sole purpose was to protect and share the work of artists. The fact that her crime was ultimately considered petty by the criminal justice system made her feel even worse.

Bringing up the mirror probably wouldn't have changed the case much in the eyes of the law, but in the eyes of the museum it would have made Brian and his colleagues seem like criminals on a whole other level. If Harry was right about the mirror—if it really was a Jamnitzer, or even a successful copy of a Jamnitzer—the department would be considered beyond negligent...not just for having overlooked a Renaissance masterpiece, but for letting it get thrown into a jumble of objects on a storage cart, then left in an office to be pocketed by a sleep-deprived spouse. Brian's job was already hanging by a thread. Bringing up the mirror would only make things worse.

When she was finally released from the courtroom, Sophie rushed outside into the chilly autumn air, eager to get back to Carly's condo so she could strip off her uncomfortable black tights and slip between the cool sheets of the guest bed, where she planned to spend at least the next twelve hours. But before she could cross the street she heard a familiar voice calling after her.

"Wait," Marjorie said, still pulling on her coat, a square purse dangling from one hand. "I want to talk to you."

Sophie winced. "Hi, Marjorie."

"I need you to explain how you can just walk out of here."

Sophie wasn't sure if Marjorie was asking about her

conscience, or the law. "I was a cooperating witness. I helped them catch a bigger fish in exchange for immunity."

"But that's ridiculous. You're a criminal. You should be locked up!" Marjorie hitched her purse over her shoulder. "It's disgusting, what you did. Making us look so…unprofessional."

Part of Sophie wanted to turn and walk away from this. Marjorie had never given her the time of day; why did she deserve an explanation? But she decided to accept this fresh punishment. "I'm sorry. If it matters, I didn't do it to hurt the museum, or you, or anyone."

Marjorie didn't seem to hear. "Anyway, I don't see how that dealer is important enough to let *you* go scot-free. Come on. What about the objects? Where are they?"

"That's what the FBI is trying to find out. That's why they're squeezing Harry. He's supposed to tell them where the stuff is, but he won't talk."

Marjorie waved her hand at this. "Regardless, you belong behind bars. Look at you. You don't even care." Marjorie lifted one side of her upper lip. "You got away with it. You're *smug!*" She jerked her chin in Sophie's direction, then turned and marched away.

"I am not smug!" Sophie shouted after her, adding, "I feel terrible!" But Marjorie kept walking, her broad shoulders and thick neck stiff with indignation.

Sophie walked slowly to Rittenhouse Square, where she found herself drawn to the bench where she'd seen that homeless woman months ago. Scot-free, Marjorie had said. Where did that expression come from, anyway? Sophie sat down, her body heavy with exhaustion. It was basically true, she thought; she was free to start a new life. Free to disappear.

Was this how her mother had felt, after Randall's funeral? Hollowed out by guilt, a numb husk, ready to sail off on the wind? Had she thought about her daughter, who was wrapped in her own confused grief, before setting off? Or had she flipped a switch in her mind? Sophie knew how that switch worked; she'd always done it right before a move. Letting go of her school, her friends, her favorite bike routes. Putting the car into reverse, backing out of her life. She knew how to do it: start fresh and unfettered. No weight of responsibility, no need to control other people, no more secrets bogging her down.

People were always asking why she didn't try to find her mother. Hire a detective, they always said. Search public records. But Sophie knew her mother didn't want to be found. She felt this, now, more keenly than ever: Maeve didn't want to be taken care of, and she certainly didn't want to take care of anyone else.

Sophie looked up into the reddening branches above her head. She'd once heard that a tree was a natural fractal: a pattern that keeps making smaller and smaller copies of itself. There was so much of Maeve in her, and now she saw so much of herself in Lucy. But if she quietly backed out of Lucy's life—could she break the cycle? Elliot, too, would probably be better off—free to become his own person, without her meddling influence. He was such a fine person. More like Brian, really, than like Sophie. Patient, loving, and kind. Innocent.

Sophie shook her head. She needed to steel herself, control her thoughts. She needed to do what was best for everyone. Think about someone else's happiness for a change.

Grief welled in her throat. It was ironic, really. Maeve hadn't been responsible for Randall's death, no matter how much she blamed herself. It was a structural flaw, a maintenance issue, something unconnected to her design. Sophie, on the other hand, had brought Brian crashing to the ground through genuine stupidity. If anyone deserved the full luxury of guilt, it was Sophie. She deserved to be exiled...and clearly, Brian didn't want her back. She'd waited for him to make a move in her direction, to make some sign of warming or thawing...but there was none. He had set her free—or rather, she remained as free as she had always been.

Sophie stood and walked into Carly's building, giving the doorman an apologetic smile. Upstairs she got into bed and pulled the silky pillow over her head. Here, there were no small voices to listen for, no demands on her consciousness. Here, she could sleep for as long as she wanted. If only sleep would come.

Nineteen

Minimum two bedrooms, maximum three. Washer/Dryer. Air-conditioning. Philadelphia. Radius—twenty miles? Fifty? One hundred? Sophie clicked "100." The rental site delivered several pages of results, but she didn't look at them. She erased "Philadelphia" and entered "San Francisco." She didn't look at those results, either. She closed the browser. Reopened it. She read some headlines, checked her RSS feed, scrolled through some blogs. She felt time slipping comfortably down the Internet funnel.

She latched on to a passing thought the way a drowning person grabs a branch: how was Brian filling his time, now that he couldn't go in to the office or access his museum email? Was he looking for another job? Could he write articles from home, separated from his filing cabinets and books? Sophie had fully cooperated with the head of security, telling him everything (or almost everything) about the few times she'd had access to the objects. She'd assured him that Brian's only real crime had been trusting his wife. She'd pleaded with the museum to let Brian keep his job, but his fate still hung in the balance. The Board of Trustees had to meet for a vote, and the FBI was still trying to recover the objects. That's what people seemed to care about most—the objects.

Sophie slumped in her chair, staring at the computer screen. Then she sat up and went to Yahoo's home page.

Hacking into Harry's email turned out to be surprisingly easy. Resetting his password was a simple matter of finding his birth date and the name of his primary school. Both were available in public records, for a small fee. She was surprised to find that his account was still up and running, then figured the FBI must be monitoring his incoming mail. In any case, his inbox was a mess, which was good in a way: he'd kept every message ever sent to him. But he only had a few folders set up, and had neglected to sort most of his emails. Sophie idly clicked through them, scanning notices about antiques fairs, auctions, exhibitions. Mixed in with his business messages were hundreds of personal emails: notes about dinner plans, travel itineraries, terse conversations with his brother about Christmas. There were even a few messages from Sophie, from the early days of their friendship, before she'd decided to limit their communications to the prepaid phone. She opened a thread she'd started on the train home after their first lunch together:

From: sophie@codemonkey.com
Date: June 28, 2005
To: harry_mcgeorge@yahoo.com
Subject: the spins

Thanks again for lunch. And drinks. I caught my train; slightly worried I won't get off at the right stop. Where do I live again?

From: harry_mcgeorge@yahoo.com
Date: June 28, 2005
To: sophie@codemonkey.com
Subject: re: the spins

I believe it's called Philadelphia. Don't worry; you'll smell it.

From: sophie@codemonkey.com
Date: June 28, 2005
To: harry_mcgeorge@yahoo.com
Subject: re: re: the spins

Hey now.

From: harry_mcgeorge@yahoo.com
Date: June 28, 2005
To: sophie@codemonkey.com
Subject: re: re: re: the spins

Sorry! Kidding. Hope you make it home in one piece.

From: sophie@codemonkey.com
Date: June 28, 2005
To: harry_mcgeorge@yahoo.com
Subject: re: re: re: re: the spins

Thanks Harry. I love you. That's the martini talking. My martini loves you.

From: harry_mcgeorge@yahoo.com
Date: June 28, 2005
To: sophie@codemonkey.com
Subject: re: re: re: re: re: the spins

My martini loves you too.

Sophie sighed and went back to her search. There was a folder called "Clients," with a few hundred messages in it. She typed "tazza" into the search box, but this yielded nothing. "Snuff" brought up twelve results, all unrelated to the box she'd brought to Harry. She tried "Jamnitzer." This brought up one exchange, with a curator at the Met. Harry had asked for a photograph of the master's mark, which the curator had provided. Sophie opened the attachment and saw a slightly blurry photograph of a lion's head in a shield crowned by a W.

She went into his Sent folder and scanned messages sent around the date Harry had made the Jamnitzer inquiry. There was a flurry of giddy exchanges with Jeffrey about their plans to move in together; a weekslong correspondence about a collection of spoons; a rather nasty note to a Dutch curator who had apparently asked him to bid on something at auction, then failed to come up with the funds to pay for it. There was also an apologetic email to someone named Mrs. Hathaway, thanking her for bringing her "very interesting" Coach watch to his attention, and informing her that due to extensive part replacements and regrettable problems with the condition, he would be unable to offer more than eight hundred dollars for the piece.

Sophie frowned and went back to the Clients folder. Hadn't she just seen something with the words "Coach watch" in the subject line? She located the message, which had been sent to Harry a week after his note to Mrs. Hathaway:

From: hbergman@foxrothschild.com
Date: September 8, 2005
To: harry_mcgeorge@yahoo.com
Subject: Louis XIV Coach Watch

Harry,
Thanks again for bringing the watch by my office. It's a magnificent piece. Per our conversation, I'm having my secretary courier a check to you today in the amount of $14K. Please return receipt by same

courier. I'd also appreciate a copy of your dossier on the piece, for
my insurance agent.
Yours truly,
Howard

Harry. The scoundrel. Sophie quickly looked up Howard
Bergman on the Fox Rothschild website; he was a partner
specializing in mergers and acquisitions. There was nothing
remotely nefarious about him; and anyway, the FBI had probably already paid him a visit.

Sophie rubbed her eyes. This exercise wasn't giving her much
she could use. But the hospital website job had been put on hold for
a few weeks, so there wasn't anything to keep her from wandering
as far down this rabbit hole as she could go, other than the nagging
feeling that she shouldn't be snooping in Harry's private messages. Then again, Harry had broken into her house. Fair was fair.

Sophie logged in to her calendar and searched for "NYC." She
wrote down the dates when she had delivered the snuffbox and
the Irish setter, as well as the date Harry had driven to Philadelphia
to pick up the tazza—just before her FBI interview. Then she
returned to Harry's Sent folder and started reading through all the
emails he'd written after receiving the objects. The more she read,
the more she began to understand about Harry's business model.

From: harry_mcgeorge@yahoo.com
Date: November 22, 2005
To: annahoffman@hotmail.com
Subject: Water Pitcher

Dear Ms. Hoffman,
It was a great pleasure to meet you earlier this week. Thank you
for sharing your family's unusual water pitcher with me. While it

is a fine tribute to late-nineteenth-century hammered silverwork, I'm afraid it is not an authentic Tiffany & Co. piece. My research shows several similar examples of pitchers created in the latter half of the twentieth century with fake Tiffany marks. This pitcher, unfortunately, shares many characteristics with those forgeries. My best guess is that it was made in China.

I understand what a disappointment this must be for you; I encourage you to seek a second opinion to confirm my conclusions. In the meantime, I am acquainted with a decorator who happens to be looking for this type of silver for a project she's working on. I would be happy to buy it from you, on her behalf, for $300.

Thank you again for sharing your piece with me; I'm terribly sorry I didn't have more felicitous news.

Warm regards,

Harry McGeorge II

McGeorge & Fils, Antique Silver

A quick search for "Water Pitcher" turned this up:

From: harry_mcgeorge@yahoo.com
Date: November 22, 2005
To: jjgorham@mcneil.com
Subject: call me

Screening your calls, darling? Call me back. I've turned up a Tiffany hammered water pitcher for you. Beautiful condition.
H.

He really was incorrigible. Sophie mulled over the paltry sums Harry had paid for her treasures, then quickly tamped those thoughts down. This was not the kind of revelation she was searching for.

She clicked through email after email, scanning the text for anything remotely related to her pieces. She skipped ahead to the date in January when Harry had come to Philadelphia to pick up the tazza. There was one brief exchange:

From: harry_mcgeorge@yahoo.com
Date: January 9, 2006
To: sergei@secondsight.com
Subject: meeting

I've finally got my hands on something; I think he'll be pleased. Any chance I can talk to him tomorrow or the day after?
Harry

From: sergei@secondsight.com
Date: January 9, 2006
To: harry_mcgeorge@yahoo.com
Subject: re: meeting

Tomorrow. 2 pm.
S.

Sophie squinted at the screen, then rechecked her calendar. The emails had been sent an hour and a half after Harry picked up the tazza in Philadelphia. What else could he possibly be talking about? She did a Whois search on the email address and came up with someone named Sergei Kumarin, living on the Upper East Side. She clicked over to Amtrak.com and bought a ticket to New York.

Twenty

Sergei Kumarin lived in the kind of building where a doorman had to announce you. "He doesn't know me," Sophie said, half hoping she'd be turned away. "We have a mutual friend." But after a quick call the doorman gestured toward the elevator, and in a moment Sophie was standing outside of apartment 7B.

"Hello?" she said, tapping lightly on the door, which stood slightly ajar. Inside, the living room was darkened by thick drapes and a cloud of cigarette smoke. A television flickered, the sound muted.

"Yeah." A large man entered the room, pulling an undershirt over his head, just clearing the cigarette in his mouth. A few long strands of hair lay across his mottled scalp, and his belly surged over the front of his pants. He was wearing slippers.

"Sorry for barging in," Sophie said, disoriented by the contrast between the apartment's address and its occupant. "I'm Marianne." She'd spent the whole morning trying to come up with a name that didn't sound fake. Hearing it out loud, she decided she'd failed.

Sergei beckoned, and she entered the apartment and stood uncertainly in front of the TV while he closed the apartment door, then turned and squinted at her. Sophie hugged her middle, wondering if the door was locked from the inside.

"Tea?"

"No. Thank you."

Sergei shuffled into a small kitchen. "Beer?" he said over his shoulder.

"No."

He emerged with a can of Budweiser in his hand, then gestured toward a small table with two straight-backed chairs. Sophie sat down, and he lowered himself into the other chair with a groan and popped the top of the can open. "Oh wait," he muttered, getting up to turn off the TV.

"Harry McGeorge gave me your address. I hope you don't mind."

"Who are you looking to talk to?" Sergei sat down, lit another cigarette.

"Um, you?"

"Okay, but then who. I'm just the go-between."

Right. The go-between. The fence. Or if Harry was the fence, this was the subfence. One of what was probably a long, tangled string of unsavory characters involved in the dispersal of stolen goods. Sophie had seen *Law and Order*. "All right," she began slowly. "Let's say I have some silver. Sixteenth century, Dutch." She paused. She had no idea how to ask this. "Can you point me toward someone who might be interested?" Sergei had lifted the beer can toward his mouth, but paused midway. "I need to talk to him. Or her. Well, I'm pretty sure it's a him."

Sergei put the can down. "You mean like a former owner?"

"No. Someone who collects. Someone who would want to buy it."

"In this world?"

Sophie waved smoke away from her face. "What?"

"Did you say Harry McGeorge sent you?"

"Yes."

"Seems like you should ask him." Sergei leaned back in his chair, cigarette dangling. "That's his line of work, ain't it?"

"But don't you—don't you work with Harry?"

"Not like that, I don't."

What had Harry's email said? Something about good news, needing to talk to somebody about it. There hadn't actually been any mention of the tazza. Sophie felt sheepish and disoriented, like the victim of a practical joke who hadn't quite come up to speed. "Oh."

Sergei pointed his cigarette at her. "You're here for the same reason the FBI was, ain't ya."

Okay, so she wasn't the only one who could hack into a Yahoo account.

"I told them to get lost," he said. "Goddamned government."

"I'm not from the government," she offered.

"I know." Sergei drained his beer. "You're Sophie." He crumpled the can and got up for another. It seemed to take an eternity for him to shuffle to the kitchen, pull out a beer, and shuffle back to the table. Finally, after sitting and taking a long drink, he said, "You're trying to figure out where Harry fenced your goods."

"Do you know?"

"I told you, that ain't my line of work. Harry came here for a different kind of service."

Sophie wasn't sure she wanted to know what that was. "All right, well, sorry for wasting your time."

"They talked a lot about you."

"Who?"

"Him and his dad."

"Harry's dad? No. He died before I met Harry."

Sergei nodded, drank, then released a sonorous burp. "I put them in touch. I'm the go-between."

"You put Harry in touch...with his dead dad."

"Yeah."

Sophie thought about this a moment, then looked around the shabby, smoke-drenched apartment. No candles. No lamps draped with scarves, no crystal balls. Just a threadbare La-Z-Boy and stacks of newspapers. "You've got to be kidding me."

"I don't exactly do it for fun. Harry Senior's a mean son of a bitch. Makes his kid feel like shit. I keep telling Harry he should talk to some of his nicer relatives, but..." Sergei shrugged. "Fathers. Sons."

"Can I have one of those?"

"Help yourself."

Sophie went to the refrigerator and took a Budweiser.

"Why do you—they—talk about me?"

"They talk business. Harry's dad wants to make sure he's running things right. It was his idea, grooming you. He loved the idea of a curator's wife chiseling."

"Jesus."

Sergei was becoming more animated. "And anyway, Harry Junior really needed you. After his dad died everybody ditched him. His dad tried to teach him how to keep thieves in his pocket, but Harry was too greedy. He always underpaid. Nobody wanted to work with him."

"Except me."

Sergei took a deep drag on his cigarette, then stubbed it out in a beanbag-bottomed ashtray. "Except you. You were supposed to help him make things right with that collector."

"You know about him? The collector?"

"Seems like Harry Senior was working for him before he died. The guy had a big appetite for stolen art. He paid up front for a job at the Cleveland museum—gave Harry Senior a shopping list. But the thieves fucked it up, didn't get anything. The collector didn't want his money back, though—he wanted the goods." Sergei lit another cigarette. "He still wants the goods."

"So I gather."

"Harry Senior died right after. I guess the stress got him. He's a very tightly wound son of a bitch. He won't rest until Harry Junior makes things right with this collector. I guess he's a good customer. Important to the business."

Sophie drank her beer, mulling it all over. What was Sergei's angle in all this? Was he working for the collector, pushing Harry to deliver the "goods"?

"Was it Harry Senior's idea to blackmail me?" she asked.

"To hide the piece in your house?" Sergei gave her a slow smile. "Yeah. That was cute, wadn't it."

"Goddamn it," Sophie cried. "Do you know what I did to my house, looking for that bowl? Couldn't you have come up with something more...conventional?"

"I told you," Sergei said loudly. "I'm the go-between." He crumpled his beer can. "Don't shoot the goddamned messenger."

"Please. You're manipulating Harry. He's got issues, and you're taking advantage of it. If you ask me, that's a shitty way to make a living."

Sergei reached over and grabbed her hand, squeezing it hard. Sophie tried to pull it away but he wouldn't let her. "Nobody makes Harry come here," he said. "He needs time with his dad, I give it to him. I don't like it—I fuckin' hate it—but if that's what he needs, it's what he needs." He released her hand.

"Fine," Sophie said, rubbing her hand and trying to breathe normally. "So can you tell me who the collector is, or not?"

"No. They never use his name." Sophie got up to leave, but Sergei stayed seated, leaning back in his chair. "What about you?" he said.

"What?"

"You want to talk to your dad?"

Sophie stared at him.

"Anything you wish you'd told him? Anything you want to ask?"

Sophie felt a rush of love for Harry then, with his freckles and his nervous knuckles and his face pressed against the bars of boyhood. Maybe it would do him some good to spend time away from this charlatan. See how it felt to be free from the past.

"It's too late for that," she said, walking to the door.

"Randall could have something to say about your mother's whereabouts. You never know."

Sophie paused, turned. Sergei had disappeared into the kitchen. She shook her head and left the apartment, plunging into the hallway's bracing rush of clean air.

⚜

Sophie strode furiously down Eighty-Fourth Street. When she got to Lexington, instead of turning toward the Eighty-Sixth Street subway entrance, she kept going west, toward the park. She wasn't ready to go underground. She needed to breathe.

Sergei knew too much—about the business with the collector, about her. Was he engineering the whole operation, and somehow funneling the proceeds into his own pockets? Or was he just milking Harry's constant need for conversations with his father? Either way, it was sick—Sergei clearly enjoyed playing the role of the abusive authority figure, watching Harry dance like a puppet on a string. Just like that last comment he'd made, about Sophie's parents. He loved messing with people's minds.

Sophie stopped at the corner of Fifth Avenue, the Met to her left, the park to her right. She hadn't been in the museum since that day with Harry, when he'd given her the tour of the

Nuremberg gold and silver. It was one of her fondest memories of him, even now that she knew he'd been "grooming" her, per the instructions of some chain-smoking fortune-teller. They'd had a good time, the two of them, wandering the galleries, Harry going on and on about the Habsburgs and their treasuries, Sophie taking it all in.

She climbed the steps, zigzagging around encampments of students, lovers, and exhausted tourists, and found her way through the entrance hall and into the Renaissance galleries. Browsing the cases again—seeing the cups and plates, the tankards and ewers—brought memories of that day into sharper focus. Harry had been so inspired, holding forth on the fluidity of the forms, the lyrical expressiveness of the motifs, the chasing, the etching. She remembered how he'd explained fire gilding, which involved mixing mercury and gold, then evaporating the mercury into the air. "Every last one of 'em got mercury poisoning," he'd said darkly. "They turned all twitchy and mad." Then he launched into a flailing, yelping imitation of a poisoned goldsmith, lurching across the floor, Sophie laughing and begging him to stop; it was awful, people were staring, but he'd kept going, dragging his left leg into the period rooms.

Harry. This was where he belonged—among the art, immersed in beauty. Not in the shadows of his father's murky, rotten world. Maybe she could persuade him to go straight, turn the shop into a real business. He had the connections and the know-how; he just needed a little help with the business side. Maybe a website.

Sophie found herself standing in front of the case with the silver ginger jars. "Anonymous Loan," the label said. A number of thoughts snapped together in her mind. Didn't Harry say he knew the donor who gave these? A client of his father's— someone with terrible manners? She frowned, pulled out her phone, and took a photo of the label. Here, at least, was a piece of information the FBI didn't have. She'd look up the accession number on the museum website later, see if it led anywhere. After the day she'd had, anything seemed possible.

⁂

Marjorie looked almost comical sitting on the tall stool at the coffee shop, her feet barely reaching the footrest, her square bag standing pertly on the tabletop. "I don't know why you feel like you have to explain yourself to me, of all people," she grumbled. "What I think doesn't matter."

"I know. Well—I mean, of course it matters." Sophie batted some stray hairs away from her eyes. "But I'm actually not here to explain myself. I need your help."

"You need *my* help?"

"I think I can figure out where the objects are. You know, the missing objects." Sophie locked eyes with Marjorie for a moment, then dropped her gaze.

"Shouldn't you be talking to the police instead of me?"

"The FBI? Maybe." She'd already picked up the phone a dozen times, then put it back down, feeling silly about playing detective, realizing she didn't have anything substantive to report. Yet. "I just want to make sure I'm right about this before I talk to anyone."

"I really think you should go to the police. I don't want to have anything to do with this."

"The FBI. I know. But, Marjorie…" Sophie placed a hand on her chest. "I need to do this myself. I've done something terrible—unforgivable. But I think I've been given a chance to, you know, redeem myself. At least, to the extent that redemption is, uh, possible."

"Ha!" Marjorie rolled her eyes.

"You can help me," Sophie said, reaching for Marjorie's hand, which was quickly withdrawn. "You have connections, you know how things work. Your registrar experience is… indispensable. I know the museum doesn't appreciate that."

Marjorie blinked at her.

"And you have connections with the Met. That's key."

"I do?"

"Your friend Helen? I met her at the One Big Family party."

"Oh, Helen. Right."

"You said she volunteers for the Met registrar."

"Yes. She doesn't have actual staff experience, like I do, but yes, she's been there, I don't know, ten years now." Marjorie sniffed. "Sort of a junior volunteer."

"I was hoping you could ask her to find out some information about a Met donor. An anonymous donor. I would just need a name and home address."

"Oh, no, I don't—" Marjorie squinted her eyes as if trying to read a faraway vision chart. "Why would you need that?"

Sophie leaned forward. "I know I don't need to tell you how these things work—the world of collectors, their egos, their insurance schemes."

"Oh, the insurance schemes." Marjorie rolled her eyes.

"It's all connected," Sophie continued in a low voice, circling her forefingers around each other, mysteriously. "And there's a chance it could lead me to the guy who's been buying our museum's treasures."

"Oh, you definitely need to go to the police."

"FBI." Sophie sighed deeply. "Let me tell you something about the FBI, Marjorie."

"What?"

"They do not appreciate art."

Marjorie waved her hand dismissively. "Oh, no, I'm sure that's—"

"They care about drugs, they care about kidnapped children." She lowered her voice. "Pornography. But art is very low on the list of priorities." Sophie paused, sending a silent apology to Agent Chandler. "They've had many opportunities to find this collector and recover our objects, but do you honestly think they're putting their best people on the case? I have given them so much information. So many leads. And nothing."

Marjorie pursed her lips. "Well, I have to say I was shocked by the light sentence they gave that British dealer. It's true that people have no appreciation. No appreciation at all."

Sophie nodded solemnly. "And like you've always said, sometimes you have to take things into your own hands. Otherwise nothing will get done." She pulled a small piece of paper out of her pocket and slid it across the table.

"Here's an accession number. I need to get in touch with the donor. Ask Helen for his name and address," Sophie said. "That's all I need."

❧

Harry had been moved to a low-security federal prison in a town called White Deer, Pennsylvania. Sophie drove up to see him on one of those clear fall days that made the world seem freshly washed and dried on a line, green leaves still mixed in with the yellow and red, barns standing neat and square against billowing hills. Harry tried to pretend he wasn't happy to see her.

"I'm kind of busy," he said. "Those pot holders aren't going to make themselves."

"You look good, Harry." He'd filled out a bit, his eyes less sunken and dull, his cheekbones less sharp.

"Thanks. You know what they say. Khaki is the new khaki."

On the drive up, Sophie had debated whether to tell him about her visit to Sergei. Seeing him now, looking more like his old self despite the shapeless polyester clothes, she decided not to embarrass him. Instead she chatted about Philadelphia, Carly's condo, her work. Harry complained about prison food and prison furniture and prison lighting, but he also said he was getting daily letters from Jeffrey, who'd decided he enjoyed the romantic possibilities of Harry's incarceration. "Did you know California just approved same-sex conjugal visits?" he exclaimed. "I need to put in for a transfer. This is not the sexual wonderland I was led to expect."

"So that's why you were so intent on going to prison."

"Ha."

"Harry," Sophie said then, reaching across the table to take his hand. "You can still talk, you know. They can probably clear the charges. You could go legit, get your shop back up and running, maybe start fresh in a different location. Get back together with Jeffrey? Wouldn't you be happier?"

Harry pulled his hand away, turned somber. "No."

"Goddamn it, Harry." Sophie threw herself back in her chair, crossing her arms. He was like Elliot, refusing to listen. When would he learn that she knew what was best for him? She was so tired of all the manipulation.

"Yoshiro Hansei," she said.

Harry cracked his knuckles, looked around.

"Nineteen Gramercy Park South?" Sophie watched Harry's jaw work back and forth. "It's him, isn't it—I can tell!" She laughed, then slapped a hand over her mouth.

"Just—" Harry held up his palm. "Where are you going with this."

"Your collector—your precious client. I'm giving you a

chance to be the one who takes him down. A chance to get out of here. Call Chandler, tell him about Hansei." She paused. "Or I will."

"Sophie, I can't. I can't do that to one of my biggest clients. I'd never do business again. And my dad—it would kill him. I mean, you know what I mean."

"Oh, Harry, cut that out. Your father is *dead*, all right? This is your chance to start fresh, turn your life around, let go of the shame."

"Shame?" Harry laughed. "You think I'm ashamed?" He rolled his eyes dramatically. "Look around yourself. You think the museum pays a fair price for everything they acquire? They pay what they think they can get away with—even if it's highway robbery. And what about all that art that turned up on the market after 1945. You think the museums sat on their hands, saying, 'Oh, no, that would make us feel ashamed'?"

"They're giving that stuff back."

"When they're made to. My point is, everybody's on the take, Sophie. Banks. The bloody government. Your friend who likes other people's husbands. How are you supposed to survive in a world like that, if you're not taking the opportunities that present themselves?"

"I tried that. It didn't work out so well."

"You didn't exactly distinguish yourself as a thief. Rule number one: thou shalt not snitch."

"Okay, okay." Sophie felt confused. She'd expected Harry to congratulate her on her detective work, realize he had no choice but to roll over on Hansei, then thank her for escorting him onto the path to righteousness. "Look," she said slowly, "all I really want is to get that mirror back. The museum didn't realize they had it; if I can get it back to Brian, he can return it to the department without anyone noticing. It's not enough, but it's something. I need to do something."

"Well, I'm afraid I can't get it for you. My schedule's full for the next thirty months."

Sophie sighed, tapping her foot. "Does Hansei keep the stuff at his house?"

"Most of it, yes."

"Does he use a cleaning service? Or I don't know—an IT consultant?"

"I have no bleeding idea, Sophie. I've only been to his house once, and it was like Fort Knox. I don't know what you're thinking, but you can't get in there."

She thought a minute. "What about kids? Does he have kids?"

Harry pressed his knuckles into his palm. "Yeah. Two little ones, like yours. No mum around, just a nanny."

"Perfect. Do you know their names?"

"Jesus, I can't even remember the names of my brother's kids."

"That's all right. It's good, it's a start. Thank you, Harry."

"Look, Sophie, I don't know what you're thinking, but please don't screw things up for me, all right? You're making me nervous."

"Don't worry. I have a talent—remember?"

Harry bit his lip, then leaned forward. "Just promise you'll be careful. I don't want this coming back to me, but I also don't want anything happening to you."

"Why, Harry, that's so sweet."

"Yeah, well." He gave her a sly smile. "Maybe when I get out we can have another go. Like old times. What do you say, love?"

"Oh my God, Harry. Good-bye."

"Be safe, Sophie."

"I'll try."

Twenty-One

S ophie's rear was freezing, but she willed herself to stay a little longer on the brownstone stoop. In five minutes, she decided, she could have her sandwich. She'd eat slowly, to take up time.

She'd been sitting on this stoop, and others like it, all morning, because the gates on all four sides of Gramercy Park were locked. Inside the iron fence she could see thick black tree trunks and long branches crouching over some comfortable-looking wooden benches. A gardener gathered fallen leaves from the tops of some carefully pruned boxwoods, but otherwise the park was empty. She wondered what time it was supposed to open.

She stole another glance at the brick house on the corner of Twentieth and Irving. It was, she'd decided, the most beautiful house in New York, with its stately air of restraint, its massive proportions tempered by a soberly geometric facade. Four rows of neatly trimmed windows marched up the brick walls, crowned by a string of sturdy corbels. Above the cornice a row of hooded dormer windows peeked out of a slate mansard roof, interspersed with three proud chimneys. The roofline was crested with lacy ironwork, and above the ironwork, like flames leaping into the sky, Sophie could see the red-leafed branches of some large trees growing in a rooftop garden.

So far she hadn't seen anyone coming or going from the house. For all she knew, the Hanseis were on vacation and she was sitting there for nothing. She looked at her watch and pulled out her sandwich, then noticed a squat woman in a barn jacket unlocking one of the gates to the park. Sophie hurried across the street.

"Sorry," said the woman, giving Sophie a sharp look. "It's a private park. Only residents have keys."

Sophie laughed in surprise. "Oh! Do you mind if I follow you in? I just want to sit and eat my lunch." She lifted the sandwich in explanation.

"Sorry," the woman said again, closing the gate and locking it behind her. "It's against the rules. And anyway, there's no food allowed."

Sophie let the bag drop, feeling her listless mood sink lower. This was why she'd never wanted to live in New York. This right here: this gorgeously manicured park, with its gilded ceiling of autumn leaves, its plush grass carpets unstained by orange peels or wayward napkins, proudly on display yet impenetrable to all but a select few. In this city, you always lived with your face pressed up against someone else's window.

Sophie returned to the stoop and ate her sandwich quickly, half expecting the woman in the barn jacket to appear and shoo her away. Brian had always said that someday he would like to work at the Met, but Sophie had never encouraged him to act on those fantasies. They would never be able to afford a decent amount of space in Manhattan, and she knew that adding a commute to Brian's life would result in the working parent's nightmare: getting home every night after the kids' bedtime. Of course, considering everything that had happened, a job at the Met was probably no longer within the realm of possibility.

The sandwich gone, Sophie rubbed her hands together and

considered walking to a coffee shop to warm up. That thought led to thoughts of walking to Park Avenue and catching a cab to the train station. Her fact-finding mission had begun to feel more like impotent loitering, and anyway, she wasn't sure what facts she was expecting to find. It would be easier to just go home and call Agent Chandler.

Still, her mind kept turning back to the mirror. Nobody knew it was missing; nobody even knew it existed. It was right there, within those brick walls. She felt an intense need to hold it in her hands again, to slip it back into the museum, as if it could reverse time and events. She couldn't retreat to the carpeted hush of Carly's apartment without trying something. Anything.

She stood up. She'd just ring the doorbell, ask to use the bathroom; she could improvise from there. She strode toward Irving Place and stood at the corner waiting for the light to change, her sights set on the imposing double doors flanked by curved brass handrails. Then, from the corner of her eye, she noticed some movement on the Twentieth Street side of the house. A mass of frizzy curls was slowly coming up a small stairway that led from a basement entrance, dragging something heavy. The curls belonged to a young woman; she was pulling a wide double stroller. She left it on the sidewalk, then descended the stairs again, reappearing with two small, black-haired children, whom she strapped into the stroller with practiced efficiency.

Sophie waited until the woman had pushed the stroller past her up Twentieth Street, then turned and followed. They walked to Park Avenue, turned right, then left onto Twenty-First Street. It took some effort to stay behind the woman, who was slowed by the weight she was pushing, but Sophie matched her pace, trying to look like she was taking a leisurely stroll around the neighborhood. Finally the woman stopped in front of a limestone apartment building with a shop window on the first floor, and bent down to unstrap the kids. Sophie ambled past, reading the bright red awning with an inward groan.

Music for Me.

⁂

1. *I'm sure you got word about the conviction. We'll see what happens with sentencing; I heard they want Michael to testify at the hearing. I hope you'll be able to go back to work soon.*
2. *Goldmeier wants to get together next week to go over our legal options. Can you come see him on your lunch hour? Say, Tuesday?*
3. *Carly thinks she found me an investor to help get my database idea off the ground. I'm meeting with him next week to show him some wireframes, and go over my business plan. I'm pretty nervous/excited about that.*
4. *If it's all right with you, I'd like to take the kids to New York on Thursday. I've been missing them, and I thought it would be fun to go to the Museum of Natural History. Elliot's into dinosaurs these days.*
5. *I miss you. I want to make things right. I'm trying.*

This time, when she handed the notebook to Brian on the doorstep, once the kids had run inside, he sighed and let his arm drop heavily. "Thanks."

"What?"

He looked sideways and up, into the ginkgo tree, then let his gaze fall back to the sidewalk. "Nothing. I'll see you in a few days."

"Seriously, Brian."

Brian held out the notebook as if it were incriminating

evidence. "This is nice and all, but don't you ever think it would be good to, you know—"

"What?"

"Talk?"

"Talk!" Sophie laughed. "You never want to talk."

"No, *you* never want to talk."

Sophie jerked her head back with a furrowed squint. "I want to talk. I love talking."

"No, you don't."

"Yes, I do. I love it. This right here, what we're doing right now, I love it."

"Okay then."

"What?"

"Let's…" Brian waved the notebook around in circles.

"What, out here?"

Brian shrugged and pushed the front door open. Sophie brushed past him into the living room, where she sat, like a guest, on the edge of the sofa. Brian sank into one of the armchairs across from her.

"So what do you want to talk about?" she asked him, a smile escaping, momentarily, from her tense lips.

"Very funny."

"Let's hear it then. You hate me."

"Christ." Brian rubbed his mouth. "Okay, a little. But no, not hate, really, just…what the hell, Sophie? How could you do this to the people you—supposedly—love?"

"I don't know." Sophie bent forward, tucking her hands between her belly and her thighs. She realized this was the first time Brian had asked her, point-blank, to explain herself. She also realized she hadn't prepared an answer. "I guess…I thought, I don't know. This house was the key to everything. I thought it would keep me from becoming someone I didn't want to be." She paused. "Someone like my mother." Brian was look-ing at her with his usual nonexpressive expression. "I thought it would give our kids a better life. And when it looked like it was going to be taken away, I couldn't think about anything else. I was fixated on the house." She straightened up, avoiding Brian's gaze. "The wrong thing." She was still holding back... still tightly wrapped around her darkest secret—the thing that "filled the hole," as Harry put it.

"I just feel like we could've avoided all this if you had included me," Brian said. "If you'd told me what was going on. If you'd asked for help. Now I feel like an idiot."

"I'm so, so sorry." Sophie wanted to reach out to him, but she didn't. "I was trying to protect you. I was trying to just take care of things, to fix things so you wouldn't have to worry." Brian pulled the corner of his mouth ever so slightly to one side. "And okay, yes, I was ashamed," Sophie continued. "I didn't want you to know how royally I'd screwed up. It's not easy, you know. Being married to Mr. Perfect. While my career falls apart. While my life turns into something I wasn't ready for. Always feeding someone, cleaning up after someone, carrying someone, wishing someone would carry me for a change, wishing I could just do some work—*my* work, the work I'm actually good at. Blah blah blah, the oldest story in the book. Everybody goes through it, but I'm the only one who used it as an excuse to sabotage my entire life." She hiccupped, and tears came in a gush—dammit! Again with the tears! But her frustration only made them come harder, and soon she was sobbing into her hands.

"Mommy?" Lucy and Elliot were standing in front of her, identical worried expressions on their faces. Lucy patted her knee. "Are you okay, Mommy?"

"Oh, Lucy," Sophie cried. "Elliot. I'm okay. I'm sorry, don't worry. I'm just having a bad day." She pulled them onto the couch, kissing their heads and breathing in their salty-sweet scent. The weight of them against her, the clambering jabs of elbows and knees, the heat of their high-pitched breath against her neck—it was what she needed; it was what she'd always needed. She'd been so focused on the giving, she'd completely forgotten about the taking. She looked over the children's heads at Brian, who seemed almost on the verge of a smile. "I hope you know how much I love you," she said. "I hope you all know."

Taking the kids to New York on the train by herself was doable; taking the stroller along with them was another story. In Philadelphia, at least, a redcap let her take an elevator to the train platform, but then she had to put the kids on the train ahead of her, ordering them to stand motionless by the door while she fought her way through boarding passengers to retrieve the folded stroller from the platform and hoist it into the narrow luggage compartment at the front of the car. In New York the elevator wasn't working, so she had to hold Elliot in one arm and the stroller in the other, leaving Lucy to fend for herself as they rode the narrow, crowded escalator up into the station. Taking the subway uptown, she realized, was not an option, given the obstacle course of turnstiles and stairs. So they stood in the Eighth Avenue cab line for twenty minutes, Elliot strapped into his seat against his will, unmoved by promises of dinosaurs, Lucy dancing all over the sidewalk, touching everything.

The three of them relaxed once they arrived at the American Museum of Natural History, a stroller-friendly haven busy with children in various stages of joy, exhaustion, and outrage. They wandered through the dinosaur halls, where Sophie did her best to read some of the labels, causing Lucy and Elliot, bristling with impatience, to abandon the stroller and run ahead, rushing through the Eocene, Cretaceous, and Jurassic periods with the impetuousness of creatures who have only been on Earth for five and three years.

After lunch, Sophie announced that she had a surprise for them: they were going to Music for Me! In New York! But the kids received this astonishing news with mere shrugs, probably imagining, quite reasonably, that New York and Philadelphia were part of the same vast metropolis, and that it was perfectly normal to find Barnes and Noble, the Lego store, and Music for Me just around the next corner.

She'd signed them up for the same early-afternoon session she'd seen Hansei's nanny go to: Rhythm Makes Me Happy! Sophie had often taken the kids to Rhythm Makes Me Happy! in Philadelphia, but she'd never personally experienced actual happiness during the class—just irritation, existential angst, and a rhythmically pounding headache.

She had the cab drop them a few blocks north of Twenty-First Street, then walked the kids the rest of the way in the stroller. When they arrived she could see the curly-haired nanny with her two small charges already inside, sitting on the rug. Sophie hurriedly parked the stroller, then ushered Lucy and Elliot toward the spot just next to them. As the teacher began strumming the familiar tune to "Good Morning, Farmer George," Sophie grabbed a maraca and began shaking it with brio, singing the words she could—and probably, on occasion, did—sing in her sleep. Lucy and Elliot, inspired by her sudden enthusiasm, sang and clapped loudly; Lucy even twirled around a few times in the center of the circle.

Afterward, Sophie followed the nanny outside and popped open her stroller next to hers. "That was so fun," she exclaimed. "Your kids have great rhythm."

The nanny looked up with surprise, her face pillowy with

youth. "Oh, they're not my kids," she laughed. "I'm just the nanny. But thanks, I guess."

"Have you guys been coming to this class for a while?"

"Oh, sure. Well, they've been coming since last year. But I literally grew up coming to Music for Me. My mom used to bring me and my sister. My sister didn't like it, though, so my mom would leave her in front of the TV and bring me because if I didn't get to go she said I would literally drive her nuts."

Sophie smiled at her, a little dazed by this flood of information, then bent down to greet the two children in their stroller. "Did you like that class? Was it fun?" The girl nodded solemnly, but the boy squirmed and turned his face away. "This is Lucy and Elliot," Sophie said, turning her stroller to bring the kids face-to-face. "They're about your age, I think."

"This is Mina and Takashi. Say hi, guys." The four kids looked blankly at each other. "They don't spend a lot of time with other kids," said the nanny. "That's why I've been bringing them here. They don't go to preschool or anything. Their dad's kind of a control freak. I mean, I don't mean that in a negative way or anything, he's great, but sometimes, you know, I think kids need to socialize a little. I try to keep them entertained and all, but I'm probably pretty boring. To a four-year-old."

"I'm Sophie, by the way."

"I'm Becca." She wiped a hand on her jeans and offered it to Sophie. "Nice to meet you. I guess we should go—we're creating a traffic jam." Annoyed-looking pedestrians were piling up behind the strollers. Becca turned toward Park Avenue.

"We'll walk with you," Sophie blurted, wrestling her stroller around to follow Becca. "We're going this way." She walked behind Becca's bobbing curls until they got to Park Avenue, whose sidewalks were wide enough to accommodate the strollers side-by-side. "So how long have you been their nanny?"

"About a year I guess. I started last fall. I was a camp coun-selor all summer, then I took a break for a few weeks 'cause I was burned out, and then I literally went broke so I started answering nanny ads. This is really just a way to make money while I work on my writing. I'm going to be a writer some-day. I mean, I already am one, just nobody knows it." Sophie nodded and smiled, doing her best to seem politely interested in a noncreepy way as Becca continued rambling from subject to subject. Eventually they pulled up in front of the Gramercy Park mansion, where Becca stood, still talking about her writing, her boyfriend, and her night classes at CUNY, for another fifteen minutes. "Well, anyways," she finally said, gesturing toward the house, "this is us."

"You live here?"

"Yeah, he gave me a room on the fifth floor, and there is no elevator, so you'd think I wouldn't have these thighs, ha-ha."

Sophie craned her neck to see the fifth floor, then looked back at Becca. "What would you think about having a play-date? It seems like they all get along really well." She pulled back the sunshade so she could see Elliot and Lucy. They were fast asleep.

"Mmm…." Becca's lips momentarily disappeared inside her mouth. "I'm not supposed to have anybody over. Their dad is such a control freak about stuff like that. Like, this is literally the only park we're allowed to go to." She nodded toward Gramercy Park's iron fence. "I honestly think he bought the house just for the park key. Doesn't want them mixing with the riffraff. Not that you're riffraff, of course, but you know. He's strict."

Sophie felt the day's investments—the train, the singing, the nap-deprived kids—on the verge of evaporation. Her mind rifled through Becca's previous monologue, searching for something to use. "Do you think I could check out your writing sometime? Do you have a blog?"

"Oh, gosh, no. I would have no idea how to—"

"No blog?" Sophie widened her eyes. "Every self-respecting writer has one. It's how people get discovered these days. Seriously, you can't not have a blog."

"Really?" Becca pulled a strand of her hair straight, then let it spring back. "I guess you're right. I should get one. Or make one or whatever."

Sophie leaned on the stroller handle, gazed into the distance. "You know…"

"What?"

"I'm not doing anything this afternoon. I could set it up for you. But I understand if you're not allowed to have anyone over."

"You know how to do that?"

"I'm a web developer."

"Oh my gosh!"

"Is their dad home? Maybe the kids can play a little while I set it up, then we'll be on our way."

"No, he's not home…"

"I mean—if this is really what you want to do," Sophie said. "Be a writer. Because if that's really your dream, then you have to just do it. You won't always have this kind of time. This…passion." Sophie took a deep breath. "Don't let it go to waste."

"Wow." Becca wound another strand of hair around her finger. "Maybe we can do it on my day off? Are you around this Sunday? We could go to Starbucks or something."

"Sunday." Sophie drummed her fingers against her lips. "Oh, you know what, I'm out of town."

"Oh."

"I'm sure you can set it up yourself," Sophie said brightly.

"Just decide which open-source CMS you like best, like Movable Type, or Blosxom if you'd rather work in Perl. I'm really liking WordPress, now that widgets are included by default in the core code."

Becca blinked at her.

"I'm sure you can figure it out." Sophie picked her diaper bag off the sidewalk, slinging it over a shoulder.

"I guess I can try." Becca fiddled with her stroller brake, then cocked her head and gave Sophie a wavering smile. "Oh, who am I kidding?"

Inside the townhouse, Becca showed Sophie a closet under the main staircase where she could put the stroller and pulled out a basket of white cotton slippers. "Can I keep these?" asked Lucy, rubbing the sleep out of her eyes, when Becca handed her a tiny pair.

"No," said Sophie.

"Yes!" laughed Becca. "Come on, let's have a snack first. The kitchen's down here."

Sophie scuffed slowly down the corridor, peering into a series of formal rooms while the kids, energized by the thought of snacks, ran ahead. The house was like an oyster shell: the walls and floors, darkly textured with complicated woodwork, were lined with gleaming white upholstery, rugs, and furniture. The tall windows were shuttered at the bottom with dark wood, while light fell through the upper panes in blinding quantities.

Becca led them through a heavily carved door to the back staircase. They filed down the steps and into the kitchen, which was long and low-ceilinged, with two blocky marble islands in the center of the room, the air sweetly perfumed with sesame oil.

"Danny!" cried Mina and Takashi, running toward a wiry man who stood chopping vegetables at one of the islands.

"Hey, guys," he said, handing each of them a slice of red bell pepper, which they devoured. Sophie felt a twinge of jealousy. Her kids would never touch a red pepper.

"Hello," he said with a nod to Sophie.

"We're here for snacks," Becca said. Danny thoughtfully pressed his bottom lip upward for a second, narrowing his eyes almost imperceptibly at Becca, then gave Sophie a swift smile and resumed chopping.

"What?" Becca said. "It's just for a little while. Everybody come sit." She slid into a banquette that curved around a large round table at the far end of the room.

They sat, and Danny brought them a tray of colorful, doughy-looking balls. Lucy frowned at the balls, then turned to Mina. "Is he your daddy?"

Mina laughed, popping one of the balls into her mouth. "No, silly. He's my *Danny*."

"Danny cooks for us," said Becca, pushing the tray toward Lucy. "Wagashi?"

Lucy shook her head vigorously. Danny reappeared, this time with a bowl of Goldfish crackers, which Lucy and Elliot began scooping out of the bowl like ravenous bears.

"Danny keeps telling me I'm going to get in trouble," said Becca, sticking her tongue out at him. "He says I'm careless."

Danny walked back to the chopping board without responding.

"Nice artwork," Sophie said, looking around the walls of the eating area, which were covered from floor to ceiling in framed pictures drawn, apparently, by Mina and Takashi.

"Their dad literally frames everything they draw," said Becca, pushing the tray toward Sophie. "He's really into art." Sophie took one of the balls, which was starchy and subtly sweet. She pinched off a piece and tried to interest Elliot in tasting it, but he remained focused on the Goldfish.

After the snack, Becca led them up the dizzying central

staircase to the third floor. "We can hang out in here," she said, breathless from the climb. "Can you believe this playroom?" They entered a ballroom-size space lined with dark wood shelves and cabinets neatly stocked with baskets of toys. The high front windows looked out over the park; under Sophie's slippered feet a plush, pale green carpet fit perfectly within the wood floor's inlaid border. While Becca went to get her laptop, Sophie wandered around the room, peeking into cabinets and admiring the toys, which were the expensive European kind—sleek and glossy, cleverly crafted of wood and enameled tin. There was a sumptuously painted Noah's ark, with dozens of carved animals; an Italianate dollhouse strikingly similar to the house they were in; a bin filled with nothing but windup robots. One set of shelves displayed an impressive collection of vintage toy fire trucks. It was foolish, Sophie decided, to feel jealous of two small children. But the fact that they probably weren't even aware of their privilege, had never been afforded the opportunity of comparison, somehow made it worse. She combed her fingers along the carved fluting of one of the wooden pillars that edged the cabinetry, wondering if it was original.

"Let's sit over here," Becca said when she reappeared with her computer. Sophie joined her on a love seat and went to work setting up a new WordPress account. She showed Becca how to pick a theme, post a new entry, assign tags, and manage comments. "It's really not that complicated. Just make sure you post a lot, to keep your readers interested. Do you want to learn how to add pictures?" While she led Becca through the process, finding photos on her hard drive, uploading them, and writing captions, Sophie's mind worked its way toward her next move. Maybe she would ask for a tour, or sneak away during a trip to the bathroom. She needed to get a look at the rest of the house.

Elliot had found a wooden train set and was methodically

assembling track, but Lucy, after pawing breathlessly through several toy baskets, had apparently become paralyzed by the number of choices. Now she was pressing herself against Sophie's knees, staring at her over the screen of the laptop. "I'm bored."

"You're bored. In the world's most fabulous playroom. That's the most ridiculous…" Sophie trailed off, then set the computer aside. "How about a game of hide-and-seek?"

"I love hide-and-seek!" cried Becca.

"I'll count," Sophie said. "Elliot, you can stay with me. Everybody else go hide."

After counting slowly, to give everyone a chance to run to the furthest corners of the house, Sophie carried Elliot from room to room, whispering, "Do you think they're in here?" as she peeked inside closets and chests and wardrobes. "What about here?" she said, sliding open a desk drawer in a small study.

"Nooooo Mommy! Too small."

"Here?" She eased open a filing cabinet.

"Maybe."

The house was impressively absent of clutter, and most of the walls were bare. In the drawers and cabinets she found neatly organized files and office supplies, but nothing resembling a work of art. She checked the kids' rooms, the minimally furnished master bedroom, a small gym. She went downstairs and searched quickly through a media room and a sitting room, then pushed through a pair of double doors to find herself in the cavernous shadows of a large library.

Darkly furnished with leather sofas and club chairs, the room was lined with mahogany shelves tightly packed with books. Here and there, glass-fronted cabinets glowed among the bookbindings. Behind the glass, like babies in incubators, shapely objects gleamed under recessed lights: vases, statues, chalices. Sophie's eyes skittered across the shelves. Bowls, more vases, a jeweled dagger.

Elliot pointed to a corner of the room. Sophie heard giggling, but couldn't tell where it was coming from. She walked toward the sound. In the shadows, where the shelves met the wall, a narrow, nearly invisible door was tucked into the woodwork. She ran her hand down its edge, finding a recessed metal plate. With a light push, the door slid behind the bookshelves.

"You found us!" shrieked Lucy, Mina, and Takashi.

"What is this?" Setting Elliot on the floor, Sophie entered a windowless room, about the size of a generous walk-in closet. A low-slung swivel chair occupied the center of the floor. All around, from floor to ceiling, the dove-gray walls were covered, in the same jigsaw manner as the kitchen walls, with paintings. Taking in the mosaic of thinly crackled portraits, lush landscapes, and dark religious scenes, Sophie felt her eyes choking on the overly rich, unexpected feast.

"It's the hiding place," Mina said.

The children were clustered in front of a low, utilitarian glass case. Sophie crouched, gently pushing Lucy aside. The glass shelves were lined with objects: a golden stag; a set of enamel boxes; a strikingly familiar silver tazza. In the middle of the top shelf, its glass a winking oval of light, stood the Jamnitzer mirror. Sophie sucked in her breath. She'd forgotten how beautiful it was.

"Found you," she whispered.

"You guys?" Becca's voice floated faintly from another part of the house.

Sophie stood up. "I don't think we're supposed to be—"

"In here!" shouted Mina and Takashi, jumping up and down. "We're in the hiding place!"

Becca's face appeared in the doorway, her youthful features sharpened by worry. "Oh geez, what are you doing in here?

Everybody out. Mina, Takashi, you should know better. Oh my God." She shooed them into the library, where Mina and Takashi started chasing Lucy around the sofas, giggling wildly. Becca waved her hands at them, frantically shushing. Then, somewhere deep in the house, a heavy door thudded shut.

"Daddy!" cried Mina and Takashi, running into the hallway.

Becca wiped her upper lip with a shaking hand. "Okay. Okay. Oh my God. Okay."

"Becca." Sophie put a hand on her arm. "What's wrong? Are you sure that's him?"

"Nobody else would come in the front door like that. Crap. I'm so dead."

"It's fine, we'll just wait in there." Sophie pointed toward the hidden room. She used her extra-calm, mother-in-a-crisis voice. "You come tell us when the coast is clear, and we'll zip out the front door. He'll never know we were here. I promise." The voice seemed to be working on Becca. She nodded, put her hand to her forehead, briefly closing her eyes, then hurried after the kids.

Back inside the hidden room, Sophie set Elliot in the chair and gave Lucy a quick squeeze. "Let's be quiet, okay?" she whispered. "We're playing hide-and-seek with Mina and Takashi's daddy now." Lucy nodded with a sly smile. Sophie went to the door and put her ear against it. She heard Becca's chattering voice come close and then recede.

Sophie turned; the wall to her left was dominated by a large, dark picture of a ship in a storm. Tiny contorted men clung to the heaving boat. The rabidly foaming waves; the whipping clouds; the torn sail lashing a timid beam of light...the scene was troublingly familiar to her, although she didn't know why. As she stared at it, she could almost hear the crack of the violently flapping sail as it threatened to knock the sailors into the water's black depths.

Maybe Harry was right: they were all just thieves stealing from thieves. Who could ever know where the mirror had come from in the first place—how often had it been bought, sold, stolen, bestowed, lost, found, treasured, ignored. On the subject of provenance, the mirror was silent. The only truth it could tell was the artistry of its maker, the deftness of his hand, the whimsy of his mind. She slid open the glass cabinet, pulled out the mirror, and turned it over to look at the maker's mark: a proud W hovering above the head of a fierce lion. "This is mine," the mark seemed to growl.

"What are you doing?" Becca was standing in the doorway, her mouth puckered with worry. "Put that back!"

"This belongs to someone I know," Sophie said, clutching the mirror to her belly. "I'm taking it with me."

"You can't!" Becca gasped. "Put it back! He's upstairs now—you have to go."

"We're going," Sophie said, clumsily lifting Elliot out of the chair with her free arm. Becca reached out to grab the mirror, but Sophie held it tight against herself. Elliot whimpered, his arms clamped around her neck. "Stop it, Becca," Sophie said. Becca was working the fingers of both hands around the edges of the mirror, her face turning red. "He's going to hear us. Let go."

"Give it to me. Give it back."

"No. Becca, listen to me right now. That's enough."

"Give it. Give it!"

"Stop it!" Lucy howled. "Stop fighting!"

"Shhh!" Sophie and Becca both hissed. Becca backed away, looking like she wanted to cry. "Get out of here," she pleaded, holding out her arms, her hands open, spread wide and helpless. "If he sees you, he will literally kill me."

"Becca, literally means—oh, never mind." Sophie grabbed Lucy's hand and led her out of the library into the hallway, urging her down the steps, the mirror digging uncomfortably into her chest as she held it between herself and her son.

"Mommy," protested Lucy, who, for some reason, still descended the stairs like a toddler: two feet together, one foot down, two feet together.

"We have to hurry," said Sophie, sorely tempted to try carrying both children. After another moment she released Lucy's hand, hurried down the stairs, and set Elliot in the entrance hall, then ran back up, two stairs at a time, hoisted Lucy into her arms, and rushed back down, panting, the mirror still clutched in one hand.

"Mommy, my slipper fell off!"

"Don't worry about your slipper."

"Becca said I could keep them!"

"She was kidding."

"No, she *wasn't*. I want my slipper! My slipper!"

Sophie had the stroller out of the closet; she shoved the mirror into the diaper bag, along with their shoes. She opened the vestibule door and heaved the folded stroller through it. Lucy headed back toward the stairs, but Sophie caught her by the arm.

"I WANT MY SLIPPER!!! IT'S MINE! I GET TO KEEP IT!" screamed Lucy.

"Lucy, hush!"

High above them, a man's face appeared over the banister. It disappeared, then reappeared as he rounded the staircase from the second floor, stopping to pick up Lucy's slipper. Sophie stared up at him, choking back her breath, which was rushing out of her chest in hoarse gusts.

Yoshiro Hansei's skin was dark, his features thick without being fleshy. Short, sparse eyebrows angled upward like accents, but they were so disengaged from his eyes they did nothing to add levity to his expression. A mustache pronged sharply down-ward around his full, stern lips, which sat atop the sheer cliff of a chin. He finished descending the stairs and offered Lucy the slipper. She snatched it, shooting Sophie a triumphant look.

Sophie swung her diaper bag over the shoulder closest to the front door. "I'm so sorry," she said, taking Elliot's hand. "We didn't mean to disturb you. My kids...we're friends with Mina and Takashi."

"Friends?" He said the word curiously.

"We go to Music for Me together."

"What is that?"

"It's a music class. For little kids. It's...awful. Anyway, we just had to use your facilities." Hansei furrowed his brow. "Becca asked us to leave right away. You know, she is a wonderful nanny. You're very lucky. Your children are in excellent hands."

"Thank you."

"We're going now."

"It's chilly outside. Where are your shoes?"

"In my bag," said Sophie, yanking the front door open. "We'll put them on outside. We're late." And with that she hauled the stroller down the front steps, threw it open on the sidewalk, strapped both kids into their seats, and set off down the street, her slippers scuffing flimsily over the purplish-gray slabs of slate.

Twenty-Two

S hadyside Orchards, Sophie had heard, trucked in pumpkins from Maryland and scattered them in their drought-ravaged fields, then charged people to ride out there in a wagon and "pick" them. This was where she drew the line. This year, she decided, they would drive around Bucks County until they found a farm with no haunted corn maze, no pumpkin catapult, no loudspeakers; just a barn and some dirt and a few actual pumpkin plants. Brian had agreed to the plan, possibly seeing in it, as Sophie did, a chance for the four of them to knit something back together in a photogenic context. Brian drove, and since he hated 95 he decided to take Broad Street all the way out of the city—a bleak, halting journey that increased Sophie's impatience to leave Philadelphia behind. The once-grand avenue led them past the toothless, swaying remains of the Divine Lorraine Hotel and the Metropolitan Opera House, then into the optimistically scrubbed bubble of Temple University, then back into the desolation of North Philadelphia, where every row house window was filled with plywood, trees, or charred black emptiness.

In the backseat Lucy paged through a picture book while Elliot sucked his thumb and looked out the window, watching bricks turn into siding and eventually stone. Sophie followed their progress on a map and tried not to say anything about Brian's driving. Sophie was an impatient driver, always seeking her advantage, blazing through yellow lights and weaving to the front of every line. When Brian drove, he would leave too much space between himself and the car ahead, or stay in a slow lane while dozens of cars streamed by and Sophie ground her teeth. This time, though, she had resolved to loosen her mental grip on the situation and simply enjoy the scenery, which was gradually improving.

Loosening her grip: this was her assignment for the day. She hadn't even researched pumpkin-picking spots ahead of time, or planned where they would have lunch. She was happy to make suggestions, based on the map she held on her knees, carefully folded around the area surrounding the northern end of 611, but only if asked. More importantly, she would not turn to Brian and say, "So," or "I've been thinking," or "Yesterday I looked at a one-bedroom on Mt. Vernon Street." Today she was letting Brian drive.

Abington. Willow Grove. Horsham. They were passing through places whose names were only familiar to Sophie from traffic reports. Office parks, strip malls, and car dealers stretched alongside 611, interspersed with houses that had trampolines in their front yards. Eventually, after Doylestown, they found themselves in real countryside, and at some point Brian turned off the highway onto a single-lane road. They began rolling through orange-carpeted forests, where cold sunlight stabbed through the last shreds of red and yellow clinging to the branches, and stacked stone walls grew out of the mossy ground and then sank back into it. They passed a few whitewashed houses, wing after added wing rambling along the roadside, but no pumpkin fields—they would have to find some open farmland for that.

Something about the rise and fall of the road, the tight turns and sudden Ys and glimpses of houses set back in the trees, reminded Sophie of a drive she had taken when she was a child. Had it been in Washington? Missouri? She couldn't remember how old she was, just the delicious lifting of her stomach as the car plunged over each crest, the swing of the curves, the smell of wet bark and decaying leaves. She was in the front seat, probably with no seat belt, Randall on one side of her, the open window on the other. He was driving fast, veering into the other lane on the turns, snapping the huge Chevy Impala out of the way when another car happened along. Sophie could remember the distinct feeling of picking up her fear and tossing it just out of reach, surrendering to the thrill of being entirely in her father's hands.

Brian was easing their car around the curves now, hugging the shoulder of the narrow road, so when they passed the yard sale Sophie had plenty of time to ask him to stop. She hesitated, though, wanting to let Brian have the idea; she could see him turning his head to scan the jumble of furniture and terra-cotta flowerpots and baby gear. But he didn't stop, and finally, when they were around the corner and down a small hill, Sophie blurted, "Do you want to check it out?"

"Why, do you?"

"Maybe."

"Why didn't you say so?"

"I didn't know if you would want to."

Brian snorted and shook his head, then pulled into the next driveway and turned around. The sale was in the front yard of a small, squared-off clapboard cottage with a front porch and two dormer windows. There was a swing set off to the side, on a part of the lawn that pressed up against the woods. Lucy and Elliot ran straight toward it as soon as they were released from their car seats.

"Do you mind if they play on it?" Sophie asked a gray-haired woman sitting on the front step of the house.

"Not at all," she answered, in a voice that rasped between the high and low registers. "I got it for my grandkids, but they're too big for it now. I'm selling some kid stuff over there. Take a look."

The scene reminded Sophie of pictures she'd seen of a tornado's aftermath: beds in trees, couches on roofs. Here there were two armoires standing in the unmowed grass, a deeply oiled Larkin's desk, a collection of Windsor chairs. A patchwork quilt spread on the ground was strewn with rubber-banded bundles of old silverware, some pots and pans, and a toaster oven. Sophie contemplated a partially unrolled Persian rug, wishing she could remember the dimensions of her office. She wasn't sure what Brian had decided to do about the floor in there. They needed to fix it soon, before the appraiser came through. Joshua Goldmeier had, miraculously, persuaded the bank to let them refinance. Whether the process had been hurried along by the threat of a lawsuit, she couldn't be sure.

Sophie browsed some moldy paperbacks stacked on a card table, then noticed a silver hand mirror lying next to them. She picked it up. The back and handle were busy with cast daisies and violets; across the glass, a yellowed piece of masking tape said "$1.00."

Just yesterday, she'd given a slightly older silver mirror to Brian, along with a printout of the mark the Met curator had emailed Harry. She'd also handed him a photocopy of *Perspectiva Corporum Regularium*, Jamnitzer's book, whose title page design was replicated around the mirror's frame. She'd waited a little while to give it to him, letting the dust settle after the raid and the arrest and the commotion in the papers, waiting until the museum trustees, delighted about the recovery of the museum's objects, had voted to reinstate him.

"I thought we'd keep this one just between us," she'd explained. "I didn't want people finding out you had a Jamnitzer sitting on a cart in your office with no object card."

"I *wouldn't* have a Jamnitzer sitting on a cart in my office."

"But you did."

He'd laughed it off, dismissed the printouts, complained about the registrar, disputed the mark, and then, finally, lapsed into confused silence.

"Just give this to Michael and tell him you found it in storage," Sophie told him. "Let him publish it. He can take all the credit. It'll distract him from his poor little tazza." Apparently, Michael was irritated that his recovered tazza had been so thoroughly upstaged by the rest of the artwork seized in Hansei's townhouse. Among the items creating a stir were several stolen paintings, including a large and unusual seascape by Rembrandt.

Sophie eyed the woman on the porch; she was looking toward the road, watching cars drive by. Sophie turned the flowery hand mirror around and around in her hand, weighing it, taking its measurements. She smiled, imagining what Harry would say about it. Poor Harry. He was probably furious about Hansei's arrest, but he'd get over it.

She looked over to where Brian stood, one forearm across his torso, the other elbow resting on it, his curled knuckles against his lips. He looked up, caught her eye, and beckoned to her. She set the mirror down.

"What do you think of this?" he asked, pointing at a small, rustic wooden bench. "I was thinking it would be nice to have in the—"

"Vestibule. It's perfect."

"The kids could sit on it while they put their shoes on. You could keep your shoes under there, too." Maybe he hadn't meant it as an invitation, but it came out that way, and she saw his ears flush as he realized it. Sophie cleared her throat and was about to say something about the nice finish on the bench, but Brian put out his arm and pulled her against him, and she curled into his body, pressing her cheek against his chest. In the distance, one of the swings squeaked rhythmically as Lucy pushed her brother. A car drove up, slowed, then sped away with a fading growl. Brian's heart counted the seconds in its patient, forgiving way.

Sophie made an offer on the bench, the woman counter-offered. Sophie shrugged and started walking away until the woman said, "Fine, take the damn thing." Then Brian asked if she knew any places to pick pumpkins nearby, and she gave them directions to a farm a few miles down the road. They drove off, but as they emerged from the striped light of the woods into a small valley quilted with fields, they became distracted by the view and missed their turn. Brian veered onto a narrower road which rambled alongside a creek for a while, leading them past an old stone mill with a doggedly turning waterwheel and then, around the next bend, to a red-painted covered bridge.

"Look at that," Sophie said to the children. "A house we can drive through!" As they rolled through the shadowy hush, then back into the brassy late-afternoon light, she marveled at the forgiveness of the landscape, and the solidity of carefully built structures, and the cautious, edifying pleasure of gratitude.

Reading Group Guide

1. Sophie's motivations for stealing change over time. What feelings do you think compel her first theft?

2. Do you think it's significant that she chooses a mirror for her first theft?

3. When Sophie steals the snuffbox, she feels "a wave of tenderness... In a strange way, she felt almost protective of the little thing." What do you think Sophie has in common with these objects, which have been left sitting, unprotected, in a museum hallway?

4. Sophie believes that the right house can provide her family with a stable, happy life. Can you think of examples from your own life where you've focused all your hopes and energy on the wrong thing? Why do you think we do this?

5. Sophie writes to Brian that motherhood is "simultaneously the most defining and most alienating experience I've ever had." What do you think she means by that?

6. Sophie makes a lot of financial decisions without involving Brian. Do you think Brian is complicit in this behavior? Does he deserve any blame for it?

7. Do you think Brian is completely to blame for his lack of involvement with the children, or has Sophie made it difficult for him? Do you think this is a common pattern between spouses?

8. After Sophie applies for the "option ARM" mortgage, she takes the kids to Johnny Rockets, where the waitstaff dance to the song "Last Dance." What do you think the significance of that song is?

9. Sophie envies Brian's success, his passion for his work, and the fact that his career hasn't been derailed by parenthood. Has envy ever motivated you to do something you knew was wrong?

10. Value is a theme of the novel: the value we place on material goods, the value of real estate, the value of family. Brian says value is "a slippery concept," and uses that to justify underpaying someone for a family treasure. What are some other ways characters (or institutions) play with value to suit their needs?

11. Sophie thinks of mothers and daughters as a fractal: an endlessly repeating pattern. What are some of the behaviors Sophie wants to avoid repeating? Have you ever caught yourself repeating your parents' mistakes? Do you think it's possible to break the pattern?

12. Harry runs his business in deference to his dead father, who apparently gives him instructions from beyond the grave. Do you think it's unusual for someone to make decisions based on what they imagine a deceased parent might say? If you've lost a parent, do you continue having imaginary conversations with him or her?

13. Most working mothers struggle with the work-life balance. Do you think Brian feels there's an imbalance in his life? Do you think that men and women have different feelings about this issue?

14. In the scene at the mall at Christmastime, Sophie is impressed by Lucy's ability "to face the beardless, hairless truth, accept its implications, and move on." What truth is Sophie starting to face during her visit to Cincinnati? What does she decide to do as a result?

15. When Sophie learns the story of Jansz van Vianen, who gave up silversmithing to take over his father's brewing business, she begins to feel even more tormented by thoughts of the tazza. Why do you think van Vianen's story struck a chord with Sophie?

16. Sophie only half believes that the Dutch tazza is hidden in her house, yet she tears the house apart looking for it. What do you think she's really looking for? Why do you think she willingly damages her house in the process?

17. Sophie isn't the only thief in this story. Who else is guilty of stealing?

18. Sophie has trouble accepting help from others. Do you think her upbringing had something to do with this tendency? Are there people in your life who have trouble asking for help?

19. The story begins with a trip to pick strawberries, and ends with a trip to pick pumpkins. Compare and contrast the two outings. How have Sophie and Brian changed in the intervening time? How are those changes reflected in the mood of these scenes?

20. Do you think Brian should take Sophie back? Why or why not?

A Conversation with the Author

1. **Where did you get the idea for this book?**

   When my husband and I first had kids, I struggled to keep my freelance business going while nursing, changing diapers, and renovating a Civil War era row house that needed lots of work. It was a pivotal moment in my life, when everything—priorities, expectations, hopes, and fears—changed quite suddenly and dramatically. My career receded into the background as I struggled to manage the demands of motherhood and family life.

   Meanwhile, my husband was pursuing the career of his dreams at the Philadelphia Museum of Art. I loved listening to his stories of dealers and collectors and all the behind-the-scenes plotting that went into every acquisition. I loved going to museum parties, and accompanying him on trips to Europe. I envied his comparative freedom, and the stimulating nature of his work life. At times I found myself living vicariously through him.

   Thinking about the contrast between our work lives, I wondered how a less stable character might react to the tensions I was experiencing. What if someone were driven a little crazy by her new life as a mother, and her longing for a more satisfying career? What if you threw financial pressure into the mix—like a house going into foreclosure?

At the time, I was fascinated by the antiheroes who were becoming so popular on television: the drug dealing suburban mom in *Weeds*, the psychopathic forensic investigator in *Dexter*, the meth-cooking chemistry teacher of *Breaking Bad*. I love the idea of an ordinary person struggling with an irresistible secret vice. I thought it would be interesting to create a character who reacts to the challenges of motherhood by doing something awful—and then to follow her journey to redemption.

2. **Is it really that easy to steal things from a museum?**

No. The scenarios that allow Sophie to steal objects simply wouldn't happen in a modern-day museum. Storage practices are quite rigorous, and visitors—even curators' spouses—are never allowed to be anywhere near museum objects without an escort, and they're never allowed to enter storage areas at all. The system of object cards that I describe has been replaced by collection management software such as The Museum System (TMS). I based Sophie's idea for a computerized collection management system on TMS, which is widely used by most major museums to keep track of works of art.

3. **You obviously have a lot in common with Sophie, your main character. Did you base other characters in the book on real people?**

The only other "real" character in the book is Sophie's row house. My husband and I renovated a very similar house in Philadelphia while our children were very small. I shared Sophie's passion for that house's sturdy Victorian proportions, honest materials, and lovingly crafted details. I personally ripped out all the shag carpet (and Ukrainian newspapers), tore down the drop ceilings, and demolished the seventies-era cabinetry while taking periodic breaks to pump breast milk. Fortunately, I didn't get suckered into a bad mortgage the way Sophie does.

4. **Are the objects and artists in your story real?**

Some objects are real, and some are modeled after real objects. All of the artists mentioned are real. The Jamnitzer mirror is in the collection of the Metropolitan Museum of Art. The van Vianen tazza is loosely based on a piece in the collection of the Victoria and Albert Museum. The Saint-Porchaire candlestick is in the collection of the National Gallery of Art. *Het Scheepje* (The Little Ship) is a period room you can visit at the Philadelphia Museum of Art, as are the Ceremonial Tea House and the Temple of the Attainment of Happiness. The Rembrandt seascape was one of the paintings stolen from the Isabella Stewart Gardner Museum in 1990; it has yet to be recovered.

5. **With two kids and a freelance business, how did you find the time to write this book?**

For a couple of years, I tried working on my manuscript during my free time, but I found it really difficult to gain momentum—especially since it was my first book. I had no idea what I was doing, and I kept throwing out my work and starting over from scratch. That didn't get me anywhere, so I finally decided to take a year off from my job in order to focus full-time on the book. I was only able to do this because of a financial windfall, and because my freelance clients were very understanding. I realize what a luxury that year was. I have boundless admiration for writers who are able to finish novels while holding down full-time jobs, and I wonder how many talented writers will never be discovered because they are too busy trying to pay the rent and put food on the table.

6. **Was it hard to make yourself sit down and write every day?**

I sit down and write every day for my job, so that part wasn't hard. What was hard was overcoming my insecurities about my writing. I made sure to include plenty of reading time in my daily schedule. Reading good books is the best writing education you can buy. The author Donald Ray Pollock went so far as to retype stories by great writers, to get the feel of their words into his bones. When I'm trying to improve my writing, that's how I try to read—closely. Why did the author zoom in on that detail? Why did she summarize the dialogue here, instead of quoting it? How did she handle this transition? Etc.

7. **What did you read during that year?**

For pure literary beauty—lots of Updike (particularly the Rabbit novels), Paul Harding's *Tinkers*, and *Housekeeping* by Marilynne Robinson. Ian McEwan's book *Saturday* taught me about slowing down time and getting inside granular, moment-by-moment observations. Jane Smiley's novella *The Age of Grief* sat open on my desk for most of the year; I was incredibly inspired by her ability to assemble the nuts and bolts of domestic life into a story of incredible emotional force. I also reread my favorite Michael Frayn novel, *Headlong*, which is a hilarious account of amateur art theft, greed, shame, and marital implosion. Great stuff.

Acknowledgments

My deepest thanks to all the early readers, advisers, and friends who helped along the way: Amy Conklin, Kathryn Craft, Felicia Crosby, Brett and Maia Cucchiara, Nic D'Amico, Collette Douaihy, Mike Drazen, Stew Ellington, Karen Engelmann, Holly Fiss, Nell McClister, Kelly Simmons, Karen Stephenson Shore, Corey Wise, and Robert Wittman. Three cheers to my intrepid agent, Adam Schear, and my editor, Shana Drehs; many thanks also to Lucy Stille. Profound gratitude to Ed and Eulalia Cobb, Alison Cobb, and Kathy Vaughan for lending me your eyes and your ears and your quiet rooms with desks. Big kisses to Jodi Cobb, Charlie and Janet Cobb, Lauren Cobb Silva, and Ashley de Coligny for making it all possible. And most of all, my eternal love and gratitude to my devoted husband and best friend, Pierre, for your good humor, good sense, and unwavering support through it all. I love you.

About the Author

Sonya Cobb is an author and advertising copywriter. She lives in Westchester County, New York, with her two children and her husband, a curator at the Metropolitan Museum of Art.